HELPER DEATH

S E T   W A G N E R

PART ONE

CHAPTER 1

No, this couldn't be a dream! Nick could distinctly feel the body lying next to him—petite, with small breasts and lean thighs. He could feel the hands sliding over his body in a lingering caress, cool, thin fingers with slightly rough tips. Cool, even cold, but they were setting him on fire! Timid kisses barely brushed his lips—oh, how he wanted to embrace this mysterious woman who had miraculously appeared in his bed! How he wanted to burrow his face into her long silken hair and confess to her that nobody had ever shown him so much tenderness and true, passionate intimacy before. But he couldn't utter a sound or make the slightest movement. He wasn't dreaming, but some strange paralysis cramped his muscles.

He concentrated all his will in an effort to lift his eyelids. They were as heavy as if they had been glued shut and simply would not obey him. When he thought he had finally managed to pry them open, he felt an even greater fear—that he was blind!

At last he could see and stared up, sure that her face was directly over his because he could feel her panting, but—saw almost no face there! *Almost.* In the instant before she disappeared completely, he caught a faint glimmer in the moonlight: no distinct features, no shape, no fringing wisps of hair—only lips revealing in a hollow cry of disappointment large, slightly irregular teeth, one (the upper left incisor) chipped in the middle.

Nick didn't move for a long time. The heat in his loins made them throb like a raw wound, while his arms and lower legs were ice-cold yet clammy with sweat. Despite an intolerable thirst and a pressing need to calm himself under a cool shower, he could only manage to turn on the bedside lamp. Its light replaced the gleam of the full moon and disclosed the rumpled cover, his clothes thrown casually on the chair opposite the ancient double-door wardrobe, his manuscript on the small table along with an empty vase, a clock that read 3:18 a.m., and his bottle of Seconal, its expiration date long passed, which accounted at least for the foul taste in his mouth.

In his entire life, Nick had taken sleeping pills only three times. The first was just after his mother's funeral, when he took several tablets at once and slept like the dead, as if he had been with her, seeing her off on her final journey. Next was after a spiteful editor returned his manuscript to him: "Your *Future Tales* would hardly appeal to children, Mr. Edgeway. Nothing exciting ever happens in them." The third time was last night, and he had even locked his bedroom door—out of fear. All evening he had been racked by the nagging sense that someone was in the house with him, following him, standing behind him, peeping over his shoulder, and so on.

Now he was awake at half past three in the morning, and instead of fearing some abstract presence, he was painfully longing for a woman, however hallucinatory, which was much worse. It meant he was falling in love with a figment of his own imagination!

Sighing, he rose, shuffled to the bathroom, and gulped water straight from the tap before taking a shower. Wrapped in his bathrobe, he returned to the bedroom, sat in the armchair by the small table, and checked the pages—covered with scribbled notes and corrections, strewn with question marks and additions—of his latest "future tale":

A boy will be born sometime in the future with a special gift. If he chooses, he will be able to make people sing for joy instead of mourn the loss of someone dear to them. He will bring cheerful smiles to the faces of the sick, the poor, and the needy. Men and women, children and old people will tearfully tell him their troubles, anxieties, and sorrows, their decrepitude and woe. A single glance from his radiant blue eyes will transform their pain and suffering into pure, sincere, inextinguishable joy. He will never refuse help to anyone, knowing that, after meeting him, even the worst will become good. People are usually good when they are happy, after all.

The boy must share his gift for another very important reason: he will live only as long as he continues to give joy to others. Otherwise he would quickly age and die. Do you understand? That is his fate.

And so on. He knew this damned story by heart, recalled every change he had made, all the deleted passages, every punctuation mark. Yet he didn't know how it would end, although he had been working on it for months now.

Throwing the pages on the table, he stood up and shambled into the hallway, painfully aware of his appearance: a big man who had recently put on a lot of weight, forty-two years old, a pudgy face that sometimes looked naïve—or perhaps just foolish? His blond hair was thinning on top, and his blue eyes, once so clear, were now faded. A childish man who wrote dull stories for children—shy, awkward, boring—that's why nobody liked him. *Nobody*, he repeated to himself, blindly starting down the stairs.

Why didn't he turn on the lights? Was he hoping the woman would appear to him again in the darkness? Wasn't that a sign of insanity?

Reaching the landing, he stood by the window filled with moonlight, looking around expectantly. But no, of course there was no woman here. He closed his eyes and strained his senses. Even the sense of her presence had disappeared, leaving him feeling almost abandoned. If only he understood what was the matter with him!

Continuing down the stairs and through the living room, he sank into a lounge chair on the porch. Biff gave his chain a feeble clank from inside the kennel, reminding Nick that he had forgotten to feed the dog last night. *But so what? He can stand that—he's a dog.* He didn't even like the ugly mixed-breed pug that his sister Elsa had unceremoniously dumped at his feet: "I'm giving him to you so that you finally have somebody to take care of." She claimed to have bought it, but no doubt she just picked it up off the street. His sister often lied, after all. Most women did.

"A boy—will be born sometime—after many years will be born, and—will live more than a hundred years."

Think of an ending, Nick, of an ending. *The beginning was good enough in the first version; why go back to it all the time?* He tightened his bathrobe against the cool breeze. The huge, fat moon sometimes peeped through the clouds filling the sky, hanging over his head like a silver pendulum, and then vanished again, leaving the yard in timeless darkness, stripped of all forms, movements, or shadows. Even then Nick's mind's eye saw the fruit trees in the orchard that his father had planted years ago, the old rose bushes that had once belonged to his mother, the weeds that had overrun the neat rows of strawberries and vegetables, and the splendid peonies and fragile, pale daffodils. He knew the high fence still encased this whole yard, burdened with his past, as it always had, the spiked tips of the bars pointing toward where the moon had been, toward the frighteningly distant stars.

Otherwise he will soon age and die—do you understand? That will be his fate.

"Damn it!" he cursed, jumping to his feet and pacing back and forth. "Fate" or "lot"? "Destiny"? Which would be best? Or was it all the same? And why must he travail—yes, travail—to write simple children's stories? Was that some penance he had imposed on himself—a way to overcome his guilt about never really caring much for children?

He staggered for a few steps before he realized why: *she* was on the porch with him, walking toward him. Yes! Elusive, ethereal, unreal, the *woman* was still coming, approaching him. She stopped in front of him, and he slowly reached out for her. So what if he couldn't touch her? He peered toward her, straining his eyes until they filled with tears. So what if he couldn't see her? It was enough to know for certain that she was there.

Certain?

"Come...come with me! Let's...go back upstairs," he whispered brokenly. "We're both confused and exhausted. We should rest."

He hurried across the porch and into the living room and then stood there numbly for almost a minute, *waiting for her*. When he was *convinced* that she had entered the room, he closed the door *behind her* and turned the key twice in the lock.

"Come; please come with me!"

Lumbering up the cold, dark staircase as quickly as he could, he *knew* that she was following him—could sense her somehow with his soul. He felt his way into the bedroom, waited for her to pass, and then shut the door, again double locking it. Suddenly shy, he slipped into bed without taking off his robe, because she was here. *Here.* But he knew that, when he fell asleep.

Alas, the only unexpected event that night was that he did finally fall asleep. In the morning, though, he was awakened by the click of the key turning in the lock. He heard the sound, distinctly! He swung his feet onto the floor, the blood pounding in his temples, his brain drowning in the ebbs and flows of incoherent thoughts, knowing only that he had to check the door.

It was unlocked.

He locked it again and propped his back against it, barely breathing. After a long time, he came to his senses and dragged himself across the room, feeling as if he had been beaten up. With the premonition that he was going to see something eerie, unimaginable, and nightmarish, he peeped through the dirt-streaked window.

Sun. A summer sun glaring almost directly overhead, the rapacious weeds mercilessly revealing the fruit trees that hadn't been pruned in years, the driveway and kennel off to the left with the tawny, lop-eared Biff in front—only his ordinary, familiar-to-sickness view.

"Enough of this daydreaming," he ordered himself. "It's almost noon."

Unlocking the bedroom door with feigned resolve, he marched to the bathroom. He shaved slowly, every now and then frowning at his jaded reflection in the mirror. Finished, he returned to the bedroom and meticulously chose his clothes for the day, though he had no plans to go out. He made the bed carefully, dusted the room, and straightened up the wardrobe. *I don't dare go downstairs,* he admitted. *My late night "crush" has passed, and now I'm afraid. Of her—a woman who doesn't exist!*

He finally forced himself down to the kitchen, which was filled with the aroma of freshly brewed coffee. One of the coffee cups had just been washed, drops of water still on it. The front burner on the stove was still warm.

Gritting his teeth and armed with his sharpest kitchen knife, Nick inspected every room on the first and second floors, latched all windows, and even finally examined the attic. No one else was in the house.

Or was there no one *anymore?*

CHAPTER 2

"Open this window at least, for Christ's sake!" His sister started bossing him around as soon as she arrived. "We'll suffocate! Incidentally, there isn't a single drop of water in Biff's dish. It seems to me you often forget him. Annie, get that poor creature some water!"

The child obediently went to the sink, and presently Nick saw her through the window, dragging along the pot of water. She was wearing a shirred dress—obviously to disguise her thinness, but it made her look even skinnier. Her arms and legs resembled chopsticks poking out of the puffy sleeves and flounces. She walked slowly, as if shackled, but not because she was afraid of spilling the water. That was just the way the child walked. She was moody by nature, the exact opposite of her mother and a reflection of her sickly father.

"Are you going out, Nick?"

"No."

"Why are you so dressed up then?"

"Why not?"

"Come on, has something happened? Tell me!"

Yes, dear sister, it has. I'm going mad; that's what's happened, Nick thought, but said, "No, Elsa, nothing has happened to me in a long time. You know I live the life of a hermit—"

"Precisely! And I also know you don't have the temperament for it. Isolation and introspection can only bring you disappointment, Nick."

"You allude"—he smiled sadly—"to the danger of learning to know myself too well?"

"Yes," she confirmed. "Living with someone else in fact protects us from that, distracts us from worrying about ourselves, and lets us simply get on with our lives, but you—look at how you've neglected the yard, for instance. Look at our father's house! It's falling to pieces!"

He looked. *It is falling to pieces; she's right. But what about her daughter outside? She's turning herself off: standing there in front of Biff like a stuffed doll, just staring at him. But does she even see him?* "Annie has a very romantic nature. That's why she sometimes ignores reality." *What a diagnosis!*

"You must get hold of yourself, Nick! Just imagine how Mom and Dad would feel if they were alive to see the place."

Out of long habit, Nick had stopped listening. Everything she would be saying was ancient history, echoing all the banal platitudes handed down through generations or the eternal grumble against all exceptions to life's petty rules. He was hardly an exception to those rules, though: just another bachelor, whose only remarkable trait was his total failure with women. One such failure often leads to another, until all that's left is the inferiority complex, along with a variety of quirks, manias, hallucinations, and so on.

"Hey! I asked you, where's the hot chocolate?" Elsa was already bustling around the kitchen. "Ah, here it is!" She droned on, "But her best trait is that she has always been poor, always worked for her living, so she isn't just another fussy woman."

Hallucinations were certainly a possibility, but *that* woman couldn't have been just a figment of his imagination. Crazy or not, he would not have made her up, not looking like that: short, thin, flat chest, even with a chipped tooth. He must have seen her somewhere, probably at Elsa and Max's.

"Modest, as she was when she was at college. She has barely changed since then—in character, I mean. And of course I invited her over tomorrow evening—"

"Hold it! Do I know this woman? Has she come to your place before?"

"Who? Kathy? How could she have come, Nick? Didn't I just say that I ran into her this morning and that we haven't seen each other in nearly twenty years? That's when she left town, and now she has come back"—Elsa paused for extra effect—"because the late Hatcher was her uncle! Now that he's dead, the mansion on the river is hers, Nick! The Ambassador Hotel too!"

Her tone of voice and the look on her face emphasized that her visit today had been planned solely to deliver these three final announcements.

"I see," Nick murmured casually.

"Yes, yes, she's his only heir! She hasn't realized what that means yet, which is lucky for you. And what's more, she's not at all bad looking. She may not be the perfect beauty, but then you're not—"

None of Elsa's fussy lady friends, however, would appear in public with a broken front tooth, his thoughts continued. So it could have been one of her maids. She'd had at least five in the last few years. Come to think of it, what other women had he seen at their place? The hairdresser, two or three fortune-tellers reading coffee grounds or cards or the like, the "witch" who brings Anna herbs—and the seamstress! Nick could picture her quite clearly: about fifty, average height, and dark hair. *No, that's not her, of course, but—*

"Listen, Elsa, has your seamstress come to see you with her assistant, or with her daughter or sister?" he asked softly.

"Whaaat!" Her eyes widened with puzzlement.

"Please, answer me."

"Well, I don't know. I don't remember. But why—*why* are you asking?"

"It has to do with an allusion I want to use in my book."

"Oh, your book again," she said condescendingly, as if that explained every idiotic question he might ask. Then she sighed and added, "She died. I now have a tailor."

"Really? I'm sorry. What was her name? Where did she live?"

This time Elsa looked up at the ceiling, assuming an expression of utter boredom. "Her name was Alina. I never learned her second name or knew her address. I only knew her telephone number."

"Give it to me!"

"Fifty-five, seventy-three, thirty-seven," she said through clenched teeth then barked at him, "Now shut up!" She yanked the hot chocolate off the stove just as it was about to boil over.

Nick repeated the number a few times to himself and secretly smiled because, unlike his sister, he had been able to remember something: the seamstress Alina had been giving her a fitting, and the woman—or was she a girl?—next to them all of a sudden dropped a box of pins on the floor. That was it! And this so embarrassed, even terrified, her that when she started to pick them up her hands were shaking. He had bent down to help her, and she looked up at him, looked into his eyes and smiled briefly—but was there a broken tooth? Fine, but why couldn't he remember anything else about her except that smile?

"Take the napkins," Elsa ordered him as she picked up the tray of hot chocolate and cookies.

Before long they were seated around the table on the porch, looking gloomily at what was left of their childhood garden. Their appearance outside helped Anna come to herself. She finally turned away from Biff and trudged toward them, an enormous azure bow swaying grotesquely on her head like some exotic bird nested in her hair.

"Don't put such big bows in her hair!" Nick blurted out, surprising even himself.

"Why not?" Elsa screwed up her eyes at him.

Because they don't suit her—that's why, he thought. *They make her face look even paler, more like—nothing.* But he said irresolutely, "Well, they draw attention away from her face. Instead of seeing it, you look at the bow, and Anna has such nice regular features—such expressive eyes. Why hide them?"

"Hmm," Elsa murmured, scrutinizing him.

"Anna." He quickly turned to the child, who had drawn near them. "After you drink your chocolate—"

"And eat your cookies," Elsa added.

"Yes, and after you eat your cookies," he said, acquiescing, "you should go pick some apples."

"We'll pick them all," Elsa said, "and you're going to give us a hand."

"Sure."

"I'm gonna make her apple juice all winter long!" she almost shouted. "Morning, noon, and night—juice, juice, and more juice." Composing herself, she pursed her lips tightly.

Anna ate two cookies, he none, and Elsa—ten at least. Nothing ever stood in the way of her appetite. But she was no glutton. She ate as much as a healthy and energetic woman should, at least as far as he was concerned, especially since she had to take care of a sickly husband and an anemic child "with a romantic nature." Yes,

Elsa radiated strength and resilience, gave the impression of something lasting and deep, as deep as the roots of life itself.

"I don't love him," she said, turning to the subject of Max without any preliminaries, as usual. "And I see no point in concealing this fact from Annie. It would be better for her to realize some things early. Otherwise, chances are she may mistake sympathy for love someday or even get it into her head that it's a good thing to sacrifice herself and that it's possible not to be selfish at all. Do you hear me, Annie? Selfishness is absolutely necessary, as long as it's kept within bounds."

"Why, yes," Nick added. "Otherwise what will be left of you? A shrunk shadow-self that no one would like. As a rule, people despise those who live only for others."

"Do you understand, Annie?" Elsa asked. Of course she got no answer. "Does she understand what we're talking about, Nick? What do you think?"

"Of course she does, or at least she will, in time." *It'll be too late, though*, he added to himself. Actually it had always been too late for her, from the very moment she was conceived, if not before, when her genes were circulating in her father's anemic blood.

"But I'm always shrunk, even though I'm selfish," Anna said. And this from a seven-year-old child!

"Dear God!" Elsa groaned and rushed into the house as if someone were chasing her but returned before long, her face serene and composed, with one of her "work dresses" slung over her shoulder. She started to unbutton her blouse; it was typical of her not to change clothes elsewhere but to stand right in front of him "so that we won't have to interrupt our conversation." At moments like this, however, the conversation always came to a stop. Still, in this old habit of hers was nothing obscene or vulgar, nothing bad. Nick was convinced of that and, therefore, never looked away. He watched her silently, with the same old (unfortunately groundless for years) feeling of possession he had toward her when she was a little girl and he a teenager—a morass of complexes, ambitions, and grudges. He continued to look at her for another reason: he felt that the uncommon intimacy between them would become somewhat unnatural if he deliberately averted his eyes while she, his sister, changed her clothes.

"Why don't you tell him the truth, Elly? He should have been able to see it for himself by now."

She stood before him in her bikini with her "work" dress in hand, her eyes clouded. "Tell him the truth—and then?" she muttered.

"You move in here with Anna, and that would be the end of it."

"The end, the end! I am afraid of endings, Nick, even the end of a disease, because I keep asking myself what there'll be beyond the end. Nothing?"

"Or the beginning of something else?"

"Yes, but what that something else is, no one can say. And there you have the uncertainty again!"

Nick nodded his head skeptically. She was scared? Nonsense. She was only throwing dust in his eyes with her "revelations." She had wanted to mollify him from the moment she first let him down badly by choosing Max. Of course, he had pretended that he thought the marriage was a well-calculated move on her side— a textile factory, a palace of a house and another in the country, plenty of money, land, and so on. She too had tried to maintain that illusion. The sad truth was, however, that his sister had fallen in love with a feeble nincompoop—a spindle-shanked, narrow-shouldered scarecrow of a man with an even narrower mind. Snob!

He peered at her through narrowed eyelids. As always, when he beheld her provocative physical beauty, he was filled with something like awe, mixed with pain and anger. The setting sun lit her reddish-blond hair, glossy as copper, that crept down her body: solid and yet somehow almost frighteningly feminine with rosy skin and heavy breasts, thighs enclosing a hungry, maybe insatiable, womb—a primal, indomitable force flowed generously from her. How badly Nick needed that strength.

Especially now—*now*.

Shivers ran down his spine. He thrust his nails into his palms and blinked slowly once, twice, and three times. There, a little to the side of Elsa, he could again sense *something* that had appeared a few seconds ago, as he was painfully realizing. Something with form and volume, much more substantial than air—denser. Like a fine bluish haze within a defined outline, held together in some uncanny way.

The outline was a woman's profile, small, with almost flat breasts—looking pathetic next to Elsa's gorgeous, seminaked body—and nearly transparent; he could see the wall behind her and part of the window frame. Sinister. Impossible?

Nick slowly shifted his gaze toward Anna: she was looking that way! Her expression was unchanged, however—distracted, dreamy, and unresponsive.

"Come on, don't be slackers," Elsa called to them when she finally finished putting on her dress. Turning toward the window, she obviously saw nothing there but her own reflection. She slicked down her hair and called to them again, "Come on, there's work waiting for us!" She made for the driveway, walking right past the figure as it started to fade.

"Do you...do you see?" Nick whispered urgently, stooping over Anna. "Oh, please, tell me what do you see over there, child?"

But the "child" refused to utter a word. She rarely said anything and now just passed him by and clunked glumly after her mother.

Then the figure started to move too, floating across the porch away from him. It was wearing a spooky garment that reached to the ground, with a high collar and shoulders and sleeves that struck him as strangely familiar. He watched it disappear around the corner of the house.

CHAPTER 3

Elsa and Anna left by nine o'clock. After locking the door, he had come here—just for a glass of water—but he stayed on. At almost midnight he was still sitting, pressing his head between his palms, cramped by his uncomfortable position on the angular chair. Yes, he was afraid to leave the kitchen, as terrified as a child who had been told that a monster was lurking behind the door in the dark. Now he thought he heard footsteps, now stifled sighs, and once even a cough. And the rustling of a long silk dress—but why silk? It could have been cotton, linen—any material.

"It's silk!" he murmured to himself with amazement. "Light blue with golden flowers on it, a silk kimono!"

His *mother's* kimono.

The presumption was so nightmarish that his fears faded instantly. He jumped from his chair and, before he knew it, found himself in the attic, before the wooden chest where he kept some of his mother's clothes and other belongings—old photos and letters. About to open it, he suddenly drew his hand away and stood there hesitantly. What if the kimono were really not there? What then? He could not even dare to imagine what conclusions he would draw if that were so.

Still, he had to know. He stooped and lifted the dusty, rusty lid. He would later regret not having inspected it closely for traces left by someone else. He was already sorry when he took out all the clothes and the kimono *was not there.*

"Elsa. Elsa must have taken it!" He tried to collect himself as he retraced his steps and leaned weakly on the banister. Reaching the downstairs hall, he knelt, exhausted, by the telephone stand. "Please, God, let it be her who took it!"

But no! Her sleepy, angry, and unequivocally negative reply resounded in his ears long after she slammed down the receiver.

He dragged himself back into the living room and took a bottle of cognac and a glass from the cabinet. What else was there to do? He slumped down in his favorite armchair in front of the dark, silent TV and filled the glass. Gulping down the cognac like strong medicine, he waited.

Soon he was calm enough to seek some rational explanation for what had happened. It was possible, for instance, that he was suffering from a psychic disease, with periodical symptoms of an otherwise imperceptible split personality. Perhaps this morning he had not been himself when he first woke up. Then, after going to the kitchen, drinking a cup of coffee, returning to the bedroom, and falling asleep again, the second time he awoke normally. If so, his *other* self, identifying with his mother, might have taken the kimono out of the chest in the attic.

So, fine, but what about that woman? What about her figure standing on the porch today wearing the kimono? So, in his divided self, did he identify with her rather than his mother? Maybe this particular personality suited his other self better, *embodying* him, so to speak, as a small, weak, unimpressive woman? In that case, he must have put on the kimono and imagined he looked like her. Imagined it so vividly that, later on, even when he was back to normal, his own image would dissolve at times into that spectral ghostly figure. As for the presence and different noises—steps, sighs, and so on—they also belonged to his *other* self, which his normal self had imagined seeing or hearing.

That's all—unpleasant psycho business. But, most importantly, the cause certainly lay in him, not in some supernatural creature. Thank God for that! People were less afraid of themselves—although it should be the opposite, maybe.

By the time he managed to convince himself that he was alone in the house, Nick had drunk quite a lot of cognac. He went on drinking, mechanically, until he either fell asleep or passed out. He opened his eyes again to a bleak, rainy morning. He felt miserable, of course—the insidious effects of drinking cognac and spending the night in an uncomfortable armchair. He struggled to stand up, and when he finally found himself upright, he had to struggle to stay that way. So much the better! At least he could be sure that he hadn't been bifurcated or fluttering around in a light-blue silk kimono. Releasing a hoarse, dry laugh, he limped upstairs to the bathroom.

After bathing, shaving, rubdowns, and a jolting cup of strong coffee, he was ready for more meaningful actions. He sat down by the telephone in his bedroom, with a notepad and pen in hand, and dialed 55-73-37.

"Hello, I'm calling from the telephone company. We would like to send a service representative to check the connection, if you would please give us your address."

Though puzzled, the man who had answered gave him the address. Nick put on his beige suit, which made him look quite trustworthy, and then left the house. As he was about to lock the front door, he happened to look over at the whimpering Biff. There was no getting around it this time: he went back inside, opened a can of dog food, and filled Biff's water dish before backing the Ford out of the garage and heading for town.

As he might have guessed, the neighborhood the seamstress had lived in was neither rich nor poor, a far distance from downtown and filled with mostly identical tall buildings announcing "Apartments for Rent—Reasonable Rates."

After making his allotted share of inevitable wrong turns, Nick parked in front of her building and went in. The landlady, a grizzled old woman wearing a frumpy housedress and the expression of an inveterate gossip, intercepted him as he was entering the elevator.

"I'm looking for Alina," he informed her, attempting a disarming smile. "To tell you the truth, I've forgotten her family name, but I know she's a seamstress."

"Ah, I see—the seamstress. And why, may I ask, would *you* be needing to see her?"

"I was just passing through town, and—"

"Where are you from?"

"Horschlecht," Nick replied, blurting out the first city that came to mind. "I was there yesterday visiting an old friend, and she asked me to give Alina something."

"What is it?"

"Oh, nothing material—just her very warm regards and an invitation to come stay sometime before winter."

"An invitation to stay!" Her small beady eyes instantly lit up. Nick sensed that she was already savoring what she was going to say. "Alina would hardly be able to visit your friend, Mister. Not this fall, nor this winter."

"Why not?"

Making an effort to pull a mask of grief over her face, she said, "Well, because she ain't among the living no more, sir."

"Is that so? When did she die?"

"Well, I can't remember for certain. We barely knew each other. Just good morning, good-bye was all we ever said to each other. Nowadays seems nobody's got time to stop and say something nice, have a real conversation. I, however—

You, however, hag, he finished her sentence for her in his head, *are such a morbid old bore that you are trying to squeeze some entertainment out of another person's death!* "Who lives in her apartment now?" he inquired. "Her husband—and their daughter maybe?"

"Another family moved in a long time ago," she snapped, suddenly annoyed. "She had no husband. Never did have."

"How about a daughter? Or sister? Or—I need to meet a relative of hers, to tell me when and how she died. My friend will want to know more about this. Do you understand?"

"If she wanted to, she would know it. That's what I understand!"

Good Lord, do I really have to continue this tawdry charade? Nick fumed when the baggy crone shook her head and turned to go. He stood in her way.

"But you—" She looked into Nick's eyes and then softened her surly attitude. "Come; come upstairs, sir. On the fourth floor, apartment twenty-nine. The tenant there was in heart relation with the late woman, and I'm sure he'll tell you all about—"

Nick abruptly turned his back on her and, without waiting for the elevator, started up the stairs two at a time. He was relieved to find the man at home—and quick to believe his lies.

"Do come in," the man said affably, introducing himself as "just Eric" and leading Nick into his untidy studio apartment. They sat opposite each other on the two worn chairs in the center of the room. So it was with this sixtysomething redneck fatso that Alina the seamstress had been in "heart relation." How prosaic.

"She died of pneumonia, poor soul." His voice was a monotonous, feeble drone, surprisingly *thin* for his bulk. "I was with her to the very last minute—held her hand. All in all, I felt very—good about Alina. We knew each other for a long time—were friends for more than ten years. If not for her daughter, we'd probably have been married—"

"So she *did* have a daughter!"

"Oh, yes, and she loved her daughter very much. That's why she was afraid to commit herself to marriage. She thought it wouldn't be good for Kaya."

"Kaya," Nick whispered, "*Kaya.*"

"That was the name of the girl. Actually she was a girl, or child, only to Alina. I figure she must have been around twenty-five. I wonder where she is now, if she's still alive?"

"Still alive?"

"She disappeared that night, sir. About eleven o'clock, when Alina grew worse, we called Mayer, her doctor, and he promised to come over at once. But half an hour later, when we called him again, he was still at home. He said he had been "unavoidably detained" and could only come the next morning. And Alina was already dying—it was terrible, I tell you! We immediately called Emergency, and Kaya went out to wait for them and bring them up. She wanted to save some time, but her mother died only a few minutes after she left. Then the paramedics arrived, and I have to confess I forgot all about Kaya. She wasn't with them, and no one had seen her outside. She must have walked down the street to meet the ambulance. It was January; the roads were icy, and it was dark. Who knows what happened to her?"

Eric grew silent, anxiously listening to a light scratching on the other side of the hall door. He hurried to open it, closing it quickly behind him, but Nick caught a glimpse of a wheelchair holding a strikingly deformed man—with arms the size of a small seven-year-old, bare to the elbows, and legs, sticking out of a pair of shorts, as flat and stiff as if they had been run over by a steam-roller. His face seemed ghastly in the gloom of the narrow hall, and his huge black eyes set deep in their sockets looked like two deep holes.

"What's the matter, dearest?" Eric's whispered words could be heard from behind the door. "Why have you removed your blanket? Come on. I'll take you back to the kitchen. Just for a little while."

His voice trailed off, and only then, alone in the silence of this shabby room, did Nick realize how much this man must have suffered. "Redneck fatso" had been his first, harsh impression of Eric's sickly, bloated face and body. *How trustful he is*, he now realized, almost with respect. *He's a broken man, no doubt, but not because of manias or neurotic hallucinations. His misfortunes are absolutely real and in no way his fault. What's more, he is a really busy, engaged person—he has to take care of that crippled man, provide for them both, and keep the place in order. He has to! Meanwhile, I clutch my* Future Tales *because what else can I do? No one waits for me to come home; no one depends on me, other than that miserable mutt.*

When Eric came back into the front room, Nick was already up, shifting his weight uneasily from foot to foot. "Excuse me, Eric—I really have to be leaving now."

"Oh, don't worry; my brother can wait. He's not used to people coming here, and he was a little nervous, but I calmed him down. I told him I was going to tell you about Alina. She...she often took care of him."

Despite the assurances, he didn't ask Nick to sit down again. They stood looking at each other for some time, stiff and smiling, until Nick couldn't take it anymore. He guiltily averted his eyes, realizing that he was jealous of this "just Eric"—jealous of the tragedy that had given meaning to the man's life. *The time may well come*, he thought, *when I'll be a bloated sixty-year-old, but unlike him I will have no excuse.*

Only after he was standing in the hall outside the apartment and Eric was holding out his hand to say good-bye did Nick get up the courage to ask the question that had occupied his mind the whole time. "Tell me, please, what did Kaya look like?"

Eric let go of his hand. After a considerable silence, he answered, with annoyingly long pauses: "You will—find this—hard—to believe, but I don't—know."

"You don't know what she looked like!"

"No, I really don't."

"You don't know if she was tall or short, thin or fat, blond or brunette—"

"I know this sounds incredible to you, sir. The police reacted the same way. Even though I was the one who told them about her disappearance, they didn't believe me at first, since I could give no account of her appearance or of the way she was dressed—nothing."

"But you have seen her so many times." Nick was astonished. "You have spoken to her—"

"It's absurd, there's no denying that," Eric said, shrugging his shoulders, "but it's a fact! I can remember only one single detail about Kaya."

"What is that?"

"Her chipped tooth. I just remember *it* because Alina worried about getting it fixed. She knew the dentist would charge a pretty penny. But then Alina got sick, and—"

Nick took Eric's hand again and shook it abstractedly, murmuring vague words of gratitude, and then numbly started for the elevator. He had already got in when Eric clumped after him and held the door open.

"Please don't think harshly of me, sir," he pleaded. "Don't think of me as some heartless old fool who is blind and deaf to people around him. No one, and I'll say this again, not even one of the people who had seen her could give the police the vaguest description of her either, or even identify her in photos. It seems that Kaya left nothing of herself in anybody's minds but—haze."

CHAPTER 4

All morning Nick had been aware of the presence—in the car, at Eric's apartment, and then in the car again. He could sense it even now, skulking behind him, listening to his conversation with Elsa. He pressed the receiver to his ear with his shoulder while buttoning his shirt, laconically answering her questions, "It was in the chest—yes, I'm sure—no, I don't need it, but—yes, I'm OK—yes, I'm sure—I'll come—at seven. I promise—bye!"

Now that he had a plausible explanation for the presence, he paid little attention to it and wasn't particularly worried about his own state of mind either, because after all, he didn't really feel crazy. *I've always been emotional*, he rationalized. *Like any other artist, I have particularly acute senses. And since I've been stuck in the middle of that tale lately, no wonder I've been eccentric mentally.*

He was sure it couldn't last long. After all, he had already established that the woman existed and, what's more, she was a very forgettable type, since everyone had difficulty describing her after she disappeared. In other words, he had gone some way toward convincing his other identity—personality, self, subconscious mind, or whatever—that identifying with this Kaya was simply—humiliating.

Yes, keeping this in mind has to help, he encouraged himself. *After all, who would go out of his way to deliberately reduce himself to a nincompoop? Such things happen involuntarily and unwittingly. Now that*

I'm aware of what's going on, I can stop it, provided it's not too late. And in my case it's not.

There were two full hours till seven o'clock, which meant that he had dressed for dinner far too early, but so what? He walked briskly to his study, sat down at his desk, and concentrated on his tale:

He will live only as long as he continues to give joy to others. Otherwise he would quickly age and die. Do you understand? That is his fate.

And for that reason, when all the people from his own town and others who come from near and far have been healed of their pain and sorrow, the boy will have to go out into the world to seek others in misery. He will go through woods and across fields, across rivers and over mountains, will pass through many villages and towns, and everywhere he will leave joy behind him. He will continue until he finds himself facing the biggest ocean on earth. He will not waver, though. He will cross it too, for on the other side, there will be people waiting for him who are sick, crippled, frightened, and lonely.

It was loneliness, all right, that he was trying to combat by splitting his personality. Tonight, however, he would make an effort to get over his loneliness—with the help of the unknown, for the present, Miss Hatcher. Kathy.

So he will board a magnificent, fast ship and bravely sail the infinite realms of the ocean. Thanks to him, soon the entire ship's crew will be infinitely happy. The captain will stop grieving for his deceased mother, the sailors will stop longing for their sweethearts, and the navigator will no longer be embittered with thoughts of old age or his premonition that this is his last voyage.

They will ride the waves laughing and singing, having for-gotten what sorrow means. Their carefree mood, however, will vex the mighty ocean, which will hurl against the ship stormy giant waves. Too often joy makes people not only good but also careless. They forget that the world is filled with evil, storms, and mortal perils. The captain and his crew will not be pre-pared to fight the waves and will be defeated. Only the boy will survive—still immortal at this time.

But while swimming toward a solitary island in the distance, the boy will be overwhelmed by all the deaths in the storm. For the first time in his impossibly long childhood, dreadful doubts will assail him.

Nick raised his head from the manuscript, astonished by his late realization of being painfully disappointed by Kaya's disappear-ance. He felt grief for her, for a woman who was probably already dead and had left nothing in his mind but the fact that she had caressed and kissed him in a dream, a dream that had been more real to him than reality itself.

Pushing his chair back, he rose and walked to the bookshelf but did not reach for a book, frozen by his image in the glass case. He looked stern, even angry, but just enough to cover some oth-er feeling. He puckered his eyebrows more and stood straighter, taking the aggressive pose of someone determined not to bear it anymore—but determined not to bear *what?*

"I'm not going to bear *anything!*" he declared in a thunderous voice. Rushing back to his desk, he brought his fist down on the pile of written pages. As he crumpled them, they shrieked in his hands: "Only the boy will survive—for the first time in his im-possibly long childhood—dreadful doubts." He threw them onto the floor and stamped on them. The black lines of those words and phrases dirtied the pages. How could anyone create anything more perfect than pure whiteness? A blank page was filled with possibility and new chances, but once you touched it, the boundless future shrank into the disappointing present and almost as quickly sank into the past. *Future Tales* indeed—where there was neither joy nor hope!

The fifteen or so pages lay crumpled on the floor, a mute record of many hours of failure, impotence, and self-knowledge imposed by his solitary existence. *I'm not pleased, but this is me, Nick. And you? Could your name be "just Life"?*

Nick shook his head and kicked at the pages scattered on the rug, this time without anger, more tired than scornful. Bereft of an audience, Nick tended to create such "scenes" for himself; this was not the first.

He picked up the carafe empty of water, walked into the bathroom to fill it from the tap, and swallowed a few gulps. Then he washed his hands and brushed his hair in front of the mirror, deciding that he looked fine in the shirt he had on and his suit covered his imposing bulk perfectly. *After all,* he told himself encouragingly, *it's obvious that I was in good shape until recently, an athlete's build. I can get it back too, if I just exert myself a little.*

When he returned to his study to leave the carafe, the manuscript was again on his desk—all smoothed and stacked in a pile by his typewriter! Backing away, Nick bumped into the door, felt for the handle behind his back, and opened it. Then he dashed across the hallway. "Mother, where are you now? I need to hide my face in your silk kimono—and where could *it* be?"

Springing outside, he gasped like a fish washed up on the beach, mouth agape. *Damn,* he thought, *the keys to the Ford are in my beige suit.* No, not back into the house again.

"No, I'm not going back in there. No way!"

CHAPTER 5

The ride on the bus gradually calmed him down. There were about ten other passengers, just enough to feel that he wasn't another anonymous face in a crowd but an individual protected by a small, though short-lived, *community*. He struggled to find a rationale for the manuscript. No doubt it had taken just a minute to pick up the pages, smooth them out, and lay them on the desk again. If he couldn't remember doing this, then either his other self had briefly intervened—his subconscious eager to save his "future tale"—or he *un*consciously straightened up his study before filling the carafe. After all, people often did such things automatically.

He arrived at Elsa and Max's place almost calm.

"Hello," Max greeted him. "Glad you came early. Come on in; let's get ourselves something substantial to drink before the women attack us with their light wines."

Nick had never been able to figure out why Max always supposed he was in the mood for a "substantial drink." He had never given him a cause for this assumption. Not that he drank surreptitiously; he just never felt like getting drunk. As for the cognac last night, that was simply therapy, an unpleasant but necessary expedient. Nothing more.

"There, that's better." Max placed a tall glass before him, half-full of whisky. He had poured himself less than one-third of a glass.

"Well, for the first time, you're right," Nick said. "This time I really don't mind 'warming up' a bit."

"Glad to hear it," Max replied.

As usual, their conversation came to a standstill. Nick sipped at his whisky.

"Ice?" Max watched him with interest. "Or maybe club soda?"

"No, thank you."

"I see. Straight up."

Yes, straight up, you sonovabitch! Nick clenched his teeth not to utter these words aloud, but Max smiled at him and—who knows why—covered his mouth with his strikingly thin, almost spidery, fingers. A real bastard! Even more repulsive than his character was his appearance: high but narrow forehead, thin nose with nostrils that seemed too narrow to breathe through, and pointed chin jutting out above his long thin neck. Below that, of course, narrow—*very* narrow—shoulders, narrow hips and thin, unnaturally long legs.

In general, this frail-looking guy lacked breadth. Elsa, however, thought all that was "sophisticated"—insisted it was a sign of "exquisite spirituality." "Love is blind"? Yet she claimed insolently that she didn't love him. Didn't love him, my eye!

"Where's Elsa?" Nick asked.

"She's upstairs, getting dressed." A razor-thin smile cut Max's face. "You know how vain she is."

"I know—I know."

"I heard that!" She laughed as she came through the door. Nick frowned even more as he watched her cross the living room, barely making contact with the carpet in her pin-thin high heels. "Are you OK, darling?" She came up to Nick and put her arms around him, kissing him on the forehead.

"Yes, I'm fine—well, at least not too terribly bad."

He made a secret sign to her not to bring up the subject of the kimono, and she understood, naturally; they had understood each other without words ever since childhood. She nodded to him and then called out in her "motherly" voice, "Here comes our Annie!"

Today it seemed there was something not quite right with "our Annie." She wasn't wearing a bow, and that lack accentuated the paleness of her face more strongly than would have its contrast with five oversized garish bows.

"Oh, hello, Anna."

Nick knew his greeting was wasted, since she almost never responded to anybody's greetings. She walked past him as if he were a piece of the furniture and took her usual place by the little table where the drinks were kept.

The much-praised Kathy arrived at seven o'clock sharp. She exchanged pleasantries with Elsa over aperitifs before they all moved into the dining room, but not even Kathy's presence brightened the dull dinner, which passed slowly and left only a memory of boredom interspersed with awkward moments: depressing pauses, echoes of clanking cutlery, ineffectual jokes, and forced laughter that died out as quickly as it began. The maid brought in one pretentious-looking bland dish after another. It seemed that the dinner would never come to an end, yet when it did, Nick inwardly shivered at the prospect of going back to his already maddeningly lonely house.

Maybe he could get drunk enough so that Elsa would want him to stay the night? She would gladly make up a bed for him in one of the guest rooms—*no, not in Max's house!* He would rather roam the streets all night than stay here. The best thing to do would be to go home—with Kathy. Only now did he recall that she was the reason he had come in the first place. What absentmindedness! He had not even looked her over properly.

And she was already leaving.

"I'll see you off, if I may?" He jumped to his feet.

"You must see her off, darling!" Elsa pointed her finger at him in a mockingly strict manner. "And be careful—I want my friend intact. Do you hear me, you big bear?" She then turned to Kathy. "My brother may be a big clumsy bear, honey, but don't worry. He's perfectly harmless!"

Kathy blushed to the roots of her auburn hair. She was a very pleasant-looking woman, about thirty-seven, Elsa's age. She looked quite ordinary at the moment—but then, who wouldn't, compared to Elsa? A little later, when they were already in her car, Nick looked more closely, and she seemed to grow prettier.

"What kind of a see-off is this going to be?" He smiled. "I've already imposed on you and climbed into your car."

"Why not let me drive you home, then?" She smiled back.

God bless her for making his task so much easier. When they pulled up to his house, he would ask her in for a cup of tea or coffee and then get out a bottle of champagne. He would be blithe and gallant and shower her with compliments. In short, he would cajole her into drinking until he could caution her: "Oh, no, you shouldn't drive home in this condition, Kathy. After all, there are plenty of rooms here."

That's how he planned it, but what transpired was something totally different. Kathy agreed to the cup of coffee, and yes, they drank champagne, but he didn't need to be a lothario. Nor was there absolutely any sense of a "third presence." Everything developed naturally as they discovered that the two of them had something in common after all. She had worked as an editor for *Impulse* magazine for a full eleven years, and he had subscribed to it for most of those years. Well, yes, of course: Kathleen Hatcher! Eleven years, twelve times a year, that name had flashed before his eyes as he turned the first page and had waited until tonight to be pronounced by him.

"I like your magazine a lot; it has style and personality," Nick rambled on. "You've successfully resisted the temptation to fill it with cheap stories of sex and violence."

"I feel sad about leaving, really—as if I've left behind something dear to me. Does that make any sense?"

"Of course!"

"I wonder what I'll be doing from now on. I've always dreamed of having lots of free time and some peace of mind so I could try my hand at writing, and now—"

"You want to write!" Nick exclaimed.

"Well, I haven't only *wanted*." Kathy lowered her eyes, slightly embarrassed. "I've written—mostly poetry, unsuccessful, of course."

"I doubt that! I mean I doubt they were unsuccessful. Will you show them to me, sometime? Soon?"

He didn't want to tell her that he was a writer too. *It's too soon, but one day, maybe after a romantic walk by the lake. She is a sensitive soul. She will certainly feel the special mood in* Future Tales.

"I don't want you to think of me as a sentimental fool, Nick. My poetry is so trivial—all about moonlit nights, flowers, passing clouds, and such things."

There, she likes nature too!

"Have you been to the lake yet, Kathy?"

"When could I have done that? I've only been back in town three days, and I've been dealing with nothing but red tape."

Yes, she's rich now. On the other hand, he wasn't poor, so he had nothing to worry about.

"During dinner you seemed cold and gloomy, Nick, but now I can see how mistaken I was."

"I'm sorry to say I do get gloomy, far too often, but I've never been cold—although sometimes I wished I were. I think such people lead easier lives."

"More boring lives too."

They speculated a little more about all the "cold people" and eventually concluded that such people were basically unhappy, because "the light in their lives is always dim."

What had Elsa said about Kathy, that she didn't have an attractive figure? Not true! Kathy wasn't tall—rather short to be precise—but very well proportioned. She liked to keep fit, as she told him herself. A healthy, vigorous woman. She could give birth to a child—children—who would be full of life, happy, and healthy. It's not too late for her—for the two of them!

Kathy drank just one glass of champagne—her spirits improved steadily without any extra stimulation—and decided to leave around midnight, so he had no reason to insist that she stay. Still, he did insist, and she seemed glad to stay another hour, anyway. After that, despite her protests, he climbed in the car with her. "It's my turn to see *you* home. I'll take a taxi back. No, I'm not tired, not in the least! I can't even think about sleep just now."

They were silent in the car, but that silence was vastly different from the uncomfortable pauses at Elsa and Max's. Neither uneasy nor tense, a feeling of *peacefulness* had overtaken them. That was how they described it before they reached the Ambassador Hotel, which now belonged to her, and said good night at the main entrance.

"Thank you, Nick. It was a lovely evening."

"Can I call you—today?"

She nodded, took out pen and paper from her handbag, and wrote down her number for him.

"What about this evening?" Nick folded the paper carefully and put it in his inside jacket pocket. "I suppose you'll be busy."

Kathy shook her head slowly. "No, Nick, I have nothing planned. Why pretend? Truthfully, I'm a very lonely woman."

He bent toward her, and couldn't say exactly when, their lips met—the kiss was that ethereal and tender.

"Good night, Nick."

"See you soon, Kathy!"

He watched her as she crossed the lobby and stopped before the elevator to press the call button. Just before the door closed, he saw *something* get in behind her—not some ghostly figure or bluish haze but just a shadow, which somehow dimmed Kathy's face and added a slightly ashen tinge to her light-yellow dress.

"She took it!" Nick murmured to himself, dizzy with sudden relief. *Whatever was haunting me left with her, because she gave me hope.*

He decided he would rather walk a little than catch a cab. He breathed deeply, enjoying each breath of air that filled his lungs, smiling into the dark. He knew (he was certain) that tonight he would sleep calmly: no shatteringly tangible dreams, no threatening footsteps, and especially no strange presence—just his own self, at ease and undivided.

He was right: no one was waiting in his house that night.

CHAPTER 6

In the morning, an earring on his nightstand caught his eye. Gold, small, tear shaped, it looked like the ones Kathy had worn the night before. How could that be in his bedroom?

Secretly and deliberately, that's how! Kathy must have run up here at some convenient moment and left it. She had wanted to hint something to him, to create that delicate feeling of closeness she was afraid to show in a more direct way. *Well, let the earring stay there.* Apparently its owner planned to come to claim it soon—or to leave the other one next to it!

Since it was only eight o'clock, she was probably still sleeping, so he decided to call her after breakfast. Downstairs in the kitchen, he made himself coffee and toast. The sandwiches left from last night he took to Biff. "What a nice dog!" Kathy had exclaimed. "I'm glad you like animals too, Nick."

"OK," he muttered, "now let's have some action."

He took the chain off the dog's collar, and Biff started jumping around like a crazy trampoline artist. The dog slapped both his forepaws on Nick's legs, leaving big muddy prints on his pajamas, smacked his lips as if starving instead of just being fed, and then burrowed his wet nose into Nick's slippers. Nick stooped for a short stick and flung it as far as he could. As the dog galloped off to fetch it, he quickly turned and went back into the house.

He ate his toast, drank the rest of his coffee, and checked his watch: 8:25 a.m., Saturday, August 29. The last Saturday of the month! If Reno had come back yesterday, on August 28, as he said he would in his card, he was sure to come over before long. He would by no means miss their fishing day.

Nick dialed Kathy's number decisively; he wanted to talk to her before his friend showed up, knowing he would be uncomfortable speaking to her with Reno in the room. When nobody answered, he assumed she was probably taking a bath. He cleaned the kitchen and the living room efficiently, got his fishing tackle out of the closet, took out a blanket and folded it, put the chess set on top of it, and before he went upstairs to change into his fishing clothes, gave Kathy another call. Still no answer. Could she be out so early? Or maybe asleep with the phone turned off?

The honk of the Ferrari he knew so well made him jump up from the chair. Slipping the paper with her number into his pocket, he went to the window. Reno was already walking up the driveway, every now and then stopping to give a friendly pull on Biff's ears, who was obviously ecstatic at the attention. He was talking to the dog and laughing out loud.

"Nick, Nick!" he called out.

Nick waved at him and then came down to open the door.

"Good for you! You're still in your pajamas at nine!" Reno tapped him on the back in a friendly greeting. "Have you forgotten that today is *our day*?"

"How could I forget?" Nick laughed. "I've been waiting for it since the end of May."

"True! We've never taken such a long break. You won't believe how much I have to tell you—"

"You're good at telling but not so good at writing."

"I leave writing to the writers," Reno said, rejecting the reproach easily. "I called yesterday; I don't remember how many times. Where were you? Have you turned vagabond in my absence, eh? Let me look at you." Grinning, he gave Nick a nudge in the ribs. "Seems you really have become a bit of a bum, judging by those circles under your eyes. Hey, I almost forgot! I've provided for your good looks."

He hurried back to the car and soon returned with a box and other packages. He unpacked a really wonderful merino-wool sweater, three shirts—of fine fabric but so bright that Nick would never wear them except at home—and soft-leather loafers.

"*Italian*, Nick. You don't walk in these—you float! And a souvenir too—a miniature model of the Leaning Tower of Pisa. 'Lean as much as you want, my friend, but never fall' is what I'm saying to you with this little present." Reno winked at him and pushed him toward the door: "Come on! Go change your clothes. The fish may die of old age if we keep them waiting much longer."

Ten minutes later they were in the front seat of the Ferrari with Biff settled in back. "He's our lucky charm," Reno always said. "I refuse to go fishing without him anymore!"

Naturally, all the way to their favorite fishing hole, the conversation turned on Reno's trip to his "native" Italy. He talked about the relatives he had met for the first time, how beautiful and frigid the women had been, the spaghetti and pizza, the Coliseum, the canals of Venice, the songs of the gondoliers, and "that famous Luciano"—a veritable chaos of impressions that Reno made no effort to organize. His thoughts raced from one scene to the next, sometimes going back or jumping to the end without explaining the beginning, which was typical of him—a free spirit not overly concerned with rules and regulations.

"Alas, three months had passed in a fraction of a second," he concluded when they were halfway up the path to the fishing hole, lugging their gear on their shoulders. "Now it's back to work again: inheritances, property to divide, divorce cases."

"A prospect of infinite boredom," Nick said tactlessly. "But if you want to live a more interesting life, I guess you need to become a criminal lawyer. There's a psycho loose in town. If they lay their hands on him—"

"Yes, I heard yesterday that he has finished off three more."

"More? Do you mean there were others before?"

"Yes!" Reno stopped walking to wave a finger under his nose. "There were definitely others! He murdered that old man too—the same atrocities, the same sadistic methods. These victims were also found in their beds. And what's more, Nick, there's no guarantee we know about them all. I wouldn't be surprised if he's left a corpse to rot in a more secluded spot, like here, for example."

Nick gave a hollow groan, let his bag fall, and collapsed on the ground beside it. "Kaya!" escaped his lips. "He killed her! He killed her too!"

Reno bent down and touched his friend's shoulder solicitously. "Who's Kaya, my friend?"

"A young woman—an acquaintance. Listen, when exactly was the old man murdered? Do you remember?"

"About five months ago, around the middle of March."

"And she disappeared in January! She disappeared without a trace, do you understand? Oh, Reno, he must have killed her! Kaya was his first victim. The monster!"

"You can't be sure of that, Nick. Some women 'disappear without a trace' and then turn up a year later with a baby on their hands. Who knows where that acquaintance of yours went off to?"

"No! On the night of her disappearance, her mother was dying. She had gone out just to give directions to the ambulance; that's all!"

"I see. So it is possible. How long did you know her, and why haven't you ever mentioned her to me? Was she close to you?"

Nick shook his head reproachfully. *See how curiosity gains the upper hand over human suffering?* It was more important to Reno to know what Kaya had been to him, what she looked like, and if he had slept with her or not than to offer comfort now that Nick was assailed by awful thoughts about what might have happened to her. "No, she wasn't close to me," he snapped, but for a moment the ludicrous thought that he was lying flashed through his mind, that Kaya had been and still was very close to him—even though she might well be dead.

"Won't you tell me where you two met, eh, Nick? When and where?"

"It must have been toward the end of last year because that's when she chipped her tooth, and her mother wasn't sick yet." Realizing this response was confusing, Nick simply finished by adding, "Her mother used to make clothes for Elsa. I supposed that we met there but were never introduced to each other. I had a talk with their neighbor yesterday, who remembered her chipped tooth, and this completely convinced me that we had met with her, though he had no idea what we were actually talking about."

"Hmm, I see!"

Reno held out his hand, and Nick took it as an attempt at sympathy, but Reno just wanted to pull him up. When Nick was on his feet, Reno took his bag from the ground and deftly slung it over his shoulder. Then Nick realized bitterly that he couldn't tell his friend the whole truth and expect comfort or support in these so-risky-for-his-psychological-balance days. Days and nights, actually.

They continued up the path, Biff bounding on ahead, eyes alight with playful eagerness. He rushed back and rubbed up against Reno.

"Come on, Biff! On you go, boy," Reno encouraged the animal, Kaya's whereabouts, his friend's agitations, and the sadistic murders entirely forgotten. "Well done! Excellent! Clever dog! What a jump—exactly like a lion!"

That was just like Reno: a free spirit, oblivious to—well, to sum his friend up simply—everything. Nick continued to seethe with silent indignation, but gradually his thoughts took another turn, toward another, more pleasant subject—toward Kathy, alive and, thank God, not some dream or hallucination.

Finally settled on fishermen's chairs and floating their lures in the deep pool, Nick debated whether or not to tell Reno about Kathy. Reno would hardly be impressed—after all, dealing with women was a daily routine for him, and a trifle boring at that. What's more, he always chose young girls; once he knew that Kathy was thirty-seven, he would dismiss her as "past her prime."

Nick sneaked a look at his friend: disheveled hair sticking out at odd angles, high forehead, strongly curved arcs of black, bushy eyebrows that always made people think he was puzzled about something; thick, fleshy nose and full, sensual lips—all set on the neck of a heavyweight wrestler and a wrestler's stocky, muscular, and resilient body. Somewhat surprising was the kindly, serene expression of his warm brown eyes; they radiated sympathy and understanding, even when Reno wasn't paying the least attention to whom his "understanding" was being shown.

In short, Reno always caught people's eye with his burly good looks and unfathomable but undeniable charm. What that charm of his was based on Nick had never been able to deduce, possibly because there were many answers. Reno had a very positive, but not annoyingly so, opinion of himself; he was cheerful and encouraged free, unreserved behavior in others. Maybe most important of all, Reno infallibly knew exactly when and how much he would be able to sympathize with the person he was talking to.

Conversely, Nick realized, *either it never occurred to me to sympathize or, if I did, I went so far off the deep end that I made people pity themselves and resent me for forcing them to dwell on their problems. Furthermore, my self-esteem was generally low at the best of times. Instead of making people pleasantly relaxed, I seemed to make them tense and fill them with a vague sense of guilt.*

After this consideration of their differences, Nick no longer felt the least temptation to tell Reno about Kathy. It was impossible to think of introducing them to one another—not yet, certainly. Unfortunately, Nick had no reason to hope that her response to Reno would be any different from that of all other women. *All— except Elsa,* he corrected himself with satisfaction, remembering how his sister had put this "charmer" in his place, leaving him for the spindly but "very sophisticated" Max.

"Do you remember," Reno whispered, so as not scare off the fish, "that raft we made out of empty barrels when we were kids?"

"How could I forget after you fell off it when there were chunks of ice floating in the river? You could have drowned, if it hadn't been for me."

"Yes, that's true. But what about the time you almost fell out of the cherry tree? You would have cracked your head open if I hadn't caught you."

"That's true; I don't deny it."

"What about the time we threw a firecracker into that singer's room?"

"It was two firecrackers, not one."

They had started reminiscing now, and chances were they would continue until lunchtime. Then they would pack their fishing tackle, fold up the chairs, and drive to "their" little restaurant. They would give their catch to the owner, since neither of them ate fish anymore, and treat themselves to a long lunch, downing several cold beers. Then they would return to play a couple of games of chess by the side of the lake and talk some more until they eventually dozed off. When they woke up, around four o'clock in the afternoon, they would swim in the lake before heading home.

Every last Saturday of the month was like that, and this one went according to pattern, at least until they approached the house and Reno saw Elsa's Toyota parked in the driveway.

"Your sister's here!" he said suddenly and slammed on the brakes, waking up Biff.

"So what?" Nick was taken aback by Reno's unexpectedly strong reaction. "You could tell her about your trip to Italy."

"Ah, no! I'm not—in any shape for that." Reno looked almost frightened. "Let's say good-bye now, please, and quickly, before she sees us! She could be with Max, and you know—I don't like him."

"I don't think she's with him, but if you insist—"

When they got out of the Ferrari, Reno opened the trunk and handed Nick his bag. As he put it over his shoulder, Reno shoved the chess set and blanket into his hands before starting to drag out the fishing poles.

"I'll come back for them." Nick recoiled. "I can't take all this at once. Come on, don't be so touchy! Elsa's not going to bite you."

"Stop it, Nick! I just don't want her to see me—looking like a bum."

"There's nothing wrong with your appearance. You're going too far with your fussiness. You're getting obsessed with it—"

Without letting Nick finish, if he was even listening at all, Reno set—or, more precisely, threw—Nick's fishing pole down by the fence and jumped in behind the steering wheel, softly shutting the door and hurriedly waving good-bye.

Watching this awkward exit, Nick smiled slightly. *Some people can never get over rejection*, he thought ironically.

CHAPTER 7

Elsa did not move or say anything when he came into the living room. She sat slumped in an armchair, clenching a glass in her hand, the bottle of vermouth in front of her half-empty.

"Apparently you've decided to live the rest of your life as a drunk," Nick joked, though nothing about her encouraged levity. "Hey, what's going on, Elsa?"

As he approached her, he noticed the earring on the end table, resting on a paper napkin.

"It's Kathy's, isn't it?" Elsa responded in a hoarse voice.

"Yes, it's hers," he snapped, indignant that she had rummaged around in his bedroom. "She was here last night."

"Was she? And what time did she leave?"

"Listen, Elsa—"

"*What time?*"

"At one. I drove her to the hotel."

"Did you go up to her apartment?"

"Don't you think you're going a little too far?" he almost shouted, but deep inside he practically glowed at such ostentatious evidence of her jealousy. "That's none of your business—"

"Were you in her apartment? I'm asking you!"

"No, I wasn't, but I hope to be. Very soon!"

"What time did you come back here?"

"At three."

"It's much worse than I thought!" Gulping down her vermouth, she slammed the empty glass down next to the bottle. "How about this earring? How did it turn up on your nightstand?"

"Won't you tell me why you're interrogating me like this? What happened?"

"How did this earring turn up here? How?"

Elsa looked at him with inordinately widened, bleary eyes, something quite different from jealousy in her expression. Anxiety? Or even terror?

"Well, I found it." Nick fell into a confused silence. "I found it last night when I came home, right here on the coffee table, and I took it upstairs. Kathy must have taken it off because it was too tight or something and then forgotten it."

"You fool! Don't you see that this earring wasn't taken off? It was torn off! Yes, pulled by force and ripped from her ear. If you had taken a closer look, you would've noticed the blood stains on it!"

"What are you talking about, for Christ's sake? Who pulled it off?"

"The murderer." Elsa groaned and clasped his arm, turning her face away. She looked almost ugly, haggard, somehow years older. "Kathy was murdered last night, Nick. *Slaughtered…*like… like an animal!"

CHAPTER 8

"So far, so good," Lieutenant Forger said, distrustful eyes crawling over Nick's face, watchful for any twitch of a muscle, even the slightest tic. "What time was it again when you two parted?"

"One thirty."

"And after that you went straight home, did you?"

"Yes, that's right."

"Did you take a taxi immediately?"

"No, I didn't."

"Why not?"

"I wanted to walk. Take an evening stroll."

"Ah, I see—a stroll at half past one in the morning. And how long did that *stroll* of yours take?"

"A little more than an hour, because I took a taxi when I got to the bus station."

"Describe it to me. What make and color?"

"I didn't notice."

"Really? What about the driver—young or old? What was he wearing? What color was his hair?"

"I didn't notice that either."

"Well, that's OK." Forger rested his elbows on the desk and extended his frog-like lips into something like a smile. "Maybe he will be able to remember you. Especially if you stopped him, not at the bus station but, let's say, at the hotel, and not at two thirty but around four."

Nick shrugged his shoulders tiredly. "Your insinuations are quite unnecessary, Lieutenant. Just find that driver, and he will corroborate my story."

"I get the impression, Mr. Edgeway, that you aren't all that eager for us to find him," Forger remarked. "But be that as it may. Tell me how you were dressed last night."

"In a light beige suit and a white shirt," Nick replied. The moment he told this lie, he felt he was beginning to weave a sticky web around himself that was already tightening.

All this because of his own sister! She learns about the murder and heads straight for his place. She sees his car, looks for him in the house, and barges into the bedroom. She sees the earring: "If there's blood on it, there must be blood on his clothes too!" So she crams the suit he wore last night, along with the shirt, into a bag, frantically rushes to the lake and, adding two stones to the bag, throws it in!

"You'll need to give us those clothes for analysis," Forger said.

"All right."

"'All right' all right! Do you know what is really *all right* for you, Edgeway?"

"No, I don't," Nick admitted frankly.

"Well, the style of Miss Hatcher's murder is the same as in the previous four. If that weren't so, you would be the prime suspect."

Nick looked the lieutenant in the eyes but, after only a second, lowered his head. "You suspect me even now."

"Yes, but not quite enough to book you."

"What? You thought of putting me in jail?"

"Of course. Come to think of it, why not you? The papers described the previous murders in such vivid detail that you could be imitating that psycho."

Yes, the papers. Would this pushy cop believe him if he told him that he hadn't bought or read any papers for years? Or how he had learned just this morning that the old man's murder months ago, along with the next three, were all committed in the same way?

"Incidentally, my copycat theory is only one possibility," Forger added. "There's another one too."

"Another one? What are you getting at now—that I'm the sadist-psycho?"

"Well, you figured out that theory with *no* problem."

"Oh, go to hell!"

Forger rose. "After you, sir." He walked Nick to the office door, smiled derisively, and then stopped for an ambiguous parting shot. "You've shown admirable *insight* by coming here immediately and uninvited. If you recall anything else that might be useful, please come again."

"Listen," Nick began hurriedly, "as for your copycat theory, Miss Hatcher recently came into a substantial inheritance."

"We know that."

"Isn't it possible that someone interested—"

"There are no other heirs," Forger interrupted him again, opening the door but not offering his hand.

CHAPTER 9

Elsa was waiting in her car, parked near the entrance to the station. Because of reasons known only to him, the lieutenant had decided to question her the next day instead of this evening.

"Well?" she urged him impatiently as soon as they drove off. "Tell me what happened!"

"He suspects me! Can you imagine that?" *Of course she can: she suspected me herself!* Nick started wringing his hands. "Why didn't you look at those damned clothes before you threw them in the lake?"

"Even if I had, so what?"

"You would've seen for yourself that they were *clean!*"

"Some incriminating evidence is found only under a microscope, Nick."

"A microscope? But that was butchery! They would've been sodden with blood."

"Yes, if you were wearing them."

"What other clothes could I have been wearing?"

"I mean," Elsa said calmly, "that you could have been naked."

"Jesus!"

"Nick, I'm simply telling you what went through my head when I found her blood-stained earring on your nightstand."

"What about now? What do you think now? After all, nothing's changed."

"Things have changed," Elsa objected. "You told me you didn't kill her, and I believe you."

She was watching the road ahead; Nick could only see her profile as she drove, not her eyes or the expression on her face. "What if the driver of the taxi noticed?"

"What do you think he could have noticed in the semidarkness, Nick? That your suit wasn't light beige but light gray? That your shirt wasn't white but pale blue? Oh, come on!"

"I hope you're right." He sighed. "Incidentally, I've been meaning to ask you why you didn't throw away the earring too."

"Together with the clothes?" Elsa laughed mockingly and, it seemed to him, hollowly.

"Not *with* them, of course! Some other place."

"I will throw it away. I had wrapped it up in the napkin and then completely forgot about it as I was climbing the rocks there. Do you have any idea how it got into your house?"

"No doubt the murderer left it there."

"No doubt at all," she snapped at him. "The question is why? With what motive?"

"As evidence against me. I'd say that's clear, if nothing else is!"

"Evidence that he placed in plain sight on a coffee table—the most conspicuous place of all? So that you would find it and hide it right away? No, Nick, that doesn't make sense. Even if we supposed that he saw you and Kathy saying good night, how did he know where you lived? If we pursue this line of thought, we'll have to conclude that the killer knew you very well!"

"Hardly. More likely, he followed Kathy the whole evening, from the moment she left the hotel until she returned. Since I got back home around three, he had plenty of time to kill her and then go to the house, enter it somehow, and—"

"Wait, Nick. When exactly did you notice the earring again?"

"As soon as I got home. I told you that, didn't I?"

"So it's three o'clock, right?"

"Yes, yes, three," his voice shrill with tension, "more or less. I wasn't carrying a stopwatch, for Christ's sake."

Elsa swerved abruptly onto the right shoulder and slammed on the brakes. She turned to him swiftly. "Now listen to me carefully! In spite of everything, I still don't think you killed Kathy. But please, don't lie to me anymore!"

"What makes you think—"

"Stop it!" She opened the glove box and took out a newspaper, jamming it into his hands. "Take a look at the evening paper. It says there that she died at about three or four o'clock this morning. So how could you have found the earring torn off her ear at three?"

Nick gripped the newspaper and bit his lips.

"So?" Elsa insisted.

"I found it in on my nightstand this morning," he admitted quietly.

"So the killer broke into your house while you were asleep, then tiptoed into your bedroom, and put it there, right?"

"Yes," Nick muttered, fully conscious that she couldn't believe anything so preposterous. He couldn't believe it himself.

"How about Biff?" Elsa asked, and he noticed excessive interest mixed with the terror in her bluish-green eyes. "Why didn't Biff bark?"

"He might have barked, but I didn't hear it."

"His kennel is right under your bedroom window, darling. Or maybe you were sleeping with the window closed? In this heat?"

She suddenly drove the Toyota back on the road, her profile fossilized by her determination not to express anything else. Nick looked slowly down from her hands firmly gripping the steering wheel to her sandaled foot pressing the accelerator, the toenails polished pearly rose, then back up to her clearly defined calf muscles and strong thighs, bare and *silky* smooth, and put his hand on her thigh. Now, this should really shock both of them, but neither seemed even surprised—maybe because they had lived too long waiting for at least some proof that the muddle in their souls was mutual.

When he finally took his hand away, its heat left a print like a scarlet brand on her white skin.

CHAPTER 10

They parted without a word, and he headed for the house exhausted, intending to go to bed immediately, even though the sun had just set. To sleep—to sleep was all he wanted—but when he neared the door, he sensed something or someone waiting for him again.

What could it be? How could he know, since he saw nothing? Since it was simply impossible. Invisible, impossible, but still there: *I'm back, and tonight we're going into* our *home.*

Nick obediently unlocked and opened the door wide. *It* breezed past him and inside like a puff of air—the puff of a long silk kimono. The corner of the newspaper in his hand seemed to move slightly.

"Oh, no! No!" Now trembling, he crammed the newspaper into his inside coat pocket, raced to Biff's kennel, unhooked the dog's chain, and led him up to the front door, where the dog pulled back, refusing to enter. So he felt something too—but what? What?

"Get inside!" Nick kicked him over the threshold, but Biff jumped back out, entangling his flailing front paws in the chain. Nick grabbed the dog and stepped toward the threshold again. As if he were somewhere outside himself, Nick watched his fingers squeeze Biff's shaggy neck. The dog's eyes glowed in the dusk, staring point-blank at him, sending forth waves of fear.

"You disgusting mutt! Don't you want—?"

What didn't he want? Nick couldn't remember. *I'm going to strangle him, strangle, strangle* pounded in his head as he felt the hectic beating of the animal's heart, struggling to convey a final plea: "I will love you, love you; I *can* love you."

Nick gulped the evening air and threw the dog onto the cobblestones. Biff hit the ground, yipping quietly but, instead of running away, crawled back and snuggled against Nick's leg and then started growling as he turned toward the foyer. Aha! Nick peered into the dim light as Biff released a muted, prolonged howl.

"Well, OK," he said suddenly. Stooping down, he unhooked the chain from Biff's collar and threw it aside.

Nick entered his house slowly, strangely calm, closed the door, and double bolted it before going straight to the second floor. He took a shower, opened the bedroom window, and propped himself up in bed, newspaper in hand. When he turned on the lamp, the room seemed to grow cozy. He snickered, chortled, and shook with hollow laughter. *"Cozy"! Why not "intimate"? Please, come in, get comfortable, and lie here beside me.*

"I know what you are!"

You are a shadow. *The shadow of my soul, aren't you? That's why I can't see you. To be visible you need a completely different sort of light, a spiritual light, don't you? And I don't give off such light, do I?*

Nick was surprised to feel a sickly grin still pasted on his face. He hastened to wipe it off and opened the newspaper:

NEW BRUTAL MURDER:

SADISTIC KILLER CLAIMS FIFTH VICTIM

Once again our city woke up shuddering with fear... Kathleen Hatcher, recently arrived here...only heiress of our highly respected...was staying at her own hotel...The chambermaid found her at about ten o'clock this morning...The coroner established that...

Ah, here comes the important part:

> The murderer gave her a light dose of chloroform so that she would regain consciousness after he had gagged her and tied her to the bed. He then cut through her neck sinews slowly, taking care not to sever the windpipe or the aorta. His aim was to prolong the agony as much as possible. The ultimate cause of death was a rupture of the heart brought on by excruciating pain and unbearable terror. Besides the wounds on her neck and those left by the nylon cords that cut her ankles and wrists, the victim's right earlobe was torn, its earring ripped away.

This newspaper's incessant rustling was almost unbearable! He shuddered, writhed—but kept reading:

> As with the previous murders, the murder weapon was found next to the bed—this time the broken neck of a bottle, probably taken from the liquor cabinet in the victim's living room. No fingerprints remained on it, of course... Lieutenant Forger, who has been tracking this sadist since March, still has no solid leads...We can only ask how much longer...this living hell.

Kathy—murdered, tortured! A "rupture of the heart brought on by...pain and...terror." Kathy dead! Why could he realize this fact only now? He had liked her and had kissed her good night in front of the hotel: "See you soon, Kathy!" But when he first heard about her death, he hadn't been moved—just fully, entirely possessed by fear for himself: *They will accuse me, blame me.* Nick closed his eyes: he had to—was under *obligation* to—grieve for and think only of Kathy. Otherwise, what was he but an abject, heartless creature, a disgusting selfish jerk? But the sadistic murderer had been here, in his bedroom! What if he had killed him too? Slowly, slowly—*oh, Kathy, Kathy! What terrible misfortune befell you, dear Kathy!*

Yet even sadistic killers exhibit some logical pattern in their behavior—perhaps unfathomable to the normal individual but still logical. Let's take the earring, for example. Clearly it was not left here on a whim but for some purpose considered in advance.

Stop! But maybe this, too, is part of his "style"? Maybe he always takes an object owned by the victim and delivers it to the home of a relative or friend, as a kind of calling card? And because Kathy, *poor* Kathy, had been just three days in town, Nick was her closest acquaintance. Yes! He had to check into this possibility as soon as possible.

Nick tossed the newspaper aside and reached for the telephone, hurriedly dialing Reno's number.

"Are you alone?" he asked when he heard Reno's voice.

"Well, not really. Didi's with me. You don't know her. We're celebrating my return from abroad." Reno laughed, and Nick heard "Didi" giggling in the background.

"Listen, I didn't call to listen to you two driveling! I want to talk to you in private."

"Is it important?"

"Very!"

"OK. Hang on a second." Nick heard Reno tell "Didi" to take the roast out of the oven and make the salads. Then he heard a door shut. After that, Reno was back. "All right, Nick, I'm all yours."

"Listen—"

"Hey, did you hear about the new murder?"

"Yes, I *heard.* That's why I'm calling you."

"*That's* the reason?"

"Don't interrupt me, for Christ's sake! This is serious! There's a lot I can't discuss on the phone, but I need as much information as possible about the previous murders. About all four of them. Understand?"

"Of course I don't understand. What do you need this for?"

"Don't ask. Just tell me if you have the old newspapers with the—"

"Do you really think I save old newspapers? I'm no packrat. I can get you copies by tomorrow, though."

"No sooner?"

"And how would I manage that?"

"If you had them at home, I would come and get them."

"Now?"

"Yes, right now."

"Hang on," Reno whispered, "Didi's coming in."

"To hell with Didi! You're always chasing some bimbo!"

"All too true, unfortunately."

Nick heard the door shut again—this time even louder than before.

"She's gone again," Reno announced. "She's mad at me. I think I may have to kick her out, pal. Although I haven't the vaguest idea why you need them, the papers will be waiting for you tomorrow at noon—no, by ten o'clock at the latest."

"*Every* one with information about the murders, right?"

"Yes, right. Are you writing a story? Is it a short story or a novel?"

"Maybe," Nick replied impatiently. "And where are you going to get the papers?"

"I have a reporter friend who covered the cases you want. He's been collecting everything written on the subject. I'll ask him to make a copy of them from his archives—"

"OK. Bye!"

"Hold on, Nick! If you're bored—that is, if you're in the mood, I mean, come on over—"

"No, thanks," Nick interrupted and banged the phone down.

He was going to kick her out! Well, *kick her out then!* What was he waiting for? But no, he was just like Elsa, just trying to please him. Reno was perfectly aware that he was making a fool of himself with his hot twenty-year-old bimbos with makeup an inch thick. Damn it! He and Kathy had done so much better last night—so pleasant.

Sighing, Nick climbed out of bed, went over to the window, put his elbows on the windowsill, and gazed off above the dark trees. *Kathy, Kathy.* Clearly she had really liked him. She had absolutely fallen in love with him—because of his sensitivity. She could tell he wasn't like the others. She would have appreciated the special mood in his *Future Tales*. What a shame! What cruel fate! Concentrating, he pictured her gentle face, almost untouched by makeup; her soft auburn hair modestly pulled back—exactly his mother's hairstyle. He remembered best her soft, smooth neck—like a little girl's—with a tiny mole on the right side. He would kiss her exactly there, in oblivion.

So Kathy walks down the quiet hotel hall and enters her apartment, gets into bed, probably thinking of their time together, of the walks they would take down by the lake, evenings they would spend together, intimate conversations they would share. She drifts toward sleep with a smile on her face. And then—the smooth neck he wanted to kiss was sliced open with a jagged bottleneck reeking of alcohol, ripped by that monster!

At last Nick felt tears in his eyes, running down his bearded jowls. He tasted them on his tongue—his own salty tears. Real, live tears. He sobbed into the dark that was gradually deepening outside his window. "Murderer!" he shouted, choking on his wild hatred.

Murderer and thief! You robbed *me!*

CHAPTER 11

But while swimming toward a solitary island in the distance, the boy will be overwhelmed by all the deaths in the storm. For the first time in his long, impossibly long childhood, terrible doubts will assail him. Disconsolately he will drag himself ashore, but the beauty of the golden sand and the majestic evergreens against the clear blue sky will console him. How beautiful all this is, *he will think.* But the people here must be unhappy and dissatisfied too, just because they are human. So I have been called here to make their lives as beautiful as their island.

And so it will be that the first man the child will meet on his way will be a weak, half-blind old man.

"Hello, Grandfather." He will hurry up to the old man. "Give me all your sorrow and grief just for a minute, and I will transform them into happiness and lasting peace."

"Will I be young and strong again?" the old man will ask.

"No, but your old age and weakness will no longer be a burden to you."

"Will I be able to see clearly, as I once did?"

"No, but your grief at not being able to see will disappear."

"You are offering me resignation, not happiness, my child," the old man will remark.

"Does it matter what we call it?" The boy will shrug his thin shoulders. "What's important is that once and for ever your suffering will end; you will begin to notice only the good things in life and to enjoy them fully at last."

But the old man will shake his head. "I don't want to do anything fully—neither suffer nor rejoice. My bittersweet memories are the heartstrings of my life, and I can relive my past because of them."

"As you wish," the boy will sigh and sit down by him. "Now please tell me about the people here. I hope they don't all think the way you do."

"No, unfortunately not," the old man will say. "People gain the courage to think this way only when they come to expect no more from life. Until then, they are slaves to the future. They bow before it and, to propitiate it, throw hundreds of their own possessions into its mouth, although they know it can never be satiated. Finally, when the words 'will be' lose their meaning, they are sorry for the things they've sacrificed and bitterly cry for them."

"But I can free you from that too!" the boy will exclaim. "All the regrets, the grief, the disappointment—"

"No," the old man will answer sharply. "I no longer want to give up anything. I need it all!"

He needed it all. *Oooh, get out of here, old man—old man.* The sweat poured off Nick as he swung his axe again and again, driving it into the rotting, gnarled stump. He felt totally alone at the most difficult moment of his life: suspected of murder, not only by the police but also by his sister, and suffering writer's block as well. Though it made absolutely no sense, what annoyed him most was that he couldn't remember if the stump he was chopping had been an apple, pear, or cherry tree. He had cut it down himself when it was dead, and the stump had been leaning out a few feet over the driveway for five or six years now. Well, it would stick out no longer. Thwack, thwack! The axe blade whizzed through the air, splinters flew all around him, and the stump gaped at him like the jaws of a crocodile. Thwack! This had once been a healthy tree, heavy with fruit, sap flowing, leafy branches swaying in the breeze.

"Hey, Mister! Mister!" A boy was calling, as if he had been trying to catch Nick's attention for some time. "Are you Nicholas Edgeway?"

"Yes, I'm coming." Nick threw down the axe and went to the front gate, which he seemed to have locked the previous night. The boy's bike was propped against the fence, and he was holding a big brown envelope.

"This is from Mr. Marconi," he said.

"Who?"

"Marconi. Don't you know him?"

"Ah, the journalist? Yes, it's for me." Nick reached out over the gate, took the envelope, and then put it under his arm. "Thanks—but wait, let me give you something for bringing it." He started fumbling in the pockets of his pants and then realized that he was in his overalls and wasn't carrying any money on him. "Please, just a second! Let me run in—"

"Don't bother," the boy interrupted, already on his bike.

"How could I? You rode all the way over here."

"That's OK. I did it for Mr. Marconi, not for you, and not for money."

He rode off, his shaggy yellow thatch of hair billowing behind him. For some time Nick watched him with envy—so carefree! Then he returned to the house, taking the envelope upstairs to his study. He intended to open it immediately but instead forgot all about it, because…

First, he noticed that the typewriter was not where he always kept it, but on the edge of his desk, and his chair had been pushed off to the side, as if someone had been sitting on it and, hearing his footsteps, had stood up quickly, not wanting to be found there. But Nick would have seen anyone, who had really been there.

Second, the manuscript pages he had crumpled and thrown away were now even more carefully smoothed out and divided into two piles: one in the middle of the desk with the text up and the other to the right with the text down.

Third, the telephone was ringing. Numbly he walked into the bedroom and picked it up.

"At last!" Elsa began peevishly. "I've been trying to reach you for an hour now!"

"I was outside chopping up that stump by the driveway."

"What? Why?"

"To get it out of the way. You told me it bothered you, didn't you?"

"At least a hundred times, but why did you decide today of all days to deal with it?"

"Why not today?"

"Aren't you—sorry about Kathy?"

"Of course I'm sorry about her, in the same way that I'm sorry for all the previous victims. As I'll be sorry for the next victim too."

"For the next? How do you know there'll be a next?"

"I guess, Elsa; I *only* guess so. I hope I'm wrong, but because of that, I can't think of anything else, not even you."

"For Christ's sake, Nick! Don't you want to know how the interrogation went? Did you forget that at eight this morning—?"

"Oh, yeah. How did it go?"

"Well—I have to admit—it's not easy for him either."

"Not easy for whom?"

"For Lieutenant Forger, of course. But all things considered, it went very well. I explained absolutely everything to him."

"Everything?" Nick groaned and then remembered that they had agreed to be careful while speaking on the phone, since Forger was likely to have it tapped. "That 'everything' isn't much, is it?" he added quickly. "Unfortunately we can't really be of much help."

"Yes, *unfortunately*," Elsa emphasized the word. "There's nothing we can do, really. Incidentally, you'll have to hand over *those* clothes for the forensics experts, you know. He told me it was just a formality."

"Yes, they already came to claim them this morning, two uniformed—"

"Did they search the house?"

"No, they didn't. And even if they had, they wouldn't have found anything—" He almost added "by now"! He was terribly absentminded; he must end this potentially dangerous conversation. He surprised Elsa with a quick "Good-bye" and hung up.

Returning to his study, he stared with unabated alarm first at the chair, then at the typewriter, and finally at the manuscript divided into two piles. Was he supposed to blame this on his own divided self again? How much longer could he endure all these inexplicable events? While he was chopping up the stump, he had been sure he was alone, but now he no longer *felt* alone. *I must see a doctor, a psychiatrist*, was his first thought, but he immediately realized that seeking out a psychiatrist could be fatal. After all, the police were hunting a psychopathic killer, and he was among the prime suspects, maybe the only suspect. Visiting a shrink might well be a shortcut to prison!

Sweeping away the manuscript piles with a decisive gesture, he thought wickedly, *That idiot, my* other *self, will probably collect them again!* He thumped the envelope containing the newspaper clippings on top of the desk and opened it.

The articles were in chronological order, the first from March 14 and the last dated this morning. Important passages had been highlighted with a red marker. That Marconi, or whatever his *macaroni* name was, had certainly taken pains with them. He deserved a *bravissimo*.

After carefully reading the articles and taking notes, by noon Nick had prepared a few laconic comments:

1. March 14. Alexander Belloff, aged seventy-four. Throat cut in his house outside of town. Dead body accidentally found by Matilda and Isaac Shamly—neighbors and owners of gas station west of bypass. Murder weapon: old razor belonging to victim. MO: AB first given light sedative then tied to bed with cable from his home. Only neck sinews cut; trachea and aorta left intact. Death caused by loss of blood. AB lived alone; no relatives were found.

2. July 12. Victoria and Adriana Balester—twin sisters, aged sixty-six. Murdered at night in their home. Same MO. Both took slightly increased doses of Hexadorm before going to bed. Note: A often took this sedative, V never. Adjacent bedrooms on second floor. Both found tied to their beds with sheet strips, mouths gagged with duct tape. Murder weapon: large pair of scissors recently purchased by their housekeeper. V killed first. While sadist was in her sister's room, A screamed; housekeeper, who lived downstairs, heard her, ran outside, and found policeman nearby. Both returned together. When they entered A's room, she was

already dead. No trace of murderer. Only relatives A and V had were two nephews living abroad.

3. August 2. Emil Jonas, aged thirty-seven. Literature teacher at local high school, married with two children. Murdered at night—same MO. EJ and wife alone in their apartment (children at summer camp). That night both felt unusually sleepy and went to bed as early as nine o'clock. Wife woke up in morning with terrible headache to find by her side on the bed the bloody dead body of husband, tied hand and foot with cord she bought more than a year before, his mouth gagged with towel. Murder weapon: a butcher's knife taken from kitchen. It was established that both had taken Veronal, her dose three times larger than his. How they took the sedative is not known. Relatives of EJ suspected wife, since recently she had been hysterically jealous; police found no grounds to accuse her.

4. August 29...

But no, there was no use taking notes on Kathy's death. Everything he had read about her last night and today was imprinted in his mind, not as dry data but as *images*, much clearer and brighter than he would have liked.

So none of the accounts said anything about any object owned by the victim that the murderer took away. The earring, sadly, was an exception, and that was the reason why the journalists had commented on it so extensively. Kathy's case differed from the rest in two other ways: only she had been given chloroform rather than a sedative, and only she was tied with a cord brought from outside solely for that purpose. Thin nylon cord.

The same cord that he had in the basement. A whole roll of it. Elsa had brought it over about a month before; she wanted him to tie up some of the apple tree branches. But it had stayed in the basement, sealed. If it were unsealed now? Terrible! Because that bastard, the murderer, who was obviously an expert at breaking and entering, would hardly have taken the trouble of "breaking into" his basement, even though the basement door was conveniently positioned on the outside of the house. Going down there just to look for some cord stashed among a total stranger's junk would be downright stupid—except if he knew that he could find exactly what he needed.

Nick, shuffling out of his study like a condemned man headed for the gallows, walked down the hall and then the staircase. Was he alone or not? Was that importunate presence still following him? That question didn't interest him in the least at the moment. *If the roll of nylon cord were unsealed, unsealed, unsealed.* His mind repeated only this paralyzing "if" and didn't dare continue.

Once he stood outside the basement door, something in his head whispered in broken sobs, *Murderer!* He jammed the key into the padlock, turned it, and opened the door.

The cellar breathed back at him. *Murderer, murderer!* His hand trembled as he switched on the lights. As he stooped and climbed down the steep stairs, he thought he could see his own face peering up at him—pale, tired, and *cruel.* Like the face of a longtime enemy who has finally found an opportunity to denounce him, *Murderer!*

He found the roll where he had left it, on the rack above the toolboxes. It really *was* unsealed, with some missing. This was the most staggering, the most monstrous moment of his life, Nick knew. Emotionally exhausted and empty, he only managed to nod his head slowly, even lazily. *It would be no surprise,* began his next thought, *if somewhere here, in one of these boxes, is a light-blue kimono with golden flowers on it. Spattered with blood.*

CHAPTER 12

An hour later, descending the basement stairs again, Nicholas Edgeway no longer bore the slightest resemblance to a traumatized wretch. Along with the incriminating roll of nylon cord, he had dumped his horror, despair, remorse, bloody visions, and self-loathing into the deep end of the lake and had begun to feel instead an exultation and inordinate self-confidence. *So that's what really happened! I killed her!* He had marveled at himself while standing firmly on the tall gray rock above the water. *So that's how it happened!* He could not stop marveling even now. *I see her off in the evening and then come back home in the taxi. Suddenly I switch into my* other *self, jump into the Ford, and go straight back to the hotel. Creeping past the geezers dozing by the reception desk, I knock loudly on her door. "It's all over, dearest, all over with your little make-believe games!"*

"What are you looking for, Mr. Edgeway?"

Forger! He had crept to the top of the stairs like an alley cat and was now looking down into the basement.

"Something important? Something of particular interest to you?"

I'm looking for my mother's kimono, Nick imagined himself confiding to Forger, making his jaw drop with disbelief. *I want to wash the blood off it. Well, that is, if I haven't washed it already without knowing it.*

Instead, he asked, "How did you get in?"—upbraiding himself for not paying attention to the dog's barking some minutes earlier. "The gate to the yard was locked."

"Oh, I can manage to get around a lock or two."

"Why are you here?"

"I have a search warrant."

"Search warrant? For my home?"

"Yes," Forger confirmed. "So, tell me what you're looking for, and I assure you, no matter where in the house it may be, my men will be glad to help you find it."

You schmuck, Nick thought, smiling disdainfully. He felt he could afford the luxury, since he didn't really think the kimono was in the basement. More likely, it was already at the bottom of the lake. After all, his *other* self was hardly a simpleton. Far from it!

"You won't tell me what you're looking for?" Forger asked a third time.

"I feel kind of uneasy about it, Lieutenant, but mice, maybe even rats, have infested my house. I had a mousetrap down here once. God only knows where I may have put it, though."

"Mousetrap!" Forger practically ground his teeth as he spat out the word.

They climbed back up the stairs and went outside into the searing afternoon heat. By now it was three o'clock, and the sun stuck its image on Forger's baldpate like a cupping glass. He crossed quickly to the porch as Nick sauntered negligently behind him, smiling at his back.

Four apathetic subjects waited around the table, dressed almost identically, although they weren't in uniform. *More schmucks*, Nick thought, as Forger shoved the search warrant into his face. Folding it and returning it to his inside coat pocket, Forger gestured to the quadruplets, who stood up in unison, puppets on his string. Two of them made for the basement, and two flatfooted toward the front door. Biff started barking again but stopped when they were out of his sight.

Raising his eyebrows, Nick turned slowly toward the impudent lieutenant. "Do you really hope to find something here?" he asked casually.

"Not really," the lieutenant admitted.

They sat in the emptied lounge chairs. Nick leaned back and rested his head, squinting into the sheen of the sky's light-blue, silky-smooth embrace. *"It's all over, dearest, all over with your little make-believe games!"* Well, yes, he must have slept with her first. Of course! But after that. Dear God! What on earth had she done to make him turn murderous?

"Where were you last night?" Forger had been watching him intensely, apparently far from reassured by what he saw.

"Here," Nick replied. "I was here, as I am almost every night."

"Very convenient, indeed."

"What?"

"Well, the fact that you live alone. No one can prove you wrong. At least that's what you think—don't you, Mr. Edgeway?"

"I wasn't thinking that at all, if you want to know the truth."

"Did you phone anyone?"

"Yes, a friend of mine."

"I'll have that checked. What time did you call?"

"About eight thirty."

"Well, there's no need to check that. It was still too early."

"Whatever you say." Nick shrugged. "But why are you asking me about last night?"

"I can ask you about two days ago as well; that's no problem. So where were you on Friday the twenty-eighth?"

"You know that, don't you?"

"I mean during the day. Just tell me everything you did from morning till six o'clock that evening, so we can put your day and night together, so to speak."

This time Nick found it difficult to suppress a loud laugh. *Just tell him? "A girl came to me as a hallucination, but I wasn't sure who she was. So I went that morning to talk to her neighbor, a man in a 'heart relation' with her mother, to ask him if the mother had a daughter with a chipped tooth, and he said, 'Yes, she did. But the daughter has disappeared.'"*

"I was here most of the day," he actually said. "I worked until four in the afternoon and then took a walk by the lake. Then I came back, changed my clothes, and went to see my sister and brother-in-law."

"Lovely!" Forger exclaimed happily.

"Why lovely?"

"Because you're lying, that's why."

"Am I?" Nick assumed a sarcastic air.

"Yes! Beige suit, white shirt, tall, well-built, blond, a little plump, blue eyes, slightly hoarse voice, saying he's from Hors...Horshr...or some such place, but driving a car with local registration."

"Enough." Nick waved his hand. "I see the landlady has called you."

"Come on, Edgeway, talk! What did you need Alina Norris for?"

"She was my sister's seamstress."

"So what?"

"I heard about her death, and when I remembered her daughter, I decided to do a good deed, to give her a hand if she was in need—if she needed some financial support."

"You're lying again! You didn't know that Alina was dead or that she had a daughter."

"I only pretended I didn't know. I wouldn't compromise Kaya, her daughter, by confiding in that old gossip of a landlady. I was going to send her money on behalf of a friend of her mother who was concerned about her but wanted to remain anonymous."

"Oh, how delicate!" Forger narrowed his eyes. "And how noble too."

"Precisely." Nick nodded. "I've a hunch such sentiments don't mean much to you, though."

"We aren't discussing my personality at the moment, Edgeway. I'm waiting to hear what you're going to say about why you aimed your 'charity' at the seamstress's daughter."

"Well, I liked her. I mean, she seemed like a modest, decent girl."

"And she disappeared before her mother was buried," Forger broke in. "Who knows where she is now, or with whom?"

"If she's alive," Nick said morosely.

"What do you mean?"

"Well, I mean what I said, Lieutenant. It's possible that the sadist has murdered her too."

Forger pondered the possibility for a moment and then dismissed it decisively. "It isn't his style. He doesn't kill in the streets, and he doesn't hide the bodies of his victims."

"Hmm, who knows? You may be right. You've been hunting him for half a year now, after all. You should be much more familiar with his habits than I am."

"Hmm, who knows?" Forger echoed belatedly. "Who knows?"

In other words, it was clear that something had added to his suspicions since yesterday. But what? Nick folded his hands and clenched his teeth, trying to suppress his anxiety without giving himself away. It was high time he stopped fooling himself: Kathy enraged him? Nonsense! He must have known beforehand that he was going to kill her; otherwise he wouldn't have taken the cord with him. And possibly the kimono—so there was a real danger of that kimono turning up at any moment. Yes, the sword of Damocles hung above his head! Yet he also felt an unfamiliar, piquant pleasure at this ancient, *manly* game of playing with fire, which, it seemed, he played very well. He remained calm, fully in control, even slightly sardonic. How could Forger guess that, while he parried those leading questions, Nick was carrying out his own, immeasurably more difficult, "private investigation" inside his own head? Investigating his *other* self!

Well, the game goes on. He leaned toward Forger and looked into his eyes point-blank—eyes filled with dark-yellow flecks, like specks of soft clay. "You're wasting my time, Lieutenant. Why don't you try to stick to the point?"

"Perhaps you involuntarily let a little truth seep into your lies, Edgeway, by mentioning that, before you went to your sister and brother-in-law's, you changed your clothes. Do I make myself clear?"

"No."

"I'm talking about your beige suit and white shirt. You had them on during the day but not in the evening. When people go visiting, they usually change their clothes."

"Normally, yes," Nick said. "However, that's my favorite suit, so I kept it on. As for white shirts, I have at least five."

Forger ignored Nick's explanation and continued, "And yesterday, when I asked what you were wearing that evening, you unconsciously chose the easiest alibi and described your clothes during the day."

"You are trying to think," Nick remarked, "instead of finding the taxi driver."

"We found him, but, as you expected, he didn't pay much attention to what you were wearing. Light suit and shirt is all he could remember."

"Well, let me put your mind at ease. Your people can go through my entire wardrobe, even copy some of the patterns."

"OK, Randy," Forger said, turning away. "Bring them over here!"

Nick blinked, puzzled at first, then saw one of the quadruplets coming toward them with a pile of newspaper clippings in his hands. He handed them solemnly to his boss.

"It's the full set," he boomed. "He's been collecting and reading. Even been takin' notes."

"I've been doing nothing of the kind," Nick objected. "They were brought to me today. I hadn't read a single article about the killings, not one. Remember that."

Forger raised his eyebrows high and asked with unaffected curiosity, "Do you really expect me to believe you, Edgeway?"

And I, how can I believe myself? Nick thought. He already found it hard to keep the look of cool indifference on his face. He felt miserable again—felt the weight of half-forgotten facts crushing him. He could imagine himself stealing the chloroform—somehow. But wasn't it just today that he learned the details about the murders from those damned clippings? How could it have been possible for him to have killed Kathy yesterday in exactly the same way? So much for his theory of the other self, sex, and demonic possession—all an illusion, a transparent little story! He had come back that night and slept like a baby, while the *real* murderer committed another grisly murder. Whoever that was had even planted the earring to mock him.

Repressing indescribable disappointment, and at the same time realizing such disappointment was deeply pathological, Nick started feeling an almost uncontrollable fear. Now that he had concluded that he was no murderer, his audacity vanished without a trace.

"Look, I...I called a...friend of mine...yesterday," he babbled brokenly, "because I...needed the articles! I had decided to write... a novel—understand? Tense narrative, lots of suspense."

"A novel about the sadist?"

"No, no, please—about the victims. I don't know the sadist!"

"But you know the victims, right?"

"The victim, *one* victim, the latest I mean—as for the rest, only by my notes." He was now keenly aware that he was being inconsistent, was stammering, but couldn't stop himself. "Miss Hatcher...is going to be my main character!"

"Why not Mr. Schumacher?" Forger seemed to suggest the name casually. "He could also do the job."

Watch out, Nick! This is a trap, some nasty, dangerous trap!

"Who? Schumacher? I don't know such a person."

"Come on! Just think a little."

"No, I'm telling you the truth—"

"Knock it off, Edgeway! You were in his home the day before yesterday for almost an hour."

Nick bit his lower lip deeply. He was sinking deeper and deeper into a swamp of lies and misunderstandings! "If you mean Alina and Kaya's neighbor—"

"Whom you used as camouflage," Forger interrupted with a sardonic smile, "to enter Schumacher's apartment."

"Why in the world would I want to do that?"

"To make yourself familiar with the surroundings, Mr. Edgeway—that's why."

"He—" His eyes opening wide, Nick suddenly put his hands to his throat. He felt his fingers turn cold despite the sweltering heat. "Is he also?"

"Why did you lie that you didn't know him?" Forger cut the question short.

"I didn't know his family name. 'Eric'—that's how he introduced himself to me. 'Just Eric,' he said!"

"There's a nameplate on his door. All the time you were waiting for him to open the door, it was right in front of your eyes. Didn't you read it?"

"No, I didn't. I didn't pay attention. I was only thinking about Kaya!"

"To shower her with shekels on behalf of an anonymous benefactor—sorry, my mistake: benefactress—from some invented town? Don't you know how ridiculous all that sounds, Edgeway?"

"But it's true!"

"If it were true, why didn't you tell me about it straightaway? Why did you try to mislead me and say that you didn't go out Friday morning?"

After a long hesitation, Nick simply lowered his head. "I can't answer that question."

"Then I'll answer it for you: Eric Schumacher was killed that night. He was tied up, and his throat was slit. Before that he had taken two or three sleeping pills—"

"Pills just like these!" Randy broke in, opening his huge fist. He was holding Nick's bottle of Seconal.

Forger laughed and said, "Put it with the other evidence." He reached his hand inside the pocket of his baggy pants.

To get out the handcuffs?

"Wait!" Nick blurted. "Eric had a brother who must have seen, or at least heard—"

"We haven't spoken to the brother yet." Forger took a big checked handkerchief from his pocket and wiped his dripping brow and baldpate with it. "The brother wasn't home."

"That's impossible!" Nick jumped to his feet. "He was in a wheelchair! He can't even move!"

"Well, he has moved, it seems. We found the wheelchair in the kitchen, empty."

CHAPTER 13

What was the bitter truth? Probably that he had *slaughtered them all!* Nick swerved to avoid a bump in the road and checked the rearview mirror, wondering which of the cars was following him. Was it that battered Fiat or the Volvo? What difference did it make? What mattered was that they would keep him under constant surveillance from now on, because what did they have? He had been with Kathy the same night, but they knew he had gone back home after saying good night to her—the taxi driver would testify to that. Had he then gone back to the hotel? No one could say one way or another, including himself! He had paid a call to Schumacher two days ago, but did that mean that he had killed him last night? Yes, he did deny knowing him, but that was just because of confusion about the names. So what if they had found Seconal in his home? How many more homes could they find it in—hundreds? Thousands? He had been reading newspaper articles about the murders and taking notes, but he could easily prove that he had got them today. What court would even consider a case built on such shaky ground? None. So the one hope left for the detectives was that the "suspect" would incriminate himself in some way.

And he was as concerned as they were—either he would find a way to refute the hypothesis that he was the sadistic killer or he would give himself away, even if *only* to himself. If he really had committed the murders, he wanted to make sure it never happened again. He desperately needed to know the truth. If he found it, he would put his divided self together or at least gain control over his unconscious impulses. Even if he failed and slit someone else's throat, they would accommodate him in some mental institution. While people, especially Elsa, would shudder that they had dismissed him as some weak, bland mollusk, he was so accustomed to his solitary life that he would hardly notice the difference. He would go on writing his tales there, undisturbed.

"But I can free you from that too!" the boy will cry. "All the regrets, the grief, the disappointment—"

"No," the old man will repeat sharply. "I no longer want to give up any of it. I need it all!"

"All right, all right, Grandpa, just tell me then what customs there are here so I won't do anything wrong, and you can return to your ocean of grief."

"There's only one custom here," the old man will explain, "and it can be best expressed by the word 'duel.' There are two kinds of people living on the island. The people from the North call themselves Sensibles, because they are always in doubt, always hesitant, afraid of change, so they always make half decisions. The people from the South call themselves Sensitives, but they too are always in doubt, always hesitant, afraid of change and make half decisions."

"What about this duel?" the boy will ask.

"It's over two birds, which are so huge that if they spread their wings, the shadow would cover the whole island, and if they fanned their wings, it would create a steady breeze and a pleasant coolness."

"Where are those wondrous birds?"

"Well, that is something nobody knows. They probably don't exist. You see, it's always terribly hot here, my boy. The sun beats down on us day after day, troubling everyone—it's hard to live without a fight. Tonight, for example, will be the crucial fight of the year."

"I'll take care of them all!" The boy will promptly jump to his feet. "I'll ease the suffering of both the Sensibles and the Sensitives, so that they will no longer feel the heat and will have no cause to fight anymore. But tell me, Grandpa, which are your people? As a token of respect to you, I'd like to start with them."

The old man will look the child square in the eyes, and because he is almost one hundred years old—a wise man who will have spoken innumerable truths and lies in his life, often without being sure which was which—he will point due South.

"Go that way, those are my people."

Isaac and Matilda Shamly's ramshackle gas station broke the monotonous landscape on the left side of the road with its three gas pumps painted an imperative red and an elongated, weather-beaten wooden building behind them. The first floor of the building had been converted into a shop for spare parts, and the second floor housed "a childless Jewish family of humble origins," as L. Marconi, the well-known reporter, described it.

Nick pulled up past the last pump so that he would not block any prospective customers and then got out of his car. A minute later a tall, gaunt woman dressed in orange overalls, a white T-shirt, and white canvas shoes emerged from behind the building. She scrutinized him, her eyes so narrowed that he decided she was myopic, and then made her way toward him. Everything about her was squeaky clean, as if her job wasn't pumping gas but pouring water.

"Mrs. Matilda Shamly?"

"Yes, that's my name."

"Nicolas Edgeway," he introduced himself politely.

A Volvo pulled up to the second pump.

"Excuse me, Mr. Edgeway." She hurried over to service the "customers." "Your tank was practically full," she soon told them.

That's an uncomfortable situation. Nick smiled. As the woman took the money that the driver shoved at her through a crack in the window, he tromped on the accelerator and sped off. Quite a curious piece of detective strategy! Or were those people in the Volvo not cops, just ordinary people driving by late on a Sunday afternoon?

"This is a dead season." Matilda sighed, approaching him again. "Sometimes the road is empty for hours. But business picks up around the first of September."

"Have you lived here long?" Nick asked her.

"Almost fifteen years."

He took a closer look at her. *About forty, so she was maybe twenty-five when her husband brought her to this sinkhole of dust and boredom, predetermined only to be passed by—her "just Life,"* he thought, imagining those fifteen years that had stooped her scrawny shoulders: a flow of cars and gasoline and buckets of soapy water needed to keep her white shirts and orange bib overalls clean. His heart contracted in a relishing pang of sympathy: *"Give me your disappointments," the boy will say—will ask insistently—will hold out greedy hands for them.*

"I've come about the murdered old man, ma'am."

Her eyes dilated, becoming even darker, as if he had forced them to see some frightful, shattering sight. But why "as if"? Wasn't it really so? He hurried to explain that he was an author and wanted to write a novel about the murders, as a warning for the thousands of naïve people who—and so on. He was eloquent, like any other practiced liar, and like any other liar, he was happy when she believed him.

"I'm sorry, but my husband's not here, Mr. Edgeway. He could give you much more information than I can."

Though the subject was repugnant to her, she tried to answer his questions. No, they hadn't found a photo of Belloff, so there was just an inscription on his grave—no way for Nick to check if he had ever seen the man. She described him as short and emaciated, shrunk, bent with age, with thin white hair—but that description could fit at least one-third of all old men.

"Had Belloff ever mentioned anything to anybody about a *big strange man* whom he might have noticed, no matter when or where, who impressed him—no matter how—with something in his behavior or his gaze?"

"No, no…that is—" Here Matilda faltered in embarrassment.

"Tell me, please, ma'am!" Nick urged her excitedly. "Any and every detail might matter."

"Yes, only a detail, Mr. Edgeway, but since you're trying to get deeper into his personality—"

"You're right. That's my job!"

"The last few times he came around, he implied some—offensive things. He was peevish and mistrustful."

"What did he imply?"

"Well, he had got it into his head that—someone was stealing his food. He was always stashing things away, turning his kitchen into a storeroom of cans and jars. He claimed things went missing there every day, and since no other people lived nearby but us—well, he let us know in no uncertain terms that he suspected us!"

"That's understandable, a typical old man's obsession"—Nick nodded—"especially since he lived alone."

"Yes, he was a long-time widower, and Andrey, his only son, left him twenty-three or twenty-four years ago. He went back to Russia. That was where Belloff and his wife emigrated from. This gas station was his property, along with the house. He sold them to pay his debts."

So poverty had driven Belloff into that rickety house on the other side of the highway, down that dirt road. None of the reporters had bothered to mention the exact whereabouts of the old man's house, so this was new and important information to Nick, precipitating his sudden farewell to Matilda as he leaped into his Ford and drove away.

Belloff's house, though, didn't seem at all familiar to him. He could swear he had never been there before; otherwise, at least some small detail should have stuck in his memory. A rickety house like that was not so easily forgotten. It reminded him of a skull sticking out of the ground: its eye sockets filled with two windows, their panes replaced by dirty brown cardboard, and below a door of rotten clapboard. *Fine, but if I have no recollection of the slaughter of my victims, no memory of their agonizing, bloody deaths, why should I remember this decrepit old house?* Yes, this situation was complicated by the fact that, while even the vaguest memory would have been enough for him to tear off the mask and expose himself as the perpetrator of six successive murders, the lack of all memory about any of it hardly proved his innocence.

Discouraged, he drove back to town. His task wasn't going to be as easy as he had anticipated. Besides, the van driving behind him sported a suspiciously tall antenna. It gradually dropped further behind, only to be replaced by other, equally suspicious vehicles, until Nick forced himself to stop looking in the rearview mirror. It was simply insane to think that a platoon of cops were after him, wasn't it? But if we mention insanity—better not to mention it!

CHAPTER 14

His next stop was the home of the two poor sisters. He folded the map, put it in the glove compartment, and then gave the shadowy, curbed street a long look. Again nothing. Nothing stirred in his memory. Well, it was possible that he had been here as a child—back when he used to drive around town, usually with Reno and Elsa. But it seemed almost impossible that he could have been stalking around this neighborhood just a month or two ago. *"Almost!" God, how can it be that I have such little faith in myself?* He was astounded. *And to what degree don't I know myself?*

Their home was nothing special—just another white, two-story house, with a tiny porch on the second floor that almost reached the street. The low hedge in front served more as decoration than a barrier. Nick got out of his Ford and approached the gate. As he pushed it casually and entered the yard, from behind the lace curtains of one of the windows appeared a *familiar* face!

His heart instantly raced: *familiar, familiar*—but just from some pictures in those newspaper clippings, the face of the same housekeeper who, terrified by Adriana Balester's agonizing cries, had run out into the night.

She was soon at the front door—an elderly woman, asthmatic, swollen legs. When she stared at him, Nick shuddered. What if he had really been walking around the place just before the crime was committed and she had noticed him but hadn't paid any attention to him at the time? And what if she remembers now?

"How can I help you, sir?"

Her perfunctory question put him immediately at ease. He approached her with the most ingratiating smile he could produce and gave her his pitch about the new novel/warning he was writing. The woman listened abstractedly, every now and then nodding her gray head but saying nothing. He eventually had to stop, since there was no more to say on the subject.

"I live in this house in constant fear," she finally replied. "If I only had somewhere to go to, I wouldn't stay here for another second."

"I understand, ma'am."

"You could never understand unless you've seen with your very eyes what I saw."

But I could have seen even more than you have! Nick thought. *Or more precisely, I could have done what you've only seen!*

"Well, you might as well come in." She gestured listlessly. "I trust you. I don't know why, but I do."

Trust? Stupid woman! Nick followed her through the foyer, and she motioned him into the room opposite with the same indifferent gesture. This room was scantily furnished, but everything in it was tasteful, from the pictures on the wall to the scanty furniture. There was no trace of the bric-a-brac or tacky embroidery that would suggest two old spinsters had lived here.

"I'll make tea," she said after approving of the way he settled his substantial bulk on one of the thin-legged chairs.

After she left, he took a deep breath of the faint fragrance that permeated the cool room. Something about the odor evoked distant, sweet, maudlin associations in him. It was very pleasant here, very peaceful. He was instantly carried back to his childhood, when his mother would say, "I'll make tea," and then go off, soon to return with the silver tray in her delicate, graceful hands.

The return of the worn-out woman with her swollen legs cut short his reverie. The silver tray now teetered precariously in other hands, stubby and ugly.

"Now the whole house belongs to me." She smiled bitterly, placing the tray on the table and rushing to sit down, because she was wheezing again. "They left it to me years ago, but everything here reminds me of—their miserable end."

"Time will heal you of those wounds, ma'am."

"No, no, that would be even worse! I'd feel like—a traitor. I loved them. They were my only friends. We'd known each other since we were girls, almost all our lives."

"Please, tell me something about *them*." About them, not yourself was his clear implication.

She, naturally, started with the most trivial details: "They didn't marry because they fell in love with the same man. They were beautiful, wealthy, but chose to stay together—to the end. Every Sunday, children filled the house and the yard, everywhere."

"Children?" he interrupted her rambling prattle.

"Yes! We used to have big trays of cookies, cakes, ice cream—"

"Charity?"

"It was much more than that, sir. It was the *motherly* love of two aging, childless women! Did you know they almost single-handedly supported the local orphanage? They left everything to the orphanage, except for the house and an income for me. Incidentally, I've also made a will. After I'm gone, the children will come to live in this house too. That really gives me comfort.

"How about their nephews?" Nick brought her back to the point. After all, he hadn't come here to listen to her maudlin reminiscences. "They've disinherited them."

"They grew up in Australia and don't even think of coming back. They are successful businessmen, one of them the founder of—"

"So they have no plans to challenge the will."

"No." The former housekeeper's slave soul was not in the least offended by Nick's rude interruption.

Still, Nick realized that he stood little chance of wheedling anything more useful or intimate out of her if he didn't soften his tone or flatter her in some way.

"Again, my deepest condolences, madam," he addressed her cordially. "It seems you were something like their younger sister, like a friend—"

"Yes, you're right. They loved me!" she responded eagerly. "How can I ever tell you how much I miss them?"

"I can only imagine that." He sighed. "That's why I waited for some time before coming to see you. I wouldn't even think of approaching you, like others, during the most tragic days of your life—I mean chiefly the reporters, of course," he clarified to her, although he felt sure that it hadn't been them that had "bothered" her, since she posed so willingly for the cameras. "Now that your sorrow must have become a little less intense, maybe you can remember some details that escaped you then. It seems very unlikely that you didn't notice something at least a little out of the ordinary before the tragedy occurred."

"Tragedy, sir! It was certainly that. An indescribable, inhuman tragedy!"

She wiped her eyes with a tiny silk handkerchief and then, as if guided by some infallible instinct, chose this worst-possible time to start serving the strong herbal tea. Reclining his head toward her, Nick watched her, his expression sympathetic, though under the table, his fists were clenched. Her lugubrious movements and apparent reluctance to answer his questions were almost more than he could bear. Eventually she sat down across from him, slurped from "her" mug—of fine china, the same excellent quality as everything else in this former home of the unfortunate sisters. She looked at him insistently until he had tasted not only the tea but also a little piece of cake. Suddenly, seemingly having come to a momentous decision, she blurted out, "Yes, there was something peculiar at that time. It was really weird because they both started seeing—"

"What?"

"A ghost."

Nick almost choked. "Excuse me!"

"Well, I really don't know how to tell you about it. They could have simply invented it—from long grieving for their relatives, for instance. Victoria claimed that it was their father's spirit, and Adriana said their brother's. They even argued over it, but you mustn't think they were senile old women! On the contrary, they were both reasonable and rational."

"Really? I mean, of course I don't think they were senile." Since his objection sounded less than convincing, he became a bit more emphatic. "I certainly don't think of them in such terms at all!"

"Well, to tell you the truth, I had started thinking certain things about them myself. They weren't superstitious or anything like that and had never expressed beliefs in the afterlife or any mystic happenings. So, God forgive me, I was really worried that they'd fallen sick—become mentally unstable. Now, however, I can't help asking myself what if it really was their father or brother come from the dead to try to warn them?"

"God works in mysterious ways, ma'am." Nick put his palms together hypocritically. "Unfortunately, they didn't heed the warning."

"Yes, unfortunately," she said instantly, agreeing.

They sipped their tea in silence until Nick abruptly asked the most unpleasant question yet, "Would you show me the scissors that killed them?"

"I hope I never see them again! The police took them."

Of course; they were evidence, after all. He had hoped that maybe seeing the murder weapon would remind him of how he had brutally thrust the blades into the wrinkled flesh of those cracked old women. "It must have been a rusty old pair of scissors," he casually suggested. "At least, that's how I imagine them."

"No, just the opposite." The woman was taken in by his clumsy ploy. "They were almost new and quite expensive, made of some special steel. Sharp! I bought them at the special request of Victoria and Adriana. They wanted to give them as a present to their seamstress. But unfortunately she died, so the scissors stayed with us."

"Who died? The seamstress?" Nick shuddered with an ominous premonition. "What...what...was her name?"

"Alina. Alina Norris was her name. She was very good, very diligent—"

"Dear Lord! Did she come here with her daughter?"

"No, I don't remember that she had a daughter."

Was this just a coincidence? What else could it be if not that? Extremely confused, Nick shifted on his chair, which creaked tiredly. It was high time he left. His presence here had become too weighty, both literally and figuratively. It weighed down on him too, but he couldn't bring himself to get up just yet. "Do you think I could take a look at some pictures of Victoria and Adriana? The ones in the papers aren't—"

"Yes, it's true. They aren't themselves in those," she reacted indignantly. "The ones I chose were so much nicer. Just wait a moment."

She loaded the tray with empty cups and saucers, the teapot, sugar bowl, and uneaten tea cakes and left the room. When she returned, she went to the antique armoire and carefully took out a big leather album, as careful as if handling a religious relic. She brought it to the table, brushed the perfectly clean tablecloth with her hand, and set the album down.

Nick started turning the thick pages, checking only for the two sisters. At first he was startled—he had forgotten that they were twins. And amazingly similar, even as they aged. There they are, with their heads together—laughing, long-haired girls. And here, young women with faces already solemn, probably having just endured their painful, all-too-ordinary love affair with "the same man"—maybe not so ordinary after all? Who knows? He skimmed the brown-paper pages that chronicled the years of identical life, hurrying to reach the end.

Finally he found it: their last photo, taken only four months ago. Nick stared at it. No, they were hardly "wrinkled old women." While they were no longer young and had lost their youthful glow, they had become truly beautiful exactly in this way: ennobled by their undeviating course through time, by the little Sunday interludes when, tired after the trays heavy with sweets and cakes, they had sat at this very table, side by side, smiling across at "their" always-hungry children. Those smiles were no doubt completely sincere, as testified to by the tiny, fanlike wrinkles around their eyes and lips.

Innumerable tiny fanlike smiles around those eyes and lips, and now a gaping scarlet smile of death carved with a pair of scissors around their necks. Nick held his head in his hands. He felt physical pain as if someone had started cutting at him too, tearing through the thick veil of fantasies that had protected him until now, protected him from *seeing*. Shattered by the "view," he caved in for a moment and shook with throaty, convulsive sobs.

"But who are you, sir?" The former housekeeper retreated to the door, her face contorted by suspicion and fear. "Who are you really!"

She was ready to run away as she had on that terrible night. Her asthma and swollen legs would hardly slow her down on her way out. "Who are you really?" He would *love* to be able to answer that question, to be confident that he hadn't murdered those two tired old women—that, if it were up to him, they would still be sitting placidly together on their slender-legged chairs. He would like to yell at her, *"No, It wasn't my arms spattered up to the elbows with their blood! It's impossible—because my mother had the same little wrinkles, do you understand? The same!"*

He stood up, wiping his eyes with the back of his hand and still sobbing when he reached the door. The woman drew back or, more precisely, jumped aside. He would have liked to yell something else at her too, *"Why weren't you scared of me when I was rude to you, you obsequious soul, asking absurd, nasty questions about scissors and seamstresses? No, you only grew suspicious when you saw my tears! And why is it that you only have wrinkles between your eyebrows?"*

CHAPTER 15

Nick made his last stop at the high school where Emil Jonas had taught until his death and which turned out to be suspiciously close to the home of the ubiquitous seamstress Alina Norris. He clambered out of the Ford, a little nervous because of the late hour—already past nine o'clock. Not midnight, after all, but the security guard stared at him through the glass and bars of the entrance gate as if asking himself whether he were some vampire, maybe even the sadist himself. Sad but true, everyone in town was now in a state of constant fear.

Nick tried to calm him down with the friendliest gestures he could think of, but to no avail. When no other option occurred to him, Nick began explaining in detail why he had come—that is, he began lying again, and in quite a loud voice. Still, the man inside the security booth gave no hint that he had even heard, as if he were deaf.

As usual, however, the problem had a simple solution: Nick opened his wallet, and the guard opened the gate, tucking the twenty-dollar bill into his shirt pocket. His face dotted with punctured capillaries, and the purple nose unmistakably indicated how the money would be spent. The guard led him to the basement, where the school records were stored, turned on the lights, and sat next to the door.

Nick rummaged through the seeming chaos of old papers and documents, mildly surprised to discern some order, and found the files he needed—quicker than he had expected. He occupied himself with checking first the names of the graduates of eight years ago, then seven, six, and five.

Until he found her name: Kayara, but not Kayara Norris.

Kayara *Belloff.*

The name of a girl who disappeared without a trace somehow connected with all five murders. Perhaps with the murderer as well?

CHAPTER 16

Nick's car's headlights revealed the road ahead as if it were a rolled-up scroll of space beyond which gaped only *nothingness*. He gazed into that nothingness with tired eyes, almost instinctively resisting the sensation that someone was staring at him insistently—from the empty backseat! That stare drilled through his skull, into his thoughts, which seemed to travel to nothingness too.

"Kayara *Belloff*," he whispered.

The name couldn't be a coincidence in this small town. Reviewing earlier coincidences, his only explanation was that Andrey Belloff, the son of the murdered old man, was Kaya's father and Alexander Belloff her grandfather. Emil Jonas had been her teacher; her mother had sewn clothes for the Balester sisters and was in "heart relation" to Eric Schumacher. Was Kathy related to Kaya in some way as well? Given all the other connections, that seemed likely.

Nor could he help but assume that all the victims—including Kaya—had something else in common, something that had led to their deaths, to the series of inhuman murders.

So I'm the sadistic psychopath who committed these terrible crimes, eh? Nick asked himself, tapping his forehead with his finger. *But I don't remember anything about it, because it was my other self? What an improbable scenario!* He laughed out loud and put an end to the self-interrogation. He no longer suspected himself of anything—except that, even earlier, he had only been pretending to suspect himself, for some perverse thrill.

The living room light was on! Nick was so startled that he slammed on the brakes, which screeched like animals being slaughtered, eliminating any chance of sneaking up on the intruder. Fighting off the temptation to step on the gas pedal and just get lost, he parked the Ford along the road next to the fence, quietly sneaked into the yard, and raced for the house. He tiptoed up the front steps to the porch and, with his back against the wall, inched to the closest living room window, and tripped over something! Jumping back, he managed to hurt his ankle and bang his elbow. *Damn!*

It was Biff, leaping around him wagging his thinning tail.

"Get out of here!" Nick whispered.

Kicking him aside gently so he wouldn't yelp, Nick moved to the window and cautiously peeked through a slit between the curtains. Shaking his head with indignation, he retraced his steps and, deliberately and loudly, rattled the door.

"Nick, is that you?" Elsa called from inside.

"Who else would it be?"

She unlocked the door and greeted him—holding a knife in her hand. Nick stepped back, grabbing his throat. His reaction seemed to surprise her, and she looked down, as if just *noticing* what she held. She casually tossed the knife on the shoe cabinet.

"Sorry, I picked it up by mistake," she murmured. Then she quickly went on the offensive. "May I ask why you were creeping around outside like—"

"Like *what?*"

"It's perfectly obvious like what."

"Really?" Nick also chose the offense. "How about you? What are you doing here at eleven o'clock anyway?"

"Yes, we've been waiting for you for hours! Where have you been all this time? I've been going nuts in this spooky house, alone with the child!"

"Did you say 'spooky'?" He trembled. "Have you noticed something—out of the ordinary?"

"What do you mean?"

"How would I know! You're the one who said 'spooky.' I thought you might have heard or seen some ghosts or a presence—"

"Oh, come on, Nick, we have so much to talk about, and all you can do—" She turned her back to him and headed for the living room.

"Wait," he asked her to stop. "Have you had dinner yet?"

"Yes, *we* had dinner, *Annie* and I. Do you hear me? *Annie* and I!"

"Why act like this, Elsa? It was Anna I was worried about. Anyway, if she's already had dinner, why don't you spend the night here, so we can have that long talk? Just put her to bed."

"You're right." She turned her head and called out sweetly, almost slimily, "Annie, oh Anniiee dear!"

The child popped out into the hall, blinking like a mouse, and looked like a mouse as well, if she looked like anything.

"Hello, Anna."

"Come, say good night to your uncle, honey."

But she said nothing and shambled after her mother up to the second floor. Her skinny legs in white stockings, as unsteady as her father's, seemed like wobbly ropes that might at any moment get tangled up with each other—even knotted up!

Puffing his cheeks in full disapproval, Nick locked and bolted the front door, hung his jacket on a hook, took the knife, and went into the kitchen. He squatted by the stove and opened the oven door: a few cutlets, French fries, and mushrooms. On the table waited a big bowl of fresh salad. He didn't think he was hungry, but after he washed his hands, he sat down at the table and practically inhaled it. Tension always increased his appetite.

"You coming?" Elsa called from the living room.

There she goes again! No peace for him when she was around! He left the dishes on the table and joined her, slumping into his favorite armchair grumpily.

"Where's that roll of nylon cord?" she began, skipping the preliminaries.

"Which roll do you mean?"

"The one I brought so that you could tie up the branches of the apple trees."

"Oh, that one. It's in the basement."

"No, it isn't there. It's nowhere to be found. I looked for it."

"I remember now. It must be somewhere in the backyard. A few weeks ago, I was going to tie up the branches with it, but something interrupted me, and I forgot about doing it. Incidentally, why don't you give Max a call? Tell him you're staying here so he won't worry about you. Although, come to think of it, he's not the kind to worry easily."

"I called him while you were eating." Elsa sat across from him and folded her arms. "Aren't you going to ask me why I'm so interested in that roll of cord?"

"No, I'm *not* going to ask you that."

"Fine! That's enough in itself to give you away!"

"What I'm giving away is my unwillingness to respond to your arrogant, insinuating tone. I'm tired."

"Ssstop it!" she hissed, like a snake. "Guilty! That's what you are, not tired but guilty, with no defense. All the facts are against you!"

She's here to accuse me, Nick realized, slightly shocked. *Or even worse: she came to* pretend *to accuse me.* "Listen, Elsa," he responded, "it's perfectly clear that you don't really suspect me. Otherwise you wouldn't spend the night here, let alone bring Anna with you. No one trusts a psychopath to that extent, even if the psychopath happens to be one's brother. Don't suspect me, but your questions suggest the opposite. Why? What's happened since I talked to you last?"

Instead of answering, however, she unexpectedly launched into how she had fired her maid that morning. "I told her...she says...then I...but she." Elsa's gesticulating and melodramatic grimaces weren't really connected to what she was saying, as if she were reacting to something else, some insistent thought that her words were covering up.

"And when I reminded her of the broken vase—"

"How much longer are you going to continue this pointless performance?" Nick cut her short after he finally understood that she was just trying to make him uneasy before she told him something particularly unpleasant. "You've fired her—so what? She's not the first and won't likely be the last."

"I fired her with the hope of her going back to her village, so that Forger won't be able to interrogate her about the clothes you wore *that* evening. Unfortunately, though, he doesn't need her testimony. Very unfortunate for both of us, Nick!"

Pressing her hands to her temples, she gave him a desperate look, as though she were about to weep for him or looking at him in his coffin.

"But what had happened?" He surrendered to panic. "What *else*? Tell me!"

"Well, I...I lied to you," she finally mumbled. The truth is that I hid the sack with your clothes under some stones down there, under the big rock, and hurried back to search the house for other possible—clues. The police were likely to show up at any moment to search! Then I couldn't bring myself to go back and throw the clothes in the lake. I was worried that they might already be following me."

"Oh, is that all?" Nick pretended to relax, though he felt sure there was more to come. "Tell me exactly where you've hidden them, and I'll find a way to get rid of them once and for all."

"Don't hurry, dear; there's more. Forger showed up at our house around six this evening."

"That means he went there right after leaving here."

"He interrogated the two of us separately, and Max—told him everything: about the hidden clothes and that we'd agreed to testify that you had come to our place dressed in your beige suit. Forger pressured him, told him that another man you'd visited on Friday under some pretext was murdered that night, and that you had denied knowing him! That's when Max decided to tell Forger everything."

"'Decided,' eh? The treacherous sonovabitch!"

"I can't blame him, Nick. It's quite understandable that he wouldn't want to be involved in anything so dangerous. What's more, the two of you have never been on—the best of terms."

"True, but as far as those clothes are concerned, he would be covering for you, Elsa, not me!"

She blinked fast at him, pretentiously and with childish naïveté, which didn't suit her at all: her fluttering eyelashes, heavy with mascara, long and artificially curled, gave her a vicious doll's appearance. Tiny drops of sweat had appeared on her upper lip, delineating the fine hairs there, turning them into some preposterously rakish blond-auburn moustache as she slowly continued, "I really didn't want Max to know what I was doing, what I was thinking about my own brother, so I told him you had hidden the clothes there yourself."

"You lie too much, dear sister," Nick remarked dryly. "You lie to your husband and to me. But—" Suddenly he jumped up as if jolted by an electric shock. "So the police think that I—do you realize what that means! If I hid them myself, that would mean there really was blood on them! The police are now convinced that I'm the murderer!"

Another long silence followed, deliberately prolonged on Elsa's part—apparently calculated to fray his nerves to the point of snapping. Then she gave him a wan smile.

"Don't worry. I told Forger what actually happened and even showed him the place."

"Wonderful! Now they will make their analysis, and everything will end!"

"Well, yes, it would be wonderful!" In her voice Nick sensed a triumphant lilt. "But the clothes weren't there, Nick. Somebody must've found them, although I can't imagine who or how. I had hidden them very carefully, honestly!"

"Maybe you forgot which stones they were under—"

"No," Elsa interrupted. "I remember exactly where I left them. They're gone."

Nick bent over her. She raised her head, and their eyes met. Never, even in his darkest moments, had he dreamed they could become so estranged so fast and so—irrevocably. *She's not such a beauty*, he thought irrelevantly, and it was as if he were seeing her for the first time. *Besides, she's growing older and will soon get that middle-aged spread. And those watery-green eyes, at this moment absolutely expressionless, like cheap glass marbles.*

"As far as I can see," he commented quietly, "you're not particularly worried about the damage you've done me with your lies and stupidity."

"No, I'm not very worried," she countered with a brutal bluntness that was almost more than Nick could bear.

"Where's the earring?" he asked in an even lower voice. "I suppose you kept it, despite your promise."

"Yes, that's true. I kept it."

"What if they search your house?"

"They won't find it. Don't worry about that."

"Don't worry?" Nick impulsively stepped back, far from her. "What the hell do you plan to do with that damned earring?"

"It depends."

"Depends on what?"

"Depends on who I'll choose, if it comes down to making a choice."

A barely audible creak made them turn to the closed door. Annie stood there. How had she entered unobserved? And what for? To eavesdrop?

"How long have you been standing there, Anna?" This time Nick's resentment toward her was unmistakable from the abrupt tone of his voice. He collected himself and made an attempt to be more civil. "Can't you sleep? Are you thirsty?"

Naturally Anna didn't answer him. "Choose yourself," she said to her mother.

She was barefoot, dressed in a long nightgown—pink and thin as a cobweb. Nick could see her naked little body through it. Her loose hair fell in dry, colorless locks over her sharp, narrow shoulders. *She'll never be a woman*, occurred to Nick. *She'll never walk toward her lover barefoot, her hair down. She'll never be embraced by a man, caressed and kissed, desired. She has no future; no life awaits her.*

Nick frowned as a shiver of consternation crossed his face. No, these thoughts could not be his! They came from outside him; they were so obdurate. Only a sadistic monster would condemn a child to a sterile, loveless life. Or was it a spontaneous insight, a voiceless, gloating insinuation from the future? From the near future.

"Annie, my darling!" Elsa was also watching her, and her eyes were no longer watery-green glazed marbles. Instead, dark and abysmally deep pain shone through them.

She walked toward Anna, smiling desperately, and held her close, as if cradling a precious, very fragile jewel. "Of course I'll choose me. Only me...only us," she whispered brokenly.

As she picked her up, Nick felt the abyss that opened up beneath that "only us," a fitting conclusion to their vapid, even *slimy*, conversation. He hurried to open the door for them, somewhat obsequiously.

"Good night, Annie," he said quietly.

CHAPTER 17

The gray suit and light-blue shirt hung crumpled on two of the hangers in his closet.

"Stop this. Stop this!" Nick groaned.

Instead of hanging up his pants beside the suit, he put them back on. Why try to sleep? He had to think, to think—and do something! He slumped onto the nearest chair and stared transfixed at the incriminating clothes. Who had left them there?

Elsa? Maybe she did it because Forger ordered her to; then, if Nick tried to get rid of them, it would be as good as "admitting" his guilt.

Or the murderer himself? He could have been following her on Saturday when she hid them and then taken them. It was possible that he had marked them with some barely detectable substance that would incriminate their *owner* but had retrieved them too late to plant them for the detectives to find, so he brought them back here after the search.

Yes, both possibilities were equally plausible, and both left him in the middle. If the first were true, he had to submit the clothes to the police straightaway, but if the second were true, he had to destroy the "evidence"!

I won't even touch them, he finally decided. *I haven't opened the closet, so I never saw them. That's what I'll say, and I'd like to see anybody prove otherwise.*

But he knew this attempt to frame him would hardly be the last. He could assume more would follow, even more drastic.

That's it! He shook his head, knowing he couldn't sleep now, while he was still free to find the murderer and turn him in to the police. This was not impossible: after all, he had collected valuable information the previous afternoon. For example, he already knew that the victims were connected in some way and whatever they had in common had led to their deaths. So they weren't murdered by a maniac but by someone with a *motive*. Thus, by leaving his "handwriting" at each crime scene, the killer was only attempting to give the impression of a sadistic psychopath, which he definitely was not.

A diabolically clever ploy, which had led the investigators on a wild-goose chase. What that schmuck Forger and his cops were seeking didn't exist, while the real clues remained unnoticed and probably even untouched—especially those to be found at Belloff's house, which since his murder had not even been lived in.

Nick leaped up, excited by the conclusions he was coming to. He closed the closet and put on his shoes and jacket before tiptoeing past the room where Elsa was sleeping, hopefully *not* awake and eavesdropping traitorously behind the door. Once downstairs, he groped for the cabinet and rummaged through its drawers for a flashlight. In the darkness, he almost knocked over the telephone. *No, Elsa didn't call Max while I was having dinner,* he realized. Elsa had recently given up her mobile, since its waves were bad for Anna, and if she *had* called from the phone upstairs, this one would have been clicking audibly while she dialed the number, which he would have heard in the kitchen. Yes, his sister had lied to him again, forgetting about that archaic feature of the telephones in her former home.

So she had told Max in advance that Anna and she were spending the night at Nick's and had even taken pains to bring Anna's nightgown along. Why then did she pretend she was making up her mind to stay on the spur of the moment? Angry that he had taken so long to figure this out, Nick shoved the flashlight in his pocket, crept out of the house, and locked the door behind him. Thank God his car was parked on the road by the fence. Wasn't that another sign that Elsa had planned in advance to spend the night?—she had parked her Toyota in the garage instead of in the driveway as she would normally have done.

He released his brakes and started pushing the Ford down the slightly inclined slope. On his way back, he would take the roundabout route and use the momentum to coast from the upper part of the road with the engine and lights off, so Elsa would never know about his late night ride—not that he really cared whether she knew or not!

About forty yards down the hill, he slipped behind the wheel and started the car. The road was completely deserted, so he would certainly notice if he were being followed. If so, he would just take a little drive. *"I couldn't sleep, gentlemen. Any decent man would develop a case of insomnia from all your interrogations, searches, and allegations!"* But when no tailing car appeared, he felt absurdly hurt and humiliated instead of relieved. What did they take him for—a half-wit dwarf caught, because of his stupidity, between the fists of the giants? A blank bullet that the cunningly smiling murderer, safe in his hiding place, had deliberately aimed in the wrong direction? A clumsy puppet at the mercy of blind fate?

Unfortunately, he fit each of these descriptions, at least at the moment.

The drive took no more than fifteen minutes, since he drove far too fast, either because of his eagerness to show himself that he was an "individual" or simply to suppress his characteristic indecisiveness. He swerved onto the dirt road about two hundred yards from Belloff's house and parked the car behind some bushes that hid it from the road, reasoning that, while this precaution was probably unnecessary, it couldn't do any harm. Grasping a pair of pliers and a screwdriver from his toolbox in the trunk, he took a shortcut across the field without turning on the flashlight.

The grass was bone dry from the dog days of August, springy and tall, as high as his knees. That and the sea of gopher holes slowed his progress considerably. To top it off, the stars were completely blotted out by a huge, dark cloud that resembled the dome of a gigantic cathedral coated with thick gray paint. Why not paint it with saints and other symbols to complete the picture or simply with a moon and stars, goddamn it?

Next time he stumbled, he finally switched on the flashlight. The beam darted straight ahead and lit up the weathered facade of the house. Then he shone it on the remains of the barn next door and over the rotten planks of the stable. The roof had long since collapsed. A few crooked stakes remained of the fence. Shifting it back to the house, he focused on the rickety, crumbling door, which disclosed two rusty padlock rings, suggesting how Belloff had locked it when he went to town or visited his only neighbors down the road. Now the padlock was gone, along with the handle.

Nick gave what was left of the door a slight push. There followed a tremendous grating sound and much creaking and crunching. Obviously he needed no pliers or screwdrivers to break into an abandoned house half-collapsed with time. After forcing himself into the miniscule foyer, Nick hesitated, wondering whether to shut the door behind him. He decided to leave it ajar. On the inside of the door, he noticed more rings—obviously the old man had been serious about his safety, which was only natural in such an out-of the-way place. So how had the murderer entered the house that night? Probably just by knocking and saying something like "Please, open the door! I've hurt my leg!" or some such excuse. Or maybe he was an acquaintance? Then he could have simply said, "Hello, it's me." And then. Well, that was something Nick preferred not to think.

The house had only two rooms—a kitchen and another room that, it seemed, hadn't been used for quite some time. Its trash heap of old and broken belongings were so far gone that it was difficult to guess what they originally were.

Clutching the flashlight far more tightly than necessary, Nick stood at the kitchen door. The air reeked of mold, mice, decay, and—death. He held his breath as he examined the chaos. Nothing but dirt and clutter was his first impression. Then he saw the oil lamp hanging above the bed and slowly approached it, noticing that it was almost half-full and on the shelf beside it was a matchbox. After a few clumsy attempts, he managed to light it. On the window were some cardboard plates that took the place of windowpanes, so the light would hardly be seen from the outside. Who would see it anyway? No doubt the cops and the killer were asleep at the moment, miles and miles away from here. Those miserable gas station attendants down the road were asleep too, as were even the crickets in the fields. Maybe he too was sleeping, asleep and dreaming this stinking dream filled with garbage and badly lit by a dusty oil lamp.

On closer inspection, he noticed that the lamp wasn't all that dusty. In fact, it wasn't dusty at all—in contrast to everything else in the room. Nick was more puzzled than alarmed at that discovery. Yes, somebody had dusted it recently, yesterday or even today, maybe only a few hours ago—why not *minutes* ago?

This last conjecture shook him, hit him in the stomach like a pair of brass knuckles. Nick doubled up and took a step back, while almost on its own, without the help of his rational mind, his hand removed the screwdriver from his jacket pocket. He gripped down on the handle, ready to use it as a weapon. That made him feel less threatened. Still, he found it hard to believe that there might be someone close by. *Whoever had been here has left,* he encouraged himself, *so this may be my good luck: to get here hot on his heels, while the trail is still fresh.*

More calmly, he looked over the room again. First the bed— oversized, with wooden panels. It wasn't just old—it was ancient. Noah himself might have built it for the ark. At its lower end, there were two moth-eaten blankets humped in a shapeless pile. The mattress was without a sheet and was covered with rust-brown stains, which were larger up toward the pillow. The pillowcase was almost entirely rusty brown.

"Blood," he whispered to himself. "His blood!"

It must have spurted out. Good God, what butchery that must have been! How could a shriveled seventy-four-year-old man have bled so much—like a stuck pig? With his free hand, Nick touched the pillow and then ran his fingers over it. As he bent over, he felt that infinite repugnance that transfixes human eyes to every ugly, horrifying sight. His nostrils quivered; he snuffled loudly. But no, the stains had long been dry—no rank smell of blood remained.

His head must have been there. He was half-asleep, doped by the sedatives, but only enough not to be able to struggle against the murderer as he tied him to the bed with the cable. And af- ter that? No doubt he had been fully conscious! In fact, none of the newspaper accounts mentioned anything about any gag in his mouth. For the other victims, yes, but not this one. Who could have heard him in this remote place? And when the blade of his own razor began to cut, to slice through his throat? He must have been whimpering, wheezing, begging for mercy, while the slimy bloody bubbles streamed from his toothless mouth.

No! No mercy for you! Nick swung the screwdriver at him. Again and again, staying his hand exactly where the metal point reached the defenseless bare neck, jabbed at it, and poked slowly inside.

"You will die, because I've *decided!* You good-for-nothing foul old man!"

There it was! He could clearly see his victim—a pale, face-less squirming form, desperately swinging his head left and right, large scarlet drops of blood—falling over white downy hair.

His hand froze in midair. What was that? Squinting his eyes, he stared at the pillow.

Nothing. The phantom was already gone. He looked warily at the screwdriver, almost surprised that it wasn't stained with blood. He put it in his pocket mechanically.

"I was playing again," he croaked at himself reproachfully.

But what could he do? Writers are like this, people who culti-vate the dreamy child in themselves, who like playing games and can even become totally absorbed in them.

Yes, that was it: Nicolas Edgeway is a writer!

But neither the time nor the place was appropriate for such make-believe games now. He wiped his forehead with the back of his hand, reminding himself that he was here to work, and moved away from the bed to the door, thus taking in the whole chaotic room.

Overturned chairs and an armchair, with a circular cut, that had lost half its stuffing. Drawers flung randomly onto the table, all their contents—forks and spoons, nails and studs, cork bottle stoppers, matchboxes and candle stumps—dumped on the floor and kicked around. Heaps of cans, obviously swept roughly off the makeshift shelves. Broken jars of stewed fruit. Nick walked over to them, noticing they had *really* been broken very recently, no more than an hour ago! The fruit was lying in small puddles of still-gooey sugar syrup, and mice hadn't touched them.

How was this possible? Half a year since the murder, nobody had come near the place for months, and now suddenly two at almost the same time? Perhaps that other person had come here often, but if so, why on this night of all nights had he turned everything upside down? What was he looking for?

Kaya. It might have been Kaya! For a moment he was overwhelmed with hope, both unfounded and unexpected. If she were alive, which was—unfortunately—hardly likely, she would never come here, to this place where her grandfather had been so brutally butchered. Furthermore, it seemed obvious that no woman had wreaked such havoc in the victim's kitchen. Wreaked, but apparently he had done this as a false lead—to cover something up.

His eyebrows arching in bewilderment, Nick squatted to look for recent footprints on the dirty floor. The first thing that caught his eye was a folding pocketknife under the armchair. It looked brand new and could hardly have belonged to Belloff. The other man could have cut the armchair with it, and after that, well, it could have slipped out of his hand somehow.

Nick took his handkerchief and carefully picked it up with two wrapped fingers so as not to erase any possible fingerprints. He stood up and looked more closely.

It was his own pocketknife, given to him by Elsa for his last birthday. It was gilded and had three blades made of some special alloy, with a bottle opener. Most importantly, his initials were engraved on one side.

He was so taken aback that when the front door creaked, he did not even budge, just kept staring at the knife. Finally he put it in his pocket—and then froze. The creaking continued and was definitely not from the wind. *There is no wind! The killer's coming! And there is no way out. Except through the window. Maybe the window, the window.*

Nick rushed for it, banged it open, jumped over the window-sill, and landed heavily on the ground. He ran blindly toward his car. He heard no footsteps following him, at least not *yet*. He stumbled into a gopher hole and fell, hitting his head against a pole. Leaping to his feet, he grabbed the pole and, with a single abrupt movement, yanked it out and grasped it tightly with both hands. He turned around and looked wildly at the house, just in time to see somebody turn off the oil lamp and close the window. *Now he'll try to get me! Well, let him try! I have to see who it is.*

But the moment the front door clanked shut and he heard the other man start running toward him, Nick threw down the pole and fled. It was pitch dark, but if he turned on the flashlight, he would be a sitting duck for the killer. Almost certainly he had a gun—why not? Still, Nick felt he was moving in the wrong direction. His car had to be more to the left. He slid down onto the grass and took out the flashlight—but didn't have to use it.

His car suddenly lurched forward toward him, with the head-lights on! It swerved drunkenly over the uneven ground, the engine roaring and whining. The keys! He had left them in the ignition. But who was driving it?

Somebody. The car stopped maybe fifteen yards from him, and the driver's front door swung open. *"Quick, get in, save yourself!"* was the unspoken command. As if obeying, Nick rushed toward it, just wanting to escape whoever was lumbering through the springy grass, closing on him with implacable resolve.

The car was empty.

There was no one inside or near it. Nick bounced in behind the steering wheel, slammed the door shut, and tromped on the acceleration pedal as he shifted into reverse. Whoever had started the car was long gone, it seemed—trying to help but without revealing himself or herself.

"Well, OK!" he announced, veering toward the invisible highway. For a fraction of a second, a man loomed in the headlights, so bent over that it was impossible to get even the vaguest idea of what he looked like before he slid back into the dark.

CHAPTER 18

When he finally reached the highway, trailing clouds of dust, Nick did not head for the nearest police station to report what he had seen but drove straight home instead. Noticing that his speed wasn't just excessive but life threatening, considering the state he was in, he immediately slowed down. But he couldn't as easily slow down the hectic flow of his thoughts, which were like floating debris after a shipwreck, bobbing in stormy seas of panic, consternation, and fear. Gradually, something surged to the surface, like a monster of the deep, breaking through to his consciousness.

"Remember those moments," it ordered him, *"the most frightening ones!"*

So there he is again, sprawled on the grass, clutching his flashlight, when just in front of him are his car's headlights, coming toward him. The car stops next to him; he can see it quite clearly. The driver's door opens, *only* that door. He runs toward it without taking his eyes off it for a second. Before he gets behind the steering wheel, he takes time to look in the backseat. Then he slams the door shut and speeds away.

Did anyone get out of the car? *"No,"* the monster answers for him—the monster he'd been trying to bury in the deepest parts of his consciousness, but in vain. *"No one got out."* Well, what could that possibly mean?

One thing only—whoever started the car is still *here.*

"But I'm alone, alone," Nick whined. "I can see that!"

"You see, that's true. But what do you feel? Come on, answer!"

The *presence.*

Dark and light splotches spin before his eyes in a sluggish dance. The dark ones increase in number. Never in his life has he lost consciousness, but some particle in his brain which is still working tells him that's exactly what's happening. He slams on the brakes instinctively, the tires squeal, and the engine bucks and stalls. Then comes the terrifying feeling, mostly by its expansiveness in time, that the silent darkness is growing thick and resinous and is closing in on him, flowing all over him, beginning to solidify, tightening its slimy, painful hold on him. He can't breathe anymore and feels as if he is surrounded by a huge black chunk of amber, trapped like a bug.

A car appeared behind him and whizzed by, breaking the spell with the indifferent glare of its bright eyes/headlights. Nick caught his breath and slowly moved his body. But a few more minutes needed to pass, devoid of sound and light, before he dared drive again. The rest of the way home he mumbled children's rhymes and hummed old tunes, anything that popped into his mind, to force down into his subconscious what he refused to think about—for now. He succeeded because he believed that, when he was calmer and more lucid, he would find some plausible explanation.

When he got home, he was working so hard at staying calm that he remembered his plan to drive the long way and shut off the engine so that the car could coast down to the house. He again parked the Ford outside the fence and crossed the yard so quietly that even Biff didn't hear him and then unlocked the door and bolted it behind him. He put the car keys on the cabinet and the flashlight, screwdriver, and pliers in the drawer before he moved toward the staircase.

Just as he reached the first stair, someone's bony fingers sank into his shoulder.

"Husshhh!"

CHAPTER 19

"Quiet!" Someone's hot breath hit the back of his neck.

Nick froze in midstride, one hand on the banister of the stair-case. *He told me to be quiet,* flashed through Nick's mind. *That means Elsa and Anna are alive. He's come for me! For me.* His knees wobbled; his whole body seemed stripped of its bones and muscles, sagging down as if made of warm jelly.

"Hey, what's the matter with you?" the whisper behind his back asked as a hand grabbed him under his armpit. "Nick, Nick! It's me!"

Max.

Yes, it was Max who pushed him and propped him against the wall, as unceremoniously as if he were a sack of sawdust. For a while they stood face to face in the darkness, barely able to make out each other's silhouettes, each listening to the other's shallow breathing. Then Nick felt an influx of galvanizing anger pump through his veins, bringing him back to his senses and giving him strength to stand on his feet and talk, though almost inaudibly.

"Damn you! You intended that!"

"Shush, don't talk," Max repeated unnecessarily. "Come with me!"

He struck his lighter and walked toward the library. They crept in together like two criminals—or at least one of them. Max turned on the end table lamp by the sofa and sat next to it.

Nick took the chair opposite, whispering, "Why are you here?" He immediately realized the absurdity, or at least redundancy, of the question, because he would have already known the answer.

"And why were you not here?" Max responded, pursing his thin lips into two bluish-pink lines.

"I took a stroll. I was nervous and couldn't sleep."

"Really?"

"Listen, Max, how can you not feel any discomfort here?" Nick was again intrigued by Max's arrogance. "After what you did to me!"

"After what I did?"

"You told Forger that I hid my gray suit and the shirt! You knew perfectly well that you could have sent me straight to jail by saying that—"

"Oh, come on," Max interjected, and his thin, almost hairless, arm made a tentative brush, as if Nick were an irksome fly that had to be chased away. "You're too full of yourself. Did it ever occur to you that nobody takes you seriously?"

He's trying to insult me, Nick noted vaguely.

"I mean as a killer," Max clarified, after a pause long enough for the more general implication to stand. "Otherwise they'd have arrested you by now, or at least there'd be a tail on you."

"Wait a minute! You talk as if you're absolutely sure I'm innocent. Despite all the evidence!"

"What evidence, Nick? Elsa might buy all this because, in the first place, you'd make up any story just to make yourself more interesting to her. That's why you lied to her about your idiotic clothes. Very stupid, indeed—you expect me to believe that you crammed them inside some sack, rushed out, and hid them behind the rocks?"

"I didn't lie to her, but she seems to have lied to you. Yes, yes! It was Elsa who hid them there after she learned about Kathy's murder. She did it because she thought I could be the murderer, get it?"

"Nonsense," Max declared imperturbably. "Even if she did hide them, it was for other reasons."

"And what could those reasons be?"

"Because, ever since your childhood, she's taken it upon herself to bolster your self-confidence, in *every* way, to protect you from the truth about yourself—the simple truth that you're a person incapable of doing anything, either good or bad. Nothing. To keep you from realizing this, Elsa is always trying to convince you of her faith in your—how can I put it?—your presence in life."

Presence. Just to hear the word pronounced out loud sent shivers down Nick's spine, nerve wracking but also pleasant. He could imagine saying, condescendingly, *"Well, you know, my 'presence in life' happens to be double, so—"*

"If it hadn't been for her continual efforts," Max continued, "you'd feel like you were a shadow, and in fact you are a shadow: a dim, barely discernible shadow that still manages to pollute the environment."

"How ferociously you must hate me!" Nick muttered, bolstered by the thought that he had inspired such a strong emotion in somebody. "You totally hate me!"

"Hate? You?" Max stuck up his "aristocratic" nose. "Again, nonsense. I just got tired of you hating me, for no reason at all, and decided to give you some reasons."

This is all so absurd, Nick thought tiredly. *I endured so many nightmares, I'm totally exhausted, and now I'm sitting here at two in the morning tolerating this. Tolerating* him*!*

"You still haven't told me why you're here, Max. Or how you got in."

"I used the duplicate key, the one you keep outside under that cobblestone. As for why I'm here, well, I was worried about my wife and child, Nicolas. Just imagine this: I come home and find a note, 'We're sleeping at my brother's, *my love*.' 'Terrifying!' I told myself, 'They're alone with that raving maniac!' I jumped into my car, and hither I flew. 'Please God, let me not be too late; let it not be too late,' I repeated, almost mad with fear. Well? Was that how you wanted me to answer you?"

Nick involuntarily put his hand over his eyes, trying to protect them from the leering curiosity in Max's gaze.

"Well, that's not how I'm going to answer you, Nick, because I'm certain you didn't kill anybody. As I see it, you're one of those perverse scumbags who can commit crimes only in their minds."

"Only in their minds?" This time Nick managed a chuckle. "There are too many facts that you don't know, Max—facts that would make your hair stand on end!"

Max also laughed. The lamp lit only half his face, his right shoulder, right arm, and right leg as far as the knee that he had crossed over the left one. His entire left side blurred into semi-darkness, and momentarily Nick had the revolting sensation that this gaunt fop was being born before his very eyes: still half-stuck like some human chrysalis making its way out of a dark cocoon, pushing its way into the light, sucking his strength from him, trying to choke him with its contempt.

"You're a worthless scumbag too, Max," he heard himself say, adding to himself, *Otherwise you wouldn't be wasting your time with me.* "Besides, I know that Elsa didn't write 'my love' in her note. She—"

Nick fell silent, suddenly alarmed by noticing—he couldn't say exactly what. A single detail had caught his attention for a fraction of a second and had then faded back among the multitude of other details that added up to half-black Max. Ignoring his accuser's puzzled grimace, Nick continued to scrutinize Max's appearance. His outfit was quite unusual for him: a black cotton T-shirt, the pants of a baggy tracksuit, also black and frayed at the cuffs. And across the back of the sofa lay a worn black leather jacket—a jacket Max hadn't been wearing when they entered. *He must have been here in the library even before I got home. He was waiting for me, stalking me. But why would a dandy like Max, who always chose bright colors, dress like this?*

As Nick examined him more closely and with even greater perseverance, Max started to remark that, but then stopped before he could get it out. Instead, he just squirmed a little on the sofa, though only seconds ago, he had changed his position. Now his left leg was over the right one, so the lamp lit it from the knee down to the surprisingly white sock peeping below the leg of the black sweatpants and on his suede shoe with a metal buckle, around which was entangled—a blade of dry, resilient grass!

"Jesus!" Nick groaned.

"What's the matter?" Max followed his gaze and understood. But instead of being startled or at least alerted, he sighed with relief. "You've solved my problem! All this time I've been wondering whether to tell you or not—"

"You're the murderer!"

"Well, didn't you just say you were?"

"*You* are the murderer!" Nick repeated.

He felt a huge, desolate emptiness gaping in his heart. He had been robbed of something, something he didn't even dare confess, not even to himself. He couldn't deny that it had become important to him. *Nourishing.* Now it was gone. He was back in the old prison of selfless self, no longer at the center of terrible events, no longer needing to encourage himself with *Come on, Nick, do something, Nick! Don't give up!* He would no longer imagine—what he had been imagining. It was back to writer's block, to his boring future tale that had nowhere to go and whose only purpose was to while away his time.

"That's too bad, really...you...fiend!"

"Come on now!" Max grinned insolently. "I take a walk in the field at a somewhat unusual hour, and off you go: 'murderer,' 'fiend.' You don't sound convincing, my dear friend Nicolas." He glanced at Nick from under his eyebrows, smirking with his typical bullet-proof self-confidence.

But I will get behind that smug mask! Nick suddenly fumed. "I can assure you I'll 'sound convincing,' Max, when I *testify* against you, because I know much more than you can imagine. And Kaya? What about her? Is there anything you can say about her? You were hoping that the relationship between her and your other victims would remain hidden, but I've discovered it! Do you understand? Yes, Kaya is the key figure. She used to come to your place with her mother, and then she accidentally stumbled on some nasty secret of yours. That's why you decided to do away with her. You weren't successful, though. She kept escaping you, as she still does, *doesn't she?* So, while you were after her, you went after the people closest to her, for good measure: you killed her grandfather, the twin sisters, her teacher, and her mother's friend! You were afraid she might have shared your secret with them!"

Craning his long neck forward, Max was motionless, listening and looking at Nick with his eyes wide open and unblinking—listening almost voraciously.

"Through Kathy's murder, you aimed at diverting the suspicion in my direction, because I was the last one with her that night. To frame me even more securely, you tied her with a rope from my nylon roll!" Reassured by Max's tense attention, Nick had risen from the chair and was pointing at him with his index finger straight up. "And what about *the earring*, Max? You finally ripped it from her ear and came here. Using the garden ladder to climb up to my open bedroom window, you casually tossed it, since it was bloody, onto my nightstand. You wanted to scare me, confuse me. Oho! Come to think of it, my unfortunate visit to Eric's two days before you killed him also turned out in your favor."

Still there was something amiss in Max's reactions. True, people don't take much interest in a story that describes their own actions, because nothing surprises them.

"Maybe you've also stolen Seconal tablets," Nick added, carried away with the momentum, and then lapsed into alarmed silence.

Was there really nothing surprising in this description of the killer's actions? Or more precisely, did that description really correspond to what Max had done? If not, what's the conclusion? Nick had just armed the man who was possibly his most dangerous enemy with a lethal weapon! He had revealed to him all the details of the murders—the earring, the rope, and so on.

"Where's the earring now?" Max asked in a businesslike manner.

"In the lake. Sixty feet deep, at least!"

"How about that girl you mentioned, what was her name? Kaya? Who is she exactly?"

He's just pretending he doesn't know, Nick told himself, although he was already seized with misgivings. *He is the murderer! That's why he went to Belloff's tonight—to erase all previous traces. What other reason could he have had?*

"The pocketknife! You threw it there. That's what you went there for!"

"I'm glad you finally got it." Max leered at him again. "I picked it among your other possessions because your initials are engraved on it."

"When did you take it?"

"Yesterday afternoon. I set off in your direction as soon as Elsa left with Forger to show him the place where you told her you hid the clothes."

"*She* hid them, not me! How many times do I have to say that?"

"Anyway, it's all the same to me. What interested me was that, through your lies about those clothes, which were quite out of fashion incidentally, you aroused the strongest suspicions in Forger."

"Suspicions you decided to augment even more by trying to frame me in that house!"

"That's also true," Max confirmed, as if they were discussing some very ingenious action. "I, however, never considered the possibility that you'd turn up there too. A curious coincidence, wasn't it?"

"Yes, very curious," Nick muttered through gritted teeth.

Max, still relishing the memory of the recent "adventure," explained, "It was pure chance that we saw each other. I had already started for my car when I heard footsteps! I lay down in the grass, wondering who it was. And then, click! Someone turned on a flashlight no more than thirty feet away from me. I couldn't believe my eyes. 'That loser brother-in-law of mine,' I said to myself."

"Watch it, Max!"

"I was watching you look everywhere around, dying with fear! When you entered the house, I didn't know what to do and made a mistake: I didn't act at once. If I had made some noise, you would have run like a rabbit and wouldn't have rummaged around the kitchen and found the knife. Then I would have been able to give Forger an anonymous call, suggesting another search of the place, for instance. Well, anyway, I enjoyed watching you squirm. Ha-ha-ha! That was some getaway you made there!

"Watch how you talk to me, Max!"

"Yes, just like a rabbit. A fat, rump-heavy rabbit. Scared to death! You didn't even take time to notice that your pursuer had no desire to catch you, that he was barely jogging and making as much noise as he could. Ha-ha-ha!"

He had long passed all tolerable limits. Nick realized it was high time to jump up and grab Max by his turkey neck, but he didn't really feel any anger at him anymore. Worse than that, for the first time, he felt only—understanding for him.

"So it was your car that whizzed by me when I stopped by the side of the road," he said. "You were in a hurry to get here first; otherwise I'd have bolted the door behind me. You wanted to put back a couple of my things here that you had 'borrowed.' Well, did you find something else that would do as well as the knife, or did I mess up your plan?"

"You did mess it up, yes," Max nodded, "but when you crept into your own home, I couldn't resist the temptation. I just had to startle you again."

After a short silence, his eyes half-shut with pleasure, Max went on in the same confiding tone.

"I never dreamed that you would play into my hands like that. You, Nick, revealed yourself as much more dumb and naïve than I ever thought. You incriminated yourself with facts I didn't know existed. Now you are in my hands entirely!"

"So now you're going to turn me in?"

"Maybe. Depends on how you behave. Incidentally, tell me, what wild whim made you go out there? Who was with you? Who started the car and drove it up to you?"

Who? Nobody, Nobody! The terrifying memory somehow lifted Nick's spirits, supplied a background against which his fear and failure before Max became quite insignificant. He pondered the situation for a moment and then stared at Max with mysteriously veiled eyes. "I really hate to let you down, dear friend, but this time *you* were dumb and naïve. You're really in a sticky mess!"

"What do you mean?"

"Now isn't the time to supply you with such information. All I can only tell you is that the person whose 'wild whim' we didn't manage to *accomplish* because of you is involved with—a very important institution."

"An agent? A secret agent—"

Nick interrupted him quickly and abruptly, "Let's skip the details for now, Max! It'd do you good to realize the situation at the moment. The sadist has been very busy lately, and the entire town is in a panic. The police are still unable to uncover anything but their own incompetence. Don't you think it's logical that authorities at a higher level would eventually get involved?"

Naturally Max didn't answer, but it was obvious that he was less sure of himself now. How easily he had swallowed the bait! Now Nick grinned at his long face, which had always resembled a haggard horse but now even more so because of his rising alarm. Well, that was how a quick-witted man could take advantage of his own nightmares!

"Come on!" Max prodded him. "Tell me more about the 'mess' I'm in."

"I told you, didn't I? A *very* sticky mess it is. Because my partner, Max, not only drove the car up to me. He's a seasoned pro, as you could figure out for yourself. So all during our 'chase' and before that, when you were still in the house of the *murdered* old man after I ran out, he was taking pictures of you, pictures—"

"Ha! Big deal!"

"You'll be able to judge that soon enough. Not that I want to discourage you, but I don't think you'd be able to convince anybody that the *sole aim* of your nocturnal activities was to frame your good-natured brother-in-law, who has never harmed you. With such evidence against you, my version of the story would outweigh yours, don't you think?"

Max's forehead wrinkled in tense, apparently fruitless and less optimistic, speculation. "No, I don't believe you," he announced finally, though his voice lacked conviction. "Listen, Nick, even you must realize that your version of the story, as you call it, is no more than a soap bubble! You'll just make a fool of yourself if you tell it to other people. Some girl named Kaya, whom I've never heard of, some nasty secret of mine that I'm supposed to know—"

"But you do have a nasty secret," *Anna* interrupted, "and I know what it is."

CHAPTER 20

"Jesus!" both exclaimed simultaneously.

Then Max groaned with a voice made weak by the unpleasant surprise, "Anna, Anna! How many times have I told you, Anna... asked you...not to come into a room like...that?"

She stood leaning against the door, which she had both opened and closed noiselessly. She was silent. In the gloom beyond the light shed by the lamp, her figure beneath the thin nightgown looked evanescent, neither in this world nor quite in the other. It was impossible to say where she was looking at the moment: whether at them or somewhere *else*. At something only she could see? Her eyes reflected flitting shadows on their mirrored surfaces, though at the moment, there was not a trace of movement in the room.

"She always...she...does that all the time, Nick!" Max held out his hands palms up, as if looking for comfort. "This child simply appears, and every time all of a sudden. I can't get used to it! I keep asking myself why she does it, but I haven't got a clue. I just can't get used to it."

"I know, I know—I mean, I know that she does it," Nick blurted, staring at Anna. *But who was she watching now? Maybe the spirit of a dead man?* "What woke you up, Anna? "*Who* woke you up?"

"She won't answer you!" Max whined again. "You know she won't. Oh Lord, why do you punish me so? I haven't deserved—"

"You haven't deserved!" Max's self-pity spurred Nick's dormant hatred. "Who else is to blame, if not the sickly loser who conceived her—"

"There you go again!" Max interrupted, clapping his hands "That's the reason for my recent actions: I just couldn't pass up the opportunity to destroy you! Otherwise you'll continue to poison my life, always blaming me—"

"Shut up and look at her!" Nick drew his attention toward Anna, who had started shaking, while her expression didn't change. Indeed, it resembled a death mask—unblinking, no sign even of breathing. She looked like the mummy of an ancient child, shriveled by millennia and doomed to fall to pieces at any moment, returning to dust! Nick instinctively rose, feeling that he had to help her remain standing while that was still possible. Yes, he would certainly have made a rush toward her if he hadn't noticed, at the very last moment, that the *door* was giving her slight pushes, opening at small, barely noticeable intervals, and a mournfully depressing crack was forming inch by inch behind her. Everything had slowed to a snail's pace, as though the crack were filled with something other than air, some solid, transparent substance, which was gradually being overwhelmed by the *inhuman* efforts of the person outside.

At last Anna was forced to step forward, and the door opened wider so that Elsa could squeeze into the room.

"A late night family reunion, eh?" Nick snickered, but he was drenched by a cold sweat.

Nobody answered him. Elsa pushed the door shut behind her with a casual gesture. But how cautious she had been just a second ago! She must have known her daughter was leaning against the door, seized by another break with reality—had to be as certain of that as the mother of a normal child would know when her child was looking for a snack before dinner. Maybe Anna had been come here from hunger: not in the ordinary sense, not physical hunger, which seemed almost impossible for her, but a desire for something far less tangible, the same hunger that killed certain animals kept too long in captivity or deprived of light.

First Elsa wrapped her tightly in the cardigan she had brought especially for that purpose, and then she took her firmly by the hand, as though afraid that Anna might try to run away. The third thing she did, which took the longest, was to examine her carefully from head to foot. Only when she was sure that Anna was fully conscious again did she turn her undivided attention to Max. "What are you searching for here?"

"Exactly, *searching*!" Nick remarked bitterly. "You have no idea how precisely you expressed yourself."

Max gave him a resentful but also imploring look, and then, though he had absolutely no chance of getting away with it, started lying, "I was worried, honey—so worried about you that I came here almost without realizing what I was doing. Such terrible things have been happening lately—"

"Why are you wearing those rags then? Did you get them from the shed?"

"It's immaterial where he got them; what counts is they're black." Nick couldn't hold himself back. "Perfect for a disguise, for merging into the nighttime background."

Once again Elsa ignored him. Perhaps she was pretending for Max that he meant nothing to her? But if so, why? Maybe simply because she didn't want to hear the truth, with him in the room. Or was she afraid to hear it, or afraid of Max himself?

Meanwhile Max continued, "Yes, darling, I found these clothes in the shed. I was looking for some tools, and when I spotted them, I decided they suited the dirty work I was going to tackle."

Extremely dirty, I'd say! Nick could barely suppress his fury. He was at a loss to understand how this man could act like that *in his presence*, as if he were mute, knowing all but unable to speak a word.

"What dirty work, Max?" Elsa was looking at him hopefully, as if to say, *"Speak plausibly, dear; that's all I ask!"* Yes, she was trying to suggest something like that.

Max, in his turn, blurted out in one breath, as if managing a tongue twister, "I had started to fix the shelves in the basement, darling, when suddenly I grew concerned about you, as I already said."

"You were fixing the shelves?" She sounded disappointed with his answer. "Wasn't it a little late for home repairs?"

"Yes, it was…the thing is…you know…I often can't sleep at night."

"No. Max, I didn't know that. As you are perfectly aware, I haven't known what might disturb your sleep at night for a long time." Elsa uncovered this fact, which stunned and pleased Nick, as if she had suddenly decided no longer to withhold any number of revelations. Hesitating briefly, she then produced another, "And I've long wanted to know also what disturbs you during the day!"

Nick couldn't tell if her distorted grimace was an expression of fear, replacing the momentary agitation, or the result of some sudden desperation, but she quickly regained her self-control and placed one hand on Anna's head, while with the other, she firmly held her tiny, almost invisible, wrist as if in a handcuff. "Tell your father and uncle good night, honey," she concluded, after which mother and daughter left the cluttered library without another word.

The door remained wide open behind them, spilling a flood of bright light from the hall. The scrape of their slippers gradually trailed away up the staircase, soon completely dying away.

"Maybe you better spend the rest of the night in the basement, eh?" Nick said spitefully. "Get a start on those shelves of yours."

Max blinked as if Nick had thrown sand in his eyes. Eventually, however, his gaze became piercing as he came to an undeniable conclusion, "This game has turned really dangerous, Nick. For both of us. So I suggest we call a halt to the thrust and parry. It's still not too late to cover up our childishness."

"Is that what you call your attempt to incriminate me of six sadistic murders? Childishness?"

"Come on, now. After all, I didn't incriminate you of anything. You retrieved your pocketknife, and you have a witness—whether a secret service agent, which I strongly doubt, or some lover of yours, which I doubt even more, doesn't really matter."

Max really shouldn't have admitted those doubts! With a false smirk, Nick retaliated, "Really? And do you also doubt the photographs?"

Clearly dead tired, Max chose not to return to what he considered a very unpleasant topic. The enervated fop would have done much better to stay home in his "long time" lonely bed, battling his insomnia rather than making malevolent nocturnal "excursions." Presently he stood up, took his shabby jacket from the back of the sofa, and started to leave the home he had entered like a sneak thief, slanderer, traitor, and perhaps even murderer?

Rising reluctantly to see him off, Nick suddenly realized that he didn't really want Max to leave, no matter how maliciously he had acted. More importantly, Max was a man, another human being to sit with and talk to. True, their conversation was far from friendly—could hardly be called a conversation at all. Only an exchange of threats and insults, but didn't he prefer even that to the silence of his *loneliness?*

He walked down the hall behind Max, his gaze intensely fixed on the narrow back and skinny shoulders that were about as imposing as vestigial chicken wings. He could picture himself holding out his hand, tapping those scrawny shoulders, and saying, *"You're right, let's stop here. Come on, let's go back! We'll have a 'strong drink,' as you like to say; then we'll go to your place and tackle those rickety old basement shelves."*

In the foyer Max suddenly turned and almost stuck his face into Nick's. "I strongly advise against," he rasped, attempting a brutal stare. "I strongly advise you against telling Elsa about any of this. If you do, I promise you will be very sorry! I can be a merciless adversary."

"Perhaps!" Nick shoved him back abruptly. "But you can't keep your nasty secrets to yourself. Even your family secrets are revealed now!"

As Max left, Nick slammed the door and double bolted it. He was sweating again, his outraged heart thumping against his ribs in a savage tattoo. *I'm going to kill him! I'm going to slit that bastard's throat at last!*

Climbing the stairs, he redirected his anger at his sister. When he passed by her door, distraught and lonely, pushed to his doom by inexorable, fatal circumstances, he knew that, if he knocked, he would get none of the consolation due him. *Night, night! She's there, behind that closed door, lying in her bed, probably listening to my footsteps—unwilling to move an inch!* His troubled mind, knowing she must be perfectly aware of the excruciating pain he was suffering at the moment, became convinced that she was totally indifferent to him, might even have come to hate him—simply because he was in trouble.

Fine! But why in the hell wouldn't she get up to ask him what her husband had really been doing in the dead of night? How could she not be curious about what had transpired, after she had seen for herself how false his behavior was, after she had listened to his bald-faced lies?

Or was she conspiring with him? Against her own brother!

CHAPTER 21

Before turning in, Nick took a hot shower to ease his nervous tension. Then, instead of going straight to bed, he opened his bedroom window, propped his elbows on the windowsill, and stared blankly into the dark, his eyes teary with fatigue. Gradually his head emptied of everything.

The boy won't walk for long. As soon as he passes the cliffs along the coast, the little cottages of the Sensitives will come into view. Built close together right down on the sand, they will look like nothing more than a mirage in the wavering haze, and just behind them will be a majestic evergreen forest.

"Why do you live here?" he will ask the first person he meets.

"Where else could we live?"

"Well, over there, in the forest shade, on a carpet of pinecones, with the serene whisper of a light breeze."

"Oh, that will happen someday," the stranger will reply, his voice filled with conviction. "The decision has long since been made. All that is still to be decided is the exact date. However, now we are occupied with a much more important problem: the Sensibles continue to insist that the birds belong to them. Can you imagine that?"

"But why should you care about some fictional birds, when you have a forest paradise just a stone's throw away from you?"

"What good would that paradise be if we can't defend our rights to our fictional birds?" the Sensitive will reply, continuing on his way.

"Continuing on his way." And I will also continue on my way, Nick told himself. "I'll keep moving in some direction after all! Damn Elsa and Max—it doesn't really matter whether they are conspiring against me or not; I don't even care if Max is the murderer. And damn their weird daughter too, and Kaya—missing without a trace, and that bastard Forger and—"

His car loomed white in the darkness, like the snarling grin of some huge ghostly face glaring from behind the latticed fence. He stared at it against his will, when all he really wanted to do was to turn his back on it and go to bed. He wished he could forget, at least for a few hours, how that grinning ghostmobile had careened toward him across the field, and how, when it stopped in front of him, no one was inside.

No one? You'd better rethink that; do something to solve your problem, *Nick. Don't waste your precious time! If you can't cobble together some plausible explanation this very night, if you just sleep on it, tomorrow you'll be a candidate for the insane asylum.*

He had read somewhere, probably in an issue of *Impulse* magazine, that two scientists had developed a theory about our "constant companions." They claimed that every person has a twin—no, not exactly a twin, a double—not symptomatic of a split personality or alter ego or such psychiatric categories but a personality, quite real, created by the sum total of energy emitted by an individual. In other words, an *energy*-identical self "coexisted side by side with each of us." Nor had the article insisted that "side by side" was absolutely obligatory; rather, it speculated that, if the living person were in extraordinary danger or suffering from great emotional stress, the identical self might separate from its host and undertake some action of its own.

Now let's apply that scientific theory to this case. Nicolas Edgeway normally coexists with his identical self, but then comes the terrible tension of these sadistic murders. His identical self, which must have far more acute senses—it's made of pure energy, after all, not matter encumbered by thousands of flaws—foresees the danger that threatens its host self much earlier than he does and starts pulling away, because every sentient being seeks to preserve itself. It pulled away, *pulled back*, and of course Nick can sense its presence, simply because it's already connected to him.

Applying the same logic, it is possible to account for what happened in the field. The identical self was off at a distance and saw or sensed Nick jumping out of the window of that rickety house and that someone was running after him. *He is going to kill him*, it realizes, *and I will also perish. However much I may separate myself, I remain an identical self, and that terrified matter running toward the car is essential for my continued existence.* At this crucial moment, the identical self acquires new—supernatural or simply extraordinary?—abilities to influence material objects, like the Ford. And off it goes—off it goes.

Carried away by these speculations, Nick only half-heard the soft click below him. But as he leaned a little farther out the window, he almost fell out. He didn't want to believe it, but the Ford's front door on the driver's side was open. As he told himself that he must have forgotten to shut it and only now notices this, rubbing his eyes in the desperate hope that, when he looked again, the front door would indeed be closed, the car began to creep noiselessly along the fence. Somebody had released its emergency brake and pushed it down the sloping road—as if somebody had telepathically tuned in to his speculations and decided to lend them further credence.

Puffing out his cheeks, Nick released a long, wheezing sigh. His feelings were reduced to boredom, enough to make him sleepy. *Now stop with all the mumbo jumbo. It's getting duller by the minute—beyond all limits.*

Although the Ford was hidden by shrubbery, after a few seconds, Nick heard its engine turn over. Beautiful car, quiet and powerful. But wait, wait a minute! What just happened?

My car's just been stolen! Right in front of my eyes!

The drowsy boredom, created to defend his tortured brain, evaporated, blown away by the stormy wind of panic, or rather a panicky optimism: common thieves! Nick rushed down the hall, slippers flapping, and dashed toward the first floor. *Come on, Sister, wake up!* his mind yelled as he flew by her room. *It's about time you joined the game!*

He stopped his headlong rush at the cabinet in the foyer. The car keys were *missing. Vixen that she is, she has already joined the game.* The sardonic realization almost calmed him. The front door was unlatched. *So she's taken the car and driven off somewhere—maybe.*

Chuffing like a steam engine, he lumbered up the stairs to Elsa's room in practically no time and turned the handle. Locked. Anna—she had made Anna lock the door when she left.

"What do you want?" Elsa whispered from inside.

No luck! "Op...open up," he stammered, disappointed.

"Why?"

"I need to talk to you."

"About whom? No! I don't want to know *anythhhing*!" She had been doing a lot of hissing lately. "Leave me alone!"

SET WAGNER

"But Elsa—"

A wild conjecture insinuated itself into his brain and sucked all his thoughts—like a vampire!

"Where's Anna!"

"You must be crazy! Where could she be? She's trying to get some sleep, the poor thing!"

"I must see her, just to look at her! Please Elsa, just for a second, from the hall. I won't come in."

There followed a deep silence from the other side of the door, which, even Nick could feel, was filled with enough strong emotion to explode at any moment. Then the door slowly opened. Elsa stood in front of him, her eyes brimming with tears. Her chin was trembling, and her lips quivered for some time before she found the words she was looking for.

"I didn't know...I...didn't know you had such affection for her, darling. Even at times." She waved her hand, somehow expressing both pain and joy at the same time. "I didn't know!" she repeated. "The dear child's right here; you must have had a bad dream?"

"Yes, a bad dream," Nick repeated, looking over her shoulder. God, what a fool she was sometimes! But he really was having a very bad dream. Only he couldn't wake up, because it was *real*. "Elsa, step aside. I can't...see...her!"

Elsa, again overcome with wild emotion that distorted her face, drew aside with an expansive, comforting wave of her hand. *Here's our adorable Annie!*—sitting on the bed in front of him, the nightcap on her head a riot of frills and pleats. Her eyes were fixed on the glowing chandelier. How could she stare at it like that after waking up in the pitch dark?

Nick awkwardly nodded his head. "Well, well—I'll be going. Go back to sleep."

142

Before closing the door, Elsa moved close to him, ran her ice-cold hand across his forehead, and kissed him on his stubbly cheek. Her lips rustled as if made of paper—dry, hard, and chapped. "Good night, Nick. Soon it will be light out."

Nick went back to his bedroom, muttering under his breath, "Dawn. Already half past three. I'll wait for the day. Soon it will be light out." Then he picked up the receiver and dialed Max's number. The phone rang seven or eight times—nothing. He hung up. Max wasn't home. *He* had been driving the Ford! That was the why the dog hadn't barked. He must have left his car somewhere close by, and Elsa must have given him the keys! And then she had forgotten to bolt the door.

But what did Max want with *his* car?

He'll commit another murder with it! That's what he's going to do. Then he'll drive it back to where it was parked, by dawn. Around the scene of the crime, he'll leave clear prints of the tires.

"Lovely, just lovely!" Nick snarled.

This time I'll catch him and call the cops on the spot! He yanked off his pajamas, quickly donning the clothes he had worn to Belloff's house, turned off the lights, and quietly left his bedroom, its purpose becoming a distant memory. Walking down the hall again for what seemed the hundredth time that night, he didn't worry if Elsa heard him or not. Even if she did, she would just hug her Anna, chanting, "I don't want to know anythhhing!" Ah, but she does know things, terrible things. That's obvious by her looks and actions.

The early morning coolness greeted Nick as he stepped outside. He didn't even bother to lock the front door—had grown tired of such apparently pointless precautions. People entered and left his home without the slightest scruple, as if it were an inn—an inn for bastards with nasty secrets, bleary-eyed lying sisters, and evanescent nieces. Above all, an asylum for presences—shades, shadows, second selves, and sometimes resembling a barely discernible girl in a kimono, sky blue with gold trim!

Grinning sarcastically, Nick walked along the house, planning to cross the yard diagonally so that Elsa couldn't see him from her window if she happened to look out. Soon Biff joined him, stretching his forepaws and yawning like—well, like an ordinary, sleepy dog.

When he chose an appropriate vantage point by the fence and lay down in the giant weeds, the animal snuggled up to him as if they were life-long friends, even pushing his muzzle under Nick's armpit. A surprisingly ugly dwarfish dog, a stupid mutt without an ounce of charm, but not a vicious bone in his body. Biff deserved respect, after all, for being so open minded. Nick patted him on his bushy back, though not without distaste. *I'll give him a bath tomorrow.*

And so they waited.

"What good would that paradise be if we can't defend our rights to our fictional birds?" the Sensitive will reply, continuing on his way.

You won't be making up anything from now on, *the boy will smile to himself behind the man's back.* And it won't be long before you forget all the things you've made up in the past. *Then he will walk confidently by the houses where on that day there will only be women, old men, and children. He will continue on his way to the military camp.*

Seated in a deep hollow among the dunes, their armaments gleaming and naked torsos glistening with sweat, the soldiers will be singing their usual war songs in an effort to stifle the piteous whimper of fear that troubles their souls. Yet none of them will realize that the fear is necessary, that they polished their armor only to feel that fear, which blesses their meaningless lives with a halo fashioned from defeat and death: "What if I perish? I will lose everything!" And instantly the squat hovel hunkered in the sand becomes a home, the withered woman is transformed into a desired beloved, and the irksome, slovenly brats become "my dear children."

"Hello there!" The boy will address them, and his sonorous voice will put a stop to the songs of the warriors. "Is there something that oppresses you?"

"There are very many things that oppress us," they will answer almost in unison.

"And do you want to be free of them?"

"Who wouldn't want that?"

"Come over here to me, if that is really so!"

Then the boy will briefly explain his gift. The multitude will throng around him, tired of the everyday tedium, of the fruitless monotony of labor, of yearning for the unattainable, of disillusion, unfulfilled dreams, anxieties, scruple. Men tired of grieving for lost relatives, diminished abilities, aging features, tarnished beliefs, thwarted ambitions, dubious merits, competitions, first loves, and last comforts. Disturbed, oppressed, unbelieving, heartbroken. A vast array of men, made nervous by the incessant scorching heat of the island.

"You will no longer need to plant seeds of fear in your souls to give birth to illusions," the boy will say to them. "You will no longer need to wage battles so that you can return to your homes filled with the joy of victory. You will no longer make your life meaningful by fighting over imaginary birds!"

They will pass one after the other beneath the powerful gaze of his azure-blue eyes and become amazingly alike: their faces serene, their smiles broadening, a new crystal-clear calm filling their eyes, eyes grown practically transparent from indifference to the blistering heat.

After half of the army has received its dispensation, however, the boy will grow tired. Despite the grumbles and entreaties of the rest, he will postpone their total happiness till the next morning.

Before that "next" morning comes, as we know very well, the decisive, inevitable battle will be fought.

CHAPTER 22

At first it seemed to him that his whole body was trapped by braces and plaster, especially around the neck. In truth, his muscles were just badly cramped. Opening his eyes, he immediately remembered where he was. Before he had time to be astounded that he had managed to fall asleep, he realized what had awakened him: the quiet, swishing sound of a car coasting toward him. His car, coasting down the hill with its lights off, like some creeping thief in the early morning haze. It stopped exactly where he had parked it, just as he had anticipated, so he had the best possible view. Again, the driver's side door was open, but it obstructed his view so that he couldn't see who was steering. Well, so what? The driver would have to get out any second. *Let it be Max!*

Nick waited and waited, but nobody got out. Then, curiously, Biff jumped up, sniffed the air and, vigorously wagging his tail, scooted out onto the road through the fence's metal slats. He ran around in circles, welcoming with pure joy—whom?

A-aha-a-a! Nick stared stupidly from behind the bushes. They have become very good friends already.

With whom?

He took his knife out of his coat pocket, opened its longest blade, and crept along the bushes until he was directly opposite the open door. The front seat was empty. Had the driver climbed into the backseat or? Nick rose to his feet, unable to bear the suspense any longer! He had to unravel this mystery at any cost, even if it meant his life.

But how to proceed? Heading for the gate would give the mystery driver time to slip out of the car and hide; judging from Biff's antics, however, the driver had already made his escape and need make no attempt to hide because he was—invisible!

"No! No, I don't believe in ghosts," Nick muttered through clenched teeth. "Nor in energy second selves!"

He approached the car without making any attempt to conceal himself. Clenching the knife between his teeth, he took off his jacket and threw it on the ground. Then he grabbed two metal fence bars. Covered with rust, they were still solid, but his hands were stronger. Oh no, he hadn't lost his strength! He pulled mightily, his chest heaving forcefully enough to pop two buttons on his shirt as if they had been shot out of a slingshot. *Come on, Nick, let's see what you can do!* He could imagine thunderbolts shooting from his eyes as his biceps swelled up like balls under his bursting sleeves. *He's watching me now* flashed through his mind—only a mind coming up with a thought like that, at a moment like *this*, wasn't quite right.

The metal slats gave way, and Nick quickly pushed his body through the fence—but he got stuck in the middle. The insanity exploded in his head with ravaging might. Swinging helplessly, his gaze still fixed on his car's front door, he finally managed to force his bulk through to the other side. Jumping onto the road, he pulled the knife from between his teeth. His shirt was in tatters, stripped of every button, and his raw, bare chest was covered with blood—blood dangerously mixed with the rust from the fence. What did that matter if he was about to die anyway?

However, he would instead go on living *this* way. The car really was empty, while Biff now cavorted on the path to the lake, apparently following his new-found "friend."

Nobody.

Yes, a mystery.

Nick confirmed that this was a real mystery by returning to his bedroom and dialing Max's number again. This time he answered, "Hello, hello!" His voice was anything but sleepy, which meant nothing now, because one could cover the distance from here to Max's place in ten minutes only by flying—really fast at that!

Nick hung up without a word, poured iodine on his scrapes and cuts, and plastered his chest with Band-Aids before going to bed. He was inordinately tired and pleasantly unhappy, feeling as if he were in the middle of—well, it didn't really matter what.

PART TWO

CHAPTER 23

Reno tried to say something again, but Nick shot him a glum glance and read even louder:

> "*I can free you from that too!*" *the kid exclaimed.* "*All the regrets, the crying, the grief—I come to bring you joy.*" *But the old geezer ignored him, acting as if the kid didn't even exist. Perhaps he had sunk deep into his own reminiscences, finding comfort there. Then the kid got angry, bent over the old geezer, and pierced him with his pale-blue eyes.* No, I have no gift to bring people joy, *he suddenly realized.* But I have the power to kill them! I can, and I want to do this right now!

Nick slammed the manuscript onto the desk.

"Reno, this overflows my cup of patience! Not just a cup—a cask, a barrel, a cistern of patience!"

Reno didn't understand. "What's the problem, Nick? Why did you read that to me? Is there some connection between it and everything you told me about?"

"Well, there must be, though I can't seem to figure out what! All those tricks—with the earring, the nylon cord, the clothes—show clearly that he wanted to make me the prime suspect. But to cross out passages from my own story and revise it so ludicrously—why would he? He's even changed the tenses. I write in the future tense to make the story more original, and he's put it all in the past!"

"Wait, wait! Hold on a minute—"

"And besides, *my* old man is wise, venerable, and this nincompoop calls him 'old geezer'—a clear implication that he considers my character a banal, senile dotard! And what 'kid' for God's sake? As if the boy were some teenager! My character is young, completely innocent, still untouched by the burdens of maturity. Then how about 'I have no gift' and other nonsense? Of course he has a gift! He—"

"Nick, please stop!" Reno eyed him with apprehension. "Just who do you think did this?"

"Who! Isn't that clear? He even goes so far as to confess: 'I have the power to kill them. I can, and I want to do this right now,' he says. Further on, he says, '"The past isn't just years and years ago," the kid said angrily, "but also seconds ago. In these last seconds ago, in the final seconds of your life, I will force you to find not comfort and peace but MY IMAGE!"' In other words, the murderer is writing about himself!"

"The murderer," Reno murmured. "The sadist?"

"Exactly."

"He sneaked into your study, read your manuscript, then revised—"

"'Revised' is putting it too mildly! This morning, when I read his corruption of—"

"So he sat down at your typewriter and started tinkering with—your tale. The killer?"

"Who else would have done it?"

"You."

"No, I wrote the first version, which he crossed out, but this—"

"Look." Reno assumed a solemn tone, as if breaking a heavy piece of bad news. "From some details of what has happened to you in the past few days, one could draw a conclusion, not—alarming— but not too pleasant either. After all, thousands of people suffer from a similar condition—not a disease, exactly."

"What are you talking about? Get to the point!"

"I'm talking about somnambulism, Nick. Sleepwalking. I think that you've developed this—peculiarity. Who can say how long you've been walking in your sleep? After all, you've lived alone for a long time. Or perhaps the condition was only latent but was activated by your strong reaction to your friend Hatcher's death."

"So you're saying that at night I get up, cross out entire passages in my favorite creation, and rewrite stupid, contradictory variants?"

"Well, why not?" Reno snapped. "Who else would take the time to revise such—well—childish stuff, Nick, if I must be blunt?"

"Not everyone *can* write 'such childish stuff,' let me assure you!" Nick flushed with anger. "Creating a tale is not as cut and dried as pleading a divorce case: 'My client is obviously innocent because the plaintiff is impotent, and therefore the house and all the furniture go to her, but the mother-in-law will have to vacate.'"

"Do I really have to put up with your sarcasm?" Reno shot back indignantly. "You take me away from my work, call me over here at this inconvenient hour—"

"Work? Your friend's dying, and you—"

"Dying from what, Nick? Just write your tales when the mood strikes you, when you're awake! As for the revisions you make in your sleep, simply throw them away and that's that."

"Reno, you simply refuse to admit that this"—Nick slammed his fist on the manuscript—"this *could not* have been my doing.

Awake or asleep. I'm not so perverse as to trample on my inmost ambitions! You have no idea what this tale means to me."

"All right! Even if we assume that the killer did revise it, so what? That's nothing compared to his attempt to shift the guilt on you."

"You still don't understand! It's one thing to implicate me by his tricks—that, at least, is playing by the rules, making cunning moves to get away and blame everything on me. I can make my own countermoves and try to defend myself. But this hits below the belt; it violates my author's honor!"

"Nick, Nick, come on!" Reno gave in all of a sudden. "I don't really want to argue with you anymore! I left my office and rushed over here, despite important appointments. Sorry, no need to bring that up again. I'm ready to help you anyway I can! The only thing is—I don't really think you need my help. Or if you do, what exactly is it that you need from me? Just tell me! Let's get down to cases, eh?" Reno gave Nick a wan, strained smile and raised his arms in the air, those hairy arms that he could have borrowed from a gorilla.

How shallow he is, Nick thought, a wave of boredom washing over him. He regarded Reno reproachfully through half-closed eyes, drooping from lack of sleep. *He's only concerned about his office and important appointments. Yes, my friend is superficial and annoyingly, even repulsively, businesslike.* But maybe this "virtue" can be of some use?

"So," Nick dove in, "as I mentioned, since last night my suspicions are strongly connected with Max because—"

"No, it isn't Max," Reno interrupted. "As far as the clothes are concerned, I can agree that he might have followed Elsa when she hid them and then took them in an attempt to incriminate you. But he's not the killer."

"Yes," Nick said, suddenly galvanized, "my intuition tells me the same thing, despite ample evidence against him. He's too much of a snob."

Reno stood up and walked around the office, his new shoes rhythmically creaking at every step. "Well, well, well," he intoned, stopping opposite Nick, then sternly demanded, "enough beating around the bush. Now tell me plainly and simply: Alina wasn't married to Andrey Belloff, was she?"

"No, she wasn't."

"And Kaya's twenty-three?"

"Yes."

"Good. In that case, Andrey Belloff, who left the country twenty-four years ago, might not even have known that his lover was expecting a baby. Am I right?"

"Well, admittedly he *might* not have known."

"Therefore, his father Alexander wouldn't have known either. And if he ever did learn about Kaya, it was near the end of his life. Otherwise he would have told his neighbors that he had a granddaughter. In other words, Alina chose to keep the father of her child secret.

"How secret, Reno? She gave Kaya her father's surname, Belloff."

"Yes, but soon she must have regretted that. Why? That's the question. If we take into account the fact that all victims were one way or another connected with this Kaya—"

"All except Kathy," Nick reminded him.

"Very likely Kathy had something to do with her too. We just haven't found out exactly what. Yes, I think it's safe to assume that all the victims knew Kaya and were killed by the same person. Whoever that person is was originally after her. Kaya must know something incriminating about him, and he's afraid that she told the people she went to for help. What could that incriminating information be? Of course it must be a crime, Nick, a serious crime committed in the past, a crime that only Alina knew about—until the day she died, when she told the whole story to her daughter."

"Who then disappears without a trace—to save herself? According to your version, Alina's death was not caused by pneumonia!"

"Certainly possible," Reno said. "How, though, do we account for the subsequent behavior of Kaya? The killer's hot on her trail for months on end, leaving behind a pile of corpses, yet she doesn't go to the police to turn him in. Why not, Nick? What do you think?"

"Well, I don't know."

"The answer is elementary!" After a dramatic pause, Reno slashed the air with his arm, as if he were cutting the proverbial Gordian knot. "Because the killer, Nick, is her father."

"Andrey Belloff?"

"Precisely. After he committed the aforementioned serious crime, he absconded to Russia, which is why Alina was so careful not to reveal the father of her child. But when he showed up again—"

"Oh!" Nick put his hands to his head.

"Yes, my friend, I understand. You're asking yourself if it wouldn't have been far more convenient for him to leave the country again than commit this string of murders. The obvious conclusion, however, is no. Not if he had too much to lose here. That is, if he is a man with a high social position, such as a famous politician or businessman. It's equally plausible that he's not doing the dirty work himself but has hired a killer to do it for him."

"The poor girl would think that the hired killer is her father!" Nick exclaimed in dismay. "And whoever that is wants to frame me? But wait, Reno. All this may not be true."

Reno stood silently for some time before bursting out, "Well, yes, it's probably *not* true, Nick! Strain yourself; try to understand! What counts is not *whether* it's true but that it *could* be true. We *consider* it true and build your defense to the police and in court on that. The murderer is Andrey, period! Let them prove me wrong if they can. Incidentally, I'm going to dig into the archives today, and I bet I'll find information about some *suitable* unsolved crime from twenty-four years ago. Oho! I'm going to cut that foolish Forger down to size! He still doesn't suspect that there is a connection between Kaya and each of the victims, does he?"

"No, he doesn't—or didn't seem to."

"Perfect!" Reno's manufactured enthusiasm was beginning to sound genuine. "As soon as I uncover an old crime, I'll go to him with it and wave it under his fat nose. No, I have a better idea! I'll go to Marconi, and tomorrow the press will announce, 'Prominent Lawyer Renaldo Aldano Shows Detective Forger the Way!' What do you say to that?"

Nick was barely listening. Instead, he was standing with his shoulder propped against the wall, his hand to his heart, looking with weary desperation through the smudged windows of the study. "It's coming back," he murmured. "It's been wandering around out there since five this morning until—what time is it now, I wonder?"

"Ten thirty," Reno replied mechanically, drawing back so that he wouldn't be noticed from outside. "Damn! You told me you were sure she'd be back no earlier than noon!"

"No, no," Nick started shaking his head.

"What do you mean *no*? Nick, how do I get out of here? But it's too late! She's seen the Ferrari. What a pain!"

"It's not *her*, Reno. It's *it*."

"It's *what*? Who's coming back? Not Elsa?" Reno faltered as he approached the window. "Is she in yet?"

"Not yet." Nick was still shaking his head. "But it will be soon; there's no chance it won't come in. Now it's by the bench."

"Aah, you mean Biff?"

"No, not Biff. Whatever is *with* Biff. At dawn he followed it down toward the lake. Didn't I mention that? It drove the car here and—"

Reno's face turned crimson so suddenly that his eyes filled with blood. Bent forward, he needed only a pair of horns to look like a maddened bull. "Are you—playing the madman again!" Seizing Nick by the shoulders, he shook him until he realized he was holding a sagging sack that would collapse the minute he let it drop. "You—are you serious? Come to your senses, for Christ's sake! Nick, Nick!"

He dragged Nick to the nearest armchair, dumped him like a bulky sandbag, instinctively shaking his hands, and got to work: unbuttoned the uppermost button of his shirt, poured a glass of water from the carafe and insisted Nick drink it down, fanned his friend's face with the manuscript, placed himself on the chair opposite, and carefully took Nick's pulse.

"Your heartbeat is irregular," Reno muttered finally, "very irregular. Then it's true. You're not insane, of course, just totally exhausted. You need a long, long rest."

"Rest? How am I supposed to rest with that *presence*?" The saddest smile played on Nick's lips. "Oh, Reno, I feel it—all the time. It lives here in my home!"

"When one is nervous and run down, he might feel anything," Reno comforted him. "You know that there are people who constantly hear voices or see—things."

"I've been seeing things too. I told you that I saw...a...ghost... with Kaya's figure—a vague image without any facial features. I heard it too."

"Yes, you told me, but that was a normal reaction, Nick, because you've been thinking about Kaya."

"I thought of her only *after* the ghost appeared for the first time. I'm not saying *her* ghost, Reno, because she...she's not dead. She's alive, isn't she?"

"Of course she's alive"—Reno nodded reassuringly—"but she's in grave danger. Maybe, because of some strange course of events, you have established something like telepathic contact with her— as if you heard her soul cry for help."

"Yes, she's been calling me." Nick feebly lifted his head and looked around, as if expecting to see her somewhere nearby, hovering amid the old furniture. "But I...how can I...help her?"

Reno unbuttoned another button of Nick's shirt. "I'll take care of that," he promised in a soft, melodious voice. "I'll find out what other acquaintances Kaya and her mother had, besides the murder victims, and get their addresses. It's very likely that she's hiding with one of them. We'll find her, Nick, before the killer does— and very soon. You just have to calm down, and we'll work this out together, OK?"

"OK, but my car; my car was driving on its own, wasn't it? Explain that to me, please. I don't believe those theories about energy second selves. That's probably what makes me feel—insane!"

"I've already told you that you are probably a sleepwalker, my friend." Into Reno's voice Nick could feel boredom creeping, though it remained gentle and encouraging. "So you saw all these *rides* your car has been taking on its own across the field and down the road in your sleep—peculiar, little pathological dreams in a part of your brain. The driver's door wasn't really open, and the car keys weren't really in the ignition. None of it was real. There was *noth-ing*!" He overaccentuated the word and then continued more cheerfully. "And it's high time you got some normal sleep!"

Then he rose from the chair, slowly and carefully, without making any sudden movements, trying to avoid his friend's eyes, as one would ease away from a very sick man, a man on the verge of death, and picked up the pile of newspaper articles from Nick's desk. "I'll just throw these away," he said. "It's obviously harmful to you to read them. That's what brought on your emotional collapse just now. Bye, Nick. We'll stay in touch."

CHAPTER 24

Although she tried not to make noise as she walked, still Nick could distinctly hear the familiar sound of her slippers slapping softly against her bare heels with each step she took on the carpet. How pleasant her footsteps were, and how soothing the rustle of her fine silk robe! He had heard those sounds thousands of times before, when he was drowsing and she came to tuck him in, turn off the lamp, or just look at him and stroke his ruffled hair. Here she comes now: slap, slap, slap...

He was suddenly overcome by great gratitude for her. Her proximity made him feel safe and cozy, blissfully knowing that there is—there is!—somebody in this world who would never, under any circumstances, betray him. Faithful unto death! To the very grave.

She stood quietly above him, her breath lovingly caressing his cheek, like the fluttering of a fragile bird's wing. She bent over him, probably smiling the smile of love.

His *mother*.

She kissed him on the forehead. *Sleep, sleep, Nicky. Sleep well, my azure-eyed boy!* She started unbuttoning his shirt slowly: he must have dozed off in his clothes again, as he so often did. Her hands reached for the buckle of his belt, undid it, and then came the top button of his pants—then the zipper. He could barely feel her hands.

But Mother, I'm not a little boy anymore!

She kissed him on the forehead again and then the cheek. Her soft hair fell loose over his face, bathed him with the odor of—of Elsa's perfume.

Elsa—it's her! Oh, Mother, is it really possible that you've been gone so long?

Elsa's breath came in short, rapid gasps. Maybe she was crying? Or was she sorry about some of her recent actions and hoping for a reconciliation? She would tell him she loved him as much as ever, or even more! She hated Max and had finally made up her mind to leave him. *"I'm coming back to our father's home, Nick, and from now on, we'll be together always. Inseparable!"*

Her hands reached down again, taking his pants off little by little. He felt those hands on his trousers, pulling them off his legs—very carefully, so that she wouldn't wake him up. But was he really asleep? And if not, why couldn't he open his eyes?

Total exhaustion. Every single particle of his body ached, down to the smallest muscle. He lay absolutely still, numb, practically corpse-like.

She tucked him in, just as their mother had done. Then he sensed her robe falling to the floor. She lay down beside him, her body barely touching his, only her fingertips softly stroking him. It was very pleasant, but he began to grow hard, even though he knew it was wrong.

He had to stop her! How could she dare take such liberties with him? Or was she testing him somehow? *"I've long suspected you; I could feel it—I knew!"*

She let her head lie on his chest. She was light as a feather next to him and much smaller than she should be—now.

When is this "now" anyway? Could it be possible that someone had turned back the hands of time to years ago? If so, everything was fine, still nice and pure, with uncorrupted relations
and intentions. *My sister's just taking a rest beside me. She's a loving,
boisterous, somewhat spoiled, little girl, with reddish braids sticking out
from both sides of her sweet golden freckled face.*

"I look like Pippi Longstocking, don't I, Brother?"

Yes, but you're more beautiful than she is.

"But I don't have my Villa Villekulla, and I don't even have a horse."

*I'll buy you one, Elli. Just wait until I become famous writer; you can
have anything you want!*

"Anything you want," he repeated drowsily.

Her lips were suddenly pressed to his, and her tongue, parched
and chapped, almost feverish, was trying to force itself through
his teeth.

Girl with braids, my eye! This was a woman hot with passion,
her hair hanging down in a mane, apparently trying to mount him!

"I want you," she whispered in his ear.

"You've always had me. Oh, Elsa!"

Her angry, catlike hiss almost deafened him. She jumped off
the bed, dragging the bedspread with her.

Nick realized that he was stark naked now. When had she tak-
en off the rest of his clothes? "But this is—disgusting, perverse!"

He snapped out of his stupor, jumped up, and opened his eyes
to discover he was standing beside the bed, his feet on the rumpled
bedspread that lay on the floor, covering his nudity with a pillow.
A preposterous picture. And of course there was no one in the
bedroom but him. His ear was still buzzing from that imaginary
hissing scream, or had he dreamed it?

Nick threw the pillow down next to the other one and looked
around for his clothes. How absurd! Now he was a "somnambulist

stripper"—in broad daylight, at three in the afternoon! He lifted the bedspread to find his clothes lying in a heap: boxer shorts, socks, trousers, and shirt.

And, a little to one side, his mother's slippers. The *last* ones she had worn before she died, almost new. He knelt down and wonderingly picked them up, pressing them against his bare chest.

It hurt. Some of the bandages had come off, and the skin was raw. Raw from the rusty bars of the fence, last night! Belloff's house, the empty car, and then the car again.

Everything suddenly came crashing back into his memory like a heavy load released from above. He threw aside the slippers convulsively, as if he had been holding giant insects in his hands. He felt sick and reeled off to the bathroom, stumbled over his shirt, and kicking it out of his way.

Then he saw the *kimono*.

No, that was no somnambulistic experience, he realized too late. It had really happened: her robe had fallen to the floor when she removed it. She had really lain. But who, for Christ's sake? Small with almost flat breasts and thin thighs. Long-haired, gentle, young.

"Kaya!"

She had been here and possibly still was! Shaking with nervous tension and impatience, he put on his shorts, hurried to the bedroom door, and opened it. "Kaya! Come here, my darling; don't be afraid of me!" His entreaty echoed down the empty hall.

Returning to the bedroom, he quickly walked around, looking under the bed, behind the curtains, in the closet. The window was closed. Well, fine! He walked out into the hall, locked the door behind him, and took the key with him. Now what? The search should begin downstairs, of course! He took the stairs two or three at a time. Glad to find the front door had not been unlocked after Reno went home, he turned the key in the lock once more, double locking it, and then clenched the key tightly in his cupped hand. He took the box with the rest of the house keys out of the cabinet, though the other doors were almost never locked, and first searched the pantry, then the kitchen, the bathroom, the living room, the library, and so on.

He looked high and low, in every nook and cranny, behind every piece of furniture; he checked all the windows—they were all shut tightly. He kept jerking his head this way and that, so that she couldn't sneak up on him. Eventually he found the key to each door, double locked it, and returned each key to the box. She was nowhere to be found on either the first or second floors.

Since there was no doubt that she hadn't left the house, she could only be in the attic. Once there, Nick locked the door from the inside before he started his search, because the attic was too spacious to take any risks with the door open. There were about a dozen keys in the box by now. With no pockets in his boxer shorts, he had to keep the box under his armpit. If he set it down somewhere, Kaya could steal up to it, unlock the doors he had locked, and escape again. He wandered around until he came upon a piece of old string. He threaded it through the holes in the keys and tied the string around his neck like a necklace. Then he took a long time burrowing into the nooks and crannies in between the piles of old furniture.

No, she wasn't in the attic either—as hard to believe as the equally clear fact that she *had* to be somewhere in the house. Or...

"She must be on the roof!" He was startled by his own voice, hoarse and almost unrecognizable with its manic undertones. Raising his head, he examined the two round windows under the roof's south cornice. Yes! One of them was slightly ajar. He couldn't squeeze his way up to it, of course, nor would that have done him much good. To reach the roof, he would still have to hang onto the cornice first, and it would never bear his weight. Kaya, however, since she was cornered, must have had done just that rather than wait for him to catch her. "Good Lord, is the girl an acrobat? Or am I even crazier than I thought?"

He looked apprehensively at his mother's old chest and then opened it—but no Kaya. He closed it again and pushed it right under the dormer, through dusty cobwebs, before stepping on it and squeezing his way onto the steep roof. No one on that side—how about the other? He moved cautiously toward the ridge. The tiles, overgrown with moss and very slippery, rattled under his bulky body like the chattering teeth of a dying dinosaur during the ice age. His teeth chattered too, but not with cold. He was becoming hysterical.

"Calm down, calm down!"

Finally he could scan the whole roof. Empty. Idiotically, he even checked down the chimneys, which were black and covered with soot that had clogged their throats for years. *If I don't clean them, I won't be able to use my fireplace*, he realized and then giggled sinisterly. He was worrying about the winter, as if he expected to be still alive then. *And why not?* He stood up, propping his back against the tallest chimney. Why shouldn't he be alive, really?

Because the killer always followed Kaya!

"But Kaya's not here. She's just not here; you made that perfectly clear to yourself, didn't you?" Nick spread his arms wide with such an abrupt gesture of conviction that he lost his balance. Staggering, slipping, falling, he hit his elbow and tumbled part way down the roof before clinging dangerously close to the edge. If he hadn't caught himself, he would be lying on the stone porch by now, probably with a broken spine at the very least.

For some time he didn't dare move a muscle. "The roof of my own house—*my world*—as slimy as if a thousand snails had been crawling on it!" Sprawled on his belly, filthy and half-naked, wretched and terribly aware of his wretchedness, Nick whimpered quietly. There was no sun above him. Indolent gray clouds crept sluggishly across the low domed sky.

"Damned clouds!" When he finally moved, *something* cut into his neck. *A knife?* He groaned with surprise and terror, raised his head and heard a clanking sound. The keys! Some keys flew right off the roof; others slid first to the edge and then fell to the porch with a mournful clang. Only two remained—accidentally, not because he instinctively grabbed them as they slid away. He was again lying on his belly, barely breathing, his heart palpitating wildly as he tried to shake the sensation that someone had started slicing his neck!

"'Someone'—but in fact nobody, nobody," he started muttering feverishly, mustering his courage as he realized that the string had hooked on the edge of a tile when he tried to rise, so naturally *it* had cut into his neck. Naturally, yes, but it was frayed! Even if it had been new, the mad shaking of his head could have snapped it.

He tied it, with the two salvaged keys, around his neck and began to pull himself up again. Standing was out of the question; only a snaillike crawling enabled him to inch back safely to the dormer, where he lowered himself through the narrow opening. After a few kicks in the air, he landed heavily on the chest. He sighed, not with relief but the bitter sigh of a man up to his eyes in trouble. Not only had he not found Kaya, which seriously put into question his mental health, but he also would probably have to break down his attic door.

He clambered down to the floor and pushed the chest back to its former position, brutally struck by his bare footprints conspicuous on its dusty lid. That chest housed cherished memories of his late mother along with her reminiscences—photos, letters, pressed flowers, and the pictures he and Elsa had given her when they were still children—and now he had trampled all over these sad, silent bits of the past, leaving his rude, present footprints.

"I must wipe them off. Right now!"

Upset and disgusted with himself, Nick crossed to the old dresser, where their mother had stored their baby clothes, opened it, and took out a little sweater that had once been his. He chose it deliberately to torment himself, remembering how much he had liked it back then, over thirty years ago. It was so soft and fluffy, sky-blue. *It matches your eyes, Nicky!* He balled it up in his huge man's hand, almost obliterating it, while the stench of mothballs contemptuously hit him full in the face.

"No, I don't have the gift of bringing joy to others, *the kid realized.*"

Stop it! That's not my tale. The boy in my story doesn't belong to the dead past. His world is the future, *and everything still awaits him. He is my unborn son, the son I will someday conceive! Yes, yes, that's not impossible.* "Because not only will I be alive when winter comes," Nick muttered through clenched teeth, "but I'll also live to see it gone!"

He wiped, scrubbed, and polished the dresser, darkened from its many years in the attic. The sweater was now no more than a dirty rag. A dirty rag, like his once azure-bright childhood optimism. *"What's most important is to bring joy to yourself, my son."* *That's what I'll tell him!* "Not to others, but to yourself; *remember this! Everything else is just—empty 'future tales.'"*

Nick scrubbed and scrubbed the old chest. Scrubbed! *I'm sick, mother, sick and very lonely. I'm sick with loneliness. And I'm afraid. Afraid of nothing! It has become alive—holds me, caresses me, kisses me. It wants to possess me—to swallow me. I...I almost want that too. Do you understand, Mom! It attracts me so much—because only it caresses me, only it holds me, caresses me, kisses me.*

"*Nothing*, is it? How about the slippers and the kimono?" But were they really in the bedroom? Nick angrily threw the sweater onto the floor and crossed to the door. He tried both keys in the lock, but neither fit. Just what he expected. He would have to break it down. Thank God it opened out; that would make his task considerably easier.

A few powerful shoulder slams landed him headlong on the landing, on top of the attic door. What a battering ram he was! However, he had badly bruised his shoulder in the effort. He rubbed it briskly. "It will be blue, even black before long," he pronounced in a grim, prophetic voice as he started down the stairs.

Even if he succeeded in unlocking some other doors, he would still have to climb through the window and collect the keys that lay scattered on the porch. After that—after that, he could go to his bedroom and try to maintain his sanity. The way things were going, he couldn't tell if he were living in a dream or sleeping in some alternative reality—if he ever slept at all—or, when he was awake, whether he *lived at all*. He could only wander in swampy gray mists of vague conjecture. With no definitive answer, he justifiably leaned on "maybe" or "hardly" like rickety crutches for a crippled man.

Now he felt crippled both spiritually and physically. He was limping on both legs, his sore muscles cramped him further, and the elbow he had hit when he fell on the roof was clicking discordantly. His bruised shoulder was the least of his problems right now, but his neck was sore where the string had cut in, and the raw skin on his chest had become inflamed by the dusty, sooty roof. That's the way things go: after hope is lost, all the earthly ills descend at once.

It took him forever to figure out that one of the keys was for the pantry and the other for a room on another floor. Most unlucky, since there was no window in the pantry. From bad to worse! He dragged himself up to the second floor and stopped opposite the door to his bedroom, preparing to break it down too. Just as he readied himself, he was pierced by the *presence* nearby—clearly from inside the bedroom, more palpable than ever. It seemed to stream forth through the very walls—or was it through the keyhole?

The keyhole, the keyhole—he inserted the last key in it. When it fit, the thought that he would have broken down his bedroom door while holding its key in his hand unnerved him more than anything else he had been through. Shivers ran up and down his spine as he became aware of rustling sounds coming from the bedroom, followed by footsteps.

Slap, slap, slap—*it* had put on the house slippers.

More rustling—*it* had put on the kimono.

Astounded, Nick fell to his knees before the still locked door, which now looked more enigmatic than a sphinx. He pressed his ear to it and listened with his mouth wide open, his eyes bulging like a night bird in the gloom of the dark hallway.

The *nothing* inside *kept moving.*

Aha, that's *it*! There's no one else in the house. But he knew that, when he locked the door to that haunted bedroom, no one was inside.

Did Kaya have a duplicate key? That must be it! She had been hiding out here since Wednesday—the day he first sensed the presence—her presence! The day all the shocking incidents had started happening, which weren't really so shocking—God, things suddenly seemed painfully obvious again. The girl had gone back to the bedroom after he left it. That's why he couldn't find her. Fool that he was, he almost killed himself up on the roof, while she—she's inside!

Nick put his hands on the door and pushed, straining himself to the fullest to regain his feet, as if weighed down by the insupportable burden of his twisted emotions.

"Kaya? Kaya, it's me. Don't be afraid!"

But how could she not be afraid? His voice sounded coarse and mean. And the poor girl—she must desire him, as she has unequivocally shown, but he had given her absolutely no reason to trust him.

"Please, trust me, Kaya! I want to help you—I'm coming in now; don't be afraid!"

But how could she not be afraid? A huge bearded man, slimy and disheveled, almost naked! Well, after all, she had taken his clothes off—what a temperament!

"Don't run from me, dear! I like you too. I like you a lot!"

He unlocked the door and opened it abruptly and then slammed it shut behind him, locking it again with a trembling hand. He spun around, looking everywhere. Not a living soul inside, but his clothes were folded in a tidy pile, and the bed was neatly made. On its snow-white pillow was something else: a lock of auburn hair, lying like a small, coiled snake.

CHAPTER 25

How long had he been staring at that lock of auburn hair? Probably no more than a minute, though it seemed like an eternity—or no time at all, which was the same thing. He bent down and rested his knees on the bed frame, looking for the kimono on the other side of the bed. It wasn't there, nor were the slippers. But what was so extraordinary about that, after all? Obviously Kaya had really been in this three-time-locked bedroom and perhaps still was. The lock of hair was her calling card. That fact led Nick to the stunning conclusion that he was suffering from—how to put it? Partial blindness? Localized or selective amnesia? He could see perfectly fine, but not everything, or he saw things and immediately *forgot* them, over and over again—in this case a human being!

Biff's angry bark interrupted his reverie. Nick crossed to the window, drew back the curtains, and opened it. The intruder turned out to be Detective Forger, standing on the lawn with his hands in his pockets, flanked by two of his stooges.

"Good day, Mr. Edgeway."

He was craning his neck up at the window and smirking; obviously he had noticed that "Mr. Edgeway" wasn't feeling exactly "good." He rocked back and forth with annoying raffishness, shifting his weight from heel to toe, his bald pate glistening even though the sun was behind a cloud. It seemed to give off a light of its own, though more likely Forger had simply applied something to it. *Give up, baldy; you've grown your last head of hair!*

Motivated by the sour look on his master's face, Biff sank his teeth into Forger's baggy pants, whereupon Forger gave the mutt a swift kick.

"Hey! Don't kick my dog! " Nick yelled, suddenly choked with justifiable rage. "Don't kick him, or I'll come down and—"

"Yes, please *do* come down," said Forger. "We need to have a little talk, and I can return your clothes." He made a wide ceremonious gesture, and one of his stooges promptly stepped forward, a beige suit and white shirt draped across his arm.

"Here," Forger continued, "we have no need of these, as you very well knew. But if you would be so kind as to show us the other suit, the one you *really* wore the night of the murder."

"Yes, I will be so kind." Nick snorted. "Why not?"

"Perfect!"

"Would you go to the back porch first?" Nick leaned out of the window, pointing to the spot with his index finger. "There are some keys on the ground there. Lots of them."

"Excuse me?"

"Keys. One of them is to the front door. I'm locked in."

"I see." The lieutenant looked up at Nick suspiciously, apparently assuming this was another example of his weird sense of humor, but motioned his second stooge to take a look.

"There should be ten," Nick added.

The cop took his sweet time picking them up, then walked back to Forger, and poured them into the detective's hands.

"Yeah, there are ten, boss," he reported, returning to his post behind Forger's back.

"Is that where you usually keep your keys?" Forger raised his head again.

"Yes, always," Nick confirmed vindictively and then crossed to his closet and took out the "real" suit. Had he made a mistake by not destroying it and about to make another by handing it over? He answered himself out loud, "I don't know." Then limped downstairs.

This was all so wearisome—especially the questions that had no answers. Normally, when people come to a wall, they simply change direction and go around, while the idiot starts smashing his head against it. *Enough! No more head smashing. I'll go around the wall*, he decided. *It has to end somewhere, even if this place is hell!*

Nick heard the key turn in the front door, he unbolted it, and Forger strolled, uninvited, into the foyer.

"Here are the clothes that you're so hot to get your hands on." Nick shoved them into Forger's hands. "There's no point in questioning me about them. My sister told you the first part of the story—that she hid them somewhere, but they somehow disappeared. I can only add that I found them in my closet last night. Who put them there and why, I don't know. But if I find out, you'll be the first person I'll call."

"Jack!" the lieutenant barked. Cop number one immediately appeared, handed Nick the beige suit and white shirt, who hung them carelessly on the hall stand. The cop took the gray suit and the light-blue shirt from his boss and went out. The exchange of objects continued as Forger poured the remaining nine keys into Nick's hands. The two then approached the locked living room door. The fifth key Nick tried fit. After they entered, Nick placed the rest of the keys on the small end table and remained standing, arms akimbo, as Forger settled into the sofa with a sigh.

"This time my men would like to take a little look around your yard, with your permission, and check your car. Incidentally, why did you park it out there by the fence?"

"Why not?"

"Randy!" Forger roared like a deer in heat, and cop number two hustled into the living room. "He'll need the keys to your car, Edgeway. Are they on the porch as well?"

"No, they're on the cabinet in the hall."

Randy closed the door behind him.

"Will he take fingerprints?" Nick perked up. "From the steering wheel, for instance?"

Forger leaned his way.

Is he using some sort of hair restorer or not? I'll ask him!

But Forger spoke first, "Why not get dressed, Mr. Edgeway? You'll catch cold like that."

Damn! He had completely forgotten that he was practically naked! Barefoot, wearing only his boxer shorts, covered with dirt and soot. He grew nervous and confused, his determination to act aloof and bored evaporating, and began excusing himself profusely, "I had just come down from the roof when you drove up. I was trying to clean out the chimneys. 'Winter is coming,' I was thinking, but I dropped my keys."

"Why did you take them onto the roof at all?" Forger asked, understandably curious.

Nick couldn't think of an answer, so he just shrugged his shoulders noncommittally and muttered, "Excuse me for just one second." Then he started for the door, well aware of his grotesque appearance. Even the sound of his bare dirty feet on the floor made him blush. In his mind he visualized the way he had behaved: showing off, putting his hands on his waist, pretending to be impudent. With his figure! Maybe a few years ago, he could have pulled it off, when he still had his athletic physique, but now!

He left the living room under Forger's interested gaze and headed straight up to the bathroom but paused on the landing between floors. What was he doing? The bathroom key was still on the end table, so he would again have to become ridicule for this second-rate cop.

Even the second time he left the living room, grasping all the keys, the absurd situation wasn't over. Meanwhile Elsa had arrived, and he literally bumped into her in the hallway. She gasped.

"Everything's OK!" he whispered. "I've just been cleaning the chimneys."

"But why are you nearly naked?"

"Why, why—so as not to dirty my clothes, of course. Come on!" He took her by the elbow and dragged her up the stairs. "Forger's here!"

"I know. I saw the patrol car. I'm so worried, Nick! There are rumors going around town—"

"I'll be right back!" He pushed her into the bedroom, ran to the bathroom door, and unlocked it. After a quick shower, he put on his bathrobe and went back to Elsa.

"We must make some arrangements," he began but didn't finish.

She was standing by the bed, her hand pressed against her chest, terribly pale, gazing down at the snakelike lock of hair on the pillow.

So? How much longer can I stand all this? Nick asked himself. *I'm going to buckle before long, like some overloaded old horse.*

"That...that—" Elsa was trying to mouth the right phrase. "That's Kathy's hair!"

This accusation floored him. Or worse: his soul collapsed, fell into a terrible abyss of hopelessness and dark, leaving only an empty shell, perishable and devoid of spirit—a stick figure in the middle of the room, blinking hard against the drab, dank day.

"It's Kathy's hair." Elsa repeated. "Her hair was long and auburn. Where did you—find it? Nick! Do you hear me! Where?"

"Here," the perishable mouth wheezed.

"I see!" Elsa suddenly pull herself together. Her expression even betrayed grim satisfaction. "That explains your bizarre appearance. You woke up, saw *that* next to you, and didn't take time to dress, because you assumed the killer left it on the pillow and was still in the house. You rushed out of the bedroom to look for him. You searched the attic and even climbed up on the roof, didn't you?"

His head nodded woodenly in agreement, emptied of thoughts.

"What a nasty sonovabitch!" Elsa exclaimed. "Sonovabitch! I knew it. It's a good thing you didn't catch him—oh!" She cut herself short, taken aback by her own words, and started to qualify them: "I just meant that...in the sense that...you know...that this killer is capable of anything, and with *huge* sadistic experience!" Pulling herself together again, she straightened her hair. "Listen dear, I'm going down to Forger, and you"—she pointed at the lock of hair imperiously—"hide that *at once*! And get dressed!"

Passing near him, she patted him encouragingly on the shoulder and marched out of the room.

Nick's battered body dutifully, mechanically, started to drag his sunken soul back into it, managing slowly to bring it round after that horrible experience, and Nick finally found the strength to do something. First, he took the lock of hair with two fingers and put it between the pages of the book on the nightstand. Second, he put on clean clothes. Third, maybe he really *came* to his senses—something that wasn't all that wonderful.

"Sonovabitch!" he heard himself say as he descended the stairs. "You may have outsmarted me this time, but we aren't through yet!"

CHAPTER 26

When he walked into the living room, Elsa was sitting beside Forger on the sofa. That struck Nick as strange at first, baldly suggesting some intimacy between them. Still, Nick was quick to grasp the strategic advantage her position gave her—sitting next to him, she could avoid his point-blank stares, which she would probably find hard to take just now.

But that left Nick no choice. He sat down facing them both.

"Did you go out today, Edgeway?" Forger interrogated him immediately.

"No, I was at home all day."

"Well, that's OK, but you made up for it yesterday with quite a little outing. Seems you took a tour of some of the crime scenes."

"'Tour' is hardly the word I'd use, Lieutenant. After all, we're not talking about museums or exhibition halls here, are we?"

"Precisely!" Forger snapped his head. "You think you're a wise guy, huh? Sticking your nose where it doesn't belong, lying to people that you're writing some sort of novel, sweet-talking them into confiding in you! Incidentally, you frightened Mrs. Lang out of her wits with your maudlin little fabrications."

"Oh, you mean the maid?" Nick laughed quite naturally. "Who knows what story she's made up this time! She's not quite all there. She 'confided' in me that, shortly before the sisters were murdered, some troubled spirit came to them, either to warn them or to take them—"

Forger waved him off impatiently. "How about the high school? What do you have to say about—"

It was Nick's turn to interrupt. "I'm really tired of all this! What are you driving at, Forger? You seem obsessed with me, conducting regular searches of my home and having me followed wherever I go. I've had just about enough! From now on I talk to you only in the presence of my lawyer."

After this declaration, he turned to Elsa for support, but she didn't seem to have been listening. Shouldn't she be listening very carefully, even intensively, if she really were worried about him? Or could it be that she was worried about someone *else*? She looked more than worried—even petrified with fear: sitting on the edge of the sofa, hunched over with her shoulders pulled back, staring straight in front of her, her lips set, and her fists clenched in her lap. And she was strangely silent, as if dozens of voices were arguing in her head, making it impossible for her to speak.

"Well, fine." Forger broke the short silence. "Have it your way. Actually, all I want to know is where you were this morning just before daybreak, from three thirty to five. Think about it and answer me if you want to."

At first Nick felt relieved at Forger's question: they hadn't followed him during the night; they had missed his escapade at Belloff's place. Then he was shattered as if by a blow: his car had been gone exactly from three thirty to five o'clock! Could it be possible that the killer had taken his car—to commit another murder?

"Home. I was right here at home. And, thank God, this time there's someone who can confirm this! Elsa, tell him!"

Elsa, however, remained silent.

"She and my niece slept here last night," he was forced to explain. "And it so happened that I had to wake them up at about three thirty. Come on, Elsa, tell him! I came to your room. I was... I'd had...a bad dream and wanted to see how Anna was. Tell him!"

"I don't remember anything of the sort, Nick," she replied. His own sister!

Forger now looked at her and then back at him. Nick could almost see his ears perk up, like a hound on a fresh trail. Then he turned abruptly to the door, where Anna had silently materialized. *What a family I have!* Nick groaned to himself, dismayed by this latest development.

"Ah, the child's here too," Forger remarked unnecessarily. "Perhaps she will remember? Did your uncle come to your room last night, dear?"

She won't answer him, Nick assumed, his heart sinking further. *She never answers anybody's questions.* Oh, what a family! Of course Anna just stood there by the door, holding in her hands some twig with leaves that had been half-eaten by insects, staring down at it—or at the insects? She gave no indication that she had heard the question.

"Elsa, how can you deny it?" Nick pleaded with her. "You know perfectly well that Max left at around two thirty and that about an hour later I—"

"Max?" Forger broke in. "Your husband was here last night? Is that true, madam?"

"Yes, he came at around two," she began with surprising readiness. "We'd had a fight yesterday, and that's why I decided to spend the night here at my father's home with my daughter. I hope you understand, Mr. Forger. But since we rarely fight, my husband couldn't sleep. He couldn't 'close his eyes,' as he admitted to me, and wanted to make up as soon as possible. Well, we did make up, of course, and he *stayed with us till morning.*"

"You're lying!" Nick cried in amazement, stunned rather than dismayed. "Why are you lying?"

"Easy, Edgeway."

"Easy, my eye! She's lying through her teeth!"

"Or maybe she's fed up with lies?" Forger gave him a piercing look. "Like with the clothes? She didn't want to do it, it seems, but she was forced to lie about them too. My impression of you, sir, is that you're constantly putting pressure on your relatives to corroborate your threadbare alibis. Perhaps you're threatening them."

"That's not true! Just the opposite! She forced me to lie about the damned clothes because she had hidden them without my knowledge, while I was out fishing! As for last night, Max was here until ten to three and then left. I saw him out myself! Do you hear me? And at around three thirty, I went to their room."

"I don't remember that," Anna piped up out of nowhere, loud and clear.

Elsa nodded at her approvingly and turned to Forger. "I wouldn't claim that my brother wasn't home at that time. I would assume that he was in his room asleep. But we didn't see him. Do you understand?"

"Yes, entirely, madam." Forger boldly leaned toward her. "I'm sorry if all this disturbs you."

"That's all right." She smiled at him! "I know you're just doing your duty. But if you have no more questions to ask me—"

"I have questions to ask you!" Nick exploded. He had the inordinately acute sensation that his skin was about to rip apart, not figuratively but literally. He was suffocating, popping at the seams! "At least tell him about that day before Schumacher's murder. Tell him that then I asked you about Alina. And when you told me she was dead, I immediately asked you for her telephone number—but not to call her!" He pressed his head hard between the palms of his hands, as if trying to smash it. The pain helped him to concentrate. "Tell the lieutenant that I was interested in Alina *only* because of her daughter!"

"I'm sorry, Nick," Elsa said with hypocritical embarrassment. "I don't have any idea what you're talking about."

"I'm talking about the seamstress! You gave me her telephone number last Thursday!"

"What phone number, for Christ's sake? Alina died seven or eight months ago, and this is the first time I've heard of a daughter."

"OK, maybe you didn't know she had a daughter, but…Ah, you…you damned liar!"

"Excuse me, Mr. Forger," Elsa stood up, pretending she was holding back her tears. She went over to Anna, put her hand gently on her daughter's shoulder, and departed the battlefield—as the victor. Nick half-closed his eyes, gnashing his teeth. *I'll kill her! I'll cut the bitch's throat!* This murderous desire pierced his brain but didn't surprise him.

"It seems you're going down, Edgeway," Forger announced cheerfully, "but why drag your sister along with you?"

"You shut up!" Nick snapped at him. "You have no evidence against me. What gives you the right to browbeat me? As for Alina and Kaya, ask the man who's now living in their apartment. He'll tell you a certain telephone repairman called on him on Friday. Is that clear?"

"Not in the least."

"I can't believe that someone with your amazing lack of insight could do this job!" Nick demonstrated genuine astonishment along with his rage. "That repairman was me! Now do you get it? I pretended I was from the phone company so that I could get the address."

"So what?"

"That's *proof* that I was looking for Alina—or more precisely for Kaya, not Schumacher!"

"I'm not here about Schumacher, or about Kathleen Hatcher." Forger sighed suddenly, sounding like a big burst balloon. He rested his elbows on his knees, put his chin in the palms of his hands, and then blurted out, "I came here right from one doctor—"

"Doctor?" Nick repeated stupidly, even as the name Forger was fishing for appeared in his mind's eye in big, bright bloody letters: MAYER. "Mayer." He sighed. "Doctor Mayer."

"Ahaaa!" Forger exposed him with a shout. "How did you guess?"

"No, no. I didn't guess. Just—"

"Oh, I see. Your sister. She had told you then. Yet she claimed that she hadn't heard anything about that murder."

Forger's words jumbled in his mind with those of Eric Schumacher: *"the doctor who took care of her."* "Your sister?" *"Alina was already dying."* "She told you!" *"He had been unavoidably detained—Mayer, the doctor who."*

"Hey, wait a minute!" Nick waved his arms, as if trying to snatch a passing thread of logic out of the air. "If I killed Mayer, why would I have to learn his name from my sister? What kind of game are you playing with—against—me now, Lieutenant? You just gave yourself away—you don't suspect me!"

Forger arched his eyebrows thoughtfully. "Yes, you're probably right," he admitted, "but to be honest, I don't know if I suspect you or not. I don't know anything lately! Except one thing: the psychopath has picked up the pace. It seems he's become insatiable lately, committing a murder every night for three nights in a row. I wonder how he can manage it? If nothing else, it must be *exhausting*, wouldn't you say, Edgeway?"

Forger hurled his heavy look of the cop in a deadlock against Nick's *exhausted* face, doughy with lack of sleep and anxiety. Nick practically shriveled in his armchair, as if he'd sustained a heavy blow. The next moment, however, he somehow found the strength to jump to his feet and vigorously pace the floor, as if to say, "Take a good look at me! I'm not the least tired," until tripping on the edge of the carpet startled him. *My behavior probably seems downright insane! Though it's—just very stupid.*

"Enough!" he yelled at himself. "Enough!" he yelled at Forger too. "You're constantly making mistakes, and then you have the gall to come here with your absurd questions! Well, yes! If you'd ordered your people to follow me not only during the day but also at night, you'd know perfectly well by now that I'm not the killer!"

"You're probably right," Forger said, acquiescing. "Still, Edgeway, it's more than obvious that there are—some very strange things going on around here. Why don't you try to explain them to me—to tell me the truth, for a change, huh?"

The truth? Nick attempted an awkward smile from somewhere deep in his own hopeless confusion. Forger got up from the couch and came over to him.

"I'm looking forward to the results of the lab tests on the Seconal," he said, looking deep into Nick's eyes. Then he nodded his gleaming head and finally did something good—he left.

Nick eagerly saw him to the front door. "From now on, I want you to place me under continuous surveillance," he said. "Night and day! After you finish inspecting my car, leave the keys in the ignition. I'll get them later. Yes, follow me, but don't disturb me anymore! Understand?"

Forger made no reply other than to stare deeply into Nick's eyes, as if trying to decipher some secret message he saw there. Nick put a stop to this exercise by slamming the door in his face.

As usual, like some neurasthenic old spinster, he locked and double bolted it.

Elsa intercepted him on the landing between the two floors. "Nick, I'm very sorry!" She was crying, and as far as Nick could tell, this time the tears were real. "Forgive me!"

"Forgive you?" He couldn't believe his ears. "For trying to destroy me!"

"Yes, forgive me for everything!"

She was trembling now, her face pressed against his chest. Looking down at her profuse honey-blond hair, he was torn between a desire to grab her by it and an almost equal desire to stroke it. He put his hands behind his back.

"OK, of course—I forgive you!"

She drew back and looked at him through tear-blurred eyes. "And I forgive you, my dear. I don't know why you're constantly asking me to lie for you these days, but whatever the reason is…I won't…I could…never hate you."

CHAPTER 27

If he had been sentenced to death and given one last wish, Nick would have answered without hesitation, "To sleep for at least half an hour!" Nothing else. But as he had not been sentenced *yet*, he could indulge himself in a much longer sleep, right now, though it was barely six o'clock in the evening. He closed the bedroom curtains tightly, put on his pajamas, and sank gratefully into his bed. It and it alone was always ready to enfold him, warm him, and caress him, no questions asked. Only in his bed did he feel entirely wanted.

He slept without dreaming and so deeply that, when the telephone started ringing, he felt like a deep sea diver forced to rise slowly and painfully to the surface through layers of dark and heavy oblivion in order to reach it. He propped himself on his elbow and groped for the receiver and then uttered a hoarse, inarticulate grunt.

"Listen to me, Nick!" Max's voice echoed in his ear. "Where's Elsa?"

"I don't know."

"Go check on her!"

"Why?"

"She might be eavesdropping, that's why. Come on, move it, man! You sound half-asleep, damn you!"

"I *was* asleep," Nick replied, awakened by Max's rudeness. "I *was* asleep!"

"Good for you. You must have a tough conscience to sleep that soundly. Now go check on her."

"No need, Max. If she picks up the other phone, we'll know right away. It makes a very distinct crackling sound. So, speak!" Nick switched on the bedside lamp and, narrowing his eyes, read the clock. Barely nine o'clock in the evening. "But keep it brief!"

"Yes, I'll be brief. All I have to do is say one brief word and you go straight to jail!"

"Maybe. But only until the next murder."

"You're wrong there. Even if there are ten more murders, you'll stay in jail until you sit on the chair. *The last chair*, with very high voltage!"

Ah, this is Max, with his—how did Elsa put it? Yes, his 'exquisite spirituality.'"

"'The copycat.' That's what they'll call you from now on." There was no stopping him now. 'The copycat writer!' Another possibility is that the murderer leaves you all his deeds and moves on to some other town, where he might change his style—maybe stop cutting their throats and start skinning them alive."

"How eloquent, Max, but if that's all you have to say, hang up. You know your position is far worse than mine."

"Oh, really?" Max's laughter crackled through the receiver like a whiney buzz saw. "Because of those nonexistent pictures you mentioned?"

"Just try to frame me again, and you'll see if they exist or not."

"That's exactly what I plan to do! Now listen to me carefully. Last night I didn't go straight home. I watched you from the street, to see if you'd drag yourself to Elsa to give her all the details about the pocketknife and all. You turned on the light in your room pretty quickly, so I assumed you regained your reason. But I decided to watch a little longer, and what did I see? Your Ford going down the hill! At first I thought that the hand brake might have released, but a few seconds later, I heard your accomplice start the engine—"

"Accomplice? Why not simply say the car thief?"

"Because as your car drove away, Nick, you were calmly watching it leave from your bedroom window."

"OK, make this short, Max!"

"I'd hidden my car down the road, so I ran to it and I followed, which wasn't all that easy to do, especially in town. Toward the end I almost lost it, and when I finally caught sight of it again, whoever had been driving had already parked and left." Max was providing all the petty details, sure that he wouldn't be interrupted. "I hid nearby and waited for more than an hour. I hoped to catch a glimpse of whoever was driving, but I guess my attention wandered at just the wrong time. I didn't see him return, just saw the Ford drive off again. Then I gave up the chase and went home to get some sleep. And this morning, Nick, I found out *exactly* where your car had been parked—just down the street from a very stately mansion. Would you like to know who lives—that is, who *lived*—there?"

"Dr. Mayer."

"Oh!" Max was surprised. "How did you know?"

He doesn't suspect me either! Now it was Nick's turn to be surprised. *What an offensive trust I've been granted lately!*

"What do you mean *how did I know*, Max? My accomplice told me, of course."

"Oh, come on, cut it out! He's no accomplice of yours. I just called him that to startle you. I wanted you to realize how things stand, how it would all look to an impartial observer, to an *outsider*."

"And how does it look to an *insider*?"

"Like that other guy has used you, Nick—like he only pretended to be a secret agent. And you, with your typical childlike faith, believed him. You even let him take your car! So off he goes to satisfy his pathological lusts, meanwhile arranging all the evidence to point to you!"

"Or to you," Nick countered.

"There you go again, threatening me with your insignificant photos. Even if those pictures do exist, they are worth exactly nothing now. I'm in a far better position to frame you than you are to frame me!"

"How? By saying that my car was parked near Mayer's house? Don't be ridiculous, Max! If the police swallowed such hearsay, we'd all be in jail by now."

"True, but my accusation won't be merely circumstantial! Listen, whoever was driving your car parked half on the sidewalk, and he had to back up to do that. But there was a tree in front of him and another one right behind him, Nick! That so-called agent may be a skillful killer, but he's a bad driver. But then nobody's perfect, right?"

"Yes, yes! So what?"

"So he scratched the Ford on the tree behind him. I figure the dent must be just above the rear right fender. I checked this afternoon and found a very noticeable mark on the tree too. If those two marks are compared, along with the paint—"

"OK. I get the picture. So what do you want?"

"I want you to come by my place tomorrow, at least by noon, with the photos. If you don't come—for instance, because there *are* no pictures—at twelve one, I leave for Forger's office!"

"Understood. I'll be there." Nick hung up, murmuring, "Yes, Max, expect me, but not *as late as* tomorrow!"

He jumped out of bed and dressed as quickly as possible, thinking, *Yes, God certainly works in very mysterious ways.* His worst enemy was the only person who had offered him any help during this nightmare. Without intending to, Max had rid him once and for all of his last doubts about his sanity; clearly everything connected with the car had really happened. He wasn't a somnambulist, and that realization suggested an answer to another most painful question: Why had Elsa acted so treacherously?

Clearly the *killer* had made her do it! He must have threatened her—or threatened Anna. Why else would she falsely accuse her own brother? No doubt he also forced her to play that little game of giving back the clothes, to hand over the keys to the Ford last night, and to lie again and again, using her to set his vicious trap. Still, whether by accident or design, the trap could only be sprung by Max.

"But it won't be sprung!" Nick asserted resolutely. Wearing a pair of comfortable, light shoes and a dark sweatshirt that he thought suited a man regularly and easily deceived, completely on the wrong track, with absolutely no intentions about anything, he settled into a weary slouch and knocked on Elsa's door.

But he soon learned she wasn't in the house anywhere. She was gone, with her precious Anna, and had left behind a note for him. More like an epistle, and in such a fine, flowing, steady hand, extraordinary for a sister and mother being blackmailed by a ruthless killer!

Nick,

I still want to believe you, but after the way you behaved in front of Lieutenant Forger today, it is getting harder and harder to do so. I keep asking myself if you really are innocent, why all the lies? No, I can't lie any longer to protect you. I can't remain with Anna here in our father's house without being afraid, and with good reasons. You've become a complete stranger to me, Nick. I just can't trust you anymore. And my mistrust, Nick, didn't start today, or even yesterday, but almost half a year ago, though I've been trying to suppress it anyway I could. But lately that has become impossible.

I defended you with all my heart and soul to Max, who from the very beginning has suspected you. I fought with him only yesterday, and that was the first such fight we've had in our long and happy married life! Now more than ever, I'm convinced that he was right, not me. Only my pride keeps me from going straight to him and admitting that I was wrong. I have to confess that I still hope you really are innocent, even though that hope grows dimmer and dimmer. Please find a way to prove your innocence, Nick, if you have any innocence left to prove!

Annie and I are going to spend the next few days or maybe weeks at our place in the country. I'm ashamed of Max; I fear you! Oh Lord, I never dreamed all this could happen to me!

PS: Don't try to reach me! I'll keep my phone off the hook, and if you come to the door, I won't open it. I don't need to tell you why.

PPS: Help me to trust you again, my dear Nick!

"Sheer nonsense!" Nick folded the note with disgust, as if it were a used handkerchief, and stuffed it angrily into his pocket. He had never read anything more hypocritical and unconvincing. While it was addressed to him, it was in fact destined for other eyes. No doubt Elsa expected her brilliant invention somehow to find its way to Forger.

But why Elsa? Obviously this was the killer's next move, though the handwriting was certainly hers, and she had written it with great care! Well, no wonder—with a knife at their throat, who wouldn't? *Including me*, Nick admitted, immediately angry at his old bad habit of unnecessarily taking the blame for something he hadn't done.

"Stop this!" *You have a tough job to do, Nick, so don't get off the track. Act; act!*

He left the house and tied Biff up, since the stupid dog insisted on clambering all over him when it saw him come out. Then he went to the Ford, parked outside the fence like a sated predator. The keys were in the ignition as per the instructions he had given Forger. Sniggering, he climbed in and put his hands on the steering wheel, which felt strangely rough, so he turned on the dash lights instead of starting the engine. His palms were covered with something black with the consistency of fine sand—probably some stuff for fingerprints—but Nick had no doubt that the butcher, who drove the car last, had worn gloves.

Yet Nick couldn't figure out why he had killed Mayer too. After all, Kaya hadn't sought Mayer's help. The good doctor had even refused to help her mother when she lay dying. Maybe he had refused because he had been afraid? Afraid because, as the family doctor, he already knew—something—that eventually caused his own death, just last night. With this same car!

Nick drove the car onto his property and parked it in the garage. Climbing out to close the wrought iron front gate, he automatically turned on the garage lights and couldn't help noticing the deep scratch above the rear right fender. Yes, that was most unfortunate.

"Most unfortunate for *you*, Max!" he warned in a funereal tone.

Then he took more decisive action—checked the gas gauge, glad that he hadn't filled the car lately. After the psycho's excursion to Mayer's place, there weren't more than a couple of gallons left in the tank. He located a small gas can and, with the help of a hose, managed to siphon almost all of the gas out without spilling a single drop on the garage floor. Replacing the gas cap, he put the can next to the shuttered window that looked out on the backyard. Next he dug out his old bike. He put air in the tires, long flat with years of disuse but hale, adjusted the brakes, and oiled the chain, which took him almost an hour of well-spent time. He would definitely need the help of this long-neglected old friend.

Remembering how he had insisted that the police keep him under constant surveillance, Nick turned off the lights and then opened the window. Trying not to make noise, he hoisted the bike through the window and lowered it onto the grass, propping it against the garage wall. Then he set the can on the bike seat, closed the window, and turned on the garage lights again. Finally he left the garage, turning off the lights yet again, and with studied carelessness left the front gate open as he went back into the house. *If my car's here, I must be here too. Right, Lieutenant Forger?*

He came back out with some food and water for Biff to keep him from whining, but the dog wasn't impressed by this generous gesture. Apparently Elsa had fed him before heading for her hideaway in the country. Not only that, she had also taken pains to feed her *untrustworthy brother*, leaving a whole roast chicken in the oven, with rice and vegetables. After washing his hands, he sat down at the kitchen table and ate very slowly—the chicken was cooked to perfection—relishing every bite. He didn't eat because he was nervous, as was usually the case, and that puzzled him because, now of all times, if only for the sake of propriety, he should feel some distress. But no! Serenity washed over him like high tide over an offshore reef. Was this sense of contentment a sign that he had finally found his *true calling*?

By now it was already eleven thirty.

I'll take nothing along that could implicate me, he decided, finishing his coffee. *At the crime scene, I'll find—whatever I need.* He went upstairs to his bedroom, opened the window, and flung out his arms, shouting at the top of his lungs, "Help! Help!"

After waiting anxiously for some response in vain, he yelled again, even more desperately this time, "Help! Help!"

But no cops dashed into the house brandishing their weapons. Not even a twig cracked. Apparently, in spite of his insistence—or maybe because of it—Forger hadn't put the usual tail on him. It seemed equally clear that his phone wasn't tapped since, if it had been, they would have contacted him by now about the conversation with Max and also have taken some precautions to guard the latest circumstantial evidence against him—the car with its telltale scratch.

This was just great! With his humiliating trust in Nick's innocence, the totally incompetent Forger had robbed him of his alibi, contained in almost every word of his little talk with Max. Robbed him of the last possibility to save his humanity! *But my humanity is something I can easily do without*, Nick admitted to himself. *My humanity isn't much more than a mask of endless, cowardly endurance anyway.*

He gave one last forlorn cry of "Help!" and closed the window.

Leaving the light on in the bedroom, Nick stepped into his study, took out a manila envelope, and put it into his back pocket. As he started back down to the ground floor in the dark, he hesitated: Should he leave through the front door or through the bathroom window? After all, the window faced the darkest part of the backyard, and the tree in front of it blocked the view. True, it seemed completely absurd that the cops could be watching the house after his heartrending cries for help had generated absolutely no response, but how could he be certain? Considering all the stupidity and irresponsibility around him, logic began to seem like a drowning cat: you feel pity for it, but you realize that it can't catch even a limping mouse anymore. So he chose to exit through the bathroom window.

He let himself down as quietly as he could and, as soon as he felt ground under him, sank into a crouch and started running, keeping close to the house. This was the most dangerous moment. *"Freeze! Where are you sneaking off to, Edgeway?"*

"Well, I'm running from the killer!" Yes, that's what he would say! *"I thought I heard someone in the house. I called for help, but when nobody came—"*

He reached the bike propped under the garage window. Grasping the gas can, he put the bike over his shoulder and made for the gate at the far end of the yard. Since it hadn't been used in a long time, it was covered with vines. He tried opening it inch by inch but still couldn't keep it from creaking. He pushed the bike and can through the narrow opening before somehow squeezing through himself. When he closed the gate, he was pleased to see the vines return to where they had been. If he could manage to keep them intact on his return, by morning it would be almost impossible to tell that the gate had been opened.

He carried the bike all the way to the path that wound around to the main road. When he reached it, he tied the can to the handlebars, settled himself precariously on the dangerously rickety seat, and gave the pedals a mighty push.

CHAPTER 28

When he reached the end of the path, Nick hid the gas can behind a bush and then rode his bike down the path and across the moon-lit road. He sped down the right-hand lane, planning to cover the distance in under an hour, though he knew he would be limping in the morning from the exertion.

But before that "next" morning comes, as we know very well, the decisive, inevitable battle will be fought. The armies, each numbering exactly two hundred soldiers, would meet at a specifically prepared place on the beach. In the deepening night, the moon will take on the aspect of a pharaoh's golden mask, haughty and unfeeling, bathing the scene in its magnificence. The sky will be spangled with stars, allowing each man to be easily recognized by his comrades and to appear frighteningly determined to his foes—that determination no more than a mask itself for the entire army of the Sensibles and half the army of the Sensitives.

For the hundred that the boy has enlightened, though, this determination would be really frightful, because they will have forgotten their physical and spiritual torments and no longer bear in their hearts images of the wonderful imaginary birds that have inspired these battles for ages—imagistic battles but plausible enough to cool hot human dissatisfactions. These one hundred men now feel no dissatisfactions; in their forever cool eyes, neither the battle nor the men facing them will be merely plausible images, rituals on a ritualistic battlefield designed to resurrect, for God knows which time, their dream birds.

*Everything will be **real** for them. They will see before them real **enemies**.*

Enemies? For example, Lieutenant Forger at the head; Nick could imagine that conversation as well:

"It's almost midnight, Edgeway. Where do you think you're going?"

"I'm going to see my lawyer, Lieutenant. I've decided to file a formal complaint against you, and tomorrow morning I plan to submit it to the DA. That's why I'm carrying all my IDs with me."

"But why on a bike? Did you leave your car in the garage so we'd think you were still at home?"

"Nonsense! There's almost no gas in the tank. Check for yourself."

Nick finally negotiated the steep hill and rode with no effort along the straight flat road. Things were going better than he had hoped for. No one was following him, and despite its years of disuse, the bike had performed beautifully on the toughest part of the trip. He had managed the hill better than expected. Most importantly, only two cars had passed him so far, and he had hidden from both of them behind roadside trees.

He was lucky that both Max and Reno lived in the same upscale neighborhood. May they both be cursed forever—pompous upstarts! If he were confronted on the way there, he would claim to the last that he had been going to see his lawyer. On the way back, however, the situation would be far more complicated:

"Where are you coming from, Edgeway, at this time of night?"

"From—my brother-in-law's."

"And why were you there?"

"He called me. He said he had the feeling someone was stalking him, that he was frightened and wanted me to come over. Of course, I rushed out to the garage, but when I found that my car was almost out of gas, what else could I do but ride my bike?"

"Ah, I see. And what happened when you got there?"

"Nothing. Nobody was home. At first I was worried, but then I decided he probably went to their place in the country. My sister's there with their daughter. So I started back home."

Nick reached the suburbs of town and maneuvered the bike skillfully around the potholes on the dark streets. Now he was absolutely calm and ceased his imaginary conversations with Forger. Instead, he went over basic precautions for getting away with a perfect crime: no incriminating fingerprints or footprints, no strands of hair, no shirt buttons or other clues always found in all those movies, and not a single drop of blood on any article of clothing either.

Damn! He swerved to miss a pothole, lost his balance, and ran into the curb, coming within a whisker of taking a tumble. Only his catlike reactions had saved him. Everybody thought of him as slow and clumsy—had he even just sprained an ankle, his whole plan would have gone up in smoke! But nothing like that had happened. He pedaled off again, thinking, *So as soon as Max opens the door, I show him the envelope that supposedly contains the photos: "Yes, the pictures are all inside, dear brother-in-law, but before you look at them, I'd like to have a word with you." I take off my shoes, pretending that they hurt my feet, put on a pair of his house slippers. I go into the bathroom and take a few sleeping pills from the medicine cabinet. "Pour us a glass of cognac, Max, will you?" I say invitingly and then drop the tablets into his glass. I wait for him to fall asleep—wait for him...*

Here his thoughts grew confused and tangled, at the edge of some chasm, while the bike continued to travel on. He had passed through the poorer quarters and was already crossing through immaculately groomed Three Stags Park, though the stags were long dead.

All the people seemed to have died too; at least, he didn't meet anybody along the way. The actions of a serial killer were not so strange, given the complete absence of accidental witnesses.

Stupid, snobbish town! Nick thought angrily, returning to his plans. *I wait for Max to fall asleep, drag him into the bedroom, and tie him to the bed. Then I put on the longest of his raincoats, find some gloves, get a knife from the kitchen, and then—well, everybody knows what happens then! The End.*

The brutal conclusion he avoided imagining, however. At the moment, only the end of the road was clear. Nick slipped off his bike and hid it inside a shack filled with garbage cans on the far side of the street. Then he walked to the front gate. That it was unlocked didn't mean much; Elsa and Max weren't in the habit of locking it except when they went on one of their snobbish vacations.

He pushed open half the double gate with his elbow and then closed it behind him the same way. Taking the biggest steps he could, he strode to the front door. He took out his handkerchief with some reluctance, worrying about what he had to endure, and then pressed the doorbell through it. The result was a powerful warble, reminding him of a giant canary, echoing through the large, elegant home. He rang repeatedly without pausing until the warble was loud enough to wake the dead, and even they would yell, *Stop!* But from Max came absolutely no response: probably he was afraid to open.

"Hey, Max! It's me!" Nick shouted.

Yes, let him hear and see for himself that his visitor wasn't the sadistic killer but merely his beloved perfect wife's nonthreatening, nonnoticeable, nonsociable, nonentity of a brother. Hadn't Max said as much once, only half-jokingly, "Your only flaw, my darling, is your—luckily only—brother."

"Max, I've brought you the pictures! Open up!"

But this didn't help either. What if he really was at their place in the country?

His wrinkled forehead lit by the moon, Nick slowly walk around the house, still not ready to admit that, along with his anger and disappointment, he felt relief. Well, what else could he do? *This crazy man is lucky. He will live—or wait.* A chandelier on the second floor was lit! That probably meant that Max was up there but had no intention of opening the door. Interesting, however, that his "perfect" wife had chased him into that west—sunset—wing: Is his bedroom there now? And how *long* has it been? Nick grinned and shouted again, "Hey, Max, it's me! Come out—it's all right!"

Come out, and we may understand each other, he added to himself. Nothing happened—not a sound or movement behind those sheer curtains. Outraged at this latest demonstration of disdain, Nick rushed back to the front and angrily pressed the doorbell again, pressing it until his ears started ringing and he began to resent all birds, real, mechanical, or imaginary.

"Quit playing games with me or—" Nick grabbed the knob, shook it, and unexpectedly the massive door swung open. He tumbled inside, carried by his momentum, and then instinctively jumped back. Was Max waylaying him? Planning to kill him and then plead self-defense? What a convenient occasion. He might be poised in the darkness behind the door, biding his time with an axe raised above his head!

Nick visualized the bloody scene—his cleft skull, face swimming in pulpy gray matter. He held his breath or, more precisely, lost it and, step by step, backed over the threshold and onto the porch, ready to turn around and...

"*What a great escape.*" Max seemed to snigger in his ear. "*Like a rabbit.*"

Nick froze, opened his mouth to protest, but managed to produce only a gurgling hiss.

"*An overfed, fat-assed, scared rabbit. Ha-ha!*"

No, he wouldn't give Max such satisfaction again. He catapulted back toward the door and hit it hard, so that anybody hiding behind it would be smashed against the wall. But no one was there, so the gory scene he had imagined gradually faded, like some garish chalk sketch scrawled by a child driven crazy by horror movies. What paranoid nonsense! Max was simply absentminded. He had probably left in a hurry and simply forgot to lock the door behind him, or turn off his bedroom lights.

Calmed by this uncertain conjecture, Nick felt his way to the switch and turned on the lights. The frightful mouth of a cave was instantly transformed into the familiar spacious hallway. He crossed it, his footsteps muffled by the plush autumn-yellow carpet. The huge surrealistic canvas on the far wall now seemed to him not just hanging but *hanged*, squinting back at him with its many freakish images—multieyed, goggle-eyed, one-eyed, with no eyes at all—perhaps imbued with some deformed *sight* by the artist. And pressing its monstrous black face against the window for a closer look, the night blindly peeped in.

At the foot of the stairs, Nick leaned against the banister, panting like a swimmer caught too long underwater. He concentrated on the smell of his own cologne prickling his nose, only slowly realizing what exactly puzzled him about it. He had been using that cologne for almost a year, since Reno stopped using it and had given him a supply, but during the last frantic days, he hadn't even bothered to open the bottle.

Turning on the staircase lights, he started up with narrowed eyes and lips pressed tightly together, sniffing like a bloodhound following a scent. Yes, someone had recently climbed these stairs, leaving as a calling card the unmistakable aroma of his rare Italian cologne. But what "someone"? Was this person known or unknown? Had he been going up or down the stairs?

Following the scent on the second floor, Nick's nose led him toward the west wing, bringing him up short, admittedly with a twinge of panic. He stared at the narrow strip of light under the door at the end of the dimly lit hallway. Who was in that room, or who had *been*? Where was Max? And why was this damned house so obtrusively, tangibly lifeless?

Get away from here! his instincts screamed. *Run! Run!*

No, see if someone's there, his curiosity argued, or his humanity maybe.

He stood frozen, his skin covered with goose bumps and his hair practically standing on end. *Run! This house is not completely lifeless. Death has broken in and* hasn't left yet.

"Max!" he shouted suddenly, heedlessly. Recklessly.

Why does it always seem that a man can't rely on himself exactly when he most needs to? Why can't he simply leave this place that he knew he should leave? Why was he drawn to exactly *that room*, from which it would be the most difficult to exit? Or impossible—

Quiet! What was that? A sound.

"Max, is that you? Hey, Max!"

Alas, another sound from "that room" crushed the hope that he had misheard, scattered it, left his heart aching. Other, *inhuman* sounds followed: wheezing and a strange gurgling.

What, what was happening there?

As if in answer, something resembling a growl, wheeze, and groan all in one propelled him down the hallway. With only his bare hands—against whom? Or against *what*? He stopped short at the door of the cursed room, the overpowering odor of his cologne again filling his lungs.

He heard the sounds from here, but it was impossible to say whether their source was human or animal. Max! It's him. Was death really in the house, with him at this very moment—the sadist slowly cutting Max's throat?

Aaah! Come on, Nick, do something! Even a second's delay could be too much.

But his hand shook and wouldn't obey, refused to turn the doorknob—and not only out of fear. He vaguely recalled a handkerchief—whose was it? What was it for? Then there were glasses full of cognac—sleeping pills, gloves, and house slippers. His head felt like an inflating balloon, ready to pop, incapable of containing the chaos inside. In that chaos, like a rat searching in panic for an escape fissure, his mind raced in its futile effort to understand what was happening.

Slowly, he turned the knob. *Oh Lord, at least let this door be locked.*

But it wasn't locked. When he opened it and gaped into the emptiness, for an endless moment, he seemed to see a river of blood flowing across the carpet: thick, yeasty blood that he could feel pouring over him, choking him with its rank alien taste.

Nick reeled back drunkenly. *Stop it, stop it now!* he ordered himself. *Back off, greedy imagination! The scene is plausible enough without your help.*

Plausible? It was *real*.

"It's real," he murmured, smacking his lips as if tasting some unknown exotic dish. "Real."

The word seeped into the corners of his mind, strangely numbing him. His panic and trembling disappeared, leaving him suddenly weary. He yawned widely and stepped back again. *Re-al, re-al*, some clock deep inside, perhaps in his ancestral memory, ticked in a lulling rhythm. *Re-re-re-al.*

Then stopped. Why? Hey, what about those other sounds? Why had *they* stopped too? And the "clock" inside exploded like a time bomb.

"Let go of him!" Nick hollered. "Don't touch him anymore!"

He ran headlong into the room, balling his heavy fists. Now anger had completely replaced his lethargy, sharpening his reactions as if they were knives. *Murderer! Let's see how you deal with me!*

"Here I come, Max! Hold on!"

Wheezing.

More wheezing from the bed, which, to make matters worse, was hidden in a corner right of the door behind a crenellated tulle curtain. *To hell with your damned snobbish interior decorating!* No silhouette shadowed the curtain, but maybe the murderer was hiding someplace else in the room; with so much furniture cluttering it up, that would be no problem. Nick took a quick look around, but the sounds from the bed were so heartrending that he forgot any precaution and flung himself at the curtain. He jerked it so forcefully that the rod fell out of its stays and hit him on the shoulder, while the curtain covered him like a shroud.

Now would be the perfect time for the murderer to strike. Nick squirmed beneath the curtain. *He'll stab me dead.*

The wheezing stopped. The now endless silence was even worse.

"Max?"

He finally managed to pull the curtain off and looked down at the huge mahogany bed just a step away, where Max...

CHAPTER 29

Max was tied with a long, thin nylon cord. It had cut deeply into his bare arms and legs and cinched his loins beneath his exposed, shaking belly. The cord crisscrossed his flat chest, his skeletal ribs jutting out and dotted with the bold, bright pattern of his silk summer pajamas—very bright, *joyfully* bright, cheerful.

Nick concentrated his *full* attention on the shirt, which was wet with *sweat*, he decided, and stuck tightly to Max's body, like a second skin, or Max's own skin tattooed by an overly ambitious— was it tattoo artist? There were circles, rhomboids, triangles, and strangely enough, totally out-of-place, small sailboats. Dominating the many and varied colors was red. Of course, red would be the dominant color *now*.

Nick couldn't take his eyes off the shirt. What he had momentarily seen when he first pushed back the curtain, he wouldn't—he refused to—see again. That's why he locked his eyes far below the pajama top's collar.

As Max moved feebly, the tiny sailboats floated on the wrinkled, colorful red sea filled with geometrical figures. Had Max bought those pajamas himself, nostalgic for his lost childhood, or were they a gift? There could hardly be a keener irony: lanky, scraggly Max in his little boy's pajamas covered with diamonds and sailboats! How grotesque! *Let him survive, and I'll give him such pajamas forever.*

If he survived.

"Try not to move, Max. You'll just make it worse. You're going to"—*Look at you!*—"be fine. I'll help you, my friend!"

"Ni...i...ck." He choked, spitting blood.

Nick fiercely closed his eyes. *I just need a second, Max!* Such dainty little boats—childhood—and above them a deep gash in the long, thin neck.

A chicken's neck. *I would never even cut the neck of a chicken!* Truth overwhelmed him with its frightening force, a truth he had to face before this wheezing, half-dead wretch. The realization crushed him like a pitiful, insignificant bug. *You weren't going to kill him under any circumstances, no matter how much he humiliated or insulted you. Deep inside you* knew *you couldn't, and all the resolve, preparation, plans—they were all* a game.

A game is a way to cope with reality, but what if a man couldn't stop playing games, even at the age of forty-two? "You're incapable of doing anything, Nick, neither good nor bad," Max had told him once, the same Max now dying before him with a neck gaping grotesquely like the grinning mouth of a monstrous clown.

"*Neither good nor bad,*" Nick repeated to himself, stunned and hurt. *I just stand aside and look at life. No, not even that! I don't dare even look.*

He somehow managed to meet Max's bloodshot eyes. Everything about him was bloody: his ascetic high-browed face streaked with rivulets of clotted blood, his head "resting" in a puddle of blood slowly soaking into the sheet, turning it almost black. Nothing bright—here all is *real*, not simply plausible: no "geysers of thick foamy blood" erupting through the gaping wound, only a mere trickle dripping almost apologetically. His neck was the most bloodless site of the entire scene, with its taut bared sinews and pulsing bared veins, also almost black, and precisely above the wound, the jagged Adam's apple rising and falling with the broken rhythm of Max's labored breathing—just like a little boat. Sail, sail on, in this sea of clotted, tattered tissue!

Nick covered his mouth with both hands, feeling violently sick, and turned sideways, barely able to suppress his stomach convulsions. Tears came to his eyes; he doubled up as his guts tightened into a fiery throbbing ball. Eventually he tried to collect himself. *It's bad enough to want some perverse insight from these death throes; I can't also make his last view of earth that of me obnoxiously belching up my substantial dinner, alive and obscenely healthy!*

Turning to Max again, he asked, trying to sound terribly concerned but managing only to sound terribly hypocritical, "Who did this to you, my friend? Who!"

"Hel...p...p me...e...e!" The Adam's apple bobbed up and down in a frenzied rhythm, and the lips—they were tattered too! He must have bit them from the unbearable pain and his strenuous efforts to tear through the cord while his murderer *carefully* cut his throat.

"OK, there now! Stay calm—try to keep still. I'll call Emergency right away." *Yes, I will, "dear friend," though if you kick off before they arrive, all the suspicion will again fall on me. "The killer in a moment of remorse makes a futile attempt to save his victim" is how Forger would interpret this.*

"Who did it, Max? Just tell me that, and I'll do anything to help you. Did you know the person?"

Max strained to half-close his livid eyelids, implying that he did know. Then his eyes opened wide, staring up at Nick without blinking, glazed with consternation—the look of a man suddenly realizing he has made a fatal mistake.

"N...no," he tried to correct himself, and his efforts proved *really* fatal. While Nick's mind found no explanation and even his intuition failed him, something seized him bodily, burned into him like a disease, collecting its devastating strength.

"Say the name, Max!" he insisted in a hoarse voice. "I have to know!"

"He...e...l...l...p!" Max was able to say very clearly—as he could have clearly said the name.

He could have, but he wouldn't. Why?

Why? Nick asked himself, yet dreaded, knowing even before his mind recognized the only possible answer laid out before him—poisonously bright and indisputable—in some inner infinity. Multiplied a thousand times, this answer filled that infinity, an *indestructible fact* that—like all real *facts*—left in its wake a widening web of consequences, thinning out in time but never disappearing. Ineradicable.

The first in that string of consequences was the fact that Nick was *not* going to call Emergency.

"Oh no." Nick breathed, shaken not so much by the answer/ *fact* as by the next truth about himself, which revealed that he was now about to commit his most revolting, inhuman act.

But how, dear God? How can I? Leaving him like that is even more hideous than the murder itself!

"No!" he screamed but couldn't smother the insistent *Yes, yes, yes.*

Seized with the pangs of a terrible remorse that would follow him to his last breath, Nick fell to his knees before this helpless creature whose sickly, solitary life was ebbing away through the cut throat, drop by drop.

"*I* haven't known what might disturb your sleep at night for a long time," Elsa had said. *Who else is to blame, if not you, Max, who conceived that lifeless child?*

The blood continued to soak into the already sodden sheet. "But you do have a nasty secret!" Nick clasped his head, heavy with unwanted, unavoidable insight. *Whatever nasty secret you have, Max, will be nothing compared to mine, because right now I'm going to leave you, to your death—maybe to long hours of cruel, ugly agony. I have to leave you, and you know it.*

"That's how things stand, Max. Why did you make that fatal mistake?"

Nick rose and rounded the tulle curtain heaped on the floor, his eyes riveted to that gaunt, bony body so meticulously trussed in nylon cord. An unbidden thought haunted him, terrible in its infinitely inappropriate sarcasm, *How little meat on his bones. How fast he will become a skeleton.*

CHAPTER 30

Normally Nick would have cowered in fear on the way back, terrified of being seen. Instead, he felt numb, an automaton riding his bike utterly instinctively: at a normal speed through the park, successfully circumnavigating obstacles in the slums, pedaling somewhat harder when he found himself on the road, and turning off when he recognized the path through the trees. Finally he stopped at the wicket fence that led to his backyard. He squeezed through again without disturbing the creepers and pulled his bike in after him, hiding it in the tall weeds by the fence. He entered his house the same way that he had left—through the bathroom window.

He was pleased that, with almost 100 percent certainty, no one had seen him either in town or on the road. God takes care of drunks and idiots, as the old saying goes. "Well, I don't know if I'm an idiot or just not quite all there," he murmured, closing the window softly behind him, "but I'll damned sure be drunker than Bacchus very soon! I'd bet my soul on that—if I still have one, of course."

He left the dark bathroom and entered the living room, groped his way to the liquor cabinet, randomly grabbed a bottle, and climbed the stairs, still in the dark. Seeing a light under his bedroom door, he recalled that he had deliberately left the bedside lamp on. The situation required these precautions, in case some half-asleep cop was keeping an eye on the house. Taking that into account, he crept into the room, pushed the door closed with his foot, and moving at the same snail's pace, crawled to his bed.

Changing to his pajamas while still on the floor, he realized that he had no glass. He chuckled: one didn't always have time for niceties. Nor could one go forever on autopilot. Soon terrible thoughts would assail him, then dreadful sensations, because his soul was probably in its ordinary place, though by a higher logic, the devil should long ago have claimed it.

"Ah, the soul, the soul," he whispered. "To hell with that pretentious woman! Concentrate on your drinking, my friend!"

Climbing quickly into bed, he uncorked the bottle: White Horse whiskey. *Well, Max, you were right—in the end. I really do need a strong drink. Well done, Max. You were a prophet. Or maybe you still are?*

"Are you still alive, Max?"

Nick raised the bottle and took a quick snort, the gurgle in his throat reminding him of—oh God! Next time he gulped slowly, doing his best to eliminate the sound, stopping only when he could feel his gorge start to rise, as it had back there. *Back* there! *Is this the way I'm going to spend the night? Take it easy, man!* He looked at the clock with some disbelief: barely one thirty. He had left at twenty to twelve, so everything had happened in less than two hours! Was that possible? It seemed to have taken forever.

After his surprise passed, which started as something spontaneous and quickly degenerated into just another diversion, Nick took a few more burning gulps of the whiskey. He waved his hand before his face as if saying good-bye, not just to fan himself, and fell into another amazement. *I called him friend, then abandoned him!*

Oh, you should never have made that mistake, Max!

214

His jaded gaze checked the clock again. *He's still alive! Or at least that was the idea—to prolong his dying. And I'm here. Here! I've got to do something!*

Leaving the bottle close at hand under the bed, he reached for the telephone on his nightstand and dialed Reno's number. As his lawyer, Reno couldn't be his witness, but very likely Reno was not alone. Some Didi, Mickey, or Kiki would raise her tousled head from the pillow and murmur seductively, "Who could be calling you at this late hour, darling?"

But Reno wasn't home—or didn't want to answer the phone. Instead, Nick heard the answering machine—a sugary sweet melodious woman's voice, "This is the house of Renaldo Aldano, attorney at law. If you care to leave a message, please do so after the beep. You have one minute."

Nick's initial anger dissolved when he realized the advantage that lay in that pretentious gadget, which would precisely record everything he said! When he heard the beep, he began reciting his message as if he were declaiming a poem, "Hello, Reno. I hoped to find you home, at least now, at this *late* hour, but I wasn't that lucky. I'm terribly upset by this series of atrocious crimes and scared too. I live so far from the town, have no neighbors or relatives nearby— even keep my bedside lamp on all night—can you imagine that? I fell asleep a little before midnight but was just awakened by a terrible nightmare, which is why I called you. But you're not there! Incidentally, Max called me last night. He sounded very strange. I'll tell you exactly what he said when we meet. One more thing, he wants me to come over in the morning to discuss some things. I'll go, Reno, and find out what he wants. Well, it doesn't matter what time you get home, if you get home at all. As soon as you hear this message, please—"

A short, shrill signal broke the connection.

Excellent! Nick relaxed, still holding the receiver to his ear. On second thought, he wasn't nearly as pleased with his performance, but so what? They wouldn't put him in jail for babbling into the "ear" of some automated bimbo.

But she had sighed!

He distinctly heard the machine shut off, so where had that sigh come from? Didn't that slight but characteristic crackle answer his question?

Nick put the phone in its cradle and picked it up again. No dial tone. Hanging up a second time, he paused—until he heard the barely audible click and, when he picked it up again, a dial tone. *Welcome, so that now I can catch you at last!* He then dialed the number of his favorite bookstore. None would be there at night, but the *eavesdropper* wouldn't know that. The crackle came again. *Let her wait.*

Placing the receiver carefully on his bed, he tiptoed out of the bedroom and silently crept down the stairs. *No getting drunk tonight, after all* flashed through his mind, followed by an even more bitter thought—*I'm getting used to creeping in the dark like a bat!*

He reached the foyer and almost stopped breathing, feeling only seconds away from revelation. *Oh, Kaya, my darling, if only you knew how much I want you to be here. Right now!* He looked hard in the direction of the other telephone and hit the light switch.

And heard a crash!

Though almost blinded, he could see that no one was in the foyer. Stepping forward, he saw what had caused the crash. The telephone receiver lay on the tiled floor, its spiral cord still trembling. Nick bent over and picked it up. The earpiece was slightly cracked, and he could hear the insistent buzz on the line. He held it against his temple. The earpiece was still warm from being pressed against somebody's ear—Kaya's ear?

The ancient black telephone, a veritable bullfrog, squatted at the edge of the cabinet, its ten eyeholes staring. Terrified, Nick banged its receiver down.

"Kaya!" His own scream startled him. "I know it's you, and I know you're very close to me!" He wandered in the foyer, waving his hands as if playing blind man's bluff. "You're here, I know you are! But why can't I see you? Show yourself. Oh, come to me, please!"

Could it be possible that he was cursed, unable to see what he most yearned for?

"Oh, God, why must you punish me so?"

"And why not?" A voice thundered in his head—the voice of God himself? *"Why not, I ask you?"*

"Because I don't deserve such punishment," Nick whined pitiably. "I haven't done anybody any harm—after all."

"You will answer for the harm you've done. I seek the good in you, and I find none."

"But you would find good in me, if you didn't always refuse me the good I'm entitled to. Give it back to me! It's mine, mine!" Nick found himself unexpectedly gasping for breath in a fit of violent outrage. "You thieving old man! Old man—passionless! You have no right to punish someone whose motives you don't understand! If I were you, do you know how much good I would do? But I'm *here*, locked inside myself. How can I come out? How can I break free?"

"How? There is only one way."

"Aha! Through *death*? At least give me death, then! Give me *my death*! Kaya?"

Nick burst into tears. He wiped them away with the sleeve of his pajamas, shaking as if he had collided with a fearsome element of nature. He shambled up the stairs, sensing he was already in far too deep, almost to the core of something—preternatural, incomprehensible, and perhaps ruinous for any attempt to comprehend it. *OK, but it's in my home, so I have no chance to save myself from its secret. None,* he concluded, finally managing to replace the horror with tragic satisfaction.

Whoever has no chance has no problems to solve, right? Such a man just sinks into the whirlpool and lets it suck him under, except that no *living* creature can do that complacently. It will flail and kick, panic stricken. It will splash and rip at the surface, swallow water and gasp, instinctively fighting for the last breath of air. Unlike the spirit, the body never loses hope. It's in the blood, in each muscle, cell, and gene, a struggle to stay alive that lasts longer than life itself. Watch a decapitated chicken flaps its wings, a cat keep scratching even after its heart has been ripped out. In quiet coffins underground, people's hair and nails keep growing for at least a week after death.

Are you still alive, my friend Max?

I hope not! I hope that your pains are over. Nick had started moaning, almost eager to sink into that nightmare again and forget *his own* for a while. Such as the detectives that hypothetically had his house under surveillance. It would be good if a cop really were there. In the morning Forger would get a report confirming that the *suspect* had left his bedroom at about two o'clock, which would mean that he had been inside before then. That, strangely, he had lit the lamps backward—first in the foyer and then the staircase light. That then he had returned to his bedroom.

So he did return to his bedroom and slumped onto the bed, right on top of the telephone receiver. He jumped up as if he had been scalded with a hot iron, grabbed it, and almost threw it on the floor before collecting himself. He put it back where it belonged, set the clock for eight, and took another swig from the bottle, shifting his thoughts to the house where—where he must be again in a few hours. He choked. Strong drink indeed for an unused throat. Throat!

More tears formed in his eyes, this time brought on by drinking. Nick waited for the next wave of remorse to wash over him. But no! The White Horse was already carrying him away. Encouraged by this success, he took another gulp, giving the horse its head. And another—and another—until it was carrying him at a fiery gallop. The bad scenes along the way became more abstract, less able to divert his thoughts far from *here*, where at the moment prowled—a ghost? A vampire?

"Stop it!"

Didn't calls get mixed up all the time? Some unhappy woman who couldn't sleep might have been dialing random numbers, looking for *anyone* to talk to, and there you have your eavesdropper.

But what about the receiver? Could she have dropped it on the floor? "Nonsense!"

Nick opened his mouth, hoping to come up with a stronger argument, but decided he didn't like the sound of his drunken voice. *Nonsense! Everything can be rationalized, explained away, and I'm good at finding explanations. But not now. Later. Now I have other work. Come on, you noble steed! I'll ride you to the happy hunting grounds!*

"Ha-ha-ha!"

"Ha-ha" all right. It's all over with your mocking laughter, Max!

Two-thirds of the bottle was already gone. Nick nodded approvingly and lifted it again. "Firewater"—what a good name the Indians gave it! They invented the name, then threw down their tomahawks. Sitting Bull, eh? Felled Bison, Drunken Buffalo. Hmmm...

"Kaya...a dar...li...i...ing, come to me...e...e, pul...lease; don't be a...fray...e...e...ed of me...e...e!"

CHAPTER 31

When he woke up, his eyelids were so swollen that he had to force them open with his fingers. The clock read 9:17 a.m., so he concluded—with great difficulty—that he had slept through the 8:00 a.m. alarm. No big surprise—the pounding in his head could have passed for a mining operation. He tried to groan but could only produce a barely audible growl. His tongue was so thick that it filled his whole mouth, almost like a big cork stuffed in by some malevolent person. The worst thing was that he had to get up and had work to do—he couldn't remember what exactly but knew it was urgent. And important. He rolled over, and the empty whiskey bottle jabbed him in the armpit. Ah—the bottle!

Now to get to the bathroom, where he could rest and gather strength before adjourning to the kitchen. After two or three cups of black coffee laced with aspirin, he should be able to achieve at least partial communication between his addled thoughts and his bodily functions. The bathroom, however, was still so far away. He felt like tumbling out onto the floor and covering the distance on his belly—that would minimize the risk of falling in this cockeyed, hammock-shaped room. Wasn't that the way he entered the room first, for some unknown reason? Aha, another memory. "First" because there had been a second maybe? Or was that a dream? What a long dream! *Oh! Kaya, you are driving me crazy.*

He somehow managed to get out of bed. His joints popped as he hobbled toward the bathroom, shedding his pajamas in the ever-overflowing hamper along the way. As he splashed cold water on his face, he realized that he was thirsty—parched! Keeping his uncomfortable position, he gulped noisily, choking and spitting until his thirst was quenched. "God-awful business," he murmured, though he had nothing particular in mind. Or everything!

Next he showered, constantly adjusting the water temperature—hot, cold, hot, cold—just like his life, always running hot and cold, except this was clear water, not that muck!

Slowly he struggled back to his senses, cutting himself only a few times while shaving. He applied a styptic pencil to the nicks, and the blood stopped.

But the blood was still running, dripping, dripping, there*!*

The curtain that the alcohol had drawn across his mind was pulled back abruptly, revealing a lurid melodrama in full swing. One of the performers—Max!—was dying, the victim of a calculated operation by an imaginative executioner. The other figure onstage was himself—passive, just looking on, a captive, horror-stricken audience, but a *participant.*

"Well, now I can afford not to see anymore," he croaked feebly.

He put on his bathrobe and, as he was leaving, remembered the cologne. He looked at the shelf under the mirror where he always kept it, but the bottle was indeed gone! He had several more, fortunately, since they were of paramount importance for his intentions.

About twenty minutes later, dressed in old work overalls, he was drinking his second cup of coffee in the kitchen. The aspirin was already taking effect, and he felt almost normal, though the word "normal" under present abnormal circumstances struck him as absurd. Absurd!

He rose from the chair slowly, even stealthily, went to the foyer, and picked up the telephone receiver. The small crack at its upper end leered at him, totally real.

"No, I don't believe in ghosts!" he articulated in a decisive tone. It's enough that I have nightmares that I'm *forced* to believe." Leaning against the wall, he wrinkled his eyebrows in an expression of full concentration.

This is what must have happened: the call was misdirected while he was dictating his message to Reno, and the answering machine disconnected him. Then, in the ensuing silence, he distinctly heard a distant sigh. Because of his frayed nerves, he imagined that someone was eavesdropping on the other phone. He rushed downstairs, unable to think of anything but the receiver here. He fixed all his attention on it, then reached for the light switch, and, during that moment of hyperconcentration, *telekinesis*.

Why not? Many cases have been documented of moving objects from a distance! He'd even read somewhere that everybody has the innate ability, but it generally remains latent. Perhaps under the great strain, his latent power suddenly became active—involuntarily and accidentally. So what happened? He turned on the lights, which momentarily dazzled him, removing sight from the whole sense/psychological knot. Then the receiver, already suspended in the air, crashed to the floor. When he picked it up and it felt warm against his temple, that was simply the heat generated by the telekinetic force.

And that was all.

Fascinated by his rare gift, Nick stood in the foyer, enjoying both his relief—no ghost—and a strong interest in this new topic. Finally, he casually hung up the phone and returned to the kitchen.

He knew he had no time to waste but still found time to fix Biff some breakfast, feeling vaguely guilty about the dog and wanting to assuage his overburdened conscience. He brought him water, unchained and attempted to pet him, but the dog drew away, his tail between his legs. Probably because he still reeked of alcohol, Nick guessed. He resigned himself to smelling like a brewery all day.

Turning his back on the squeamish animal, he went to the garage door, still open from the night before but much wider than if it had only been forgotten. That was how a man failed in his good ideas, by overdoing them! Determined to avoid such slipups in the future, Nick opened the small garage window before exiting and walking around the house to reclaim the bike from the weeds. He put it back in the garage through the window, which he again managed without scraping the wall or windowsill.

Returning to the garage, he closed the window and then rummaged around in the clutter for older tires and inner tubes than those on the bike. He changed the tires, cursing the ones he took off for being too reliable, *Let them go to hell!* A flat on the way to Max's, and his conscience wouldn't be tormenting him now, nor would he be suffering a hangover. But no, the old bike had been fully up to the task!

He put the tires that he took off the bike into the trunk of the Ford and then stopped to admire his handiwork. The bike had obviously been greased recently, but what of that? *"I haven't been riding it, Forger, just look at the tires. They're good for nothing. But I try to keep the bike in good shape, for its sentimental value. I rode it when I was a kid."*

"My mother gave it to me," he said out loud, his voice filled with self-pity.

Poor woman! When she gave it to him so many years ago, not in her wildest dreams would she have imagined that, years later, her darling son would place his 220-pound body on it with murderous intentions—and then return, after most inhumanely abandoning his half-slaughtered brother-in-law bound and slowly bleeding to death.

It amazed him that the creaky antique of a bike really had carried him to town and back! Maybe his mother's spirit had helped support it, neither knowing nor caring where her "dear Nicky" was going? *"It doesn't matter where he's going. He's my son! Let him ride safely."*

You shouldn't have loved me so blindly, mother! There are those who see through me now, and they certainly don't love me. Even worse, I have begun to see myself.

As he headed back to the house, feet leaden with remorse and shoulders guiltily hunched, he heard the telephone ring. He felt as though a needle had pierced his heart. *I'm too late; they've found him!* In his head something began to swing, heavy and stinging like molten lead—his brain still sunk in whiskey. He burst into the foyer and grabbed the receiver.

"Nick! Hello, Nick!" It was Elsa.

"Yes?" Now his stomach clenched violently, causing him to double up with pain. "What do you want?"

"Are you alone?" As usual, she disregarded the anguish in his voice.

"Who could I be possibly with, goddamn it?"

"With—Max, for instance."

"With *Max*?"

"Yes, with Max! He's not with you then?"

"No, he's not with me." Nick sat on the floor, clasping his knees with his arms as panic flooded him. Then he felt it change into—something new to him—a *free* sense of hatred toward his sister.

"Did he come looking for us at your place?" she asked.

"No, Elsa, he didn't come looking for you." He did his best to sound sardonic. "Strange man, isn't he? Supposedly he suspects me of being a sadistic killer, yet it doesn't trouble him in the least to leave his wife and child in my clutches. Or maybe you told him you'd be at the summer place, after all?"

"Yes, I did tell him that."

"Then why ask me if he came looking for you here?"

"Because we're not at the summer place, Nick. We spent the night with his aunt because—I was so worried about Annie!"

"Really? Is there something wrong?"

"Oh, I don't know! She fell asleep last night while I was making dinner, and when I tried to wake her, she just wouldn't wake up. No matter what I did, she wouldn't budge, as if she wasn't asleep but having some kind of seizure—"

"So, instead of taking her to a doctor, you chose the tender mercies of his aunt?"

"She was a nurse once, Nick, and you know her place is close to ours."

"But town was only another fifteen minutes' drive. Anyway, was your aunt able to help?"

"Yes, she was," Elsa snapped, "which is exactly why we spent the night at her place. But I've been calling Max since eight this morning, and he doesn't answer!"

"Maybe he's gone out," Nick said, thinking with terrible cynicism, *but that's highly unlikely.*

"Gone out—so early? Without his mobile phone? It's much more likely that he's sick, Nick. You know how sickly he is anyway."

"You should've stayed at home and spared yourself all the anguish."

"We argued because of you—"

"I know; I know! He suspected me, and you argued with him, but you also had your doubts. I've heard this little tale before, or at least read it. The note you left yesterday should be diligently studied by every would-be Pharisee—a real masterpiece of hypocrisy."

"Oh, I don't even remember what I wrote in it." She sobbed. "I was so confused!"

"Were you?"

"Nick, don't be so rude with me, please. I'm terribly worried!"

"OK, OK. What do you want me to do?"

"Well, go over there and see—see if Max—just see if he's doing all right."

Just!

"Why don't you check yourself? This could be the perfect excuse for you two to kiss and make up."

"That's exactly what I don't want—for him to think that I was looking for such an excuse. Can you answer me yes or no? Will you go over there or not?"

Nick looked at his watch: already five after eleven. He had lost track of time, but maybe that was good. "I'll go," he said with mock reluctance.

"When?"

"Right away."

"Great!" she exclaimed. "Give me a call when you get there, OK? Meanwhile I'll keep calling him, and if I get through to him—"

"Bye, Elsa," he cut the conversation short as curtly as he could.

Bye. He wanted never, never to hear her voice again.

CHAPTER 32

Dressed in the same clothes he had worn the night before and reeking of cologne, Nick coaxed the Ford out of the garage and drove off, wishing himself good luck and strong nerves. He made it to the first turn on the road with the drop or two of gasoline he still had in the tank. Then he swerved onto the shoulder, pulled over, and waited until the bus and jeep behind him passed before he ran to the bushes at the end of the path and claimed the can he had hidden there. Returning to the car, he made sure no one was watching and quickly poured the gasoline into the tank. He stashed the empty can in the trunk and drove off.

As he passed through the slums on the outskirts of town, he disposed of the bicycle tires in two separate trash containers and left the gas can by a lamppost before circling the park and pulling up in front of Max's place, which now reminded him of a huge, three-story sarcophagus. Leaving the car, he looked around quickly to check that the street was deserted, though he knew perfectly well that someone might be watching from a hidden vantage point. He entered the yard as he had the previous night, walked down the same path to the front door, and then, exaggerating the gesture, pressed the doorbell. That ghastly canary warble pulled him back to the same scene twelve hours ago: his finger glued to the doorbell, his vain hope that Max would answer the door.

He stepped back, pretending that he again expected Max, that he didn't know it was open. Just now, when he most needed a witness, luckily two elderly ladies, dressed as if they were going to the opera, toddled by. He called out loudly, "Max, hey, Max!" and pounded energetically on the door, immediately attracting their attention. They even stopped and peered at him through the fence. They were primped, yes, but particularly well mannered, as Nick was relieved to see.

He continued pressing the bell, pounding hard on the door and calling Max's name as if he hadn't noticed them. Then he turned around so they could clearly see his face, and they reluctantly walked away, their head still craned in his direction. Nick assumed that the two resplendent old cuckoos lived nearby and could easily be tracked down. They would tell Forger, "*Yes, that is the same gentleman who was ringing the doorbell, calling out for somebody named Max and looking terribly concerned.*"

The sun hadn't reached the west side of the house yet, so the lit chandelier in Max's bedroom was still noticeable, also in Nick's favor. "*I was a little worried, Lieutenant, when my sister asked me to go over to check on him, but when I saw the chandelier still on at nearly noon, a fearful apprehension struck me! That's why I didn't just leave when nobody answered. I even considered breaking down the door, but fortunately it wasn't locked.*" Still playing the worried brother-in-law, Nick went back to the front door, shook the knob, and opened it.

He entered the vestibule and passed the surrealistic canvas on the wall, its many eyes still disorderly popping out, before reaching the staircase. After climbing only a few stairs, he stopped and put his hand to his pounding heart, afraid it would burst. After all, he was forty-two, twenty-plus pounds overweight, had barely slept for a week, had rode a bicycle a long distance last night, and to top it off, had downed a bottle of whiskey in record time. Not even mentioning the stress caused him by anticipating the view that awaited him. Now.

Right now his most pressing concern was what to do if Max, by some diabolical miracle, were still alive.

He climbed the rest of the stairs to the second floor, deliberately smudging the banister with his clammy paws, and then clumped down the hall to Max's door. He listened hard, his hand pressing even harder against his chest to keep his heart from being wrested out—still beating!—by his potentially fatal suspense.

If he's not dead yet, I'll have to kill him was the overwhelming upshot of all his agonizing.

He crossed his heart devoutly, fixing imploring eyes on the ornate ceiling, and then ventured into the quiet room, now bathed in both natural and artificial light. The tulle curtain was still heaped on the floor where he had fought it, the curtain rod beside it. Trembling, Nick took a few more steps forward.

There lay Max, seemingly immovable, but just to make certain—no, no closer! If he were alive, the sound of his breathing would fill the room. Even comatose, he would still be wheezing, choking. Besides, his head was unnaturally tilted backward, the mouth—wide open, teeth bared, as if in his final moments he had snarled at death. The huge neck wound had already turned black, and the brightly colored sailboats were finally in dry dock on that feeble chest bound by nylon cord.

Nick covered his eyes and ran from the room. He didn't dare release the screams echoing inside; even the smallest sound in this room of death could literally break his heart.

The heart, the heart! His living, beating heart warned him with frantic jumps that he must regain at least some control over himself or—a heart attack. He returned to the vestibule downstairs and approached the telephone, insanely exultant because *at last* he was going to call Emergency. *Because I'm not completely certain he's dead. I'm not certain. I'm not at all! I'm not*, he told himself hysterically as he dialed the number. When someone answered, he almost shouted the address before hanging up quickly to avoid having to explain anything. Then he dialed the police.

"Put me through to Lieutenant Forger," he said, panting, as if after—a murder. They gave him another number to call, but he couldn't remember and asked them to repeat and then scribbled it down in enormous crooked letters on the notepad. He dialed it.

"Forger!" He groaned when a woman answered. "Please, quick!"

"One moment."

He stiffened. "One moment"? *So he must be there!* Then he realized that he had subconsciously hoped the detective wouldn't be in. He even reached down to end the call, but...

"Yes? Forger speaking." He was chewing something. Nick, fighting for every breath of air, even heard him swallow. Was this belated panic, or right on time?

"Hello—it's me, Edgeway.

Another gulp on the other end. "Now what has—?"

"It's my brother-in-law!" Nick screamed. "Another brutal murder!"

"Where?" Forger asked, always cool and logical.

"Here, in his house...I...I'm here—"

"In your brother-in-law's house?"

"Yes, that's right!"

"And *he* is the one who's been murdered?"

"Yes, that's right, but there's a chance he might still be alive! Quick! I've called Emergency. Please get over here!" Nick dropped the receiver and slumped heavily to the carpet.

What is happening to me? And why now—why? A heart attack! *Aaah, I'm going to die of—overreacting.*

He remained sprawled on his back by the small telephone table, threw his hands out palms up, and breathed deeply and evenly. *Am I really simulating? Or more precisely: Was I only simulating?* The question wiped his mind clean—emptied it by its complete absurdity. It was normal and at times even advisable to simulate strong emotions, but to commit oneself to them to such an extent that they became real? That was sheer lunacy, wasn't it? *So cut out the crap about the imminent heart attack!* "With a heart like yours, sir, you could work two shifts a day in a foundry" is what his doctor had said. What was his name: Lansky? Polansky? Just a month ago.

Nick breathed as deeply as he could, turning his face to the side. Deep, even breaths. Focus on the carpet, on the warm, autumn-yellow pattern. Autumn was coming; it was already September. The day outside was peaceful and clear, sweet and serene. Probably rain would be better—but no matter, he had erased all evidence of his late-night visit. The scars in his soul would remain forever. "Forever" may seem an infinite notion, but actually it could mean tomorrow, or even a moment later, if right now he. What? A heart attack? He continued to take long deep breaths until he drifted into an early-autumn, golden-leaved, cerulean-blue nap.

CHAPTER 33

Somebody slapped him on the cheek.

"He must be out, chief." Then a few more slaps.

Nick moved a little, groaning faintly. *Out, my eye!* He had just fallen asleep, but who would assume that, under these circumstances? No sane person, thank God! He opened his eyes with almost genuine astonishment and stared at Forger, who was bending over him. Forger stared back with the usual distrust in his eyes. Then up popped Jack with a glass of water, which he gave Nick after helping him into the nearest armchair. A humane act indeed! Nick gulped down the water and sighed. Meanwhile, Forger was waiting, but for what Nick had no idea.

Presently Randy came in. "It's the same butchery upstairs as in the other cases, chief."

"Good." Forger nodded.

"How can that be *good*?" Nick protested feebly. "How can you say that!—is he still alive?"

"Didn't you see him?" Forger asked.

"I wasn't sure."

"He's as dead as a log, chief," Randy continued, "rigor mortis and the whole nine yards."

"But, you, Edgeway, weren't so sure, eh?"

"I just glanced at him, just a quick glance!" Nick buried his face in his hands, not even sure himself if he were playing a role or not, but who could really draw the line between sincerity and falsity in such a situation? "I called Emergency."

"When?" Forger arched his eyebrows.

"Before I spoke to you."

"If that were so, they should be here by now. Jack, give them a call and see what's going on. But first, get forensics over here."

While Jack went off to do Forger's bidding, Randy blared, "Shall we go upstairs, chief?"

"No, not yet." Forger's expression was unreadable. "Is everything according to the usual pattern?"

"Mostly, yes. Other than the curtain on the floor."

"I did that," Nick muttered. "I pulled on it, and the—curtain rod came off."

"Why did you pull so hard? What kind of curtain is that, Randy?"

"A tulle curtain, chief. Like a mosquito net. I assume it was around the bed—"

"I'll do the assuming around here," Forger interrupted him. "Go on with your story, Edgeway."

"'Go on' with it?" Nick echoed indignantly. "You act like we're here for a game of cards. A man has been murdered!"

"Of course you're right," Forger said with untypical oily tractability, "but in our line of work, you either get used to these *events* or you go nuts."

I think that people like you get used to them because you're already nuts, especially you, Lieutenant! "Don't you at least feel how inappropriate it is to question me just now? Sending your puppets—your subordinates—to check the body and report to you. Why not just go do your job yourself?"

"I'll answer that question, sir, even though I don't really have to. I think right now my job is here. The body can wait. It's stiff as wood and not going anywhere."

"Aah, I see! You want to gauge my initial reactions and—"

Jack popped up again. "He did call Emergency, chief, but he gave them *his* address by mistake."

"Good Lord!" Nick slapped his forehead, really astounded this time.

"I told them they needn't bother to come over," Jack added, "and our coroner is on the way."

Forger waved Jack and Randy away. When they left, he turned his undivided attention on Nick again. "It wouldn't be a bad idea, I think, to finally concentrate, Edgeway. You're a man, after all. Come to think of it, your brother-in-law didn't like you very much, did he?"

"I didn't like him much either!" Nick snapped. "But, unlike you, I'm far from accustomed to 'events' like these."

"*Really?*" Forger gave him a look that probably tried to pass for incisive but came across as just another dumb cop ploy. "Incidentally, could you explain the altercation with the curtain to me in a little more detail?"

"I tried to pull it back to look at Max's bed, and after I...I... saw Max...I almost fainted. I grabbed it without realizing what I was doing. Otherwise I would have collapsed from the horror of it all. Then the curtain rod came down on top of me and I...I got tangled up in—I don't want to remember anymore."

"Well, it's no great strain to remember what happened twenty minutes ago," Forger said. "Or was it hours ago? Sometime last night, perhaps?"

"There you go again with your insinuations." Nick hunched his shoulders. "I'm sick of them, and of you!"

"And I'm sick of you, Mr. Edgeway. You're hovering over three corpses, so to speak. You walk Miss Hatcher to her hotel, and the next morning, she turns up dead. You visit Eric Schumacher, and two days later, his throat is slit. Now once again you present us with a dead body. So why not make an effort to provide us with a few more details about this latest unfortunate event?"

So with a reluctance, he did his best to exaggerate, Nick related how Elsa had called him at about eleven that morning—not from her summer place but from her aunt's place—and asked him to go over because she was worried about her ailing husband, since he didn't answer the phone; how he came here an hour later and, when there was no response to the bell or his shouts, walked around to the back of the house, where he noticed that the bedroom chandelier was still lit. "I was seized with a very dark premonition, Lieutenant!" And so on.

Forger kept nodding as he listened, like a horse dipping into a feedbag into which Nick was pouring large amounts of chaff, but as he finished, shocked Nick by turning the conversation elsewhere, "Now tell me, Edgeway, why you were calling for help at eleven thirty-two last night?"

Nick opened his mouth, producing nothing but a groan. The horse had given him a hard kick and left him gasping for air! Forger threateningly lowered his head until it was almost up against Nick's.

"You don't seem to remember that call, eh?"

"That's not true—how could I forget? I heard a suspicious noise and thought that the sadist—"

"Knock it off!" Forger cut him short. Again, out of nowhere, "You've way too much cologne on, Edgeway, way too much."

How could he argue with the obvious?

"You can't fool me, though," the cop continued authoritatively, causing Nick to question his dim-wittedness. "A Siberian tiger would envy my sense of smell, understand?"

"No, I don't."

Damn it! Could he possibly smell the difference between what was left of *last night's* cologne and *today's*? Without climbing upstairs, without even going into Max's bedroom, which must be the only place where the old smell still lingered? Nick felt drops of sweat forming on his forehead. "I haven't the least idea what you're talking about," he complained, resolved to deny—everything. "What are you getting at?"

"Just that you drank yourself senseless, like a sailor on shore leave."

"A...ah, I see."

He is *dumb, praise the Lord! Dumb!* Nick exclaimed joyfully to himself, while arranging his face to express two feelings appropriate to the moment: confusion and admiration for the Siberian tiger's keen sense of smell.

"I hate drunks," the lieutenant added, staring at him sullenly and somewhat enviously. "I'm a teetotaler myself."

"Sorry, I obviously can't hide anything from you. I drank a lot last night."

"I can't help but ask why—because of joy, anguish, or to ask God for repose of the soul—"

"What!"

"I'll tell you straight out what I think, Edgeway. I think you knew what was going to happen to your brother-in-law last night and, to drown the last shreds of your humanity, drank yourself senseless. You also called for help last night because you were driven by a momentary desire to prevent this murder—a desire that resulted only in a few drunken cries—all the moral resolve you could muster!"

"That's pure nonsense!"

"What? That for a moment you felt a desire to prevent a brutal murder?"

236

"No, no! I didn't mean that!"

"Ah, I see. Then you did feel such a desire—"

"Forget the cheap lawyer tricks, Forger!" Nick burst out, choking with indignation. "How could I have known that my brother-in-law was going to be murdered?"

"Let's assume from your *accomplice*, Edgeway. Yesterday my men found fresh fingerprints on your steering wheel, and they aren't your sister's! Why don't you tell me whose they are?"

Nick, however, was speechless. This time *truth* had descended on him like a mythical bird of prey that, resist as he may, was determined to carry him to its infernal nest strewn with human illusions stripped clean to the bone! *It's* her. *Kaya!*

"I'm waiting for an answer," Forger insisted, clearly excited by his lucky bull's-eye. "Who is the woman you were with the night before last? Where were you headed—for Mayer's perhaps?"

"No, no!" Nick waved his arms in despair. "The night before last I was at home, all night long. It is from you that I learned my car had been driven by—someone. I don't have any idea who it was, believe me!"

Forger grinned nastily and nodded his head in mock understanding. "Yes, definitely a noble deed, Edgeway. How chivalrous of you to cover up for your lover, especially if she's married. But this is a matter of crimes committed, of murders."

"You must be crazy!"

"Why? She isn't your lover? Or she's not married?"

"You're crazy and—professionally careless. Of course, if your bloodhounds were sniffing around—"

"Tell me her name!"

Nick, however, adamantly changed the dangerous theme. "*Bloodhounds* sniffing around my house and heard me calling for help—why didn't they come help me?"

"Because they contacted me instead. I ordered them to stay where they were. I thought it was another of your little tricks, to see if you had a tail on you and, if not, to go—somewhere."

"What if I really did need help? What if the sadist—"

"Come on now, the 'sadist'! A minute or two later my man saw you close your window, perfectly calmly."

My man. Not *men*. He admitted that only one cop was tailing him, so Forger's "man" could only have been watching the front of the house. Nick sighed with relief. He had definitely done the right thing to climb through the window both on his way to Max's and on the way back.

Meanwhile, Forger sighed with disappointment. "I overestimated you, Edgeway. It wasn't clever strategy at all, just drunkenness. Come to think of it, why did you deliberately leave your garage door open last night?"

"Deliberately?" Nick smiled ironically. "I don't even remember when or why I went to the garage. I was surprised to find it open this morning. I started drinking at nine yesterday evening, Forger."

"Fine, fine. I've heard about your kind of boozers. But I wonder if you started drinking at nine in the evening or in the *morning*? Anyway, back to my previous question, who is the woman? There's no point denying—"

At that critical moment—finally some good luck!—the vestibule was literally jammed with idiotic faces perfectly matching the eyes of the surrealistic painting. The police photographer and coroner, accompanied by their crews, just walked in together and in the nick of time, at least for Nick.

"So you finally made it, Doctor Chadwick," the lieutenant hissed, his eyes fixed upon the small red-haired man wearing horn-rimmed glasses with inch-thick lenses. "We've been waiting quite a while, but we're thankful for this now!"

"Yes, I'm a little late," the doctor said pointedly. "I was working on the last corpse you sent over when you called, so I had to park it in the vault next to the one you sent over day before yesterday. It's getting hard to keep up with you, Forger, I must admit."

Forger turned to Nick. "Edgeway, you're free to go! Please give your sister my condolences. Tell her also that I'd like her to come see me as soon as she has recovered."

Nick was already on his feet and heading for the door. He was very happy to be going but also felt very uneasy—now that everybody was silently staring at him. "Good-bye," he said and, since nobody answered him, he added, "Have a nice day."

CHAPTER 34

But why "The end. It was her"? Would a hardened killer leave fingerprints on the steering wheel? Could it really be possible that the murders had been committed by a woman—not even a woman—a girl, a thin, fragile, timid girl like Kaya?

"Like Kaya!" Nick downshifted the Ford and sullenly shook his head. He was deluding himself again. He had plenty of reasons to question everything about her, including her very existence, but that could easily be tested, right now!

Breaking every rule of the road, he jerked the wheel to the left, barely avoiding a head-on collision with an oncoming truck. The truck's brakes screeched, and almost simultaneously the driver laid on his horn and stuck his bony head out of the cab window, cursing. Nick gave him a friendly wave and proceeded downtown.

He stopped for a few minutes to buy a pair of scissors before driving to the city-hospital parking lot. Checking the hospital directory at the main entrance, he finally found what he was looking for: "PATHOLOGY—North Wing." No doubt the morgue would be directly beneath it. He began walking briskly toward the North Wing, but when he spotted a security guard outside the entrance, he immediately slowed his pace and lowered his shoulders, hunching over like a man broken with grief.

"Good day, Sergeant," he said politely and as sadly as he could. "My name's Edgeway. Nicolas Edgeway. Please tell Dr. Chadwick I'm here."

"He's not in the hospital at the moment," the guard answered, "and won't be back anytime soon, I'm afraid."

"Oh no, how could that be possible?" Nick covered his eyes and produced a feeble groan that he hoped would sound involuntary.

"Why do you need to see him, sir? If it's really so important—"

"No, it's not important—to anybody—to anybody but me. Nothing important to her anymore."

Of course the policeman asked, "Important to whom?"

"To Kathleen Hatcher," Nick replied. "She was very dear to me—still is. Dr. Chadwick promised to let me see her, to say good-bye one last time!"

"Well, if that's all, don't worry. As far as I know they've already prepared her—for the funeral tomorrow morning."

"I know; I know"—Nick nodded—"but I wanted to see her in a more intimate setting, not in her coffin at the cemetery." He lapsed into silence, his lips pursed. Then he blurted, "I wanted to see her here, in the morgue!"

For a moment the policeman just stared at Nick, as if dumb-struck. Then he nodded, perhaps calculating what might be in it for him. Nick interpreted the glint in his eye to mean, *Something has just perched on my shoulder. If it is luck, how can I catch it?*

"Please follow me, sir," the policeman beckoned. "I'll see what I can do to help."

Nick waited in the lobby as the policeman entered a glass booth marked "HOSPITAL PASSES" and dialed a three-digit number, obviously an extension. After a lengthy conversation that Nick couldn't hear, but which was punctuated by encouraging little smiles pointedly addressed at him, the sergeant hung up, his silence speaking volumes, "*See, I've already taken care of your problem.*"

Instead of coming up to him to demand an ID card, the duty officer disappeared behind his cluttered desk, pretending to be very busy with his paperwork. *So far, so good,* Nick said to himself as he remained standing in the cavernous lobby, devoid of chairs. Alone. Easy to observe and easier to arrest, if it came to that, especially if the front door could be automatically locked from the control panel in the booth. He felt like cackling but checked himself just in time and maintained the mournful expression on his face.

A few minutes later, a robust man with a military crew cut and very high cheekbones came up to him, energetically chewing gum. Wearing green hospital scrubs, much too short for him, and panting slightly, no doubt from climbing stairs, the attendant silently motioned Nick downstairs to the basement. They walked down a corridor lit by neon lights and stopped before a sliding metal door that creaked open sideways at the push of a button. As they entered, Nick shuddered from the cold, if for no other reason. But the ultimate chill was hidden away in the ten vaults mounted along the wall.

Silently the attendant made his way to the third vault and yanked it open, hauling out a gurney upon which, under the usual white sheet...

Nick stepped forward, choking back his revulsion, and uncovered Kathy's face. As he had expected, it seemed unknown to him, not because death had taken it over but because the pale face struck him as utterly *banal*, with ugly features. *Robbed of yet another illusion,* he thought, feeling his heart contract with pain. That vulturous bird of *truth* had pecked this illusion too—to the bone!

The corpse had indeed been prepared, or rather patched, for the funeral. The neck looked as if it had been sealed with a big crooked zipper. That afternoon she would be clothed in a high-necked dress, or perhaps a scarf strategically placed over the jagged gash. They would apply rouge and lipstick, smooth and brush the hair into a simple style. Put simply, some mortician's assistant would pocket a pretty penny to prepare her for her last assignation—with the worms!

"Oh God!" Nick sobbed, shaken by the grim vision he had conjured up, and the actor in him hurried to praise his convincing display of grief.

But the only audience, the attendant, watched him coldly from the sliding door and, instead of offering a show of sympathy by discontinuing his energetic ruminations, chewed his gum with even greater fervor, his sturdy jaws crunching rhythmically in the frosty dead silence. Under such circumstances, how could anyone experience *genuine* sorrow? Absurd! Nick gnashed his teeth. *I've even been robbed of my humanity*, he realized, *somewhere midst all these roles life has assigned me lately.*

"Forgive me, Kathy!" he whispered very softly.

He stooped and stroked her cold forehead, slipped the scissors from his pocket, and immediately sensed a commotion behind him. He turned to see the attendant standing at his shoulder, his coat unbuttoned and his right hand hidden beneath it. Obviously the sight of the scissors had mobilized him: *"A psychopath in the morgue"* or maybe *"The psychopath is about to defile the dead body of his victim."*

"What's on your mind, Susan?" Nick asked, looking with newly aroused interest at the broad-shouldered bull. "Are you going to shoot me dead on the spot and get a quick promotion? Is that your dream, Susan?"

The man stared at him, astonished and furious. *"Susan? Did you just call me—Susan!"*

"Why, sure. Who else would I be talking to?"

Nick let him heat up a little more in the freezing cold and then pointed to the name taped to the coat lapel. "Don't expect a promotion after this little blunder. The sack is more likely what awaits you, Miss—or Mrs.—'Susan Cordel.'"

The "attendant" stopped chewing gum long enough to squint down at the name tag and then looked up at Nick with new emotions, but gratitude wasn't among them. Although it should have been. Nick shook his head deprecatingly and bent over Kathy again. He cut a lock of her long auburn hair almost to the roots and wrapped it carefully in his handkerchief. Putting it in his pocket along with the scissors, he then covered her face with the white sheet.

"I'm done."

As Nick stepped away from the corpse, the badly disguised cop removed his hand from beneath the coat, tore off the name tag, and jammed it into his pants pocket. Then he shoved the gurney back into the vault and kicked the door shut, without the slightest pretense of hospital decorum or common decency.

Outside, framing the door, waited two uniformed specimens from Hospital Security. As Nick walked down the hall, he heard them rattle after him, as if they were marching in hobnailed boots. Reaching the staircase, he looked back to see that the one in Susan Cordell's coat had stayed behind and was already talking on his cell phone, no doubt phoning in his report to Forger.

I've given them the slip again. Nick smiled to himself as he passed two more security guards and a uniformed policeman in the lobby. "Shame on you, gentlemen," he taunted them. "I simply came here to pay my last respects to my beloved. I wanted a lock of her hair as a remembrance. And what do you do? You try to trap me, at such an intimate moment! What behavior! You are in a hospital— a morgue—after all! You should be ashamed of yourselves."

CHAPTER 35

After leaving the hospital, Nick headed for the nearest gas station, filled up the tank, and called Elsa. No answer. She wasn't at the summer house, and he found it hard to believe that she could be at Max's aunt's place—ex-Max, and perhaps Elsa's ex-aunt? *Everything seems to be "ex" when death comes*, he mused, and this bit of trivia struck him as very funny, as if *death* itself had whispered the very witty anecdote in his ear. Nick drove away chortling to himself. So what? Hadn't Max always hated him? Wasn't he, so to say, his sworn enemy?

Everything will be real for them. They will see before themselves real *enemies. Or to put it another way, the boy will have created on this island of Sensibles and Sensitives another race—the Satisfied, who will fight* in earnest, *as anyone would who was prevented from fully enjoying his contentment. In this case, for example, instead of sleeping soundly in their comfortable beds beside their now enticing wives, these one hundred men will be forced to participate in a meaningless (in their opinion), useless farce on the sand under indifferent stars and a tedious, yellow moon.*

"Leave us alone!" They will brandish their swords. "You're bothering us!" They will sink their glinting swords into the chests

of some gaping hot fools, who still don't believe the fight is real, and slash some throats. "We don't understand you—and don't want to understand!" Massacre!

Oh, it was true: it meant instant death to interpose yourself between the Satisfied and their contentment! Such people don't know what imagination and game-playing are. Convinced they have something to protect, they protect it in most reliable way: without feelings or thought—by blood instinct alone.

For the first time on that island after a battle, the sweltering sun won't resurrect dim, soft-winged dreams; instead, it will reveal dozens of the uncomprehending dead—terribly, fanatically disfigured "warriors."

He was almost sure Elsa would be waiting for him, but not until he saw her car parked in the middle of the driveway did he realize how difficult it would be to look her in the eye during the inevitable conversation. He took pains to park so that he didn't block her way out to—her ex-husband. She owed Max that much. "She owes it to me too," he muttered as he crossed the driveway. The front door was unlocked, so he walked right in.

Elsa was lying on her back on the living room sofa, staring at the ceiling, balancing a large mug of coffee between her breasts. She heard him approaching but didn't turn, although her breathing sharpened and her fingers tightened on the mug.

"You know what I'm about to tell you, don't you?" he whispered to her.

"Yes, I know."

Her short answer caused a kind of dry wheezing in his head, as if his brain were an overheated engine. How could she just say "Yes, I know"? Nobody should be so blunt! No tears, not the least tremor in her voice, not even a desperate glance! She didn't even blink, as if to say, *"I don't have to keep up appearances with my brother. He's a loser and can tolerate anything."*

"Well?" he said, as rudely as possible.

"I'm going there soon."

"Really?" Nick sat in the armchair opposite her. "Don't you think it would be more *appropriate* if you were too weak with grief to drive?"

"I have to go over there, Nick. Besides, I may be of some use."

"Of use to whom, Elsa? For what? To reveal the truth?"

She pondered for a moment, as if she had taken his words seriously, oblivious to their dripping sarcasm. Finally she shook her head. "In this case, there are various truths, and they are all *dirty*, so none of them should be revealed."

"But why can't truth be revealed," Nick asked, "in all its muddy and stinking appearance?"

"Which one?"

"'Which one' what?"

"Which of the four truths? Or maybe five or six? Oh, stop it, Nick! What time is it?"

"Almost three."

"Then it really is time for me to go." She sighed. "I promised Forger—"

Surprised, Nick jumped in, "You've spoken to him! When?"

"More than an hour ago. As soon as we got here I gave Max another call and—" She at last managed to tear her gaze away from the ceiling and look at him. "Why are you surprised?"

He didn't answer her, just stared at her face—it struck him as somehow gaunt, unbelievably wizened: ashen skin, sunken eyes, no longer greenish-blue but faded to a very pale, *dying* blue. Oh no! This face—for an instant—was their mother's face! The same as a day before she had died, when she was lying on the same sofa. She had turned her head toward him, just as Elsa was now. *She's stolen the moribund face of our mother—put it over her own to hide behind!*

"Nick, why are you looking at me like that? Where did you think I learned about Max? Where else if not from the police?"

She stood up, and suddenly the similarity disappeared, or just a trace of it still lingered, barely discernible. Nick sighed with relief. *What a bizarre vision!*

"Answer me!" Elsa slammed the cup on the tabletop, splashing the remaining coffee on the white marble. It reminded him of the blackened blood on *that* sheet. "Why were you surprised that I'd spoken to Forger? Answer me!"

"Leave me alone. I won't answer you. I don't want to."

As she stood facing him, Nick couldn't help but notice her legs shaking and the deep desperation in her eyes. She really was suffering—whatever the reasons. She was his sister—only that mattered now. His sister. He rose and put his arm around her shoulder, moved by an irresistible surge of sympathy.

"Stay here, Elli. Take a tranquilizer and get some rest. In your condition you can't drive a car or—"

"I have to go." She sobbed. "I have no choice!"

True. After a rest she would hardly look as *appropriate* for the occasion. "OK then"—he nodded—"at least let me drive you."

"What about Annie?"

"Where is she? In the yard?"

"She's upstairs, sleeping again. These days have been exhausting for her. No, I'm afraid you'll have to stay, Nick. Otherwise she might wake up and find herself all alone and be frightened." Elsa's body suddenly stiffened. She had remembered, but too late, "Incidentally—"

"Oh, don't!" He attempted a wry grin. "Don't start on me again. It's not necessary to simulate before me. You know perfectly well that I don't kill during the day. Any more than I kill at night. You know that even *better*."

"What are you—suggesting?"

He shrugged his shoulders, as if to suggest utter annoyance, then stooped and sniffed her hair, almost burying his nose there. She smelled of his cologne, of course, and of sweat—she, who was always so maniacal about her personal hygiene, had skipped her usual morning shower. Apparently she didn't have time to shower last night either; maybe she had been too preoccupied with her fears—about Anna's "extraordinary dream."

"Since you're going to see Forger," he said, "shouldn't you take a shower first?"

Elsa stepped back in disbelief. "Why would I do that?"

He ignored her question. "Did you take the bottle of cologne from the bathroom?"

"Yes. But is it so important to ask me *now* about it?" She feigned an accusing look in his direction but obviously could barely see him, as if staring into the dark.

"I'm not saying it's important, Elsa. I'm just wondering why you'd do that—take a bottle of man's cologne."

"Why is that so strange? I've told you a hundred times that your cologne is more suitable for a woman. It's too sweet for a man. But come to think of it, it suits you all right!"

Even if she were about to be hanged, she'd use her last breath to insult me, and it's not just bullying. She really does despise me. No doubt she has hated me for a long time, but, wise guy that I am, I never noticed. Nick felt another cherished illusion slipping away. He searched the depths of his soul, expecting to feel a searing pain, anguish, or at least emptiness. Nothing. Smooth. Obviously, having his sister's affection no longer mattered very much to him. So he must be over his feelings toward her as well—if there had been any. Maybe the problem was that the depths of his soul were not very deep. *Damn! Has something in me died? Has there ever been anything inside me that could die? I really need to know!*

Apparently assuming that he was waiting for further comment about the damn cologne, Elsa added, "Yesterday morning I couldn't find my perfume—not on the dressing table in my room or in my handbag. Honestly Nick, I just have no idea where it went, so I borrowed yours. You know I haven't been home since yesterday, so—"

"So all right!" he interrupted her. "Let's leave this story for another time. You were just about to go somewhere, as I recall."

Her teeth almost chattered as she abruptly closed her mouth in midsentence. Grimacing venomously, she turned her back on him and slammed the door behind her as hard as she could. Nick listened to her receding footsteps: she was going upstairs—to take a shower after all. Maybe he shouldn't have reminded her! It might be better for him if she had gone there with that scent on her—but who knows? He was beginning to feel uncertain about almost everything, including the *fact* that until recently had seemed indisputable to him.

CHAPTER 36

Half an hour later, Elsa headed for her house, fully prepared to play her tragic role as the "inconsolable widow." After watching her with implacable reproach from the kitchen window, Nick sat down to finish his lunch. As usual when he was nervous, he gobbled down the food as if he hadn't eaten in days and lapsed into another old habit—dawdling. Anything to keep from facing his problems and dealing with them, as a normal person would.

He pushed aside his empty plate angrily and stood up. A normal person? Nonsense. Who with a particle of common sense would decisively try to prove to himself that his house was haunted by a profligate ghost who waited for him to fall asleep and then jumped into bed with him? A specter that drank his coffee, listened in on his conversations, and drove his car—what's normal about that? Only this: that it's not proven, yet! If that lock of hair upstairs turns out to be Kathy's, that would mean the killer had dealt him another blow below the belt. Alarming in the extreme, yes, but tolerable. Real. As for the other possibility...

Otherwise I couldn't survive, Nick concluded. *I would really go crazy!*

A few unconscious gestures and the dishes were in the sink and the vase with its dried flowers was back on the table. As he caressed the flowers, their rustling sounded like whispering voices from another world. *Mother, where are you? Help me, please!* He bent down and thirstily breathed in their imaginary fragrance. Or was it imaginary? No, the dried flowers really were giving off the odor of rank herbs! He took them out of the vase. Their stems were damp, even sopping wet at the lower end. Who had poured that liquid in the vase?

It must have been Anna. Of course. Elsa had made her some tea, and she had refused to drink it, or she did she have a good reason not to drink that particular cup of tea? What could she do? Had she poured it into the vase to fool her mother? And had Elsa then been deceived by the empty cup and taken her up to bed, assuming she was fast asleep—because the tea was laced with a tranquilizer? Or perhaps the herbs themselves had been a sedative.

Interrupting his speculations, Nick took an almost empty bottle of wine from the bar and, after rinsing it thoroughly, poured some of the liquid from the vase into it. He corked it tightly and put it back with the other bottles.

He quietly started up the stairs, facing the unknown. If Anna hadn't drunk the spiked tea, she probably wasn't sleeping and would fix him with her dreamy but uncannily piercing gaze when he entered the room. Oh, what a child she was, what a *haunted* child! Nick stopped and took off his shoes, tiptoeing down the hallway in his socks. Wait!

Anna was talking to someone.

He barely recognized her voice, since he had rarely heard her utter two words at a time, but at the moment, she was waxing eloquent. Who was she talking to? That question led him to a string of not-so-logical assumptions. Had Elsa sneaked back into the house, or Max's aunt? Was it a policeman, a doctor, the herbalist fortune-teller? But why on the sly?

Nick approached the door of the room as silently as he could.

"Most of them," Anna was saying, "I didn't like at all."

After some seconds, "The same with me," Anna continued, "but then I got angry and cut his ear off. Then I checked to see what was inside his stomach. It was disgusting, and I knew I shouldn't do it because it would hurt him, so I finally put him out of his misery. When something is beheaded, it dies right away, doesn't it?"

Then silence. Holding his shoes tightly in his hand, Nick leaned against the wall. Nightmare! Nightmare!

"Yes, I even cried," Anna continued. "I was sorry, and secretly buried him in the garden."

...

"No, in the other one, at our bigger house. His grave is under our most beautiful cypress tree. I even put up a tombstone."

...

"I know, but if I put a cross there, everybody would know what was under it. I was really sorry I did it! It was just a little baby. I would never do a thing like that again, unless I get really angry, maybe."

There followed another long pause. Nick was sweating as if he were in a sauna. At the same time, cold shivers ran up and down his spine.

"Are you kidding?" Anna asked.

...

" I see. Well, I'll try it some time."

...

"No, I'll go to school next year. Mama's hiring some teachers for me in the meantime to come to my house. My father wants me to go to school now, though. He says I'm perfectly healthy, just because he won't admit that, he's guilty for what I am."

Then another long silence, much longer than the others. Then Anna laughed—something Nick would never have guessed she could do. But who was in there with her anyway, and why couldn't he hear what the other one was saying? Stranger still—why was she acting as if she were answering questions? Could the other one possibly be whispering so softly that the voice couldn't be heard outside the room?

"Please, don't go!" Anna exclaimed. "Stay awhile, please!"

She's talking to herself, Nick decided. *Children do that—invent imaginary friends to talk to.* But his rational instincts, his insidious prompter, told him that, whoever it was, the other person was real. Real? Nick wiped his forehead with his shirtsleeve. His head expanded—a scorching desert of horrors, but itself no more than a cardboard prop. Behind lay the insight, the conviction, the knowledge that Anna was having a chat with the—*ghost.*

"You'll come back later tonight, won't you?" she asked.

With the ghost, whose voice he is incapable of hearing.

"OK! I'll wait for you here. By that time Mama will be asleep."

Incapable of hearing, but not because the ghost was whispering.

"Yes, yes, I know. You go if you have to."

"No!" Nick threw open the door and blocked the threshold, his heart pounding like a tin box in a hurricane.

Anna was sitting up on the bed in her nightgown. His sudden appearance didn't seem to startle her at all. She just turned toward him and looked down at his stocking feet. *She's figured out that I sneaked up here,* he realized, *that I was eavesdropping, and probably knows I'm scared out of my wits!*

He looked into all the corners of the room, although he was sure that *it* had disappeared when he opened the door.

But he was wrong.

It, the ghost—Kaya—was standing in the middle of the room. Her small, thin figure was almost transparent, like the finest stained glass but colorless and, for that matter, faceless, hairless, and seemed to be without hands—probably because they were pressed against her breast. Yes. She spread her hands wide, and at that moment, he could see the tiny wrists, the childlike fingers. They gestured to Anna, which Nick interpreted as *"I'm sorry!"* The cut of her colorless filmy dress struck him as very familiar. Of course! Kaya was wearing a ghostly version of his mother's kimono.

When she floated up to him, he could feel the piercing gaze of her invisible but insistent eyes on him. *What does she want from me? What does she expect of me?* He peered at the filmy spot where her face should have been. The mystic horror, astonishment, disbelief—everything he had felt until now suddenly reduced to one overpowering desire: *to see her*, even for a second, because she really exists! He could even catch a hint of her perfume—actually, Elsa's perfume—and almost taste her kisses that night. He had known even then they were no dream or hallucination; he had felt them burn his lips, and her caresses had been real, *alive*. She couldn't be a ghost! It's not fair, it's mean.

But look! She raised her hands, and the flowery curtain on the window began to fade behind the figure that was taking shape. God! Something almost human, as though her own fingers were molding it with graceful movements, tracing its cobweb-fine contours: a chin, lips, nose, and eyebrows. Only the eyes evaded him, remaining two dark holes peeped from the fluttering face. Not hollow eye sockets in a skull, though: the darkness was filled with immense tension and charged with *her gaze*!

"Kaya." Nick timidly stepped toward her. The unfinished form seemed to grow soft and then melt, like a candle exposed to a flame. "No, no, please don't go! Kaya, I beg you to stay!"

As her arms, two fleshless, semitransparent outlines, fluttered rapidly, the outline of her pallid, almost childlike, features appeared again, then melted again—appearing and melting, then slowly vanishing.

In total shock, Nick knew that the being before him was waging an awesome struggle to maintain possession of *its own face*—and losing. Some unknown, inexplicable power was depriving her of her right to be fully human—draining, swallowing, sucking away her features till her figure again acquired its former undistinguishable spectral shape.

She remained visible a little longer, fossilized in the silence into tiny luminous specks dancing in the air that then feebly waved good-bye to Anna and floated toward the still-open door.

"Oh no!" Nick shouted wildly. "I won't let you go!" He stepped back to block the threshold, his legs slightly apart, puffing out his broad chest, aware that his face was frozen in a stupid, ugly grin but unable to unfreeze it.

"Move out of the way," Anna had commanded him, and as if caught in an absurd, hallucinatory dream, he obeyed. Kaya brushed by him, as insubstantial as the gentlest breeze, and disappeared. Infuriated, Nick rubbed his eyes, looking frantically for some trace of her hazy shape. Nothing—nothing except a quickly retreating *presence*, which drained his senses, wresting everything from them in a few seconds, sucking him dry. Like a leech.

Soon Nick heard the front door shut firmly, as if someone had just walked out, miffed. He hurried to his room to look out the window but couldn't see Kaya. Biff, however, could either see her or, more likely, smell her and was jumping around, practically in ecstasy, first in one area, and then he moved—they moved?—across the yard. The mangy mutt, however, stopped to relieve himself in the chrysanthemums.

"I'll kill him!" Nick groaned. "My mother planted those!" *Wait a minute*, his common sense warned. *What do those chrysanthemums have to do with anything?*

He turned away slowly and lay on his bed—if he were going to faint, it would be safer for him there. Despite everything, he remained conscious, astonished at his strong spirit! Or was he just a thick-skinned, insensitive fool?

That surly Anna was a *demon* he no longer doubted.

Pressing his palm against his feverish forehead, he headed for the bathroom, splashing cold water on his face and swallowing two aspirins but not even glancing at himself in the mirror. He preferred to keep the image of his strong spirit. Then he returned to Elsa's room, but the demon was no longer there. Her good-natured uncle closed his inflamed eyes for a moment's rest, only to see an oval rosy cloud swimming toward him when he reopened them—actually a rose-colored nightgown and above it, as if stuck on a pole, a little nondescript face, expressionless and mute, coming nearer and nearer.

"Anna," he croaked. "Annie," his voice crackling like a scratchy old record player, "Annie" was all he managed to force out.

She walked by him, not bothering to look in his direction, climbed into the bed, and turned toward the wall. No doubt she really needed her rest so that, while her mother slept, she and her ghostly buddy could conspire in the dark—maybe even find time to plan their *next* murder!

Perhaps his! A deadly chill flew through his veins, immobilized his bones, and cramped his tortured brain. His teeth chattering, Nick retreated to the door, his eyes riveted to the child's head on the pillow—to the nape of her neck with its clay-brown hair.

He slouched down the hall to warm himself and went down to the kitchen. There a quick check revealed that the vase had been emptied of the "tea" and carefully wiped dry, inside and out. Even the dried flower stems were now as dry as possible.

All in all, a very provident, cautious child, right?

CHAPTER 37

The lock of hair was gone from the book. *Somebody* had removed it, so he couldn't compare it to Kathy's lock. Yet another ominous, unanswered question to add to those collecting in his head the past few days, ever since both ghosts and murderers had decided to haunt his home.

The home to which Elsa returned with two enormous suitcases.

With a grim smile, he watched her clump into her room to her monstrous daughter, then went to the kitchen, took the bottle with the "tea," and sneaked out. On the way to his car, he checked the chrysanthemums: yes, some had been tromped on and others very recently picked. What nonsense! Was he supposed to assume that his ghost-murderer had gathered a bouquet before vanishing?

"I'll watch you all vanish into the ground!" Nick threatened as he lowered himself into the Ford and stashed the bottle under the driver's seat. He peeled out of the driveway like a racer chasing a $10 million prize. None of the various feelings raging in his chest was good.

He slammed on the brakes suddenly, right across from Reno's office, just in time to see Reno leaving, his companion a gruff guy in a checked sports coat and disheveled beard, in which a whole beehive could be breeding, who was talking his ear off and presumptuously tapping him on the back.

SET WAGNER

Nick crossed the street and stood in front of them.

"Hello, Nick!" Reno shouted, though they were only a few steps from each other.

"We have to talk, Reno. Now."

"Excellent!" Shining with joy, Reno waved his hand. "Have a fine evening, Derek. And don't worry about a thing. We'll finish them off!"

Burly-bearded Derek mumbled something to himself and walked away without a parting remark. His thickly padded shoulders, clearly due only to his tailor, still encouraged respect.

"Has your secretary left yet?" Nick asked. When Reno nodded, he immediately suggested, "Let's go up then!"

"Wouldn't you rather find a cozy little restaurant somewhere?"

"A cozy little restaurant! I'd rather go to the deepest pit of hell!"

First Reno eyed him cautiously and then suddenly winked and headed back to his office. Nick followed him and, judging by Reno's high spirits, added, "So you already know?"

"Yes, Nick. Poor Max! He was young too—"

"Oh, knock it off!" Nick interrupted. "It's me you're talking to."

"OK, OK. I don't suppose either of us will be shedding tears over the loss of dear Max. Still, it was a very unpleasant thing to happen to anybody."

"What in particular, Reno—that Max had his throat slit with a blunt knife?"

Reno stopped at his office door, keys in hand. "*Blunt?* Wow!"

"No! I don't know what kind of knife it was—even if it *was* a knife. The word 'unpleasant' just struck me as most inappropriate."

"Would you have preferred 'pleasant'?" Now Reno acted surprised. "Come on, Nick. Let's try to maintain some decency here—"

260

Nick lost the last shred of his patience. "Open the damned door, will you! How much longer do we have to stand here?"

Finally they went in, crossing the luxuriously furnished foyer to reach Reno's office, and Reno sat at his huge mahogany desk, which lacked only a net in the middle to make a very swank ping-pong table. Nick crossed to the liquor cabinet, grabbed two beers, and banged them down on the desk.

"I want you to answer me one question, Reno."

"OK, but make it quick, because—"

"Let me guess!" Nick narrowed his eyes maliciously. "Because you have an urgent appointment with 'Didi' or 'Kiki'?"

"Why are you nagging me, Nick? And that phone message you left me last night—well, it really puzzled me."

"What puzzles me is far more important right now." Nick stared at him inquisitively. "Did you *know* yesterday that Max wasn't the killer, or did you just assume he wasn't?"

"I assumed he wasn't. I knew he didn't kill Kathleen Hatcher."

"Really? *How?*"

"I saw him just before she was murdered."

"Between three and four that night? Where?"

Reno opened one of the beers very deliberately, poured it into a glass, and sipped it slowly.

"*Where* did you see him?" Nick snapped.

"I hoped you'd figure that out for yourself."

"No, I haven't!"

"We ran into each other—at their place."

"At their place? Between three and four in the morning!"

"Yes, and yes."

"What in hell were you doing there at that hour?"

"Why are you cross-examining me, Nick?"

"You should thank your lucky stars I'm even listening! Come on, speak!"

"OK. You do remember that I returned from Italy only Friday morning?"

"So what?"

"Elli and I hadn't seen each other for three months. We missed each other. So we made arrangements—for me to see her that night at half past eleven, after you and Kathleen left."

The room—no, *the world*—began spinning before Nick's eyes. No, it crashed! His well-arranged—however inappropriate—world was now crumbling into chaos.

"Nick, you really suspected nothing? I'm sorry."

"My sister and you were—you're apologizing for being?"—*I'll kill him! But first*—"How long have you two been lovers?" Nick pronounced "lovers" with a strong, very phony, Italian accent.

"Since we were in school."

"I know about then. When did you start seeing each other *again?*"

"We've never stopped, Nick. Coincidentally, that night, I had decided it was high time we brought our long relationship to a close."

"Aha, I see. So that's why you were hiding from her!"

"Not exactly 'hiding.' I was just—"

I'll kill her too! "Couldn't you two choose another place for your rutting? Did it have to be right under her husband's nose?"

"He had moved to the other wing long ago—ever since Annie was born, because Elsa insisted. So he was never around, and we never worried that he'd—interrupt us. On the whole, he was a well-mannered man."

"Well-mannered until that night, you mean?"

"Who knows? Either he really had no idea about us, or he finally decided he'd had enough. I'd gone out on the porch for a breath of fresh air—the first time I'd run such a risk! And there he was, on the porch in his pajamas! He must have come down through adjoining west-wing rooms; the damned porch wraps around half the house. Well, we stared at each other for a minute like two alley cats. He looked as surprised as I was, and very embarrassed! Then he whispered that he'd be waiting for me outside in half an hour. I don't really have to tell you how I felt, do I?"

"No, you certainly don't," Nick muttered, though he really had no idea, since he had never had such an encounter, nor was he likely to have in the future. "What happened after that? Did Elsa find out?"

"Thank God, no! Otherwise she'd surely have filed for divorce. She's been looking for any pretext. I left as soon as I could after that; I wasn't fit for anything, as you can imagine!" Carried away with the memory, Reno seemed to have completely forgotten he was sharing these details with his lover's *brother*. "When I got outside, Max was already there, waiting for me. We didn't quarrel; I just promised him I'd make myself scarce, and we agreed not to say anything to Elsa. 'I don't care how you make your retreat, sir,' he said, 'but don't let her learn that I know about your relationship. If she did, we could no longer continue to live under the same roof.' He dreaded divorce even more than I did, Nick, but for totally different reasons."

"Watch how you talk about my sister, Reno!"

"Just what's so offensive about my saying that her husband wouldn't divorce her in spite of that?"

"What's wrong is that you—that her long-time lover—didn't want her to get a divorce 'in spite of that'! And 'in spite of' *his* 'Didi,' 'Kiki'—"

"I don't know anybody named Kiki," Reno suddenly shouted, "and back then your sister refused to marry me. She married Max because I was just a poor student and the son of miserable, destitute immigrants! Why should I want to marry her now that she's past her prime and the mother of a neurotic, pathetic—"

Nick's fist caught him just under the jaw, dropping both him and his chair to the floor. His head made a hollow thud as it hit the carpet. Reno just stared up with blurred, astounded eyes, then struggled back to his feet. Panting and mechanically rubbing his badly bruised knuckles, Nick watched him tensely.

"If you'd hit me a little harder, you might have broken a finger or two," Reno commented. "You have no idea how to punch, man. It's dangerous. If you break your fingers, who will finish writing your ridiculous tales?"

"Did you say 'ridiculous'? You've never read them!"

"But I've read *you*! Long ago! You're easy to read, Nick—a crumpled sheet of paper filled with nothing but drivel."

"Why do you call yourself my friend, then?"

"Do you call this a friendship, Nick?" Reno smiled scornfully but also with pity. "Do you think I'm your bosom buddy because we go fishing once a month? Or maybe because, when you call me at inappropriate times, I don't hang up? I put up with your verbal diarrhea, even when I'm buck naked and the *young woman* beside me is getting impatient—"

"You disgusting lecher!"

"You pathetic eunuch. My parents may have been poor, but they taught me how to act like a man. Meanwhile, your refined mother gelded your soul with her sloppy sentimentality—"

"Don't you dare even mention my mother!" Nick yelled and tried to hit him again.

This time Reno was ready and jumped away so that Nick's punch missed him completely. "Don't even think of taking another swing at me, Nick," he warned icily. "I have no desire to beat you up, but, by God, I will if I have to."

"You...you." What could Nick say in the face of such pompous arrogance! He rushed Reno, crazy with anger, but Reno grabbed him by the hand with amazing quickness and pulled him against himself, so the two were locked in an utterly absurd strong embrace. The situation would have been comical if it hadn't been so humiliating! Nick made a few futile attempts to break away, jerking his head back and forth, but only got a mouthful of Reno's bristling, unkempt hair in his mouth. He felt like spitting. "Let go of me, you asshole!"

"Not until you calm down." Reno pushed him against the massive desk until Nick felt his back hit the edge.

If I try to get away, he'll just force me up on the desk, Nick reasoned. *What a pretty picture that would make: my legs up in the air among all his ledgers and legal briefs, and I could slam my head against the computer!*

"Let go of me," Nick managed to whisper, almost against his will. "Let's—cut the bullshit."

"Deal!" Reno loosened his hold with obvious relief and then held out his arms, inviting Nick to another, friendlier embrace. He got no response, of course, so he stooped to lift the chair upright and settled back into it. He drank some beer and then gingerly rubbed his jaw.

"Nick, we need to discuss some very important matters, so let's not waste any more precious time. Listen, today I found the crime!"

"What crime?"

"The undiscovered one we needed so badly. A murder was committed twenty-four years ago that we can accredit to Andrey Belloff, and I wouldn't be surprised if he really committed it—"

"Forget it," Nick interrupted, gloomy. "You'll be late for you date." Nick shrugged his shoulders and started for the door.

"Wait! I didn't really think about what I was saying; I was just angry." Reno's voice shook. "Nick, do you hear me? I'm sorry! I really feel sorry!"

But Nick heard what he didn't say, *"I really feel sorry for you!"* He kept going, not bothering to close the door behind him on his way out. What use would that be? He'd be knocking on it again soon enough.

CHAPTER 38

"You were Reno's lover," he said casually as they drank their morning coffee in the kitchen.

"Why do you say 'were'?" She arched her eyebrows, unperturbed—eyebrows far too thin, tweezed and shaped with a pencil.

Nick seemed to be noticing this unpleasant detail for the first time. A woman "past her prime"! "That's what *he* said, Elsa: 'I decided it was high time we brought our long relationship to a close.' That's what he told me yesterday."

"We'll see," Her hint of a smile brimmed with confidence. "Don't worry."

"Not worry?" Nick set his cup down and clenched his fists under the table. He really wanted to have a calm, polite conversation. That's why last night he had gone straight to his room when he got back, so he wouldn't fly off the handle at her, but her unmitigated arrogance infuriated him the minute she opened her mouth. "I learn that my sister is—was—an adulteress, and you tell me not to worry? Ha! Don't you get it? You spent sixteen years with a man you didn't love!"

"You 'learned' something that I told you a hundred times."

"No, no! You have to explain to me why you'd marry Max if—"

"I've told you that a hundred times too: because of his social standing, his money, his real estate—"

"We've never been poor. It wasn't necessary to marry him for his money!"

"We weren't particularly rich either, were we?"

"Elsa, listen to yourself! You're looking me straight in the eye and telling me you sold yourself!"

"I'm telling you again. I've told you a hundred times before."

"But I never really believed you!"

"That's your problem, not mine."

"I didn't think you could debase yourself to that extent." Admittedly, he had been convinced she said those things just so he wouldn't feel neglected—to assure him that, even after her marriage, her only brother was still the most important man in her life.

"You were wrong. Don't you see that you sound utterly ridiculous? Such archaic language: 'sold yourself,' 'adulteress,' 'debase'! You've always been ridiculous."

"Ridiculous" was putting it too mildly. He had always romanticized the most banal truisms, as if he tried to translate a merchandise catalog or a checking account into a romantic elegy! But maybe it wasn't so wildly romantic to fantasize about her proving her purest *sisterly* love for him by lying indefatigably that she had never loved her husband and had married him only out of greed. It wasn't a romantic notion, but it wasn't exactly normal either. The worst part was learning that she had always told him the unvarnished truth. *Or, no, the best was that she wasn't lying to me. No, that's not so either. It would have been the best if her relationship with Reno hadn't existed and if her feelings for me had…had…*

"What a disgusting mess!" he protested. "You—your slimy life destroys my whole system of values!"

"Who gave you the right to build a system of values on my life?" She had an irrefutable point. "Wash your hands if you played with the dog, honey."

Nick swung around, startled. Anna was directly behind them! Their eyes met for just a second, long enough to give him the shivers, as usual. Then the "child" ambled over to the sink.

"You could have *at least* put a ribbon in her hair! Give her a touch of color." He fell silent, not because he was afraid he had gone too far but because of the abrupt change in Elsa's countenance. She paled so suddenly she looked whitewashed: even her eyes turned white, glazed.

She leaned toward him, almost brushing his ear with her lips, and her almost inaudible hiss deafened him, "You *sssswine!*"

Having said that, Elsa recoiled like a snake that had just injected venom. Nick looked at her resentfully. Pathetic wretch of a woman. Since she had kept up her "relationship" with Reno all these years, she could at least have had a child with him. But no! She went childless for nine years—until Max was finally able to do his husbandly duty—out of fear. A child who looked like Reno would have been proof positive, abruptly ending her cozy arrangement.

Gradually Elsa regained her usual color, probably hoping she had misunderstood him.

"You're the one who told me not to tie ribbons in her hair, remember?" she entreated. "You said they would overshadow her features."

"Tell her to go out and play in the yard." He ignored her entreaty. "Does she always have to snuffle around underfoot?"

This time, however, Anna demonstrated an uncharacteristic willingness to be on her own by leaving without any further prompting. Her new-found ghostly friend was probably waiting for her outside.

"Last night"—Elsa sighed, a sign that she had declared a truce for the moment—"I explained to her about her father's misfortune.

Of course I didn't go into detail, and I doubt she even understood me. Death is something children can never comprehend."

"She comprehended all right," Nick muttered. *"I'm sure* she did. Now listen to me, Sister. Don't try my patience anymore! You've tried it too many times: involving me in your intrigues, hiding my clothes—"

"When I took them, I really thought there might be blood on them, Nick. Kathy's earring was on your nightstand, after all, clearly torn from her ear."

"Yet after I came back home from the damned fishing trip with your damned lover, I told you I hadn't killed her, and you believed me immediately. Then you lied to me, saying you'd dumped the clothes in the lake, so that there was nothing I could do but lie about them too. The very next evening you had another story to tell me: they weren't in the lake but somewhere on the rocks. But they weren't there either."

"No, they weren't, Nick. You know we looked for them with Forger and his men, but we never found them."

"How did you expect to find them when they were in your car the whole time, until you hung them up in my closet? You thought I'd panic when I saw them and hide them somewhere, so you stayed here that night—to follow me and then show the cops where the 'missing' clothes were. Of course, they would have found my tracks there too. Yes, it makes perfect sense to me now, except one thing: Why? Why were you trying to frame me? Last night that little point was cleared up too."

"Really? Just what became so clear to you last night?"

"That to cover up for a man you never really loved, you wouldn't hesitate to destroy your own brother!"

"Nick"—she laughed—"is this one of your tales you're trying out on—"

"You thought *Max was the killer*," he interrupted, "and, to divert suspicion away from him, decided to make me the prime suspect. So you planted the clothes and later lied to Forger, telling him that, on the night Mayer was killed, I didn't come to your room and that Max had left here in the morning. Then you also denied that I had asked about Alina—to implicate me from head to foot in Eric Schumacher's murder!"

"OK." She shrugged her shoulders indifferently. "Even if everything you say is true, isn't it all over now? Last night it became perfectly clear, in the most gruesome possible way, that Max had nothing to do with—"

"Wait!" Nick interrupted again, speaking slowly so as to savor his triumph. "The night before, I was at your house."

"Whaaat! When?"

"A little after midnight."

"You're lying!"

"What makes you think so?" When he stared at her, she quickly looked away. He whispered insistently, "Max was *still* alive, Elsa," expecting her to show at least some surprise at that fact, to say something like *"Still? Oh, Nick, do you think that the murderer attacked* before *midnight?"*

But Elsa betrayed no surprise. "Of course he was alive around midnight," she countered. "It has been established that the murder was committed between half past two and four in the morning."

It's amazing really how she can turn things around! The heartless bitch deserves absolutely no mercy! "It was established that he died during that time, but there's a very important difference between—"

"What do you want from me, Nick?"

"Just listen to me for a moment. I'll phrase it in another way: when I went to your house, Max wasn't dead yet, but his throat was already slit—"

271

"Enough!" The thick armor of her self-possession finally cracked. "Stop it!"

"The killer left him to die as slowly as possible," Nick continued loudly, "to confuse the coroner about when the murder took place. The killer hardly suspected it would go on for five or six hours when—at about nine thirty—the monstrous 'operation' began!"

"How do you know—or do you just suppose it started so early?"

"I know," Nick said. "What's more, I found him fully conscious."

"Was he able to talk?" she asked insolently.

"Yes, Elsa, so I asked him, 'Who did it, Max? *Who*?'"

"And what did he say?"

"He didn't answer me."

Her relief was so obvious that Nick found it hard not to hit her across the face. Just like that: make her cheek burn and the hair clips fly off her head, mess up her meticulously combed hair. She's been a widow only since yesterday, and just look at how well she's dressed, how quickly she regained the look of a healthy, beautiful woman!

"How about you?" she accused him. "You just gave yourself away! You were with him the night he was murdered! Oho, that will certainly be something for the police to chew on! Incidentally, what were you doing in my house at that time anyway?"

"After our telephone conversation with him *at nine*, there were some questions that badly needed answers."

"Questions, my eye! You can't fool me! He had evidence against you! He must have threatened to turn you in!"

"Something like that—"

"And you went there to kill him!"

272

"True, I was going to kill him," Nick confirmed, exaggerated, lied, or just agreed. "That must make you eat your heart out right about now."

"Is this some kind of hint?"

"Yes, a very transparent hint. Max himself gave me plenty of evidence to identify his killer, even without saying the name. His fatal mistake was not denying that he knew the killer. Then, when he didn't want, *didn't dare* to tell me the name, that told me who—"

"I don't understand a word you're saying!" Elsa exclaimed, but though she might not have picked up on all the fine points, she clearly understood the basics. "What difference would it make to Max in those last moments if you learned the name of his killer or not?"

"A vital difference," Nick said forlornly. "If he hadn't inadvertently exposed the only person in this world for whom I'd let him bleed to death, I'd have called Emergency. Yes, I would have, I'm sure of that!"

"You went there to kill him, and now you're saying you would've tried to save him?"

"There's a big difference, Elsa! I think that cutting the throat of a bastard like Max is a lot easier than leaving him tied up in terrible pain and in a darkened pool of his own blood. He didn't seem like a bastard anymore—simply a human being begging for mercy. I will be asking myself from now on if it was worth blackening myself so disgustingly for you!"

"For me?" She did her best to seem surprised. She took a deep breath, probably preparing a tirade in her usual style but suddenly gave it up. Her dignity prevented her from debasing herself further with redundant and humiliating playacting. She turned to the window and fixed her gaze on Anna, sitting on a bench in the backyard in a posture that suggested she no longer inhabited her body but had left it there and gone someplace else. The head was drooping, shoulders hunched, straw-like arms crossed humbly, legs dangling like sticks. She looked like a shriveled old woman who had died suddenly while sunning herself under the morning sky. But there were no traces of ghostly playmates around the *mortal remains.*

"It was for her," Elsa whispered almost inaudibly. "You did it for me, and I did it for her! You'll find this difficult to believe, Nick, but never even for a second did I intend to let you go to jail. I knew all along that Forger didn't really suspect you. He no doubt just assumed that, like many others in such situations, you entangled yourself in lies and blunders because you were afraid and didn't know what else to do. Otherwise he would have arrested you long ago."

"That's wonderful." Nick smiled reproachfully. "You didn't want the worst for me, 'just' the bad. Was it all really worth it?"

"Listen," she flared, "I did have to cover for Max. When I heard about Kathy's murder—well, I had reasons to suspect him. Then the earring turned up. Who could have put it there?"

Your seamstress's vampire daughter, alas, was the right answer.

"Who else but Max?" Elsa continued. That's why I decided to give him a little test by telling him you said you threw your clothes in the lake. Anyone would've jumped to the conclusion that you must be the murderer—anyone except the *real* murderer! Well, Max didn't. On the contrary, his first words were, 'He lied to you.' Then he agreed to testify that you had been with us, dressed in the other suit."

"And the very next day you told Forger all about it."

"Yes! But even then I still hoped I might be wrong, that his hatred for you was leading him on. The night I found you in the library was decisive. He told me a whole pack of lies to justify his presence there, and then Anna told me—"

"Anna *told* you?"

"Yes, Nick," Elsa snapped, "she's not as tight-lipped with me as with you. She heard Max say he had left your knife in the dead old man's house but that you had shown up there and spoiled his plan. You found it, and he immediately came here to take something else. And not only for that! Because, Nick, when you saw him off and returned to your room, from the window I saw your car drive down the road."

"I see. So you thought that Max had taken it."

"I was sure, but I asked myself why."

"And the next morning you learned that Mayer had been killed just an hour later."

She nodded and then curled up in the chair and shivered. "Oh God, Annie and I were living under the same roof with a killer!"

"To kill a killer is murder too, Elsa. And, in your case, premeditated."

"Nick, please—"

"You even dismissed the maid, to make sure there would be no witnesses. Going to the summer place wasn't a spur-of-the-moment decision either, was it? You sedated Anna first so that she wouldn't know you had gone out and that later, *after* the murder, you could say you were worried about her unnatural sleepiness, giving you a pretext to carry her at Max's aunt's. But how did you put Max to sleep?"

"Veronal," she answered mechanically. " I put three tablets in his drink."

"Bravo. So he was sleeping soundly when you demonstrated your anatomical knowledge and skill with a carving knife!"

"*Please.* I had no idea he was going to suffer so much."

"You had no idea, but you hoped he would, didn't you? You, who were always so compassionate, who used to take care of wounded birds—"

"I had to kill him. I just had to!"

"Why didn't you simply turn him in to the police?"

"I've already told you that: to protect Annie! You know she's not very well. Her life was never going to be easy, even without complications. What do you think it would have done to her if it came out that she was the daughter of a sadistic psychopath? Can you imagine her in front of the cameras or hounded by a pack of journalists? They would immediately attribute her peculiar behavior and her pale complexion to hereditary insanity! What chance would she have in school? No, I'm not sorry in the least. I'd kill him again, a thousand times, though it was a horrible nightmare, Nick!"

"Yes, but in the midst of your nightmare, you had the presence of mind to spill plenty of my cologne in the hallway outside his bedroom."

"It wasn't deliberate. I felt sick at all that blood—at everything. I ran, felt like I was going to vomit, and tried to put a few drops of cologne on my handkerchief to help me breathe, but I was so dizzy I spilled it."

"That's possible," Nick admitted bitterly, "as is the exact opposite. I don't believe you anymore, Elsa, about anything!"

"Nick, we have no choice but to believe each other and help each other."

"Did you say *we*? What do I have to do with all this dirty business?"

"Maybe nothing, but you'll be hard pressed to prove your innocence if you have to."

"You mean if it gets dangerous for you and you decide to dump it all on my back?"

"No, that's not what I mean."

"Then what do you mean? What? Why do you keep the earring and the lock of hair? Why don't we destroy them together right now?"

Elsa didn't even try to deny that she had taken the lock of hair. She just turned to look out the window. Her eyes glazed over, and her breathing became rapid and irregular, as if she were engaged in an inner battle. Waiting for her to make up her mind, Nick was suddenly smitten by an irrational hope: now their relationship could return to what it had once been, when their love and trust knew no limits. *If she could only convince me that she won't betray me again. I'd do anything for her! Anything! I'd even incriminate myself to cover up her part in all this, if she is threatened by the police.*

But Elsa said, "No, Nick. I'll keep them as a guarantee."

"A guarantee of what?" He didn't even feel disappointed. His maudlin hope was immediately replaced by rancor, as if it had been everything he had needed. "You're afraid I might inform the police unless you have evidence to use against me, but those aren't evidence anyway, Elsa! How would you convince Forger you found the earring and hair in my room?"

"I'd manage," she challenged him. "It won't be that difficult, given the corner you've painted yourself into."

"Yesterday afternoon you made another pot of that herbal *tea* for Anna," Nick changed the subject abruptly. "Not as strong as the first one, maybe, but still strong enough to put her to sleep."

"So what? The herbs don't harm her—just the opposite. They do her a lot of good. I had to go home. How else could I have left her alone if you hadn't come back? She's used to my being around when she's awake."

"I think she's also used to your lies, Sister. Yesterday, for instance, instead of drinking the *tea*, she poured it in this vase,"

Nick informed her, "so I have evidence against you as well. It's in a bottle I can show to Forger if I have to. Your *alibi* with Max's aunt would go straight to hell!"

"Nonsense!" Her scornful laughter was only too genuine. "That 'bottle' of yours is worth nothing, and so are you. You're really pathetic."

"Maybe I am pathetic," he shouted at her, appalled by his own voice, shrill and strident as any hysterical woman's. He coughed and finished his sentence, "But at least I don't go around *cutting* people's throats. It's *you* who's turned Anna into a killer's daughter. Because Max *never killed* anybody!"

"Fine!" She threw back her head. "If you don't believe, let me tell you something else. That Friday when Reno and I were to-gether, he left the house at about three thirty in the morning, and I went out to sit on the porch. Just a little later I *saw* Max sneak back into the house like a criminal, at twenty to four, just after Kathy was murdered! Well?"

The temptation was great: Nick could avenge himself for everything, once and for all could destroy this strange, self-confident woman, "past her prime," who, incredibly, was also his beloved little sister of years long *gone*. She had called him pathetic—quite often over the last few days—lied to him, incriminated him, and threatened him. It would be simple justice to retaliate, but it would also be mean. Yes, even justice had its limits that shouldn't be crossed, because beyond those limits lay only senseless cruelty.

He clamped his lips shut: no, he wouldn't say anything more!

"How mean-spirited you are, really!" she hissed. "You're keeping silent on purpose, just to put some dirty, venomous doubt in my head that I...I killed an innocent man. You cowardly insect—you *talentless scribbler*!"

So he let it out.

"Max really was innocent!" he yelled in a barely recognizable falsetto. "That night he wasn't with Kathy. He went out to meet Reno. *Re-no*, do you hear? Ask him yourself if you don't believe me."

His blow really did strike home—stunning her, crushing her. It defeated her, but far from "once and for all." She recovered quickly, no doubt aided by her deep-seated hatred. Yes, hatred of him. Nick realized with horror that he himself had summoned it, flung it like a boomerang into his sister's heart—where it *hadn't been* till this moment.

Now it was gushing against him from her entire body—her unimaginable, *true* hatred: the hatred of a woman wrested by force from her convictions that she was her child's "savior" and forced finally to see herself as a cold-blooded murderer.

PART THREE

CHAPTER 39

How could they live from now on—or should he ask himself, *How much longer will she let me live?*

Grimacing, Nick gulped down his next cup of coffee with half-closed eyes, like bitter but necessary medicine, and then froze with the empty cup in his hands. It really was bitter.

Just calm down now! When he brewed the pot, Elsa had already left the kitchen. He simply forgot to add sugar. Still, wave after wave of maddening doubt and groundless anxiety washed over him.

He rose and tightened his robe, unnecessarily. As he walked through the living room and out onto the porch, he was already starting to feel sick again. He almost lost his balance as he looked around, so sharp was the contrast between the darkness in his soul and the radiant day that greeted him: bright tinges of green, yellow, golden brown, red, and above it all, the cerulean sky. Fragrances carried on a gentle morning breeze assailed him; birds were singing, bees were humming, and the sun flooded the scene with windfall light.

Nick took a few more uncertain steps and sat on the railing. He felt suffocated. By what? Indignation? Insurrection? How was it possible that he could die and the world would go on unchanged? Birds would still sing, and bees buzz; fragrant breezes would still blow, and the sun shine. It was good that one rarely realized this *universal indifference.*

When the front door shut with a bang, he turned his head. Elsa was leaving for Kathy's funeral, wearing a very tight black silk dress, black shoes, black stockings, a black handbag under her arm, and black pillbox hat on her head. The thick black veil was still up. What coolness! Yesterday afternoon, after she had been interrogated by this sleuth Forger and less than a day since she slit her husband's throat, she remembered to pick out her mourning clothes. Off to the funeral, the hypocritical features of her unrepentant face hidden behind a veil. She would no doubt lift it at the proper moments to make a show of wiping away a nonexistent tear with her lily-white handkerchief.

Anna shuffled along behind, also dressed in darker tones, though she looked funereal even without them. They made their way down the driveway without giving him the smallest sign of recognition. And waiting in front of their car.

He jumped off the railing, ran to the corner of the porch, and leaned out. What he saw was more like a shadow or silhouette than a ghost but was possible to be seen. As they approached, its contours grew distinct. Kaya's lithe figure, but faceless, materialized slowly—from nothingness.

Nick concentrated all his attention on Elsa. Just a few steps away from the wraith, she passed literally by inches, opened the driver's door, and settled in the front seat. Meanwhile, Anna slipped into the backseat, slid over a little—no doubt to make room for Kaya—and shut the door behind her, while Elsa was calmly pulling on her long black gloves. No doubt Kaya was still absolutely invisible and intangible to Elsa.

They drove off—*three killers headed together for the graveyard.*

Ten minutes later, Nick was headed in the same direction, wearing a dark-brown winter suit, though he had other intentions than attending the funeral. What were they? He had tossed his binoculars onto the backseat so that he could observe the funeral from a distance however, convinced that something was about to happen, something terrible. But wasn't it already happening—in his mind—some uncontrollable fermentation process? Everything inside him seethed and surged: notions, ideas, memories, and expectations jumbled together and then reduced to their lowest common denominator. *Do something, Nick! Do some thing!*

I'm not going there just to watch from a distance, he realized. *No, not this time. The terrible thing that will happen will probably be done by me!*

Nevertheless he went on.

He stopped near an old part of the cemetery where visitors rarely came. Cramming the binoculars into his jacket pocket, he left the Ford and looked around. He walked up to the low fence and managed to haul his bulky body over it. As soon as he set foot on the other side, he felt—at home. He had come to this "conveniently close" cemetery so often: *I'll go see Mom on my way into town* or *I'll visit Mom on my way home.* What if it had been on the other side of town, far, far away? His life might have been very different now if he had filled it then with something else.

He shrugged his shoulders hypocritically, impotently. Of what use were such reflections on what might have been? He dusted off his clothes and breathed deeply the familiar heavy smell of *extremely* fertile soil. *Do some thing!*

Supposing there wasn't a living soul around, he scurried past the long-neglected graves near the fence to the newer ones. He grabbed a bunch of flowers that was still relatively fresh and continued far more slowly, his head bowed in what he hoped would pass for respect. Not far from the Hatchers' plot grew a huge old elm tree. He decided to make it his initial vantage point.

Dozens of—dead—"warriors"…

"It's because of the little boy," the survivors will say.

But they won't confront him in anger, for they will have realized that their island has become like any other—quite ordinary. They will hurry to place before this boy their overheated hearts in supplication, so that he can cool them once and for all, so they can go on living, and not by mere chance *as had been their lot during the previous, murderous night. To be sure they have something to cherish and protect, and protect it in the most reliable way: without feelings or thought—by blood instinct alone.*

In accordance with their wishes, within three days the boy will transform all the Sensibles and Sensitives who inhabit the island into Satisfieds—all but that one old man.

Only he *will prefer to stay the same as he was, and he will shower the boy with accusations: "Our* great ocean *could have sucked you under, but he didn't. He permitted you to come to our shores. And you?" The bent, arthritic forefinger will poke at the child's skinny chest. "You, wretched, selfish creature, drain the* ocean *dry and leave us imprisoned in a desert!"*

"What on earth are you talking about?" The boy may be pretending he doesn't understand. "I came to you with my gift to make you happy."

"No! You came here to rob us! You robbed us of our grief for our lost relatives that we have really lost; you took away the pains that taught us how to cure ourselves; you deprived us of the anguish that was the source of all our yearnings and hopes."

"If that was your ocean"—the boy will smile—"I did well to drain it."

"You did well? Now we have no island, no unpredictably changing shores! Even our imaginary birds have deserted us!"

Nick stood with his back against the tree—a gnarled, dark-brown figure protruding like a tumor from the trunk—and waited.

The funeral procession would certainly come up that path on the left, but when would they get here? They were probably still at the service, making last-minute decision about who would bear the coffin and other *final* things needed to transport that masterfully patched corpse of the woman he had imagined he was in love with, at least for half a day and half a night. Now she didn't interest him at all. He hadn't come here for her, wasn't going to throw a ritual handful of dust on her coffin, or go through the motions of placing flowers by her freshly dug grave—unless he had to.

They were coming! "Procession" was too strong a word for the ragtag group of roughly twenty people trudging more lazily than sadly behind the coffin, which swayed slightly over the pallbearers, shaking their shoulders slightly, but disgustingly, considering that the body inside was shaking too.

He squinted through the binoculars. So Forger wasn't among the "mourners." In his stead were his two puppets, Randy and Jack. Like apes in dark suits, they stuck out from the others, scowling suspiciously at the people in front of them, but they hardly expected the killer to be among them. But he—or rather she—*they* were right there: the woman with the tight silk skirt, the black veil covering her face; the gaunt girl beside her absorbed in thought, and a ghostly figure that—no, Nick couldn't see it but felt certain Kaya was there, hovering around the dead woman!

The group moved as if they were walking under water. Despite the presence of the murderers, everything seemed somehow sleepy, quiet, and peaceful. Was is really possible something could happen at a funeral? Especially "something terrible"—besides what was sealed in the coffin? What more?

Nick felt briefly tempted to turn around and go home. He threw down the flowers he was holding and began walking toward the exit, but when he reached the tombstone next to Edward Hatcher's, he swerved automatically, as if following a command, and hid behind it.

Finally the joyless procession floated up to the freshly dug grave, the moist earth piled beside it appropriately very black. The bearers took the coffin off their shoulders in perfect unison, set it on the grass across from the black mound, and simultaneously stepped back as the mourners gathered quietly around it.

Elsa was clutching her handkerchief, and her posture revealed her poorly controlled inner tension: at the priest's first words, she would launch into heartrending sobs. "The noble widow"! Only a day after losing her beloved husband, she could still find it in her sensitive soul to mourn her unfortunate friend classmate so deeply!

The priest started his annoyingly repetitive intonations, Elsa sobbed on cue, and an old disheveled crow quickly stepped up to comfort her. Letting go of Anna's hand, Elsa hugged the old woman, who immediately joined the mourners' chorus. What a tawdry farce!

The two women grew blurry, so Nick set the binoculars on his knee, puzzled that he had to blink a couple of times. Then he realized that his eyes had blurred with tears. Damn! He would give anything to really know what these unexpected tears were for, or for whom? Resting his forehead on the cool marble gravestone beneath which lay moldering human bones, he groped his way to the answer: he was crying for himself, because it's desolate and terrible to see only farce elements in a funeral!

He sniffled a little sullenly and then resumed his vigil. Aha! He had almost missed Anna taking advantage of her mother's martyrdom to sneak away. He watched her run down a path between the graves until she was out of sight.

Nick fidgeted uneasily. If he left his hiding place, he could be immediately spotted, especially by Randy and Jack with their habit of turning their eyes in every direction. But he had to take the risk. *Now or never.* He crept to the next grave, ducking behind it, and then to the next. Imagining the picture he made, huffing and puffing in the damp grass, cold sweat broke out on his forehead. How *low* he was, both literally and figuratively.

When he finally reached the shrubbery that lined the path, he stretched out and took a breath, but Anna was nowhere to be seen.

"I lost her," he gasped in disappointment.

At that moment he saw her; she had stopped by the fountain. Was it no more than that? Had the child simply grown thirsty, gone for a drink and would then return to her mother? No! She started off again, increasing her speed. Nick leaped across the path and crept between the graves. Reaching the fountain, he peeped through his binoculars—and saw exactly what he expected to see.

Next to Anna the Vampire-Child—*maybe*—the ghostly but ever more substantial figure of Kaya.

He followed them, squatting and scurrying by turns, keeping a safe distance. The two friends stopped by a grave just right of the path. Perhaps one of their victims lay there! Not the two sisters—it was a single grave—or the old man, because he had been buried at the other end of the cemetery. As Schumacher and Mayer were still in the morgue, that left only the teacher, Emil Jonas. Why had they chosen him?

As Anna stooped over the grave, Kaya bent over her, actually veiling her head. Anna's hair and face only appeared as a slightly darker oval form through Kaya's bluish-gray breasts—like a huge, inert heart. Then Kaya grew more substantial, so that shadow "heart" disappeared. Now Anna seemed *headless*! The shoulders went next. Ah! The ghost seemed to be swallowing her!

Snarling with horror, Nick jumped to his feet but lay down again. What nonsense, nonsense! Anna was intact, more whole than he was. The angle of his vision had simply deluded him.

They stood up, said something to each other, and stepped up to the tombstone, where they bent over again, their figures merging. Disgusting! Merging an immaterial and a material body? Some kind of exchange—maybe parasitism—had taken place between them, in the presence of the dead man below them. With the *help* of the dead man?

Trembling with almost pathological excitement, Nick crept closer. The binocular lenses had fogged over, so he wiped them impatiently with his jacket sleeve. Tiny brown filaments stuck to them. He wiped them with his handkerchief and then looked again.

They were looking closely at the picture behind a glass that had been inserted into the tombstone. Nick was suddenly seized with a pang of jealousy as he squatted in the grass. It's clear; Kaya was in love with Emil Jonas! She must have killed him without realizing what she was doing—obeying Vampire-Child's orders? Jonas had taught literature; perhaps he recited poems, and she—wait! How could he be jealous toward a ghost because of a dead, slaughtered man?

Nick shook his head and ran his fingers through his hair. *I don't understand anything*, he admitted to himself despairingly.

I don't understand myself! That damned vampire has sucked my understanding—but which one is the vampire?

As Kaya and Anna walked away, he hunkered down until they reached the end of the path, then stashed the binoculars in his coat pocket, and still crouching, ran toward the grave.

It was a picture of Alina Norris. Below it, strewn like a livid shroud, lay the chrysanthemums—the same purplish yellow chrysanthemums that had been blooming in their yard since his mother had planted them.

CHAPTER 40

When Nick overtook Anna, she was just passing the fountain. Was she alone or could he no longer see the ghost? It didn't matter! He put his hand on her shoulder, but it didn't startle or surprise her. Obviously she had heard somebody lumbering after her but simply hadn't bothered to look back. Nerves of steel! Or nerves of a hardened killer certain she would never be caught.

"Come with me," Nick panted, still trying to catch his breath, doing his best to look calm and friendly, even playful. "I want to show you something really interesting. I know you'll like it."

He led her toward the oldest part of the cemetery, where he knew a place to question her—well, more aggressively. Anna offered no objections and walked beside him as silently as ever, her face an inscrutable mask.

Nick looked stealthily around. She had sneaked away about fifteen minutes ago; strange that no one had come looking for her yet. Surely the instant his sister discovered that her precious Annie wasn't close at hand, she would scream to God and raise the dead, so to speak; yet nothing but silence had come from that quarter. Had Elsa so forgotten herself in her false show of grief that she hadn't noticed Anna's absence? Not possible!

"Have you made some arrangement—with your mother?" *If your uncle shows up, dear, kill him with your ghost.* "Your mother probably knows—some things? She guesses a thing or two about you, eh?"

Anna ignored him. *I'll teach you both! And stop shambling! I've seen you run, you little brat!* He was already out of patience and lifted her roughly. She was so light he could almost feel her bones sag in his hands as her gaunt, but surprisingly warm, arm slowly settled around his neck, his fat, sweaty ox's neck. He was suddenly assaulted by both shame (*What am I doing? What am I going to do?*) and despair (*No, this child is sick!*). This was the first time he had ever held her in his arms—his niece! He had always avoided even touching her. A strange, unknown emotion overtook him.

"You must be hot in those heavy, dark clothes. I'm feeling hot too. Why don't we find your mom and go home? A little girl like you shouldn't have to go to funerals anyway. What do you say we jump in the car, go home, and have a coke? Then we can change our clothes and head for the lake for a swim!"

She continued to stare straight ahead, her profile still as a skull with a leather mask pulled tightly across it, the whites of her eyes chips of mica riddled with fissures.

"You have to answer me. Do you hear me, Anna? Annie—sweetheart, you must answer me, please! It's very important that you answer me."

She didn't even blink, wasn't moving, wasn't—functioning!

"Where are you, Anna, in the other world *again*? Are you ordering the next murder? Aladdin's lamp, eh—obedient ghost, vampire-slave? Am I the next wretch? I *am* a wretch, a real wretch!"

He broke into a run, his feet crunching on the gravel as if chewing it—predators! Anna's head lolled on her scrawny neck, now striking his temple, now hitting his cheek. Her fingers pulled at his hair, but the corners of her mouth seemed briefly to curve upward into the shadow of a smile.

The path narrowed and became more grassy among a decrepit jumble of tombstones. No orderly rows here; time itself seemed to have gradually dispersed them like a slow, relentless river scatters massive boulders.

Still carrying his niece in his arms, Nick reached the remotest end of the cemetery and crept between a briar bush and a tuft of nettle to exit into a small glade. He stopped and looked around: a secluded place, damp and rank, funky with toadstools, mold, and old, hollow-boned, shallow-buried death. He came near a headstone covered with dirty green moss, opened his "embrace," and set Anna down. She stood up, not moving a muscle, as if he had stuck her in the ground.

"Where's Kaya?" he asked, attaching to his face an expression suitable for "the good uncle." "Is Kaya somewhere around now?"

When Anna looked over his shoulder, he immediately followed her glance. Yes, Kaya was nearby, and she looked—bad. Her figure, barely visible against the bush behind her, was flat and colorless, as if she had been cut out of crumpled cellophane. A step away from her lay a rotten wooden cross—the only sign that, long ago, somebody had been buried there.

"Kaya! Poor, unburied creature," Nick exclaimed. "How strange that I didn't understand you until now!" He hit himself on the forehead. "Our oldest tales say the unburied dead are doomed to walk the earth. So it's true!"

He bent toward the almost empty space. "Forgive me, my darling. You really died that January night, didn't you? In such a hurry to find help for your dying mother, you ran down the icy street to meet the ambulance, and some car must have hit you. Maybe the driver was a drunken coward who hid your body somewhere—but where? Help me find it, my darling. I'll give you a proper burial, I promise."

I've gone too far! He suddenly realized and lowered his eyes. *"Give you a proper burial"—is that the way to talk to a young dead girl?*

"Yes, I promise to take care of you. Or is it already too late for that? Maybe this demonic child, once she took possession of your spirit, won't let it—"

He pulled Anna close and, choking with rage, whispered in her ear, "I know everything! You *made* her drive my car to Mayer's and told her to tie Kathy up with that nylon cord. It was your idea that she should tear Kathy's earring off and leave it on my nightstand—all to put the blame on me!"

Anna rose on her tiptoes and then, little by little, crept—into his lap. So he had finally managed to get her attention! Now that he had it, would she try to kill him, here? Her ghostly accomplice was open to her telepathic orders. No, he was safe for the moment. Kaya always drugged her victims first. Obviously she didn't have enough strength to overpower them.

"You got her to tell you about her friends and relatives," he hissed, "and then sent her to kill them. But a year ago, you killed without her help, didn't you? I remember hearing that some baby was stolen from its stroller. You stole it! You cut off its ear, tore it apart, and then buried it under the cypress tree. Oh, I know, I know—everything!"

Kaya had approached them—of course imperceptibly. She wanted to hear what he was saying, or—he raised his voice, "Now tell me right now. Where is the girl's dead body? She must have her rest at last. She's suffered so terribly."

Damn it! He had never heard a more unctuous and servile voice than his right now. Kaya would think he was—a nincompoop!

Shoving Anna away, he stood up—sweating in his woolen suit, his stupid face flushed red, his ragged hair so thin. He ran his fingers through it as if carelessly and said casually, "I wondered yesterday why you picked all those chrysanthemums, Kaya. Today I learned with respect that they were for your mother's grave!" He eased closer to her. "Both you and I have lost the one we loved most in this world, dear." He moved closer still. "We both grieve for them."

If he could take her in his arms, she could judge for herself whether he was a nincompoop or not! Nick grabbed at the knot on his wide, old-fashioned tie to loosen it and threw open his arms to Kaya, but she was still a step away. Though he moved forward again, the distance remained the same. Slender, not flat, she wasn't made of mist but of *living* matter, something that could *breathe*. She had no face but radiated a *presence*: her figure grew more solid and turned bluish gold, with a darker tinge all around her head— her hair! Then it faded and reappeared, distinct but vibrating.

I'm going crazy, he realized. *No one could endure all this.*

"Kaya, why, why do you flee from me?" He followed after her, his arms still outstretched, his fingers clenching and unclenching, convulsively attempting to reach her. They resembled the talons of a vulture, but he couldn't stop—had lost all control of his actions.

When she reached the briar bush, Kaya swerved slightly— if she were a ghost, she would have simply passed through it, right?—and briefly revealed her profile, her arms reaching out to him as well! So she wasn't running away willingly. Even more: she also wanted to touch *him*, but every time the distance between them reached some critical point, some irresistible force pushed her away.

Nick swung around to Anna. Her eyes were open wide and had grown very dark. They were fixed on Kaya like two cupping glasses. There lay the force!

"Anna, let her go, release her," he croaked.

Give her to me was what he meant! He would have to take control of her by force if Anna refused. But how—by forcing Anna to tell him how she had gained control over Kaya? Absurd! She probably didn't know herself. They had met—Anna, who had always had one foot in the grave since her birth, and Kaya, who had one foot out of the grave since her death. Yes, they had met there, in that no man's land between life and death.

Sardonic laughter welled up inside him, almost choking him, but he somehow managed to stifle it. This situation was far from funny. *Now concentrate!* Had he simply invented another untalented tale, or did he really believe these speculations? The key to all this could be in the answer to that question, which eluded him. Was Anna controlling him as well? She was staring at him through those impenetrable cupping glasses. Her ludicrously long, dark-blue dress seemed to be turning dark gray: everything on her and around her suddenly looked gray, even her braids, thinner than his little finger. What braids her mother once had—wonderfully thick and shiny. "And your grandmother!" he exclaimed. "Her hair was so thick it sometimes made her tilt her head just to bear its weight! But you…you." *I can't stand it anymore. I can't stand the sight of her!*

As he moved toward her, she took a few steps toward him. They stopped directly opposite each other. She threw her head back, tore her gaze away, and fixed it just above his head, as if she were standing at the foot of a mountain trying to see its top.

"Stop that! Talk to me! Say anything, I don't care what! Sing!"

Why would she not sing when she is the one who could make Kaya visible, talk to her, even touch her? "I'm going to set you free, Kaya!" he called to the trembling apparition hovering over the tombstone—a spectator. "I'll set you free once and for all! I'll break this Aladdin's lamp," he promised, pointing at Anna.

Laughter rose up in him again, like bile, and this time he couldn't suppress it. "Ha-ha-ha! You inhuman child, *you* made her revise my tale—just to mock me, insult me!"

Still watching the "mountaintop," Anna seemed to see something stormy and scary that made her turn away. She tripped over the wooden cross, fell flat on her back, and her funeral dress flew up, revealing her legs. The protruding knees suddenly reminded him of Max's bony Adam's apple, twitching up and down his slit throat.

Stop! he ordered himself as he squatted beside her. She groaned weakly.

If you can't sing, I want you to scream. Yes, scream! Her livid lips curved down into a little arch above her chin as she whimpered, but he wanted more. *You pitiable little mongrel! How would it feel to tear out that heart neither living nor dead? Will you still scratch then?*

Nick looked down at his fingers with resignation. Yes, they were indeed vulture's claws. What could he do? There was no escape.

As he felt her soft girl's ribs on the *left* side, he wondered, *Is this all real?*

CHAPTER 41

Something hard and cold pressed against his temple. The muzzle of a gun. With hysterical relief, he took his hands off the child. What now? Let them shoot! Then everything would finally be over.

Still kneeling, Nick turned suddenly and grabbed a hairy wrist. He pulled it hard and heard the click as the finger pulled the trigger. No shot. Just a hollow click. Then he dragged—Forger, of course—to the ground. Nick raised his hand and struck him in the face. The blood ran from his nose. *Blood. I'm finally shedding someone's blood!*

"Why?" Nick yelled at the bug-eyed, blood-spattered mug. "Why don't you load your gun?" He caught Forger's navy-blue, button-down shirt by the collar and, with one yank, ripped off all the buttons, exposing his chest. He was naked under it. The heart, the heart. "You, dirty lying bastard, with an empty gun!" Nick dug his nails into Forger's chest.

He loved this man, this dim-witted flatfoot, who probably for the first time had arrived on time. On time, but not for himself! Nick sank his fingers in even more deeply. This wasn't like trying to tear out the tiny heart of a little girl. *She's my niece! Thanks for saving her from me! Let her slit anybody's throat; I don't care!*

As Forger flailed under the massive bulk, Nick held the detective's head with his left hand and with his right kept digging deeper and deeper.

Until Anna screamed—*at last!* He felt a sharp blow to the back of the head—maybe a stone. *Where am I falling? Why is it suddenly so dark, pitch dark?*

When he came to, he was lying on his back between tall nettles and Forger's and Randy's legs. Anna was crying over him and wiping his forehead with a handkerchief.

"Dear child! I'm OK now, darling. Don't cry anymore." He extended his hand to stroke her cheek—rather, the hollow above her cheek bone. Those sunken spaces could hardly be called "cheeks."

There I go again! What force robbed him of his humanity—his ability to sympathize with others? Had he lost the generosity to *forgive* his closest friends for their misery and the courage to reconcile with his own?

He leaned on his elbow and looked around for Kaya but saw no sign of her. "I'll bet she was here," he whispered conspiringly to Anna, "only I don't see her now."

He staggered to his feet and started straightening his torn clothes. Forger and Randy were watching him warily, finally showing him some respect. "I was going to kill you, Lieutenant," Nick told Forger bluntly. "You owe your life to your man, don't forget!" Feeling the back of his head, he winked at Randy. "You hit me just right, boy. Any harder probably would have fractured my skull. I won't forget you! I owe you a case of beer. Or maybe you'd prefer something stronger?"

"No, beer's OK," Randy growled, astonished.

Forger scowled at him as he took off his shirt and, after making certain it was ripped beyond repair, wiped his face with it.

Then he inspected his chest, where the wound proved shallow. Disappointingly shallow for Nick.

"Hand me my coat!" Forger ordered Randy. He put the long, loose coat over his naked body, crumpled his shirt into a ball, and maliciously flung it into the nettles. Then he turned and suddenly thrust his hand into Nick's coat pocket. He fished out the binoculars and shook them in Nick's face. "Let's go!"

They paraded around the briar bush: first Nick, then Randy, and then Forger, who held Anna's hand. "Why did your uncle bring you here?" he asked her. "Did you meet that girl, Kaya? Or is she dead? Did he really say that he wanted to bury her if you would show him where her body is?"

Nick smiled. Forger had heard their whole conversation but, naturally, hadn't understood any of it, and his efforts to get information from Anna were almost touching!

"Why did you go to Alina Norris's grave?" Forger just wouldn't give up. "Who brought the flowers there? They're from your garden, aren't they? And why was your uncle acting as if you were with somebody else? Who—or what—was he chasing?"

"We were playing." Anna actually responded!

The surprise was just too much for Nick. He stopped on the spot, and Randy shoved him in the back.

"Get moving, Edgeway," he barked, but not viciously.

Nick, however, waited for Forger and Anna to catch up. "No need to pester my niece, Lieutenant. It's all very simple. I was telling her a fairy tale.

"Quite a scary fairy tale—unburied dead, the 'other world' and such!"

"Unfortunately, you'd be hard pressed to hold a child's attention with pretty princesses these days, Lieutenant, because of all the horror films."

"Well, Edgeway, you might compete with them successfully," Forger remarked sarcastically. "For instance, when you shouted, 'Ha-ha-ha! You inhuman child, you made her revise my tale!' I must admit it even gave me the creeps for some reason."

"I'm glad you appreciate my acting skills."

"We'll discuss that later, *in your cell.*"

"Will you carry me again, Uncle Nick?" Anna suddenly asked.

Surprised more by her question than by Forger's remark, Nick mechanically lifted her. She wrapped her arms around his neck with a proprietary hug. No, he wasn't imagining it: this time those lips really did curve up in a smile. *Dear Lord, what am I carrying—a sphinx or a child? Or my imminent death?*

When they reached the fountain, Forger told him to release Anna and nodded to Randy. "Cuff him."

With cool indifference, Nick extended his hands. Who hasn't seen it done a thousand times in films? It took no more than five seconds, crowned with the characteristic click of the tumblers.

Then Forger splashed his face profusely in the fountain. "Now take the child back to her mother." He snorted at Randy and shoved Nick all the way to the main gate.

CHAPTER 42

At the police station, Nick was immediately frog-marched by two uniformed guards to a basement cell, where they removed his handcuffs and locked him in. He slumped onto the narrow bunk, completely isolated by the graffiti-covered walls and realizing with satisfaction that he felt safe for the first time in a week. He yawned and checked his watch: almost half past twelve, time for lunch. Since he wasn't at all hungry, he lay down, his arm beneath his stubble cheek, and fell asleep instantly.

They woke him at two o'clock and led him back upstairs to Forger's office. Forger had changed to a snow-white shirt and glanced up with an absorbed expression on his face. The swelling around his nose was less, probably thanks to an ice pack, so Forger seemed to have regained his dignity.

But how could he regain something he never had in the first place?

"Now what shall I do with you, Edgeway?" Forger spread his hands. "Book you for aggravated assault or send you to a psychiatrist?"

Facing him across his cluttered desk, Nick shot back, "An interesting coincidence—I was asking myself the same question about you, Lieutenant. After all, you sneaked up on me and put a gun to my head."

"What should I have done—let you murder your niece?"

"You just helped me decide: send you to a psychiatrist. Why in the world would I want to kill my own niece?"

"There's no point denying it, Edgeway. I saw the whole thing."

"What you saw was her trip and fall and me bend over her to make sure she wasn't hurt before picking her up."

"If that's what you were doing, how do you account for your *beastly* expression?"

"Ha! How did you expect me to look with a gun at my head—like a lamb? What's more, the moment I saw *your* beastly face, Lieutenant, do you know what flashed across my mind?"

"What?"

"That *you* probably committed all these brutal murders."

Purple rage spread on Forger's face, complementing his bruises and swollen nose. "You...are," he stammered, "you're arrogant!"

"You call me arrogant for protecting my niece? Do you?"

"Protecting! In fact, you kidnapped her! Listen Edgeway, I followed you from the time you left home—saw you jump the cemetery fence and hide there, looking through your binoculars, stalking—"

"Of course I was hiding. I hoped the killer would show up at the funeral, that I would recognize him by his behavior, so I wanted to observe those present without them knowing it. Then I saw Anna leaving, so I followed her, concerned for her safety."

"Why did she go to Alina Norris's grave?"

"She didn't tell me why, but you can ask her again."

"But you made no effort to return her to her mother. You led her—actually carried her—into the shrubs at the far end of the cemetery."

"I sensed that the funeral had upset her. I wanted to take her mind off it."

"By telling her all sorts of ghoulish tales and making horrible faces at her?"

"Why not? What could get her attention more quickly? The poor child knows how her father died and is clearly in a state of shock. I had to do something drastic to distract her from that."

"Who do you think you are, Edgeway—one of the Grimm Brothers? Your sister would have gone out of her mind with worry if we hadn't told her that Anna was with you and that we were keeping an eye on you."

"Good for you! You did at least one good deed."

"How sick and tired I am of you!" the lieutenant exploded, which seemed to calm him. He continued less belligerently, in an almost friendly tone, "I think you're abnormal, Edgeway. Yes, you are, in some weird way all your own."

"It depends on what you accept as normal."

"For example, you realized that your Seconal was a very old prescription and forensics could identify exactly those pills as the ones used to drug Eric Schumacher, so you sensibly tossed them. But why in God's name did you keep the *bottle* and fill it with vitamins?"

"Vitamins?" Nick echoed, then swiftly leaned forward, his elbows on Forger's desk. Amazement, relief, and even ecstatic exhilaration flew through him like flocks of birds, setting his head spinning. Then comprehension slowly came: Kaya must have switched the pills, as early as when the cops first searched his place. She must have seen Randy and Jack put the bottle aside as evidence and, since it couldn't just disappear, had substituted vitamins. Clearly she didn't want to implicate him in the murders, because she really cared about him! But then...

Jesus! If she remembered doping Eric with Nick's Seconal, she had not murdered in a state of hypnotic oblivion.

"Come on, Edgeway, explain!"

"What? What do want explained? Oh, the Seconal. Well, the Seconal ran out long ago, so I used the bottle for vitamins instead."

"Oh, really? I'm going to nail you, despite all your clever lies and beating around the bush, because I already know there are *two of you*. And you two invariably use the same—psychopathic MO. She made a fatal mistake by leaving her fingerprints on your steering wheel. We're going to trace those prints and then—"

Forger was interrupted by a phone ringing. "Yes?—who?—no, I don't want him here!—what?—all right, but you bring it." Hanging up, he wearily turned toward the window. "That's how I work," he finally said, overcome by self-pity. "I toil and drudge like a packhorse, barely have time to eat on duty, don't sleep, and they accuse me of—shirking!"

"Well, not eating or sleeping enough are not actions, Forger. Maybe your superiors also expect results."

"Sure, but the minute I lay hands on an extremely likely suspect," Forger argued, turning back to Nick, "up pop meddlesome, insolent lawyers, tearful sisters, idiot reporters—all hollering about legal rights. Yes, Edgeway, your lawyer's here, and your sister's been waiting for an hour downstairs. Also, we gave her your suit and shirt."

"Which were always free of blood stains, a fact that must have caused you profound regret."

"That's simply more confirmation that your mind's as disturbed as a muddy ditch after a herd of horses galloped through it. I can't imagine why you'd take the trouble to hide them and then go out of your way to turn them in to us. Do you know what I'm going to do with you right now?"

"What?"

"Get rid of you! I'm going to let you go home."

A spic-and-span duty guard came into the office, handed a newspaper to Forger, and snickered. "He says the editorial will catch your eye, chief." Then he about-faced and marched out.

Forger unfolded the newspaper, bored, but one look at the headlines brought a look of both amazement and pain, as if he had a sudden toothache. He started reading, ignoring Nick.

"That's how much you work!" Nick accused him impatiently. "Why not just turn to the crossword and send for coffee and doughnuts."

"Shut up!" Forger shook the front page of the *Express* in Nick's face. The headline of the editorial section announced in all caps: "RENOWNED LAWYER RENALDO ALDANO SHOWS LIEUTENANT FORGER THE WAY."

"What's this...this...bullshit, Edgeway!"

"How would I know?"

"Who's Andrey Belloff?"

"You're the one reading the paper," Nick snapped, "and you're asking me?"

"But is it true that—? Oh, just get the hell out of here!" The enraged lieutenant signed Nick's release form with a sweeping gesture and shoved it across the desk, along with the binoculars. "Out you go!"

Nick hung the binoculars around his neck, took the pass, and began to rise, but Forger stopped him.

"Wait! That girl who vanished without a trace—"

"She's not just some girl. She's very special and must also be very, very unhappy—I suppose."

"If she's unhappy she must be alive," Forger concluded logically, "so why were you rattling on about burying her earlier today?"

"Can't the dead be unhappy?" Nick parried.

"Try to answer me in a normal way for a change! Have you ever met the young woman? Do you know her?"

"Yes, I've met her, but I don't know her personally. But—"

"OK, is she dead or alive now?"

"I'd like to know that myself. As I told you, she's very special."

"Go on, get out of here!" Forger's face was sporting a new crop of purple blotches.

"How can you speak of *my* psychological problems?" Nick threw at Forger as he left. "Look at yourself and consider how *you* behave!"

CHAPTER 43

In the foyer, sitting at a discreet distance from Anna, Reno and Elsa were waiting for him. Their heads almost touching as they whispered—the rich widow and her lawyer, the murderer and her lover!

Nick signaled for them to stay seated as he hurried up to them and then surreptitiously took the binoculars off his neck and dropped them into Elsa's lap. "Take them apart, but discreetly!" he whispered, barely moving his lips. "There's a note inside."

They gaped at him for a moment. "But Nick," Reno started to say.

"Not now, Reno! We'll talk about it later!"

"But what?"

"Everything is written there. Leave the building exactly ten minutes after me. I'll wait in the Toyota. Where did you park it?"

"On the second level of the parking garage," Reno whispered back. *Idiot!*

"OK! Elsa, give me the keys, but make sure nobody sees you!"

She took them from her purse, looked around, and warily slipped them into his hand along with the parking ticket. *Idiot!*

Nick gave Anna a sly wink and sauntered confidently to the exit. He gave his pass to the policeman on duty, who opened the door for him, and went out. A few minutes later, he was pressing on the gas pedal, bent over the steering wheel the Toyota as if expecting to be ambushed.

They were concerned with his legal rights? Fat chance. Elsa had engineered his release because she was afraid—terrified—that he might turn her in at any moment. It wouldn't surprise him if she had shared some things—even everything—with Reno. In that case, they'll kill him together and bury the body. "SERIAL KILLER RELEASED BY MISTAKE NOW IN HIDING" would be Reno's next "engineered" headline! They're both efficient, aggressive; they'd never miss such a perfect opportunity. Good thing he had got away from them!

Nick drove aimlessly around town, his mind racing, trying to figure a way out. Escape? He had given them the slip, but for how long? He would have to go home sooner or later, and they would be waiting for him. Then their worries would be over. While his wanted poster faded in the post offices and police stations, they would be living a life of luxury, free of him and Max. Unless...

The idea dawned on him gloriously: magnificent, efficient, and simplicity itself. He turned back, drove downtown, and parked in front of an electronics store. A few minutes later, he had what he needed: a remote-controlled audio recorder and a miniature microphone.

CHAPTER 44

Nick drove immediately to Max's house—rather Elsa's house—and slammed on the brakes at the main gate, not caring if a neighbor or policeman saw him. Ironically, he feared only his sister and his closest friend right now, and they would never dare show their faces here, not today, not while they were looking for him!

Finding a shovel in the shed behind the garage, he went to "the most beautiful" cypress tree, quickly located the stone beneath, kicked it aside, and started uncovering the grave. Anna hadn't bothered to bury her victim deep. The chest, really just a narrow cardboard box, came up with little difficulty, already rotting and just big enough for a newborn baby! Besides...

Was he just imagining it, or was that really the rank odor of decaying flesh? He put his hand over his mouth and stepped back, as the lawn beneath him began to spin—on this day lavish with sun and colors.

No, Nick, don't lift the lid off that hellish box! Whatever he saw there would become a part of him—whenever he looked at a baby, whenever he passed a cypress tree and saw the grass lit by the sun. It would trouble his sleep and startle him awake in the dead of night—this thing he still might not look at.

Don't let it enter your soul!

Nick threw down the shovel, rolled up his sleeves, and lifted the lid. It drooped in his hand like a damp, rotten cloth. Yes, something definitely lay inside the box—gray and fuzzy. But it wasn't—was almost—nothing. He nudged it gingerly with his shoe. The head lolled toward him with its cut ear and red, glassy eyes.

Just a "punished" stuffed bunny.

CHAPTER 45

Nick slept badly, but at least he was safe: in a secluded place near the lake, locked in his sister's Toyota, almost as isolated as in that jail cell. His winter suit was an advantage now, keeping him warm. He woke up feeling somewhat rested and convinced that he had finally hit upon the truth—but didn't want to think about it yet.

He took a walk around the lake, but this time he couldn't feel the purifying sense of its crystal, early-morning beauty. He needed to *act*, not to lose himself in contemplation, so he hurried back to the Toyota and drove home.

He parked in front of the garage, put the box containing the audio recorder and microphone under his arm, and accompanied by the ever importunate Biff, hurried to the front door. He was worried that Elsa might have bolted the door from the inside but not so. He quietly went up to his bedroom, where he unpacked the recorder, set it, and hid it under the bed. It would start recording automatically as soon as the microphone picked up the first words of the conversation he had been rehearsing since yesterday. Then he took a shower, shaved carefully, and put on lightweight clothing, feeling much more confident.

But where was Kaya?

Let's not divert! It's time!

Cradling the tiny microphone, he resolutely walked down the hall to his murderous sister's room, to wheedle some kind of confession out of her as to how she had killed Max, while recording every word. Then he would make a copy of the recording and play it back to her, telling her that he had given the original to an attorney with the request that it be handed over to the district attorney if anything should happen to him. That should be more than enough to keep her from harming him. Instead, she would protect him, sacrifice everything to preserve his precious life!

Carried away with the favorable prospect, Nick grinned slyly and entered without knocking. Elsa was asleep, but Anna was wide awake, with Kaya sitting beside her. Good! The girl was here, at home. Nick propped his back against the door, half-closing his eyes to better make out her dim outlines. Filling them in, he could almost compose her as he chose by now. *Interesting*, he thought. *The less visible she is, the more attractive she becomes. So it must be the details in life that put people off.*

"Yes, interesting," he repeated, whispering. "Even very interesting."

He went to the window, as if to close the curtain, and clipped the microphone to it. *Now, Sister, wake up and talk!* But how she could sleep so deeply, as though she were righteous? So much for moralists who consider a guilty conscience a living hell. If that were so, Elsa would already have baked her soul. Instead, at ten o'clock in the morning, she was sleeping and sleeping.

Nick's gaze wandered to the empty glass on the nightstand. As had their mother, Elsa always drank her "morning beauty tea" before she got up. She would put a sachet of herbs in a cup to soak the night before—Nick noticed last night's sachet in the saucer and greenish drops on the bottom of the cup, still not dry. She must have awakened an hour or so earlier, drunk her tea, and gone back to sleep.

"Elsa," he whispered, then again, louder, his voice strangely quavering. "Elsa? Elli!"

No use. She didn't hear or move—just kept sleeping.

Some unconscious impulse made him bend over to study her face *in detail*. The pallid skin was swollen with sleep, her pores were sweaty and enlarged—could that possibly be her guilty conscience burning her from inside? The whites of her eyes, visible below her slightly open eyelids, were soiled pink, and strands of matted hair stuck to her damp forehead. Nick noticed as well the clearly discernible wrinkles around her mouth, her slack lower jaw, and the sagging flesh beneath her chin.

"Elsa."

A woman who had lost something of herself.

He had often watched her sleep before. Of course, after she married, he had the opportunity only when she took afternoon "naps" on his living room sofa. Then he would stand lost in admiration at the vitality—or *resistance*, as he called it—radiating from her face and body even in sleep. But now, yes, that is what was missing! Without it, Elsa looked ordinary and boring. Useless.

He straightened up, feeling somehow robbed by that tamed, unresistingly sleeping woman. Besides, she had really started to hate him. And why? Because he told her truthfully that she had killed an innocent man. Now their relationship will never be the same. After a day or two, she'll go back to *her* home, to resume her nightly assignations with *her* lover, and take *her* child with her.

"Annie," he offered, "go wash your face and brush your teeth, dear, and as soon as you're dressed, we'll have breakfast at a wonderful little café I know."

And the child—a miracle!—went to the bathroom willingly, as if she were happy. She must want to be with him—though, of course, she would forget him as soon as her mother took her away, and they would never come back. Then what would he do? He would be more lonesome than ever! Day after day.

He felt a presence behind him and turned around. *Kaya, Kaya, you're my closest friend, without even a human face.*

But no, now Kaya was gone—sunk without a trace into *her* own, invisible world. Was that because Anna, her "silhouette-donor," had just left the room? And when Elsa takes Anna away for good—if that happens?

Nick peered inquiringly at the *near nothing* in front of him. "Tell me, dear Kaya," he whispered quietly, "what must I do to be able to…to see you?"

Suddenly he felt the force of her gaze grow more tangible, her answer pierce his mind like a ghostly arrow—since it was his answer, his decision, too. He involuntary touched the cup with drying greenish drops on the bottom.

He realized that Anna had come back, not only by the quiet sound of the door shutting but also because the air in front of him was already thickening, taking on the shape of a girl's figure, which then grew almost solid, swaying to and fro—faster and faster. She writhed as if in the throes of an exquisite sensual delight. Her chimerical arms moved strangely—perhaps invitingly?—brushing his face like a gentle breeze carrying promises, caresses. Caresses that could kill *solitude*? Nick set out for them, his hot breath probably another broken, burning caress.

Kaya moved back, not to run away but because she wanted to press against the wall. Clever! There the diabolical force that separated them couldn't force her any farther away—yes, only a step separated them! But when he tried to cover that distance, he felt a *brutal* blow to his chest. Kaya hadn't moved, so?

Gasping with pain and rage, Nick turned ferociously toward Anna, but she wasn't even looking at them as she dressed at the other end of the room. *Am I going to blame the poor child again?* He was startled. *This is a spellbound circle!*

"Come on, Annie!" he said invitingly, his hand over his chest. The pain seemed concentrated in his heart, but was it of the body—or the soul? "Hurry up, sweetheart!"

The figure in the corner fidgeted uneasily, clearly discontented and radiating a *fleshed presence.*

"I'm sorry, Kaya," he said, against his will. "It's not my fault. It hurts, but I'll try again soon, tonight. The important thing is we want to be together, and I want to see you, right?" *Oh God, only a madman would say such things. I have to stop this, to shut up! Why am I not asking what this creature is? What has she done, and what is she going to do? Do I really know anything?*

Something cool grasped his hand. Anna. Annie! "Have you washed with cold water?" he babbled as he led her toward the door, doing his best not to look at Elsa, though his desire to do so was almost irresistible. There was absolutely no reason to seal her jaded image in his memory, though what he was worried about? She was just sleeping, simply exhausted after all the monstrosities that befell her—or, rather, that she had committed—recently. *Especially those she committed against me! Let her sleep then.*

When he and Annie reached the end of the hall, Nick looked back. Kaya wasn't following them.

They tied up Biff before walking to the Ford, which was still parked by the cemetery fence, and headed for the "wonderful little café."

"Even our imaginary birds have deserted us!"

"You may be right." The boy will sigh. "But what reason do you have to complain, especially you? I haven't taken anything from you, have I?"

"You're wrong!" the old man will yell at him, filled with resentment. "It was from me, of all the people, that you took the most! For I know now that when I die there will be no one to remember me. And I don't deserve that."

"You wouldn't deserve it if you had stopped me when I swam ashore," the boy objected, "but you didn't dare confront me then. Why?"

Failing to answer, the old man will simply nod his head in a gesture of helplessness and then walk away.

And the boy will remain on the shore alone.

CHAPTER 46

The café was large, gloomy, and practically empty.

"I'm surprised you have so few customers, madam," Nick commented to the waitress, a fat middle-aged woman whose face was caked with makeup.

"Are you talking about the café or about me *personally*?" She smiled at him sardonically.

Look at how sophisticated she is! Nick thought resentfully, but he was pleased to have attracted her attention. He turned to his niece. "Annie, it's just after ten. We should still be able to make the movies at eleven. What do you think?" Then he asked the waitress, "*It's ten past ten,* isn't it, ma'am?" though he could see she wasn't wearing a watch.

"If you say so." She shrugged her shoulders. "What do you want to order?"

Well, there's one way to keep us in her chicken's memory! Nick picked up the menu, took a deep breath, and began dictating an epic order. She interrupted him just as he was getting warmed up.

"Are you expecting more people, sir?"

"No. Why do you ask?"

"Well, I…just" The befuddled waitress mumbled something incomprehensible and waddled off to fill the order.

Little by little, she piled the table with all sorts of pastry, candy, juices, ice cream, and three cups of strong black coffee, to jump-start his frantic, completely disoriented brain.

Anna suddenly laughed! Soundless, but wide—the first time Nick ever saw her look happy. Apparently his epicurean epic had tickled her vestigial funny bone. Wonderful! He laughed too, with relief.

"We're going to eat all we want, aren't we? A real feast!" *Feast in a time of plague* flashed through his mind—completely irrelevant, maybe. "Bon appétit, sweetheart!"

Anna started with ice cream—like a *normal* child. "Controlling" the ghost? What nonsense! And the hypnotized ghost executing the murders she ordered—her a vampire and the ghost an unburied corpse and—how ridiculous!

"Annie, yesterday in the cemetery, did you really think we were playing a game?"

"No."

"I see. What did you think we were doing?"

"I thought you wanted to kill me," the child answered, scooping a spoonful of ice cream.

"I see!"

"Don't worry, Uncle Nick," she continued. "You were just beside yourself. Now you're back inside yourself, and probably you won't do that again soon."

"Oh, I'll never, never do that again!" A searing, painfully bright emotion flared deep inside, and Nick realized, almost with fear, what he had kept locked up for a long time—like a pearl, formed slowly, even against his will, in the spongy darkness. "Annie, do you know?" His voice was shaking. "Well, the thing is…it seems… I love you. Very much."

She looked up at him and smiled again. Yes, there was no doubt about it. They finally were together—had entered into a communion so easily! He had picked her up and carried her in his arms, and she had liked it. He had spoken a few affectionate words—seemingly insincere until just now—and brought her to this shabby café, ordering up a comical banquet, although with the most venal of ulterior motives. Yet there she was, smiling at him. They were talking, becoming close friends!

Nick contemplated her dreamily. She had brushed her hair back into a ponytail, and the style suited her. If her face was too thin, scary thin, her features were regular. Her eyes were big and radiant, her figure harmonious, with fine, long limbs. Oh, he would take good care of his niece now that she was an orphan.

That she had lost her father, *only* her father!

She would be like a daughter to him. He would take her on vacations, visit some very healthy and interesting, exotic places—do everything he could to make her happy, which turned out to be easy to do. Her weakness was due to her psychic complexity, not depression; she was simply inordinately intelligent for her age. What a lovely little girl she could be, with a little more weight!

"Annie, don't eat all the ice cream now. Leave room for these lovely pastries. Why not try the chocolate one with almonds?"

"Why do you only drink coffee?"

"Don't worry about me." He laughed. "I need to lose a few pounds."

"But you're not fat!" She looked at him approvingly. Dear God, finally somebody approved of him! "Kaya thinks you're very handsome. 'Attractive' is what she said."

"Did you say Kaya?"

They didn't need Kaya—anymore. Some glimmering, flat person. A sharp, unpleasant feeling of jealousy struck him—of anxiety. He couldn't leave *his* child in the company of—something so unidentified, could he? But to take the appropriate actions—to remove her—he needed more information, as much as possible.

"What about Kaya? What's she like, Annie?"

"A woman. Ordinary woman."

"Well, yes, ordinary—of course, but—is she *alive*? What do you think?"

Annie chose to keep silent, just looked at him with delicate but pitying condescension for his utter dim-wittedness. Which was not far from the truth, come to think of it.

Nick tried to laugh and change her impression. "By 'alive' I meant 'lively,' 'cheerful,'" he lied.

"No, she isn't very lively."

"Really? Why not?"

"Because nobody can see her, hear her, or touch her. That's all she wants."

"How long since she—became like that?"

"She didn't become like that. People *made* her like that. It's been going on for eight months!"

Since the day she disappeared. "And how do you see and hear her, sweetie?"

"I just do. I'm not infectious to her."

"So others are infectious?" he asked, feigning sympathy. "That is, everybody but you?"

"Well, everybody Kaya's met so far," Anna specified logically. "We don't know about everybody. Maybe there are more people like me. Or at least like you."

Nick sighed. "I can't hear her voice or approach her—enough."

"Yes, but when I'm there too, you can see her."

"I would hardly call it seeing! I can barely distinguish her silhouette. Really, I...guess...her."

"Oh, what a pity!" Annie shook her head, disappointed. "Kaya will be upset when I tell her. She thinks that, because of me, you two can really meet, though just look at each other and not touch. She also thinks you're in love with her."

"That's nonsense." Nick was embarrassed—in love.

"She is so sad," Annie added. "When you two are together alone, she knows you only feel her presence and think then that she's a ghost."

Nonsense again! The Balester sisters thought she was a ghost too, but this wasn't news. Because the truth is already disgustingly known. Yes, Kaya is the sadistic murderer. Nobody gives her orders; she kills consciously, of her own free will, and with a definite aim.

"Listen, Annie, isn't it best not to tell her that, even when I'm with you, I can barely see her? Why make her—sad, right?"

"Yes." She nodded understandingly.

Kind-hearted Uncle Nick—who was trying desperately to return to his former mindless, questionless state.

"My mom doesn't even feel her as a ghost, although I told her about Kaya last night," his niece continued. "'You heard your uncle say this name, so now you're inventing these far-fetched tales' is what she said."

"'Your uncle'—everything's always your uncle's fault," Nick muttered bitterly. *But what could Kaya's aim be? And how was she killing her victims when that powerful force kept her from even touching a human being?*

"And Kaya was just a step away from Mom and me the whole time!" Annie grinned. "Can you imagine that?"

Yes, I can imagine it, all right! he wanted to shout at her. Now that she had started talking, Anna was becoming downright garrulous. "So you brought her to my home?"

"No, I just gave her your address. She showed up at our place just a week ago, and when she found out I'm not infectious to her, she was really happy. Despite that, she chose to live at your place, because you attracted her most. You two met just once at my house, before her terrible accident, and then—"

"Yes, I remember, sweetie. I remember!"

What an evil, sarcastic irony—a box of pins dropped by a plain, clumsy girl; an instinctive courteous gesture by an ungainly, unartful bachelor, and look at the response! The *second series* of murders seems to be a consequence only of that gesture—because he had foolishly helped her pick up those stupid pins!

"I'm also happy I made friends with her," Anna continued the story. "She's very interesting, now that she's so sick!"

"Yes, yes, darling. Very."

So Kaya was struck down by a misfortune and began killing—without reason?—her grandfather, the kind children-loving sisters, and her elementary schoolteacher. Then she returns to where she met Nick, gets his address from Anna, and most insolently comes to live in his house! Attributing the foreign presence to his demented loneliness, he rushes out to meet Kathy, even invites her to his home.

"So what do you think, Uncle? Will she ever get better?"

"Yes, yes."

Yes, but meanwhile his *uninvited guest* hears the intimate conversation between Kathy and him and begins to see red. She leaves the living room, opens a window on the first floor so she can get back "home" later if the door's bolted from the inside, cuts a length of cord from the nylon roll, and waits for the two of them in Kathy's car. Their parting kiss outside the hotel surely added fuel to the fire. The result? An agonizing death for the unhappy, middle-aged, unmarried woman.

"Uncle Nick, eat some pastries!" the child twittered. Her loud, gratingly artificial tweet reminded Nick of that pretentious warbling doorbell. He could still hear it trilling as Max lay dying on the second floor and blamed Kaya for that death as well. If she hadn't left the torn-off earring as a token of her jealous love on his nightstand, Elsa wouldn't have become so involved and ended up a murderess herself! Without her chipped tooth, Nick wouldn't have recalled Kaya at all nor later visited Eric Schumacher while haunted by her invisible presence, who probably called down on himself her deadly anger by saying that she had left "nothing of herself in *anybody's* mind but—haze." Nor would Eric have mentioned how Dr. Mayer had failed to attend her dying mother, driving Kaya to slit his throat as well. Then Elsa wouldn't have noticed the Ford leave and jumped to the conclusion that Max was the murderer and—the circle around the box of pins grew smaller and smaller.

Grew smaller but *hadn't closed.* "Incidentally, Annie, if Kaya wants so strongly to rub shoulders with people, why doesn't she leave notes or letters?"

"She's afraid. If she lets everybody know that she exists, someone may find a way to capture her. At least she left you a—she called it a 'fairy-tale clue.' Besides, she decided she could trust you completely from the very beginning."

"Completely?" Nick shuddered. "Do you know—anything ?"

"Yes, I do." Anna nodded. "I'm almost sure that she'll write you a long love letter and sit by your side while you read it."

"Good Lord!"

"My mom never loved my father—I didn't really love him either, especially after I learned his nasty little secret."

"Really?" Nick pricked up his ears, glad to postpone his own "nasty secrets."

"What secret, sweetheart?"

Anna shrugged her shoulders. "I've kept it so far, but now that he's dead—is it OK to tell?"

"Of course! Why would he care? He doesn't have any secrets now—or anything."

"But Mom and I still have a lot of things, precious things, don't we?"

"Well, that depends." His resentment toward this too ordinary child revived with exhausting speed. What *complexity*? It wasn't enough that she inherited Max's shriveled body; she also had Elsa's devious, calculating soul. It would be better if she hadn't said anything. "It *depends*," he repeated, "on what you consider 'precious.' So what was your father's secret?"

Anna stared into his eyes, apparently to heighten the effect of what she was going to say. "At night he would watch from the porch while my mom and Reno wrestled together in bed. And he would pee in his hands."

"He peed in his hands?"

"Well, yes. He would move around in a strange way and—I guess he was peeing."

His third cup of coffee in his hands, Nick cautiously peeped into his soul, which should be ready to explode—from shock, volcanic disgust, or at least indignation—but, alas, saw nothing so scary there. Only at the bottom jiggled some dirty, nasty gloating.

"And how about your mother? Did she know his secret too?"

"No, but can I tell her now?"

Nick pretended to be thinking over it. "Yes, I think you should tell her. That would be best, and the sooner, the better!"

If it wasn't too late. If the circle hadn't tightened already. But maybe Elsa was still *just* asleep?

Anna started talking again, but in a most eccentric way—now almost shouting, then just barely moving her lips. "When Biff—and then we—I asked Kaya—we fed him—she gave me—"

Nick stood up. "Anna, this is no time for playing games! We're going home, right now!"

"The movies?—aren't we—pastries—?—me—and—"

"For Christ's sake, don't you understand? We have to go now! Come on, hurry up. Hurry up!"

"N...e-e-e-e...yow?"

"Come on, Anna, enough idiot talk!" Nick was sorely tempted to slap her hard across the face—that long, horselike, *Max-like* face. *Perverse type!* "I really don't want to guess what you're trying to tell me. We'll play this game some other time, OK? Let's go, because Kaya—and your mother—"

My sister. Elli!

CHAPTER 47

Anna finally stopped talking—namely, stopped moving her lips. She looked at him quizzically and then leaned on the table, hoisting herself up by her elbows—a child that was teetering before him like an old woman.

Her right wrist was missing.

Holes had begun to appear in her dress—actually in her chest—and were partly covered by a membrane. Now Nick could see the plush red back of her chair through them—like bloodshot eyes, eyes wormed out.

"Dear God!"

Nick couldn't and didn't want to move as he watched her right arm melt, up, up, and all the way to the shoulder, her hair turn to brownish wisps of smoke that grew thinner and thinner, becoming only a pale outline framing her face—a face hanging in the air because the neck was no longer there. The lips had become two hastily scribbled strokes, the nose two little ellipses, the eyebrows only suggestions of arches roughed in. The skin on the forehead, cheeks, and chin was pitted with holes. Something was devouring her. No, not something—*he* was devouring her flesh. Fretting her away in bigger and bigger pieces, bloodless and from a distance, unwillingly.

He was infecting her.

But her eyes, her expressive radiant child's eyes! The irises were blurring, merging with the whites, as everything around them turned dark gray. The pupils dwindled to glossy, anxiously shimmering specks. Then they disappeared too, leaving two bottomless holes, the light from the window behind her shining through them, filling them with a perplexed stare.

Dear God, I know you are punishing me; I know I deserve it, but don't…don't…why this way, God?

From Annie's chair rose part of her right shoulder, along with the left arm up to the elbow, disappearing remnants of her chest and abdomen, a piece of the dress, her legs but only from the knees up. *What's she standing on? Is she there at all? Yes, she's there, but I can't see her!*

"Annie, please stay! Don't go!" When he reached for her, she— no, not her but that *force*—pushed him back, hard. "Annie, don't move! Don't go anywhere! Don't move!"

"What's the matter, Mister?" The waitress asked from behind him.

"The child!" He sank his fingers into her shoulder with a desperate hope. "My niece—she's getting sick; I'm losing her! Stop her, please!"

"Please, calm down!" The waitress drew back, unnerved. "Calm down!"

"Calm down? I want my niece back. I don't want anything more from this life, *just that child*! And you…you're…infecting her too!"

"Your niece went outside. Maybe you didn't see her leave," she murmured in singsong tones, a voice people use to pacify the insane. "She probably went for a walk. Just go look for her. I'm sure everything is fine."

"The child's here, *here*! There she is!" Nick pointed in a certain direction, but there wasn't much left to point at—only one hand, her left hand, the one on the heart side. "Don't you see? Here's her hand, Miss! Look at her, I'm begging you!"

Humoring him, she looked where Nick was pointing to, frowned with concentration and—no.

"No," she said, "there's nothing there. Not a thing. You must calm down. Don't make me call the manager, sir, or the police. I'd hate to do that. Are you delirious? Have you been smoking—something?"

"Smoking," Nick repeated senselessly. "Annie!"

The hand that now lacked fingers swam toward the exit. She was running away, now realizing what had happened to her, *running to her mother.*

"No, don't go there; don't!"

When he tried to follow her, the big waitress, arms akimbo, blocked his way. "The bill!" she demanded. "Pay your bill!"

Nick tore his wallet out of his pocket, his hands trembling, grabbed a handful of notes, and threw them on the table over the untouched pastry and unfinished ice cream. Starting to crying, he ran after—again after—*nothing?*

On the street people passed, bustling toward their destinations, some preoccupied, some worried, pensive, and self-absorbed. Infectious people. Like him.

He wandered among them, lost in the maze.

CHAPTER 48

The doorplate read "ERIC AND DEAN SCHUMACHER" in burnished bronze, but it lied. That trusting friend of the seamstress Alina Norris who had introduced himself to Nick as "just Eric" no longer lived here, or anywhere else. What was left of him lay frozen at the city morgue, waiting to be buried—because, one week ago, Nick had knocked on this door.

You made a fatal mistake, Eric, when you let me in. Death came in behind me!

Delayed compassion didn't bring Nick back here. He stared at the door hopelessly, because of course the police had sealed it, but that didn't necessarily mean the squalid apartment was empty. If Eric's crippled brother was still inside, then the cause of Annie's inconceivable disease would definitely be…

Nick shook his head, grimacing fiercely. It was a matter of psychic survival to stop thinking, to escape from the terrible images and self-revelations, self-accusations, and self-hatred that had been assailing him for the last hour—since he had lost, maybe forever, his niece—and, *perhaps*, his sister. *Oh God, don't let me find anybody behind this locked door!*

He pounded on it like a bat seeking a rescue fissure to darkness, not trying to be quiet, not caring who heard him or even if somebody called the police. He even wanted to be arrested. Otherwise, if that "perhaps" that still sustained him became a certainty, then where would he go? *Not to our father's home, anyway!*

Stepping back, he ducked his shoulder and hit the door with all his weight. It groaned pliably, gaped.

"Dean?" Nick desperately blinked in the dark apartment. *I think you're really here! I can smell the five-day stench of an abandoned creature—helpless, crippled, human.*

He turned on the light, closed the splintered door with its broken police seals, and headed straight for the kitchen. The wheelchair, tattered and greasy near the top where Dean most often rested his head, stood by the window, but the blanket Eric had used to cover his brother's crippled legs was folded on the chair near it.

But was his head resting there now? Nick warily gave the wheelchair a little shove. Since it wasn't suspiciously heavy, Nick plucked up his courage and felt the seat. Empty, and no force pushed him back.

"Hey, Dean! We both know"—*you're paralyzed*—"that you couldn't have left this apartment on your own. Find a way to show me where you are. Use your entire *presence* so I can find you—save you!"

Nick stood next to the wheelchair for at least a minute, fiercely concentrating, but nothing happened. Maybe he was more sensitive to Kaya's presence? Or maybe Dean really wasn't here, though normally he would be near his wheelchair.

"We're going to see about this right now!"

Slowly, meticulously, Nick checked every nook and cranny in the kitchen with stretched hands but didn't encounter anything that he couldn't see. Where else should he look? Why, of course! Eric had been murdered in the middle of the night! Dean must have been in bed.

Nick dreaded visiting the crime scene, but a spider-thin glimmer of hope that he *wouldn't* find Dean there still wrapped him in a last protective cocoon. *"In situations of stress, people do the impossible,"* it whispered in his ear. *"Why not suppose that, when Dean saw Kaya murder his brother, he managed at least to crawl out of the apartment without being seen."*

Trembling with sudden lunatic optimism, Nick walked into the combination living room/bedroom and stared at the messy beds. The rusty-brown stains weren't immediately obvious on the checkered blue sheets and pillowcases of the left bed, but a closer look confirmed that they weren't Coca-Cola or spilled tea.

Since the balcony door was slightly ajar, the stench inside had dissipated somewhat, but Nick still found it hard to take. Logically, what clearer sign that the miracle of "the crippled man's escape" was just another of the inventions that had dotted his whole life?

The other, bloodless bed was messy but clean. If Dean had been in the room, he didn't stay in bed long after his brother's death. Perhaps he had crawled down during his brother's agony, either to help him or to hide. If so, now he must be somewhere on the floor, unconscious.

"Hey, Dean! Wake up, for Christ's sake, because unconscious you don't have any—presence!"

But what if Dean had crawled under one of the beds and, the next day, was still there but already unconscious? And the cops hadn't found him because of their sloppiness, not because he was invisible.

Nick quickly peeped under the bed. Nothing there, apart from an empty bottle leaning against the wall. He turned his head and looked to the left: no, not under the other bed either.

"Damn you," he muttered, then shouted: "Dean. Deeeeean!"

Nick jumped to his feet and ran to the wardrobe, flinging both doors open wide. Nothing. *Nothing!* Just some old-fashioned, second-hand clothes—damn! He grabbed the vacuum cleaner extension from the bottom shelf and brandished it like a sword, poking first under the bed of the slaughtered and then under the bed of the—sickening, stinking cripple! *Just wait until I lay my hands on you! I'll...I'll.* He had no idea exactly what he would do, but the idle threat soothed him. He stuck the pipe under the bed and raked out the bottle. No particular odor, so it was probably an empty water bottle. That's how Dean had survived! And he had gradually crawled.

To the balcony.

Nick crossed to the slightly open balcony door, but instead of going out or even looking out, he first studied the lower parts of the doorframe and the glass. Yes, they really were covered with greasy fingerprints, fingerprints made by very small hands, as if a child had been lying on the floor, trying to pull itself up, and had reached for the door handle and then tumbled down again. This seems to have been repeated many times, as evidenced by the smeared traces of his palms. Finally the child had managed to turn the handle.

But why a *child*?

Nick opened the door wide and stepped over the high threshold.

The creature curled up flat on its belly at the edge of the balcony with its hands—its little claws—dangling between the metal bars was absolutely unfamiliar to him. Yet he knew he had seen it before, had caught a glimpse of it just a week ago, here in the apartment. He knew that only because—it was indescribably, terribly deformed.

Only now did Nick realize he remembered *not Dean, but his wheelchair*, and had simply assumed that Dean was crippled because of it. But he had never imagined a face, features, or even what might be wrong with his body! Nothing about Dean was preserved in his memory.

Nothing but a *haze.*

"Dean?"

Dean was dressed in pajamas loose enough to hide the distorted back, shoulders, and pelvis, and the trouser legs were long enough to cover the twisted legs. But even hidden and covered, that tiny male body shocked him deeply. It was so mercilessly crumpled and malignantly twisted that he could imagine the whole satanic hatred for humankind having been slammed down on it in the shape of a huge clenched fist.

The bare feet resembled white, boneless fish, and the bald head was no more than a caked clod of gray clay. As for the face, Nick realized that he wasn't up to the trial of looking at it. He would leave the creature as it was, face down on the cement—on the hard, rough cement heated by the afternoon sun. Nick shivered and then bristled with his characteristic responses to painful situations: guilt and shame.

"Dean—"

You're dead, aren't you? He squatted beside the twisted husk and, struggling to overcome his repulsion, took hold of one limp arm, placing two fingers on its wrist to seek a pulse. Nothing. He was dead—but recently so, because there was no stench or other signs of decay, only the filth usual to life.

Recoiling, Nick turned his back on the dead man and ran away. He dashed through the apartment, to the stairs, and ran smack into a slovenly old hag—the landlady.

"Aauuh!" she howled, staggering back as they stared at each other. "I...I saw you go in there." Putting her hands to her neck, she slowly backed toward the elevator. "But I didn't call the police, not even after I heard you bust down the door," she gushed unc-tuously. "You're lucky that most of the tenants are at work now. Otherwise someone would have turned you in, but I thought, no—"

"You wanted to spy on me," Nick interjected. "That's why you didn't call the police! My life's been turned upside down this week, bared to the bone, but it's been business as usual for you. You only pretend to be alive, you decrepit hunk of trash!"

She dropped her hands and stood in the hall like an animal after taxidermy, her gaping mouth displaying metal teeth, while he continued.

"Why wouldn't you turn me in if you think I'm the sadist, huh?"

"I don't think you're the sadist, Mister!" she hissed vindictive-ly. "On the contrary, it's *you* who pretends to be alive. That's why you won't even be the next victim."

Nick covered his ears and ran downstairs but, before getting into the car, looked back up to the fourth floor. Squinting his eyes, he could just make out the little, lily-white arm of Dean Schumacher drooping over the balcony edge, as if waving good-bye.

Last Sunday the apartment would have been swarming with people—cops, coroners, and police photographers. Someone would have *surely* found him—if they could have seen him. But he must have become more pliable to the infection after his brother's death—the infection that had been radiating from everybody. He must have cried for help, desperately trying to attract someone's sight, to touch anyone nearby! Nick shivered as he again heard Annie's fading voice at the café. The greatest cruelty was that Dean wouldn't have had the vaguest idea what was happening to him—probably thought they were simply ignoring him because he was crippled, deformed, and useless.

"The brother wasn't home," Forger had told him that Sunday afternoon. *You're wrong, Forger. He was there, and he's still there!* he should have answered. *Come. We can save him!* Then the poor little creature wouldn't have been crawling for days, trying to cover the few yards to the balcony door. He wouldn't have clawed at that door with his pale, undeveloped fingers, which would have been invisible—until his death, just to die on that lonely balcony, no longer shouting but barely whimpering for help with his unheard voice.

Oh God, why didn't I at least have the courage to turn him over just now, so at least he could face the sky? Why?

CHAPTER 49

Nick climbed the stairs to Reno's office slowly, his chest heaving in the rhythm that he had once called *mind-fogging* once but which he now deemed not merely relaxing but vital. Entering without ringing the bell, he passed through the waiting room without encountering the secretary, who was probably at lunch, and headed for Reno's office. If Elsa were already there, he would just throw her a look of brotherly love—and run! Unfortunately, she wasn't there, and Reno was carelessly ruminating on a sandwich while leafing through the files piled high in front of him. Nick was glad he wasn't with a client. On his enormous desk, scattered with artistic disorder, were at least ten copies of the yesterday's *Express* boasting his headline: "Renowned lawyer Renaldo Aldano shows Lieutenant Forger the way."

"You've shown no 'way,'" Nick responded.

Surprised, Reno raised his head.

"Apart from being Kaya's father, Andrey Belloff has nothing to do with any of this," Nick continued. "Nor is Kaya being chased by a killer. She *is* the killer, invisible and untraceable. People like her are in the grip of a brutal force that isolates them from others. It hits them or those who try to get close to them like a fist, right in the chest, but it doesn't strike very often because most people instinctively avoid them. Take the cripple Dean, for instance. People unconsciously look away from cripples or simply block them out. Or maybe he was under the bed the whole time."

Reno, goggling at him like a carp, set his sandwich down on an open file.

"You'll leave stains that way," Nick remarked. "Yes, Dean must have been under the bed; otherwise he would have shown up in a police photograph. I think that the infected can be seen in photos; they just don't register in our brains. Another indication of Dean's tractability to infection is that, like Kaya, he left no clear mental impression—and not just because he was a cripple. There's more to it, because I've already begun to forget the child too."

"What child?"

"Anna. I can't even remember what she looks like, even though it's been barely two hours since we were sitting together in the café. Do you understand?"

"No."

"I know it's difficult to understand, believe me. Even worse, at certain times the force that pushes them away from people stops working. When? Well, during sleep, Reno. That's why Kaya sedates her victims first—then, when they do wake up, the terror and pain suppress the force even more than sleep does."

"Nick, don't you understand that I haven't the faintest idea what forces or infections you're talking about?"

"What I'm talking about is our brains' ability to repress insignificant details or trauma and things that don't concern or interest us directly. We wouldn't survive otherwise; our species would have died off, congested with redundant and disturbing information. Well, it so happens that, for some insignificant people, this feature is probably psycho-viral, Reno! Our brain's repressive function radiates an infection against which they have no immunity."

"You're not telling me anything new, Nick. Even your idiotic description of this nonsense isn't new either."

"What's new, Reno, is that a *new disease* is breaking out in our town that can't be cured by medicine or prevented by a vaccine. It flows directly from our brains and, I think, could soon become an epidemic. There are simply too many *unhappy people* in the world, my friend, far too many. And we, the others, undermine whatever immunity they might have by our rapacious instinct to…to *nullify* them in our minds! We don't *want* to see them, hear them, or hear about them—even to know they exist. Oh, yes, there will be an epidemic—a social apocalypse!"

"Listen, don't pretend you're Nostradamus. I have a huge amount of work to do—"

"Like hell you do!"

"Yes, I do. And you, Nick, are likely to be 'nullified'—not by some fantastic new disease but by idleness."

"And you, it seems, don't want to understand! Just this week I've encountered three infected people: three! And I detected a pattern: when Alina dies, her daughter Kaya immediately disappears; Eric Schumacher dies, and the same thing happens to his brother, who became visible again only in death. And today…today I watched Anna disappear, right before my eyes. She seemed to dissolve bit by bit. The last thing I saw was her left hand—without fingers. I watched it float toward the door and ran after it."

"Aha, now I get it!" Reno said, retrieving his sandwich. "You, simply, aren't 'all there.'"

"I'm not all right, I admit," Nick corrected him, "absolutely not! But I expect that, once I lose my mind completely, I'll feel much better."

"Yes, I noticed yesterday that you were off your rocker more than usual." Reno energetically munched on, making no effort to show sympathy or hide his boredom. "First you bring a pair of binoculars to the funeral for unknown reasons. Then you get it into your head that there's some note hidden inside the binoculars, take off in Elsa's car, and are gone all night nobody knows where! That lout Forger must have given you quite a scare at the cemetery."

"Yes, but he was right to do so, or I might have killed Anna for burying her stuffed rabbit. I'll tell you something about that child, Reno. She was destined to escape me—could never be mine. If Elsa were alive, she would only be yours. But now Anna's become invisible too."

Reno's face suddenly turned to stone, "'If Elsa were alive?'"

"I explained the pattern to you, didn't I?" Nick spread his hands. "Both Alina and Eric somehow protected their nearest and dearest, who obviously couldn't resist nullification without help. And Elsa *maybe* did the same for Anna. And again *maybe*, Kaya put a sedative in Elsa's tea, but she did it last night, expecting Elsa to drink her tea before she went to bed. She didn't know that Elsa drinks her tea in the morning. In other words, Kaya was planning to kill Elsa during the night."

Reno sent the remains of his sandwich flying into the wastebasket. "What are you babbling about now?" He picked up the phone and frantically dialed a number.

"You're calling Elsa, aren't you?" Nick asked. "Aren't you?" He didn't expect an answer.

While the telephone kept ringing and ringing, Reno stared at Nick with growing anxiety. Finally he slammed the receiver down, reached into his desk drawer, and pulled out a gun. He stood up. "Come on, let's go!"

"Go where?"

"To your place."

"A…a…ah, no, no." Nick shook his head. "Why don't you go by yourself? Or with a cop? I've got an alibi. At ten past ten I was—we were at the café. I was still there at half past ten, and by that time, Elsa was already, *probably*—"

"Move it!"

So Nick—moved. Once they were in the Ferrari, Reno tromped on the gas and burned rubber. "I don't believe a single word of what you told me, Nick," he snarled, though without much conviction. "If there were a shred of truth in it, you wouldn't have said it so indifferently. You love Elsa! You've been crazy about her ever since childhood, my sick friend!"

"I love only as long as I'm loved back, my *happy* friend. That's just how I am." Nick felt with astonishment a fatuous—or vindictive?—grin crease his face. He squished it between his palms, crushed it, and then heaved a deep sigh and clutched at a personal platitude. *The harder the mouth works, the more the mind rests.* "But I'm far from indifferent, Reno. To be fair, though, I admit that, if we were in Kaya's shoes, we'd probably do even worse thi—"

"Nick, shut up!" Reno interjected, driving even faster. "It'd be safer for both of us."

"OK, but please imagine what Kaya must feel like—how helpless she is. If she even gets close to someone who radiates infection—and let me tell you almost everyone does—she seem to lose all her abilities! She can't even drink a glass of water or move the smallest object. Even if she keeps her distance and somebody just looks in her direction, it happens. So tell me, how could she not become vicious? Still, I'm convinced she doesn't kill only because she's sadistic, Reno. There must be another reason, but I have no idea what!"

"You said that Anna 'disappeared' two hours ago?" Waves of hostility poured from Reno. "So what have you been doing since then? Why didn't you go to Elsa if you had such—apprehensions about her?"

"Because I went to Schumacher's first. I hoped to prove myself wrong, to hold on to my 'probably.' It helps me and leads me easily and more painlessly to *the hateful facts*. Do you understand?"

"No, thank God, I don't! To understand you I'd have to think like you, and that disgusts me!"

"It disgusts me too." Nick shrugged, not offended in the least.

"I don't believe you," Reno repeated. "I don't believe a single word of it. Everything you blathered was just more of your maniacal phantasmagoria!"

"I only hope you're right. But why don't you try to describe Anna to me? Tell me something concrete about her, some detail of her appearance or her behavior."

Reno struggled to do so, apparently against his will. He even eased off the gas pedal. Gradually his face showed signs of dismay and discomfort as he realized he couldn't do it.

"Aha!" Nick slapped himself on the knee in a ludicrous gesture of triumph. "Only mist! Mist, isn't it? And you refused to believe me!" He bent toward Reno and lowered his voice to an intimate whisper. "Ah, my friend, though you may not understand me, I understand you perfectly, maybe because all my life I relied only on disbelief. But lately it has been my undoing. Yes, we made a fatal mistake! If we had all trusted each other more, not just you and me, some people would still be alive, including our Elsa, who—"

"You clown!" Reno shouted, his eyes fixed on the empty, dusty road ahead. "Ever since you walked into my office, you've been playing this same scene! 'Impossible revelations on the verge of madness,' huh? You're trying to find a way to justify your actions that will convince even you. I swear, if something has happened to Elsa, I'll kill you!"

"Didn't you tell me yourself that you'd decided to end your long affair with her? But now that my 'past her prime' sister has turned into a wealthy widow—"

"So you suspected that she had been drugged and left her alone!" Reno refused to examine his own motives. "Even rushed to secure an alibi! You wanted her to—"

"I didn't want anything!" Nick denied. "I wanted to prove to myself that I could relinquish her. Forever! Because I knew *she* would leave *me*. At the same time, deep inside, I never believed in the possibility of...of such...a...lethal outcome. Only as I watched Anna disappear did I start putting things together, but until that moment, I hadn't even thought—"

"That's right, you hadn't thought. I know you all too well! Once you become obsessed by the impulse to do something mean, you can turn off your conscience. That's your strength. And that's the reason why you'll never step into madness. You'll remain at the threshold, even if somebody were being torn to pieces right before your eyes because of you. You'd just turn on your adaptable imagination, and 'deep inside' you'd believe you had slipped clean out of the swamp."

"Clean or not, I really am out of it." Nick felt more and more a strong need to keep talking. "But you and Elsa, *if* she's still alive, will still be stuck in a swamp of your own making forever. Remember the night you ran into Max on the front porch? That was no accident. He watched your sexual games all the time. Such entertainment."

Reno slammed on the brakes, and with a fierce screech, the car veered off the road like a wounded animal and stood there motionless. When Reno turned slowly to face him, Nick felt in his glare an abyss of utter contempt.

"Why…why…are you looking at me like that?" Nick jabbered hysterically. "If you had told her then and there that you'd seen Max on the porch, she—yes, she—wouldn't have killed him! Yes, Elsa slaughtered him! Elsa, your lover! Can you picture your lover with that blunt knife."

The fist of his one and only friend landed squarely on Nick's nose. A nasty crunching sound followed, and blood spurting from his nose spattered his summer shirt with large blotches. Strangely enough, instead of being stunned by the blow, Nick found himself suddenly in a dazzlingly clear zone of higher consciousness—*his true other self.* No shadows here: it was flat and frozen like an Arctic plain, lofty and estranged, infinitely separated from his daily life. Frozen in icy, white abstractions—how easy it was to be righteous *from here*! How easy to judge, to recognize the truth: that evil was always concrete and on the mark in everyday life.

"I'm scared." Nick shivered. "I don't want to believe a word of it either, but I'm still terrified."

As the Ferrari barreled down the old familiar road, Reno was looking straight ahead as if nothing had happened between them. They passed the last turn and the shrubbery where Nick had hidden the gas can the night he had "wanted" to kill Max, and then came the path that he had taken on his rickety old bike. Ah! How could this all have happened to him? And how was it possible that now he was *almost* sure his sister was dead? Even a dream couldn't be that absurd!

They arrived.

To save time, Reno parked the car on the road by the fence and ran across the yard, with Nick close behind him. They were greeted by an almost human whimper—Biff. He flailed and flopped around in front of his kennel as if engulfed by invisible flames.

Despite being badly tangled up in the chain, he kept pulling it and writhing on the ground. If that weren't enough, he suddenly howled piteously—as if for a death.

"Oh God—God," Reno whined as well. He raced past the dog but returned quickly to untie it. "There, there, boy," he comforted Biff—and probably to himself as well. "Calm down, please. Don't howl, like that!"

Though free, Biff didn't stop whining and moaning. Nick was almost overpowered by the burning desire to kick the mutt but forced himself to walk around him and head for the front door.

"Come on! Unlock the damned door!" Reno snarled. "For Christ's sake, what are you waiting for?"

They went in.

Reno opened his mouth to call for Elsa but didn't dare. Silence filled the musty old house like a poisonous flammable gas, as if any loud sound would trigger an explosion. They climbed up the stairs slowly, even stealthily, doing their best to muffle their breathing but not successfully. Instead, it became increasingly louder and more broken—the breathing of two men struggling with painful apprehensions.

When they reached the second floor and walked down the hall, Reno froze before Elsa's room, and Nick—Nick walked past it to his. When he entered and looked around his own room, unchanged during the long years, he finally calmed down: everything was still completely familiar and ordinary. How could something terrible have happened just a few steps away? Certainly not a murder—a bloody, sadistic inhuman murder. Ha! That's more of the "maniacal phantasmagoria," as his best friend had so tactfully put it.

He moistened his pocket handkerchief with water from the carafe and carefully wiped the blood clotted on his face and neck. Then he sat down on his bed, soon lay back. *What quiet, dear Lord, what deep, lake-smooth quiet, and today is Thursday!* Thursdays meant that he and Reno would be fishing on that woodland lake in two days. No, that wasn't so: they had gone fishing last Saturday, always on the last Saturday of the month.

CHAPTER 50

Nick heard a door open under the bed.

He jumped up and clenched his fists but released them a second later. *It's just the audio recorder, stupid! You've messed up the settings.* He had completely forgotten about it until it just turned on by itself, which meant Reno had finally dared to enter the room next door. "Thunk, thunk"—two heavy steps inside there were caught by the microphone and amplified loudly by the loudspeaker under his bed. Then...

Silence.

Elsa must be sleeping. She's asleep, and Reno doesn't want to wake her up! She's just asleep.

"No. No, no," Reno mumbled under the bed. Then wheezing, and an interval of silence. Then the loud bang of a slamming door, both from under the bed and down the hall in brutal stereophonic sound. Footsteps followed, now coming toward his room, and a double click: the loud click of his door being shoved open and, an aftershock, the recorder turning itself off.

Reno stood in front of him, but Nick shut his eyes. *Come on, my friend, just say, "She's asleep, Nick. Damn you and your crackpot, maniacal—"* A third click made Nick open his eyes. Reno said nothing; the gun in his hand had spoken instead. So it was all over! Elsa wasn't asleep.

Nick sat down again. *It's all over with you too.* His heart sensed the *other* voice within him, clear and icy white, that froze him—in dead-white relief. *Don't be afraid. Everything ended here and now. The End.*

Now this Righteous Man is waiting—nonworldly clean, at that placid white distance. Not an other self but his primal self! And this one here? Oh, this one doesn't really matter. It's only a ball of looming lights and dark shadows. And it's already condemned.

Nick looked at Reno expectantly. *He doesn't realize that, even if he shoots me, I'll still get out of this mess,* he thought with haughty estrangement. *He's trapped too tightly in one way of thinking. The poor man is one faced.*

The thought almost disappointed Nick. Reno couldn't really hurt him. "No, you can't act like me, Reno." *You want to hate me right now, just to save your sanity, but you're not able to switch off your mind. You can't save yourself from* the facts *because you lack my "adaptable imagination."* "No, you can't act like me."

Reno held the gun with a steady hand—like the hand of a dead man, his fingers on the trigger fossilized with rigor mortis. But his eyes were still seeing—whoever he had seen in the other room. Something that Nick had decisively managed so far not even to imagine.

"But you, Reno, can't act like me."

"You're right. I can't," Reno admitted and walked out of the room. It seemed that before he closed the door, he gave Nick his accustomed friendly nod, meaning *"See you soon."*

Then, the audio recorder switched on again—long enough to preserve Reno's actions with the clarity of nightmare: he entered

Elsa's room, took a few steps toward her bed, and stood there for a second or two. A groan—or a sob? That last noise was cut off, drowned out by the sound of a single shot being fired. The shot was not as loud as Nick had expected in that silence.

But the crash of the body hitting the floor shook the whole house. Reno had been a heavy man.

CHAPTER 51

"Slap, slap, slap" The recorder had automatically turned on again. Then from the hall came the same steps, very slow and tired— "slap, slap, slap"—toward the bathroom.

Kaya was going to wash off—the blood.

She had *finished* more than two hours ago, when Anna disappeared, and only now was she coming out of that room. Or perhaps she had only *started* then?

Nick took the recorder from under the bed, placing it on the nightstand. Yes, the record has lasted almost ninety-minute. He rewound it and touched the play button. He would be able to hear—*everything*.

"No!" He removed his finger.

He would never listen to it. *Never!* He felt a frantic urge to stomp the recorder, smashing it with his feet. But the recording might be the only proof of his innocence. This was no time for hysteria. He had to *act*, now, while Kaya was still washing off the blood. He went into the bathroom. Kaya hadn't even bothered to lock the door. *She trusts me—probably considers me her accomplice!*

The shower was running, water streaming around her petite— ha! her short, flat-chested—figure, which appeared only as an oval, shapeless bubble. The white tiles behind it were spattered with red specks, and rosy soapsuds washed down the drain. His mother's kimono was soaking in the sink, the water there a deep red. Under the sink was a box of "wondrous" detergent called UNI that claimed to remove "any and every organic stain." His mother's slippers lay on the floor, under a hook that held a bathrobe and one of his sister's nightgowns. Brushes and hair clips were arranged on the shelf beneath the mirror. Clearly Kaya had rummaged through Elsa's things after murdering her.

"Good!" he muttered through clenched teeth as he yanked the key from inside the door and exited, locking it behind him. He listened. From the sound of splashing water, Kaya must have stepped out of the shower and tried to open the door. But she would not be able to as long as his proximity isolated her from objects. However loudly she screamed, she would be driven back by the force radiating from him. Or should he call it power field? Or space restriction? Psycho-energetic eraser? It doesn't matter. The important truth was that his infectious proximity turned her, the murderer, into a *human zero*.

His face twisted into a mask, disguising something he couldn't and didn't want to define. After double locking the door, he thought of going to his study, but his knees suddenly began to shake. What if the door to Elsa's room were open? He didn't remember hearing Kaya close it behind her. God! How could he walk by with the two of them lying inside—dead, defaced, sunk in blood—without giving them one last look, without crying, without going mad with grief?

Or what if Reno didn't shoot himself properly? He could be still alive—may need help! The Emergency, like Max. But is such a sinister repetition possible? *Noooo!* Renaldo Aldano always finished what he started. That one-track mind of his guarantees that he did the job right: put the muzzle of the gun to his temple and blew his brains out—his skull, his brain—*ooohh!*

But why, why had he done it? Probably he hadn't even understood, had pulled the trigger out of shock, on the spur of the moment. That's right: he should have counted to ten, given his instinctive protective mechanisms time to take over. *A pity!* Nick sighed. *Reno, my old friend, you couldn't act like me—or I like you, also a pity. A disgusting pity.*

"Since I'm still alive," he encouraged himself aloud, "I know what I'm going to do!"

He ran down the hall, not even checking the door to Elsa's room, and barged into his study, looking for the only object that still meant something to him in this house haunted by pain and death: his manuscript of *Future Tales*, with the latest, unfinished revisions. Would he ever know how to end it? Probably not. But the *other* ending—to that miniature, but deadly, bit of reality into which he had fallen, maybe for no other reason than that a box of pins.

Yes, *this* End, untalented or not, he was prepared to "invent" now! Nobody else was left to do it—anymore.

He took his manuscript and pressed it to his chest, a thin sheaf of written sheets, and picked up the folder of his important documents from the desk. What else? He looked around in farewell. He would never sit here again, bent over the typewriter; never step to the bookshelves of dictionaries, encyclopedias, and his favorite books; and never walk to and fro on the carpet worn by his steps nor stare at that wall, with its stain that sometimes reminded him of a human hand and other times of a spider, crossroads, a flower, a star.

Dear Lord, bring back my boring, solitary, unsuccessful days when I was happy without even knowing it. Give me back the dreamy morning hours over a steaming cup of coffee, when everything seemed pleasant but, in my vanity and stupidity, I thought it merely commonplace and boring.

Lord, let me sit again behind my writing desk and—let everything be as before! How could a single week turn all of those years into nothing, grind away all these seemingly enduring events?

"There's no going back!"

He stumbled from his study as if after another death and hobbled down the stairs, gripping the banister like an old man. With his other hand, he pressed to his heart the tales and personal documents that proved that he, Nicolas Edgeway, was somebody: born male—with no distinguishing birthmarks—single, educated, somebody who had paid his bills by cash or checks, heir to, owner of, had credit cards.

There is no turning back, no turning. That banal phrase regained its unrelenting, cruel meaning for him, deeper and deeper until he reached its natural negative: *there* is *a turning back.* Which was even crueler, turning him to face his own inner world, a world in which every past event continued to exist but led to an unchangeable, absurd, *deadly life*—independent from him. Nick stopped to gape at his sister, climbing up the stairs toward him. She had climbed these stairs in their "father's house" in a hundred different guises, all now condensed into a parade by time. Frozen, he watched her images smile at him with died-away smiles, fix him with looks he had long forgotten, frown at him with past anger, and pass him by. Incredibly different!

All the images of a healthy, full-blooded woman, slightly past her prime but full of life, her hair loose, her hair held at the back or adorned with hats, dressed in clothes made by the mother of her future murderess! Images of a woman holding her slight daughter by the hand—a misty figure so easily forgotten; of a younger woman with an infant in her arms; of a very happy woman ripe with child. And back further, younger and younger: before she married the "rich, aristocratic" Maximilian, the man she would kill; a schoolgirl with wavy, shoulder-length hair, head over heels in love with "Renaldino," son of poor Italian immigrants, who would blow his brains in *that* room toward which his sister Elli kept climbing—but now as a young, freckle-faced girl in braids.

And younger still—half-toddling, half-crawling up the stairs, her older brother Nicky and Mama afraid that she would fall, both right behind her, poised to take her in their arms, to save her *now, now*! But she turned into a baby in her mother's arms, and he is her five-year-old brother—this infant that he would abandon thirty-seven years later as she slept because she already didn't radiate "resistance"! And later that afternoon, he wouldn't even look in at her, because he knows she is—dead. Slain.

Images, images—an endless silent procession all going up to that indifferent room. And behind the final image came the little boy with azure eyes, because instead of being the beginning of something, he had transformed everything into the end.

The End.

Nick continued down the stairs.

CHAPTER 52

Nick walked out the front door, pausing to make sure that his head was filled with nothing but anesthetic, gray silence, like a drug—gray stillness, unsounded grayness. How bizarre writers are, choosing their words carefully under any circumstances.

He walked up to the tree stump he had started chopping into kindling the day after Kathy died—and had ignored since. It stood gaping at the sky like a pair of fierce crocodile jaws, into which Nick placed the manuscript and folder.

"Just make sure you don't devour these," he warned—then laughed. He couldn't stop laughing for a long time. When he finally did, he brushed away the tears, arching his eyebrows and sneering. No time to wallow: Forger could come anytime and rob him of his grand finale!

Chasing Biff out of the yard before he could howl again, Nick then hurried to the garage. The first thing to catch his eye, among all the other junk, was his old bike, standing out to remind him of their nasty experience together, almost poking him in the eye—with its rusty spokes. *But nooooo!* Only in fairy tales did objects come to life: "the kettle said, the fork replied, the knife grinned," and "the neck of the broken bottle." This couldn't be! No time for bedtime stories.

He rummaged around for the hose he used to siphon gasoline, slung it around his neck, grabbed two empty gas cans with each hand, and hurried back outside.

First he tried Reno's car: took the keys out of the ignition, unlocked the gas cap, pushed one end of the hose inside the tank, and put the other end into his mouth, not even bothering to wipe it beforehand. As he sucked tepid gasoline into his mouth, he spat violently, almost gagging, but still managed to get the end of the hose into the nearest can—every precious drop counted. When he finally stopped spitting and wiped away his tears, the can was full. *Great, Reno, old friend. We'll have a fine bonfire before long, you and I!*

When two cans were full, he set them on the front porch and took the other two cans to Elsa's car. Her tank there was almost full. *Very good, my sister! We'll decorate the very center of the spectacle with your fuel!*

"Great, great, great," he chanted repeatedly, not even trying to stop himself. Ignoring the tears still streaming from his eyes, he chased Biff away again and wondered whether or not to fill a fifth can with the remaining fuel in the Toyota. No, four would do a good job, even a great job. *Our father's house will sigh; our parents' bed, empty for so long, will weep—remembering exactly when the brother and sister were each conceived—and burst into flames.*

Just to make sure, he returned to the garage for the fifth gas can and drained the gas from his sister's car to the last drop. It seemed unfair to isolate this gasoline from *the big fire game*!

He carried two of the cans up to the second floor, leaving one of them outside Elsa's room before remembering that the door could have been wide open. "Thank God it wasn't!" Did he have to always be so absentminded? He shambled down the hall, berating himself, and placed the other can at the bathroom door, listening for suspicious sounds. While he didn't expect to hear any human sounds, neither did he expect Kaya to take her imprisonment standing still. But what did he know? She could be steaming her invisible self in the tub: murders are exhausting, especially her kind!

Back downstairs, he divided another can's contents, beginning with the living room and kitchen. Then he entered the library, his eyes embracing the books he had collected over the years that filled the shelves as high as the ceiling. He breathed in their musty, dusty redolence until his chest ached. He felt sorry for all these— creatures. Yes, books are not ordinary objects: they become alive under the human eye, even have hearts that beat inside them with the pulse of their authors. *How can I leave them in flames?* he thought with horror. *Whatever sins I've compiled, I'm no executioner. I even feel sorry for Kaya!*

This sudden realization—or insight?—horrified him even more but didn't deter him.

He stepped up to the window and abruptly pulled the curtain, the rasping sound of rusty curtain hooks on the ancient metal rod fraying his nerves like sandpaper until he convulsed. When he mechanically rubbed his temples, he realized that he had had an excruciating headache for some time, as though a crowd of hungry little mice with razor-sharp incisors were gnawing inside his skull. It began driving him crazy—now that he was paying attention. So to hell with little mice!

He propped the windows open with the help of books at each side and then did the same with the door. In a while the house would need more oxygen—to feed the fire.

Pleased with his foresight, Nick splashed gasoline on the carpet and the lowest shelves and then trickled a highly inflammable rivulet over the library threshold, uniting the gasoline in the library, living room, and kitchen. Finally, he doused his way out the front door. He would light it from the porch: *Burn that bitch to ash and smoke!*

But which bitch? If he meant Kaya, if she really were locked in the bathroom, there were simpler ways to do away with her. No, the bitch was the house itself. It drove him mad with its crumbling old walls, its neglected—yet even originally ordinary and uninspired—appearance and, most of all, with the memories lurking in every nook and cranny: banal memories, which the present will always deform into nightmares.

The truth was that he really wanted to free himself of all of them, to "watch" all those memories shrivel and die in hellish flames! He poured a rivulet of gasoline from the foyer up the stairs, throwing himself entirely into his work until he wheezed, his tongue lolled out, and his lips pursed like a child outlining its most interesting picture.

The five gallons of fuel in the can was gone before he reached the landing. He had used far too much, pouring rivers rather than rivulets. He could sail toy boats down the stairs—*damn!* Rushing back downstairs for the next gas can, he tripped and splashed his trousers with gasoline. He paused to regain his equilibrium. He was almost reeling, no doubt from the reek of gasoline.

He considered going to the kitchen for a glass of water but dismissed the idea. Instead, he grabbed the can on the porch and resumed his work. He somehow reached the second floor and started pouring the gasoline while walking backward, unexpectedly ending up at his sister's room. He was going to pass it by, but a streak of sunlight from her window—

From her window? Vaguely sensing something wrong, Nick straightened his cramped back and turned around. Her door was partly open! He felt on fire himself—horrified because, after involuntarily glancing through the narrow fissure, he couldn't take his eyes off.

Off Reno's glistening loafers pointed toward the ceiling. He must have fallen flat on his back and hit his head hard! Nick's eyes moved to his fine white socks—what a dandy he *had been*—and the baby-blue silk of the trouser leg, a little up, accentuating the swart bare skin between cuff and sock. The leg was profusely hairy: "I have all-season padding on under my clothes," he used to joke at times. "Nature has seen to it that I always keep warm."

But right now, deadly cold crept through his flesh. His immobile leg looked tense and tight, not relaxed. Could he have stiffened so quickly? He looked as if he had been trying to get up—even after his death.

"Get up! Get up!"

Nick stopped shouting and reached for the door, slamming it so hard that the wood cracked and pieces of plaster drifted down from the ceiling.

Who opened the door, though!

Less than ten minutes ago, he had set a gas can outside a closed door—making sure it was closed, even saying out loud, "Thank God!" He checked the hall, even walked to the bathroom door. The key was still in the lock. He tried to turn the doorknob anyway—just to be sure Kaya was still locked inside. So, the other door couldn't have been shut tightly; a sudden draft must have blown it open.

A draft? On a day without a puff of breeze?

"One more proof that I need to hurry!" Nick reminded himself. He drenched the doors to Elsa's room and his study, even gave the bathroom door another slosh for good measure, splashing gasoline all over himself in his nervousness. He added a trail between the rooms and then emptied the can in his own room, at least two gallons' worth. He propped his windows open with his favorite slippers, grabbed a box of matches from the drawer of his nightstand, and clutched it in his clammy hand. Then the recorder caught his eye; he had almost forgotten about the "proof" that he hadn't killed his sister.

Oh, let it be fuel for the fire too! Otherwise he would have to listen to it, sooner or later. He circled around the bed, without another good-bye glance or thought, and left.

CHAPTER 53

In the hall he fished out the fatal match, when…

"Yes, interesting. Even very interesting." The voice was coming *from his room.*

His own voice.

"Elsa?" it continued, at first trembling, then louder, "Elsa? Elli!" Then a murmur, somewhat harsh, "Elsa."

Nick dropped the matchbox and pressed his hands to his heart. It wasn't pounding—rather, it seemed to have completely stopped beating.

"Annie, go wash your face and brush your teeth, dear, and as soon as you're dressed, we'll have breakfast at a wonderful little café I know."

Oh, that's the recorder all right: playing the recording I made this morning, the recording—

"Tell me, dear Kaya," his voice now a conspiring whisper, "what must I do to be able to…to see you?"

…

"Come on, Annie! Hurry up."

"Stop it!" Nick screamed. He barged into his room and brought his fist down on the recorder—but not hard enough: "I'm sorry, Kaya. It's not my fault, it hurts—"

The second blow choked the voice, and the third obliterated the recorder against his nightstand. Pressing his bleeding knuckles

362

to his lips, Nick stepped back. One step. His knees simply refused to bear his bulk. Completely exhausted, he realized with primal fear that he couldn't go anywhere, couldn't stand up, and he slowly collapsed on the bed. A strange, corporeal languidness overtook him, as if bursting from an open dam—or from nothingness. Perhaps *they*, the dead, were sending it to him, and they had turned the recorder on again too—as a warning:

> *"Do you understand, Nick. You're taking such great pains not to see or hear, to block all truths out of your mind—you're destroying yourself that way! Get up! Go to your sister and your friend—at least close their eyes.* Save yourself *by doing something* humane, *for once in your life!"*

He tried to raise his head, lift one of his legs off the bed, but was dazed from the gas fumes. It was their fault: they were poisoning him, lulling him to sleep, paralyzing him.

Yes, that's right; he would go nowhere. He curled into a fetal position on the bed—as the door behind him shut with a distinct sound.

> *And the boy will remain alone on the shore. A shore without an ocean. Because on the island there were no longer such people, people who would create it with their hope that beauty and bright things await them beyond.*
>
> *"But what did I do to all these people?" the boy will ask himself in surprise. Since there will be no other place to seek an answer, he will have to seek it in himself. Only then will he see himself clearly, so clearly that he will find his own true, terrifying face.*

Nicolas Edgeway. A balding, middle-aged man, overweight and ungainly, a man whose gifts had proved illusory. A man who had turned his life into a desert and, except loneliness, had no other ocean. He will have waited many years for this man, coded in every cell of the boy. Inevitable.

He had been *inevitable.*

He had looked through the azure-blue eyes of the boy with his fading, ever more near-sighted eyes and had pointed,

You will reach there, only this far—up to this very moment, and from then on it will be only me.

I am your **real** future.

And I will remember what you never expected, what you never, never wanted to happen to you.

A deafening crash came from the bathroom. After a short pause, a whole series of more blows—bang, bang, bang—as if the old house were being battered repeatedly by thunder, shaken to its foundations. Even the dead man and woman in the other room were shaking!

Nick smiled with dazed bitterness. Well, yes, of course! He, not they, had turned on the recorder, through some unconscious impulse arising from his pangs of guilt—and that was good, very good. Guilt was a very human feeling, wasn't it?

Bang!—then the sound of splitting wood. And again, and again—ferociously. Mind-boggling: what wild, savage power this girl has! And how categorically she wants to live, regardless of anything! Bang, bang—the sink, she must have broken it and was beating the door with it. The door is splitting.

The blows were rabid beasts howling from their former nothingness, racing down the hall, passing through the walls, breaking the silence.

Why did Kaya always kill with such terrible cruelty? Perhaps that was the last question Nick still couldn't answer, and no doubt he would learn the answer soon enough, because the pounding stopped. Then came the crushing noise as Kaya drove the sink through the broken bathroom door.

Get up, Nick! Come on.

The heavy, acrid smell of gasoline filled his lungs with every breath he took. His clothes, soaked with gasoline, felt sticky and cold. The ceiling appeared to be closing in on him, descending like the hard, open palm of a hand—*the hand of time.* Nick gazed at it with faded eyes.

But wait! There, though far behind, should be the little innocent boy playing in the sun. Yes, he must be somewhere. But I—why can't I find him? Where is he? It can't be possible that he's not—there. When did I kill him?!

Slowly and cruelly, in the waking dream that has passed for my life.

"You bastard," Nick snarled in impotent rage. "*Bas-s-stard,*" some distorted inner echo confirmed.

There was a scratching sound on the door.

"And in general, terrible filth." Nick sighed. He lay on his back and stared at the ceiling, without the slightest desire to look inside himself. Because the ceiling was now *impossibly* low: all the cracks in the plaster and the smudges that had collected over the years appeared as if through a magnifying glass. *So, it turns out that* time *itself is dirty,* Nick thought without astonishment. *You watch it approach all white and shiny, and after it passes you by, there's nothing clean left.*

Reconciled to this ancient *fact,* Nick slowly closed his eyes, and when the scratch on the door came again, he said, "You will come in."

CHAPTER 54

She entered the room.

He heard her prowling approach, felt her bend over and scrutinize his face. Her breath felt feverishly anxious on his cheek as her
scratchy, chapped lips warily approached his, touched his.

Kaya, Kaya...

Her hand moved, delicate and cool, across his forehead. Oh,
how well he remembered the caresses of those thin, slightly rough
fingers in those strange, sleepy moments—like now—when he
could feel her touch, discovering with guilty surprise that his desire for her was as strong as ever. No other woman had ever touched
him with such sincere—yes, sincere and passionate—tenderness.
Only Kaya, whose frail body had lit a fire in him—a fire, just like
now—when he was awake!

Her dress rustled ever so slightly as she backed away from the
bed, but he knew she wouldn't leave him. Shamming heavy eyelids, he neither feared her nor wanted to frighten her away. Nor
did he have to be afraid. He had only to wait. He smiled, realizing
that this time, finally, he risked for real. In this *supreme now*, rising before him like a lonely rock between future and past, he was
probably making his next and final mistake, but it wasn't unpleasant. On the contrary, it lifted him higher and higher, into the zone

where the biggest bets were made: bets of life and death, *risks that justified everything.*

Nick waited, listening to her feline footsteps.

She was walking to and fro, obviously purposeless—getting ready—then seemed to stop by the window. Yes, but why was she closing it? The room was so stuffy. A few seconds later, what was that prolonged rasping sound, like running—a rope across her palm?

He felt the rope slide across his shoulder, probably dropping down between the bed frame and springs. She circled the bed and did the same thing on the other side. How fast and deft her movements were, this daughter of a seamstress, who had done this to others—no doubt to Elsa too! They had been drugged, but he...

The wait was over, and his hands were still free. It was time for decisive action.

The time came and went, and Nick remained. Remained where he was, gazing, bewitched, at the darkness of his closed eyelids. Fully accepting the illusion that this darkness provided safety, shelter. He couldn't—wouldn't—leave it.

So he waited.

His strong, healthy heart beat slowly, steadily, drowning in blood thoughts of betrayers and unforgivable faults. His heart a pawn—a scapegoat.

The rope crisscrossed his chest and ran down around his thighs and calves.

Kaya, Kaya...

She tightened the slipknots around his ankles, probably securing the rope to the bed frame, so convenient for her purpose. Then, with a single pull, the whole rope cinched tight and sank painfully into his body.

Well, it was over. If he had made a mistake, he could be certain that it really would be fatal. Exactly—if! A sentence leaped to his mind that might yet save him: "And exactly there, before those last seconds of your life, I will force you to find *my image*." She had written those words herself, amending his tale, and now he fully realized what they meant.

She pressed her lips to his, becoming increasingly audacious. She would hardly undertake her cruel measures as long as she thought that he was half-asleep and thus "noninfectious." So he needed to convince her that now, somehow, the powerful repulsive force would not drive them apart—by showing her that he was already fully awake! But his will wouldn't respond to his call to action; he felt dizzy and paralyzed.

Her fingers—nimble and impatient, like those of an experienced seamstress—quickly undid his shirt.

Kaya, Kaya...

She put her palms on his bare chest, and he felt his skin crawl. Yes, he understood now, though it was probably too late.

She killed so that others could see her.

Only through the *inhuman* murders could she reclaim her *human* image! She drew near her victims in their sleep and touched them so they could sense her presence, feel her breathing, even hear her voice. But *only* in their death throes did she become visible to them. She became a human being again in their terrified, slowly dimming eyes, proving to them—or to herself—that she was flesh and blood too, a woman!

A woman who now mounted him and tightened her thighs around his hips! She trembled in every fiber of her body, probing him greedily, insatiably, reeling above him, squirming against him, panting—a woman! Overwhelmed by unremitting, never-quenched desire, he quickly became excited. This, in spite of everything—or because of everything—wasn't unpleasant at all. His loins were already on fire under her increasingly aggressive foreplay, his penis pressing against his pants like a caged predator! She unzipped his pants, pulled down his briefs, and set it free! It jumped and shook, gathering all his former strength, reborn like a phoenix from his cold ashes. What an incredible sensation!

But how could Kaya, his Kaya, not realize that he was awake—as fully awake as he had ever been in his life? His muscles bulged, and the rope sank deeper; he was enormous! His blood turned to fiery lava, his pulse a storm punctuated by mighty claps of thunder—what an incredible, magnificent *manly* sensation! Beyond anything in the world—maybe.

"Oh, Kaya!" he thundered, his enormous voice reverberating in his throat, streaks of lightning flashing beneath his closed eyelids. "Oh, Kaya!"

In reply, she grabbed him by the throat, nervously gathering the skin from right to left. Something clicked above his head, something familiar—a pocketknife? The knife his sister had given him! The blade nicked him on the side of his throat, ever so lightly, and with her other hand, Kaya pulled folds of skin tightly.

"No, wait!" he whispered. "I'll see you without—that. I can see you *now*, believe me! I've been awake the whole time. I'm going to open my eyes now, and I won't push you away, my darling. I wouldn't hurt you."

He was crazy with desire for her, desiring above all else that she would believe him. As he whispered, he was desperately trying to open his eyes. But they were heavy, sticky, obeying very, very slowly.

Kaya gave in first. Her little scream startled him, and his eyes finally sprang open—at the same second, the blade cut his throat and slit it.

Then their eyes met. Their gaze intertwined, both unbelieving, astonished, frozen; each awaiting their own cruel pain—which never came. Only the blood came, flowing from the wound. The thick skin seemed to be sliced lengthwise, but Nick was busy elsewhere now. He lay still with his head thrown back, preternaturally calm and still waiting. He knew the lack of any fear in his eyes was slowly being recognized by Kaya. She needed time.

"Do you believe me now?" he asked in an almost unchanged voice. *Do you believe me, even though a little while ago I wanted to burn you alive?*

She shook above him as if hit by regular electric shocks and clutched at his shoulder with her left hand—a girl, an ordinary girl scared out of her wits. Watching her, he saw a girl neither pretty nor ugly, with a little, long, thin face and auburn hair and olive skin. Her eyebrows were thin and slightly arched, her eyes open wide and very black, midnight ebony. Her lips were set in a tense straight line above a recessive chin, common to indecisive people. Yes, she was quite ordinary, as ordinary as he was.

"Kaya."

When he smiled, his Adam's apple grazed the slick skin of his slit throat, but he felt no pain. The warm blood ran over his ears and onto the small white pillow, but that didn't bother him either. The bright-colored sight had become familiar. *And now it's happening to me.* He was still smiling. *Kaya.*

Her lips moved slowly, their corners crawling upward inch by inch. She too smiled—with unspeakable, tragic relief. Nick caught himself waiting for her smile to widen and reveal that fatal chipped tooth.

But, God, how absurd everything is! He burst into a barking laugh, and a scarlet spray dotted her plain face. Blinking, puzzled, and embarrassed, Kaya wiped—smeared—it with the back of the hand still holding the knife. Then she frowned but was no longer shaking.

Nick reluctantly stopped laughing. *No, I wasn't going to light the match*, he realized with insulting clarity. *I never finish anything I start.*

Kaya understood that too. She looked down at him without fear, but as if she no longer saw him! Her lips formed a thin straight line again. Tense. What could possibly be going on in her ordinary, mediocre brain that had been wandering in twilight shadowlands of absurdity for eight months? What was going on there right now?

Her hand rose abruptly, the blade of the knife glinting crimson, and then darting toward his chest. With amazing precision, she cut the rope, pulled it off almost in a trance, freed his shoulders, thighs, and ankles and flung the knife to the far end of the room before coming back to her senses, horrified by the risk she had taken.

"It's over now." Nick tried to convince her, but his voice had become hoarse. How could it be otherwise, with that *not-so-shallow* gash on his throat? *It's over*, he tried to convince himself as well. "The repulsive force is gone. I endured my agony, dear Kaya, long before you cut me." *I've been going through hell for a whole week because of you!* "Maybe that's the reason why I'm no longer infectious to you. Understand?"

She kept nodding as if she understood, but her face was distorted in a fearful grimace of crying, although her eyes remained dry—and oh, so midnight black! His cramped hands tried to pull her to him, but she convulsed and pulled away wildly. Her hair poured over him in disarray, and a hair clip fell onto his chest.

Elsa's golden hair clip lay on his chest.

Nick looked at it, squeezing the girl's thin shoulders more and more. As he raised his head, the ragged edges of his wound pressed against each other, and this time it hurt. This time, *something* hurt a lot.

Now it was Kaya who waited.

I know what I want, he finally confessed to himself. *I want someone to love me—or at least to like me. Nothing more, nothing else. Just that. Is that asking too much, goddamn it?*

He freed one of Kaya's shoulders and swept the hair clip aside. They heard it fall on the floor. Their eyes met again; then their lips met unbridledly, in the semblance of a love kiss. They parted only to breathe again. *I'm better now, much better,* Nick kept telling himself, panting. Maybe he had needed this bloodletting: wasn't that the way they used to free the afflicted from evil obsessions?

Still, everything was *too visible*, especially Kaya and his incessantly running blood, dyeing his sister's pale-blue nightgown a garish red. How long would he be tormented by such intrusive *details*? Grabbing its neckline, he tore the nightgown halfway down. Kaya took it off herself. Reduced to rags, it tangled between their legs. They kicked it onto the floor, faced each other briefly until Kaya pressed herself against him.

Strangely, without the familiar nightgown, which didn't even fit her, she was less attractive—maybe because there's no mystery in nudity? Or—no matter! What mattered was that, right now, Kaya was his and obviously liked him, or at least wanted him, which—in itself—filled him with desire as well.

Their bodies intertwined, hot and sweaty, and she impatiently pulled his pants and briefs down to his knees. She mounted him, tightening and loosening her thighs as if she were a broncobuster.

That was too much! She was terribly visible—her hair still wet from *that* bathing, hanging down in long snakelike tufts, and blood drying on her face and arms! She needed to bathe *again*.

But later. Now they had to play their "game of love." Both of them moaned through clenched teeth, not just from excitement.

"Don't be so...clear. Don't be so...so...yourself!" Nick implored in broken, wheezing gasps as he stroked her small, jutting breasts and slowly, painfully, entered her tense, virgin flesh.

It hurt him to enter her—and hurt her too: he was so big. And their desires—whatever they were—were too great. Yes, everything now was *excessive*. That's why it hurt so. He tried to pull away briefly, but she pressed herself down on him, abruptly and uncontrollably. He felt her insides tear all the way up to her womb. *I'm adding more blood to that already shed*, he thought triumphantly. But no virginal moan escaped Kaya; instead, her movements became even more abrupt and rapid. She was provokingly speeding up.

"You horny little...vix...x...xen!"

He turned her under him, and they sprawled onto the carpet reeking of gasoline. End of her brutal bronco busting! He took her in mighty relentless thrusts, almost smashing her with his full bodyweight. Now she was totally silent, giving him an anthracite stare—a *nightly* look in the sunny afternoon. Her face loomed before him, spattered with blood so many times.

"No, that was wrong," Nick snarled as he crushed her with his hands and thighs, chest and belly—and not just out of excitement. "That was wrong!" She was so—dirty. As was he. "I would never have struck that match! I wasn't going to...burn...burn you...but you were going to...kill...me!"

As if triggered by his last words, Kaya again started writhing beneath him. She even ran her fingers through his hair with renewed passion and oh, finally, half-closed her gloomy eyes.

"You were going to kill me," Nick repeated. "If I hadn't seen you, you were going to—cut my throat!"

Her lips parted in a hollow scream of ecstasy, baring her large, somewhat irregular teeth, one of which was chipped—the upper front left incisor. *She wanted people to see her, so she became—a killer!* She lifted her pelvis and pushed him up, all of his enormous weight. God, she had such uncontrolled, fierce strength! Her narrow vagina contracted even more, throbbing rapaciously, hotter and hotter, smacking like a hungry, carnivorous animal.

No, this is wrong—at least now, while our dead lie in the next room. Two who had loved each other, somehow—for so many years—and had given themselves to each other, not on a carpet covered in blood and reeking of gasoline. Not like this!

But Nick found it impossible to stop. Kaya writhed beneath him like a snake, and he liked it that way. She liked it too. She liked him! *"She finds you very attractive. That's why she came to live with you."* Someone had said that to him recently, but who?

Well, it doesn't really matter. I want a woman to want me, or at least not to be indifferent to me. I acknowledge this most sincerely, so let's move on.

In fact, I just don't want to be alone.

"Oh, dear, there's so much I want to tell you," he whispered in her ear. "And this will happen, because now we're going to live together." Sentences in the future tense were dripping from his mouth like some vulgarized, soiled, dead tale.

"As for the murders, we'll impute them—to Reno. We'll say he shot himself, after he killed his lover!" The sublime moment was close. "Yes, yes, my sister was his lover; did you know that? Ooh! Do you know—that my sister Elsa, Elsa, Elsa—"

"Shut up!" Her scream cut him short, so loud that it almost deafened him. She tried to wrestle her way out of his arms.

"Oh, no!" He pressed her down. "Not yet...not...now. It feels so good...we...we're going to live together—"

"Shut up!" he heard for the second and last time. Then Kaya darted her hand toward his throat and sank her nails into the wound with insensate rage.

O...o...ouch! White and yellow lightning flashed across his eyes bulging with pain and dismay. The darkness that followed wasn't artificial or a refuge: it was pain. Nick couldn't tell if the pain was only physical or spiritual too. It filled his whole being. Kaya was grabbing at him, even after he had managed to tear her fingers away from the wound. Lying on the carpet, holding her hands in his, his head tilted backward to avoid her chattering teeth reaching for his throat, he waited. He waited for the black pain to go away.

CHAPTER 55

My blood, he thought, a little surprised as he looked up. *It's flowing—faster now.*

It fell in large drops upon the face beneath him—an alien but, shockingly, nonhateful face. Red—the shoulders, breasts, arms. What a slaughterhouse!

The thought didn't excite him. He could feel apathy rise in him like sap—physical, emotional, past, present, and dangerous, because his indifference was lulling him asleep, which somehow appealed to him. Out of habit he looked away, so that he wouldn't have to see the visible.

But he saw it.

A little girl standing in the doorway of the bedroom. Staring at them. Vaguely familiar. Wearing a badly wrinkled skirt, her legs as thin as straw in her white leather sandals. Her thin, lank brown hair pulled up in a ponytail. She was terribly gaunt. In her left hand, she held a matchbox. In her right was a match, poised to strike.

How long has she been looking at us like that? was the only question Nick asked himself, still holding the hands of the woman motionless under him. While his entrails squirmed in monstrous shame, he answered his own question: *from the very beginning.*

This girl had entered the other room and left the door ajar. She had seen…her… mother. Then she had returned to press the play button on the recorder.

Anna. Visible again.

She lit the match and held it up high above her head, as if trying to shed some light in a pitch-black room. The little flame became a playful orange extension of the child's fingers. Yes, there was a mesmerizing charm in this illusion. Nick would have been glad to contemplate that image for the few remaining seconds before the fire started, if...

If Kaya hadn't flailed in his arms, panic-stricken, still filled with lust for life.

My God, how ordinary she is! He pressed down on her, immobilizing her with his weight. *How ordinary we all are!* She scratched at him like an alley cat. *And how we've fallen from an ordinary, safe place.* He succeeded in holding her arms with his knees. *From a low place, but into a swamp.* Taking her by the hair, with an abrupt, businesslike jerk of his hand, he broke her neck.

She shook in a short convulsion, gawked at him inquiringly, and suddenly grew still.

Nick turned his face toward Anna's little flame, which had become even smaller and feebler. The burnt part of the match stuck out crookedly. Looking up, Anna watched it burn toward her fingertips—a miniscule, incorrigibly lonely figure emerging from the thick grayness of the hall. The rivulet of gasoline to her right was almost dry by now. It bisected the narrow strip of parquet flooring and petered out in the carpet, where the big stains were still dark and damp. All that was needed was a spark—just one spark! Nick waited for it with a premonition of eternal relief—painless, deadly relief—waited for the spark like a gift from this seven-year-old girl, whose childhood ended right here and now.

He didn't notice if she finally threw the match or simply dropped it when it burned her hand. Making a short, yellowish arc as it fell onto the carpet, it flickered a few inches from the nearest dark stain and then flared anew, fed by the fibers. Nick and Anna locked eyes, very briefly, before she stepped back into the hall.

In the next few uncharitably stretched seconds, Nick listened to her footsteps dying away and watched the wavering flame. *One spark is nothing if you don't give it at least an inch or two of a chance,* he realized. *Especially if you are not so sure if you want it to have a chance.*

The flame grew even feebler, gave off a few last wisps of smoke, and sputtered out.

"Oh, no, no." Nick wheezed, simultaneously overwhelmed with instinctive joy, and shook his head in reproach. "No, it wasn't supposed to happen that way—not that way."

Freeing himself from the embrace of the dead woman beneath him, he wiped his hands on his shirt and, clenching his teeth, carefully placed his hand around his throat.

Then he rose, very slowly.

EPILOGUE

Snow. Snow—and a cold that embroiders gray icy flowers on the dirty window. Nicolas has scraped a space between them and looks outside. Not that there's much to see except snow. Even the front-yard fence is barely visible, white on a white background. The trees on the other side of the road resemble huge white mushrooms, thrusting their bulbous caps into a low gray sky.

The kettle starts to whistle a shrill tune, so Nicolas reluctantly turns around. He makes tea, opens a can of mincemeat, and takes a hunk of bread from the cupboard. The bread is as hard as ice. He cuts slices, sprinkles water over them, and arranges them in the oven. While they heat he can venture out to the mailbox, though he seriously doubts that the postman would trek through all that snow. In the foyer he pulls on his "backyard" boots, wraps himself in his fur coat, and opens the front door.

Snow, snow...

He hesitantly steps onto the porch. Might it be wiser to stay in? But he keeps going. As always, Biff yelps from the kennel, but he's snowed in too and simply watches lugubriously through a pile of snow that blocks the opening. His nose is white, not only from the snow but also with age. Nicolas passes his doghouse and takes a shortcut toward the gate, sinking up to his knees with each step. He pants and gasps, exhaling air through his wide-open mouth in small bubbles, just like speech bubbles in the comics except that his breath vanishes into thin air without a single word appearing in his bubbles.

The mailbox is stuffed. He can hardly believe it. Looking down the road, he notices the footprints, nearly covered already by the drifting snow. He can almost hear the postman cursing him, though he must have been here much earlier.

"To hell with you too," he replies.

Back in his house, Nicolas takes off his boots, hangs the coat on the coatrack, and heads straight for the kitchen, where it's cozy and warm. He chucks the newspapers on the table and opens the oven. All is well—the toast hasn't burned.

He begins to eat and read:

"GIRL GHOST POSES BEFORE LATEST HORRIBLE BLAZE."

He studies the big color picture; this time Anna looks quite good. Her hair is loose, and the photographer has caught it as it billows around her head like a dark halo, a sharp contrast to the background of bright orange flames. She's dressed in a long coat and pants that hide her unnatural thinness. Maybe that's why journalists have abandoned her former nickname. Good; "Skeleton-Child" always struck him as overly boorish—vapid. Besides, his Anna was no longer a child.

"IMPOSSIBLE SPECTER OF FIRE-RAISER ONLY VISIBLE FROM THE LENS."

Only? Nick smiles, pushes the newspapers aside, stands up. He regards himself in the mirror above the sink: directly opposite the window, so his face is pasted between the gray icy flowers. His eyes are darkened by his own shadow, but he knows they aren't the way he sees them—bottomless black holes growing rounder and deeper until his own reflection slowly sinks into them. Endlessly deep. As it sinks, he understands that it's not too late—that there is still time, for him and Anna.

It's not too late for both of them together, because, wherever she is on this icy, snowy morning, all he has to do is feel love for her, and then a shapely, tender girl will pop up out of nowhere for everybody to see. Everybody. "Oh!" they will exclaim, but they won't recognize her. She will be changed, brightened by his love! Because it isn't "psycho-viral immunity"—simply *love*, ordinary human love, which he will send at all cost to her. And why not? She is his niece, after all, the only close creature he has in the whole world.

But until everything comes true...

Nicolas looks through the black holes and sees, in the mirror, standing opposite himself, a sloppy, red-faced fatso. A skunk. He beats him off, *nullifies* him, with the force of his all-consuming, habitual indifference. Then he turns and crosses the tiny, warm kitchen. He sit at the table by the window, behind which the snow continues in large, tattered flakes.

Snow.

www.ingramcontent.com/pod-product-compliance
Lightning Source LLC
Chambersburg PA
CBHW060151260626
47160CB00001B/219